Also by Emer Gillespie

Virtual Stranger

FIVE DEAD MEN

Emer Gillespie

HEADLINE

First published in 1999
by HEADLINE BOOK PUBLISHING

10 9 8 7 6 5 4 3 2 1

British Library Cataloguing in Publication Data

Gillespie, Emer
Five dead men
1. Detective and mystery stories
I. Title
823.9'14 [F]

ISBN 0 7472 2236 3

Typeset by Avon Dataset Ltd, Bidford-on-Avon, Warks

Printed and bound in Great Britain by
Clays Ltd, St Ives plc

HEADLINE BOOK PUBLISHING
A division of the Hodder Headline Group
338 Euston Road
London NW1 3BH

www.headline.co.uk
www.hodderheadline.com

For Mark, with love.

Chapter One

The cry came as we were halfway across the hot, dusty forecourt. All around was the heaving, humming noise of the busy site. There was banging, hammering, drilling, churning and the drone of heavy machinery. It was difficult to hear myself think, let alone attempt any sort of conversation with my two companions.

So why had I registered this cry?

There is something unmistakable about the sound of human terror.

Looking around, I could see nothing wrong. Had I imagined the sound? I scanned the heaving, humming, site. Everything was as normal. A hive of activity – men sawing, lugging, shovelling. As far as the eye could see, tiny figures swarmed busily about their business. Nothing seemed amiss.

There it was again.

Despite the unbearable heat, the hairs on the back of my neck stood on end and I shivered.

I stopped and turned. There, high overhead, one small figure dangled from the top walkway of some scaffolding five floors up. The man was clinging on with only one arm. The other arm grabbed for the metal bar above his head. And missed. And missed.

By now I was not the only one to have seen him. The two women I was with had also stopped to stare in horror.

People all around us had become aware of what was happening. Hammering stopped. Engines were switched off. Noise ceased.

The man was shouting. I could see his face moving. Cries

1

for help. Words, no doubt, of fear and desperation. From this far away, it was impossible to hear him clearly.

He was a young man and, with all the strength he had, he kicked with his legs against the scaffolding, trying to gain some momentum which would propel him upwards and enable him to reach the bar overhead with both hands. And again he tried. And again he missed.

For God's sake, someone had to help him! He couldn't hold on for much longer. Men began to run towards the scaffolding, shinning up the poles, scrambling along the makeshift walkways. Wait! Wait! Someone was up there already. Safe on the walkway, a second man was carefully edging his way towards the first. It was Jim Bryant, the site foreman. I'd been introduced to him by the council official who showed me round Heaven's Gate on my first visit.

Over his shoulder he carried a rope. Quickly but competently he secured himself to the scaffolding then carefully he eased himself over the side and began to reach out.

A small crowd had gathered. No one spoke. We held our breath and willed him on.

The man hanging in mid-air was aware of his hopeless situation. He looked at his rescuer and even from this distance it was easy to read the fear and panic in his eyes. He kept shouting something. It was still impossible to make out what he was saying.

For one joyous moment it looked as if the rescue would succeed. The rope was snaking down, inching closer. It dangled just out of his reach. Safe on the walkway, the second man swung it towards him, once, twice. Both times the man grabbed for it. Both times he missed. His face was twisted and contorted with the effort of holding on.

On the third occasion he managed to grab it. For one split second contact had been made. Collectively we let out our pent-up breath. It looked like everything would be all right.

Then, unexpectedly, the rope seemed to jerk out of his hand. He scrabbled frantically after it, his legs desperately searching for solid ground. Willing his body out further into a kind of limbo, he reached too far. And fell.

As he fell, his hard yellow safety hat came off. Together they plummeted downwards.

I began to run. What was I planning to do? Cover the huge distance before his body hit the ground? Catch him?

I ran, unaware of the heavy camera I carried in my right hand, unaware of the bulky layers of unfamiliar clothing. I could think of nothing other than that I must run.

I was too late. We all were. Nothing could have broken his fall. The body hit the ground and bounced. Arms and legs jerked on impact then flopped broken and grotesque when he settled for the second time.

Others reached him before I did. I'm glad about that. Some images, once seared on the retina, are impossible to scrape away.

I stopped running, aware now of the camera in my hand, the blasting heat of the sun, the grinding munching of an unattended concrete mixer turning round and round and round, the distant sound of a siren.

Something made me look up and back. High overhead stood Jim Bryant. He was staring down at the body on the ground surrounded by its group of useless observers. The harsh sunlight overhead cast long shadows. The brim of his safety helmet made it difficult to see his face properly. Otherwise why would I have the impression that the look on his face was one of satisfaction? I watched as his head ducked out of sight and he was gone.

Grace Campbell and Judy Atkins caught up with me.

'Poor sod,' said Grace.

There was no answer to that. We stood and watched with all the others until there no longer seemed any reason to stay.

An ambulance arrived and as it turned through the gates, its speeding wheels churned up clouds of choking dust.

Perhaps they would be able to do something, perhaps he would be all right.

Perhaps pigs might fly.

Three panda cars pulled into the site car park, sirens wailing, and disgorged six purposeful police officers. They strode over to where the body lay but there was nothing they could do. Instead they began to encircle the crowd.

'We will need to speak to all of you, each and every one of you, and take down a witness statement. Make sure none of you leave work today without contacting either myself or one of my colleagues.' The young officer who spoke turned on his heel and walked towards the Site Office.

In his wake people began to mutter, their shock and pity quickly turning to disgruntlement at this inconvenience.

'Come on, let's do it.'

Grace Campbell's words took me by surprise. 'You still want to go up Angel Point now?'

'That's what we're here for.'

'We have a busy day ahead of us today. We need to get a move on,' added Judy.

That they were brusque and efficient shouldn't have surprised me; in their line of work, a thick skin is essential. But I needed to think for a moment. Was what had just happened relevant? Should I pursue it further? I was here to make a short film about the demolition of the old Angel Point tower block. Since childhood I have always been fascinated by footage of the carefully planned explosions which are needed to bring down these monstrous structures. When Rob spotted the announcement in a local paper that Angel Point was coming down on 31 August it seemed like exactly the right subject for our first joint project. Hackney Council seemed quite keen. There was talk of giving the film pride of place in a local community project about the regeneration of the area.

Our own money was in this film. We'd both been doing any overtime offered and saving up for months. I've worked as a film editor for so long that I really had the feeling that it was now or never. Too many people witter on about how they would be successful film-makers if only this, if only that. It was time to put my money where my mouth was.

And that was why I was here. The body of a vagrant had been discovered only last week in an empty flat in Angel Point, three months after the block had been cleared.

It seemed like a good in. Gruesome enough to command attention, yet human enough to excite interest. I'd seen the photographs – black and white 8 × 10's of something that looked vaguely like a person. By now, of course, the body had been cleared and the autopsy done, today Judy and Grace were going to show me around the now empty flat.

You could argue that I should be focusing on this morning's tragic accident. Yet it was hard to see how invading the huddle of people surrounding the body of the young man would be justified. That was my excuse to myself; the truth was I didn't want to go any closer. If I really thought it was relevant, I could sketch in the circumstances surrounding the accident another time.

Grace was right. It was time to get on with what we were here to do.

We walked towards the huge, deserted monolith of Angel Point, the pinnacle and crowning glory of a social housing policy which had proved itself woefully misguided.

Sweat poured down between my shoulder blades as we panted up the eleven flights of stairs. The lifts were out. All water, gas and electricity had been cut off weeks ago.

The two women struggled on ahead with their own equipment. Bureaucracy meant that I couldn't help out. That suited me fine. The unaccustomed weight of the protective clothing I was wearing, and the camera case in my hand, were causing me enough difficulties.

I couldn't get the image of the man's terrified face out of my head. One moment he was a living, breathing person desperate to cling on to this gift of life, the next he was a lifeless doll bouncing and jerking off the dry earth. Shock had winded me. I wanted to sit down and catch my breath.

But to do so would seem like a sign of weakness. The other two were carrying on as if death were part of their everyday lives. In a way it was.

All around me, heavy on the still air, the stench was disgusting. Piles of rubbish lay rotting on the corner of each stairwell. Once, I could have sworn I saw the limp pink tail of a dead rat.

We reached the front door, No. 11/22. This was where the vagrant's body had been found. Judy turned the key in the lock and broke through the blue and white police barrier tape.

'Put your helmet on.'

I raced to comply but still didn't manage to avoid this new wave of noxious smell which hit me in the face as we opened the door. I waited until Judy and Grace had walked on in before I followed them. Shreds of desiccated wallpaper hung from the walls in the dark hall and sighed in the faint breeze as the door swung shut behind me. Sweat beaded on my forehead and trickled down my nose. I lifted my hand to brush it away and the rubber gloves I was wearing collided with the Perspex visor on my helmet. I raised the visor. At once the heavy scent of hospital disinfectant and putrescence made me want to gag.

'Shall I leave the door closed or do you want me to open it again?' I called down the corridor. This was less an enquiry and more a delaying tactic.

'Keep it closed,' shouted Judy. 'This block has been cleared, but you never know. We can do without sightseers.'

Inside there was no carpet underfoot. Just grey concrete. Everything of any value had been looted or salvaged long ago.

I looked around me. To my right was a tiny kitchen. No cooker, no fridge, no sink. Only dangling flexes and open pipes. The kitchen window gave out onto the concrete frontage of the building opposite, so close, it seemed you could touch it. No natural light. Eleven storeys up and in here it felt like we were underground.

I was reluctant to catch the others up. To see what they would see.

Grace appeared back out in the corridor, silhouetted against the door frame. In our white space-suits we were each physically indistinguishable one from the other. It was only when she opened her mouth to speak that I was sure it was her.

'Are you all right?' Her voice was deep and warm.

'Yes.' I sounded nonchalant, off-hand, but she wasn't fooled.

'Sorry. We should have waited for you. We've done this so many times that we sometimes forget how shocking it might appear. Don't worry, there's nothing to see. The fumigators have been here. The Health and Safety people have been here. Really, we just do the easy bit.'

I looked into her warm dark eyes and found reassurance. She ushered me through into the main living room.

Living room. A room in which to live. But this was the room where a man had died alone. And where he had lain alone, undiscovered for more than two weeks.

She was right. There was very little to see. Funny, I don't know what horrors I had been expecting.

Two huge windows faced into the blasting heat of the August sun. They dominated this small room and turned it into a slow oven. In the corner opposite was an old blue mattress. No other furniture. No table, no chairs, no curtains, no carpet. Just a saggy, blue, stained mattress and some rags of blankets. The wallpaper was heavily patterned with orange, brown and yellow fruit. In the sun-baked squalor of the room it was ripening, slowly peeling and sliding from the walls.

Judy squatted on the floor, rummaging through rubbish, gathering up clues and remnants of the man's life. Who was he? We were here to try to identify a nameless corpse. Although Angel Point had been cleared three months ago, the body had been found just last week.

'So there is definitely nothing suspicious about this death?'

Judy looked up at me. She was a scrawny woman in her early fifties with short greying hair. Judy was Hackney's Council Reconciliation Officer. Judy and Grace made up a two-woman team. The job description which went with the rather euphemistic job title involved trying to identify any unnamed corpses found within the Borough. To identify them, to organise their funeral, to attempt to inform any next of kin and to 'reconcile' their estate. Although Judy had agreed with the official request to let me accompany them this morning, that didn't mean that she accepted me here without reservation. She still hadn't decided whether my interest here was compassionate or voyeuristic.

'I wouldn't say "definitely nothing". You can never tell until we get the full autopsy results. From the evidence we have, it seems that he came up here for a private drink, curled up on a dirty old mattress with a bottle of cheap whisky, and died.'

'How will you go about trying to identify him?'

'With difficulty. We have very little to go on.' She was on her knees, her gloved hands searching through the debris surrounding her. 'We're looking for anything with a name on it – cheque book, pension book . . .' The floor was littered with a thin covering of papers – newspapers, letters, old maps, certificates. She sifted through them carefully, turning over each one. 'Birth certificate . . .' she continued.

Behind me, Grace snorted with laughter. 'We should be so lucky.'

'Are you certain our man didn't live here?'

'We know he didn't live here. This flat belonged to a Nigerian couple and their three children. They've been re-housed along with everybody else from this block. Our man was white, we think – as far as they can tell. We'll get the pathologist's final report sometime this week.'

'Perhaps he lived in one of the other flats in the block and didn't want to move out?'

'Perhaps.'

'If he didn't live here, what do you expect to find?'

'Anything we can,' replied Judy.

I turned to watch Grace working. She picked up a small, battered suitcase which lay upturned at the foot of the mattress. Her gloved hands sorting through a stranger's possessions with casual familiarity.

'Look at this! I think I've got something!' she exclaimed.

'What?' said Judy, still absorbed with the rubbish on the floor.

'This case. It's got initials on the outside. T. O. H.'

'How do you know it's his?' I said, edging closer for a better look.

'We don't,' said Grace, 'but we don't know it isn't.'

I took the case from her. It was small, an overnight case, or a weekend case. It looked as if it were made of cardboard covered with a brown and cream tweed fabric which had for the most part worn away. The colours were faded and dirty. Inside it was empty. It was lined with a beige satin material. There was one elasticated pocket with an inkstain in the corner where a pen had leaked long, long ago. The locks were rusty, and by the dark red plastic handle, I could just make out the ornate, swirling initials, T. O. H.

'This looks ancient,' I said.

'So was he, we think. The forensic pathologist at the scene put him between seventy and seventy-five.'

'I thought he was in his sixties?'

'Not necessarily. How's about we take this away with us?' Judy looked up. 'Can I see?'

'Yeah, sure.' Grace walked over towards her.

I found myself staring at the mattress. It was old and battered. Blankets were rucked and discarded in the corner. The stitching of the mattress had come undone and the blue cover was loose. The smell in the room was overpowering. I looked at the large brown stain on the mattress and thought of old age and incontinence. The stain spread outwards in concentric circles. First there was a light brown. And then a ripple of deeper intensity.

Suddenly I realised what I was looking at. My eyes scanned the room. There was nowhere else.

'Is this where the body was found?' I asked. My voice sounded tremulous. Somewhere faintly, through the sound of wind rushing in my ears, I heard Grace say, 'Are you okay?'

I stepped backwards and felt something crunch beneath my foot. I looked down and saw a mangled maggot squirming on the heel of my shoe. The corpses of a thousand bluebottles lay body deep on the window still. One, newly hatched, buzzed angrily against the grimy glass.

Desperately I sucked in air. There was none. Trapped inside my helmet, I felt that I was suffocating. Just as I began to panic, strong arms held my shoulders and guided me out of the flat and onto the balcony. I whipped off my helmet and began to retch. Toast, tea and that tell-tale bar of chocolate and peanuts glistened in the bright sunshine.

Grace stood by me and held my arm until I was finished.

'Sorry. I don't know what came over me.' I was embarrassed in front of this stranger.

She looked at me. 'Judy said you thought you'd be okay. I had my doubts. Anyway, you shouldn't be okay. Nobody should be okay looking at this stuff. Especially not the first time. I was the same. So was Judy when she did her first on-site. "Baptism of bile", that's what I call it.'

'No, it's not just that. I think it's shock at seeing that man fall to his death.'

As I spoke, I tried and tried to work some saliva into my acid mouth. In this sweltering heat my dehydrated body had little to spare.

'Here, chew on this.' Grace dug deep in her pocket and produced some extra-strong mint chewing gum. A welcome breath of air ruffled my hair and I breathed in deep.

'Can't have been nineteen.'

'If that.' Grace took off her helmet and sat down on the doorstep beside me. She was a black woman in her mid-thirties with firm round cheeks and white teeth. Perhaps because she spent her days in shapeless white overalls she wore her hair very elegantly. It was straightened and woven into a French knot fastened with a plain gold ornament. The simplicity of the style emphasised the calm intelligence of her eyes.

'How did you get into this?' I asked her.

'Research?' She smiled. 'I worked in the Register Office for eight years, you know – Births, Deaths and Marriages, filling in the certificates in my best handwriting. I got bored and wanted to see the world. So I applied for an inter-departmental transfer. I've been doing this for eighteen months.'

'And how do you find it?'

'Oh, you know – sad but satisfying.'

'Satisfying?'

'Everyone should have their own name on their headstone,' she said.

The sounds of children playing somewhere below drifted upwards on the still air.

'That stain on the mattress, was that body fluids or just stale urine?'

'No. That was body fluids. After two weeks in this heat decomposition was fairly advanced. Now that's one job I really wouldn't do. Poor bastard. Lucky we ever found him. A gas inspection team noticed a bad smell. Otherwise he would have gone up with the building.'

I stood up and looked out over the balcony. Grace joined me. The drop was vertiginous.

'What do you think of the new houses?'

'What about them?'

'Are they any better?'

'Than what was here before?' She looked incredulous. 'You obviously don't come from around here. Heaven's Gate distinguished itself by being named one of the ten worst slum developments in Europe.'

'That bad?'

'That bad. Look – you stay out here and wait for us, there's no need to come back in. We shouldn't be more than twenty minutes.' She didn't wait for a reply.

It was hot. No point in fighting it. Moving around was just too much effort. I unzipped my body suit down to my waist and leaned my head back against the peeling paintwork. Overhead the sky was a bright muzzy blue. For the last two weeks, air pollution had exceeded World Health Organisation danger levels. Children, pregnant women and those with respiratory problems were warned to stay indoors. Summertime, and the living is easy. At least going down eleven flights of stairs was easier than climbing up.

How did they get the body down? They must have carried

him down on a gurney. But with advanced decomposition, was he falling apart? Could they strap him in? They must have put him into a body bag. But how? Could they lift him? Did they roll him?

I wondered who he was, this vagrant who had died such a lonely death and who had left nothing to show for his life, not even his name.

I also wondered about the young man. I let myself think about the horror I had witnessed. Did he have a wife, a mother? Perhaps at this very moment, not far from here, a policeman and woman were standing on a doorstep ready to break the bad news.

I was wasting time: There was no point thinking like this. I wasn't here to wonder, I was here to work – to be objective, to keep my eyes and ears open and to see what I could see. With that in mind, I stood up, unlocked the case and took out my camera, a little Sony. Compact, black and very, very sexy, it could do anything. I was sure that if I knew how to work it properly, it would even bring me breakfast in bed.

It fitted snugly on my shoulder. Leaning against the balcony railing for support I turned it on. A silver line flashed across black and the scene below appeared in miniature on the tiny viewfinder. To the south were the tall towers of the City, large, air-conditioned and built for the future. To the north was the century-old deprivation of Dalston and Stamford Hill. This is the London Borough of Hackney, reputed to have the highest immigrant population, unemployment levels and street crime in the country.

Spread out beneath my feet, the building site represented Hackney Council's attempt to change their image. Block by block, slums were being destroyed and new homes, built with a mixture of European Union money, private finance and central government's budget allocation were taking their place. Down below, the ambulance had long since gone but the

police cars were still there. People had got back to work. A
bulldozer steamed back and forth with dusty cargoes of fallen
masonry. Three cranes manoeuvred huge loads of bricks and
timber, swinging them through the sky. Tiny men, stripped to
the waist but wearing their bright yellow hats, scurried around
with purpose.

It was easy to make out the police officers. Their white
shirts were dazzling in the bright sunshine. Three officers
stood talking on the steps of the Portakabin to a fourth man
who was conspicuous only because of his dark suit. As I
watched he peeled off from the group, got into a little red
Matchbox car and drove away at speed. Sunlight glinted off
his roof as he indicated right and joined the stream of traffic
heading east down the Richmond Road. Places to go, people
to meet.

By now my chewing gum had lost all its flavour. I pressed
pause and put down the camera; I ought to go back inside.
Reluctantly, I zipped myself up, pulled on my helmet and
walked back down along the balcony. I pushed open the door
of the flat and walked the few steps along the dark corridor
into the living room.

'Better?' asked Grace.

'Yes, thanks. How's it going in here?'

'We've found several bits of paper with addresses on them
but I don't think they'll come to anything,' said Judy. 'We've
bagged them and we'll take them back to the office and see if
we can make anything of them. Oh, and Grace found a book
of poetry, would you believe?'

'When?'

'Now. Today.'

'What is it?'

Grace held up a see-through plastic bag containing a very
battered Penguin edition of *The Collected Works of John
Donne.*

'Do you think it was his?' I asked.

'Could have been,' she said.

Judy stood up and dusted herself off.

'Before we go I'd like to do some filming.'

'Feel free – that's what you're here for.'

The two women moved to the corridor to get out of my way. I raised the camera to my shoulder and turned it on. In silence I slowly probed and recorded each corner of the room for maybe thirty seconds, finally coming to rest on the brown stain of concentric circles. Holding the camera as a shield I found it easier to dwell on and deal with the reality of lonely, ugly death.

Morbid perhaps, but I could make the point of how difficult it had been to establish community in these isolated vertical boxes.

We walked back down the eleven flights of stairs clutching the few clues to the man's identity; the worn and battered suitcase, the tattered book of poetry, a few scraps of letters which Judy hoped might be traceable.

'What's the next step?' I asked.

'Take these things back to the office and see if they give us any bright ideas. If not, we just have to wait for the pathologist's report sometime this week,' said Judy.

'We placed a couple of adverts in local papers like the one you saw appealing for information.'

'Does that work?'

'Yes, sometimes.'

'I'd like to follow this story through, if you don't mind.'

'Not at all. We're short-staffed at the moment as it's the holiday season – just as long as you bear that in mind. What do you need us to do?'

'Just keep me informed.'

'Shouldn't be a problem.'

The sun arched high over a hazy blue sky as we walked

back through the building site towards where we had parked the car.

Around us, men stopped to stare. We were the only women in this male-only environment, but in our white space-suits we were protected from prying eyes; and as Hackney is an Equal Opportunities employer, there are rules against wolf-whistles and cat-calls. Still, I noticed that we kept our eyes lowered to the ground as we walked by, in a form of self-imposed purdah.

'I suppose we'll have to check in with the officer in charge before we leave.' Judy led the way up the steps of the Portakabin.

Inside, four policemen sat around in a half-circle, legs spread wide apart, black shiny shoes looking out of place on the scuffed and dusty floor. They were in conference with Jim Bryant.

'Yes?'

Judy flashed her ID. 'You wanted witness statements.'

'Be right with you. Wait outside, please?'

Judy wasn't to be put off. 'If it's not convenient we'll leave our names and contact addresses. I'm afraid we have another "on-site" to deal with this afternoon.'

'You witnessed the incident earlier?'

'Yes, we all did.'

The officer in charge nodded to one of his men who pushed his chair back and walked over to us.

'I need to have your names and addresses. We will have to take a statement from each of you at some point to confirm the details of the fatality.'

So that was that then. The man was dead.

Everyone watched as we gave out our names and addresses. The atmosphere in the small room was formal and somewhat aggressive. Jim Bryant sat silent and forbidding, not meeting anyone's gaze. I'd met him on my first visit to the site and

16

didn't find him easy to talk to. Still, it couldn't have been easy, watching a man fall to his death. And the Health and Safety ramifications would be tremendous. All in all, it was a dreadful thing to have happened.

He was looking at me, or so I thought – his eyelids heavy and unblinking. I tried to give him a comforting half-smile, but he stared straight through me as if I weren't even there.

Parked in the designated area behind the Site Office was Judy's old, pale blue VW Passat. When we'd arrived the area had been in shade, but the sun had moved and now the car was sitting in full glare. We climbed out of our protective clothing and threw it into the boot. I shivered momentarily as my sweat-soaked clothes were exposed to the air, but almost instantly the heat of the sun warmed my skin and I could feel the steam begin to rise.

The silver door-handles of the car were hot and painful to touch. Grace climbed in the back seat and left me to ride beside Judy. Inside, the heat was unbearable. I wound down my window quickly and the others did the same.

We manoeuvred our way through the side streets and turned left down the Richmond Road. As the car got up to speed a breeze began to ruffle the hand I had left dangling over the side of the window, but the air was hot and dry and offered no relief. After only 200 yards of easy progress we came to a halt. A long train of cars snaked into the distance, their metal fenders reflecting the bright sun like so many mirrors.

'What's wrong? Can you see up there?' asked Grace.

I craned my neck out through the open window and Judy did the same.

'Can *you* see anything?' I asked Judy.

'No,' she said.

As we sat chugging away impotently in the traffic jam, a woman threaded her way through the stationary cars. She was wearing a white T-shirt and loose khaki shorts. Her soft brown hair was freshly washed and hung, still damp, around her shoulders. She looked cool and comfortable. Dancing round her legs was a large standard poodle, cropped close for the summer, his pom-pom tail erect and wagging in anticipation.

'Over there on the right, is that London Fields?' I asked.

Judy nodded. Speech in this heat was too much of an effort.

'Listen, would you mind if I got out here?' I went on. 'I fancy a walk through the park.'

'Not at all.'

'There is an entrance to the canal at the far end, isn't there?'

'Just follow your nose.'

'You have my work number if anything comes up before Monday, don't you?' I escaped without waiting for a reply.

Chapter Two

The delighted screams of toddlers were the first sounds to greet me as I walked in the park. Over to the right, there was an under-sevens paddling pool packed with children, adults and pushchairs. A swarming, seething, buzzing riot of colour and sun hats, floating toys and the remains of packed lunches.

For the one and only time of my life so far, I envied the young mothers as they sat there chatting with their jeans rolled up to their knees dangling their feet in the cool, shallow water. I thought of my friend Sarah, pregnant with her third child, due any day by my calculations. I hadn't spoken to her for six months. Well, I had tried, but she hadn't wanted to speak to me. We'd had a row.

No, that's not entirely true. That implies it was mutual, that we were both to blame – which isn't fair. The row was my fault. I'd let Sarah down quite badly, I'd walked out on her when she needed looking after, when she'd been assaulted at eight weeks' pregnant and was frightened of losing her baby.

I'd had my reasons, but Sarah and her husband John didn't think they were good enough.

No, again that's not fair. It wasn't that they didn't think I had good reasons, it was just that Sarah was one of my oldest friends and she had needed me. She had bailed me out on countless occasions, and just this once I could have returned the favour. It was my choice. And I had chosen to walk away.

Afterwards, I wrote them a letter to try to explain. John wrote back. He said that they quite understood, that they both did. But he said that he and Sarah would have a lot on their plate for the rest of the year, and that they had decided to batten down the hatches and keep their social life to a minimum.

That was the phrase he had used, 'batten down the hatches'. That's what you do to keep the enemy on the other side, isn't it?

He said that as I was one of Sarah's oldest friends he was sure I would understand. After such a traumatic start he wanted her to have as anxiety-free a pregnancy as possible. To try and get in contact after that was impossible. I'd been barred from the house in the name of friendship.

I sent her a card for her birthday in June, a picture by Matisse called *Formes*, which shows two abstract female figures standing side by side. They are blue. One is a light blue and the other is a very, very deep blue. I couldn't have made the symbolism more overt. I still hadn't had a reply.

Nature's fresh colours of early summer were looking jaded, and the park, although an oasis of green in this heavily built-up area of tower blocks and Victorian terraces, was obviously struggling under these last few weeks of merciless heat. The grass was scratchy and yellow. Patches of hard red earth were showing through underneath. Wilting roses lolled in the flower beds.

The park was crowded. It was lunchtime and people had escaped from their claustrophobic offices. Secretaries peeled off their tights, showroom salesmen undid their ties and stripped off their shirts. Pink flesh turned rapidly to lobster red, oblivious to all the government warnings on skin cancer.

A gang of boys chilled out in the shade of a large tree passing around a bottle of water, an abandoned football at their feet. I made my way over to the avenue of plane trees. The relief was immediate; I could even feel a faint breeze. Above me the dry leaves rustled, faintly whispering their appreciation.

I was going to have some explaining to do when I got

home. Job was already pissed off when I told him he couldn't come this morning, and when he sniffed around and found out I'd been for a walk without him, my life wouldn't be worth living.

A life not worth living. The ease with which we throw away these words, these thoughts. What makes a life worth living? I thought about the rotting remains of the old man found in Angel Point. I thought of the young man who had just fallen to his death. What had their lives been like? Had *they* been worth living? What does that mean?

If I wanted an answer to these questions, who could I ask? Perhaps I could get in touch with their families. Well, obviously not the family of the vagrant.

I thought of what Grace had said – that everyone should have their own name on their headstone. Only those dead from war or famine or plague lie interred en masse in unidentified graves. Twenty years ago, to die lonely and abandoned and then lie undiscovered was a relatively unusual occurrence; it made front-page news. Now it happens all too frequently. What did that say about our world today? What did that say about the disintegration of social responsibility and community?

Something I had read somewhere long ago teased my mind. What was it? About London Fields. It came back to me, how London Fields was a plague pit. Three hundred bodies had been buried here, four hundred years ago. All those bones now rested below the pleasure-seeking feet of playing children.

I looked out across the expanse of jaded green just as a gust of wind scattered dry dust in my eye. I tried to wipe away the grit. Instead it scratched across my eyeball. A huge, protective tear drop welled up and washed it away.

What happened when they tried to lift him onto the stretcher? Did he fall apart like overdone meat? The final indignity. I thought of that room I had just come from. Out here, despite the sights and sounds of summer, I still had that stench in my nostrils. I pictured him lying there, slowly cooking in the midday sun . . .

I forced myself to focus on something else – the peeling bark of the plane trees, the distant sound of a train on the railway bridge. Interviewing the family of the young man. There was an obvious symmetry here, the thought occurred to me suddenly. The death of a young man who was just starting out; the death of an old man who had lived his long life. Both united by the place in which they died, which in turn was being revitalised to provide new homes, new places for more people to live.

I started to get excited by the possibilities – *Seven Ages of Man*, our journey through life . . . I wanted to get home quickly and phone Rob. I walked out the other end of the park and into Broadway Market. The place looked familiar. Had I been here once, years ago? The memory was distant: I couldn't catch hold of it. But I knew that the canal ran along the bottom of London Fields somewhere. And the canal was the quickest way home.

The market was packed and to make any progress I had to push through the crowd. The cobbled streets were lined with wooden stalls piled high with wilting fruit and veg. Canvas awnings provided some protection from the ferocity of the sun, but couldn't prevent the slow bake. Queues of women stood languidly in the heat waiting their turn. Piles of colourful oranges, strawberries and apricots jostled with the pink and silver of their Indian saris and the green and gold of Nigerian batiks. Visual colour therapy.

'Three for a pound yer straws, best English strawberries,' bellowed a young boy.

Despite my eagerness to get home, I paused at a street corner, hoisted the camera onto my shoulder and switched it on, letting it rest on the changing scene for a few minutes.

This footage would be useful in establishing the wider community surrounding the redevelopment of the estate. The area definitely felt familiar but I couldn't work out why. I pushed my way through the crowded streets. Teenagers, bored by the holiday from school, clustered on street corners.

'Is the canal down this way?' I asked a group of girls. Blank eyes flickered in vague assent.

Then I saw the sign. POPPINGHAM ESTATE. A small signpost in the shape of a hand pointed the way.

Memories came flooding back. My aunt used to live here – my dad's sister. Her husband walked out and left her with my two cousins, Carol and Sylvia. Carol was the same age as me and the last time I saw her Sylvia was a shy baby of about three or four with golden ringlets and black patent-leather shoes. I had a doll that looked like her. The doll's name was Victoria. I had forgotten all about that doll. And about my cousins.

I used to visit them years ago, when Mum was still alive. After Mum died they moved. I remembered the address. The card lay open on the table in the hall. I saw it briefly, then it disappeared. By that time my aunt and my dad weren't speaking. I'd never been to her new flat, but I remembered the address. No. 23 Poppingham Gardens.

Without thinking I followed the pointing finger and turned left off the main street. What the hell. It was worth a look.

Poppingham Gardens turned out to be a block of flats, four storeys high, built round three sides of a square. In the centre was a lush grassy lawn; in the middle of that stood a shady lime tree. No. 23 was on the second floor.

Now that I was here, I didn't know what to do. I didn't want to go and introduce myself. Twenty-one years was a long time. Water under the bridge. And yet . . . And yet . . . These people were my relatives. If my aunt had argued with my dad, that wasn't surprising. I myself found him difficult to get on with at the best of times. Steeling myself, I walked up the stairs and along the balcony to the front door. Perhaps they'd moved. Perhaps she'd died.

No. I'd have heard about that.

The door had been personalised, which meant that whoever lived here now had bought the flat. Instead of the regulation council door there was a panelled mahogany one with diamond pane windows and gleaming brass fittings. I rang the bell.

No answer.

Well, that was that then. Old history. Best kept that way.

'Can I help you?' A woman came out of the flat next door, carrying an armful of wet washing.

'Maggie Wilkins, does she live here?' I stuttered.

'She does. And who shall I say called?'

'Don't worry, I'll come back another day.' Perhaps I would, perhaps I wouldn't.

'I can pass on a message,' she persisted.

'No, it's okay.' I escaped along the walkway. What was I doing? I needed to get home, I wanted to speak to Rob. Besides, Job was waiting for me. He wouldn't thank me for being late.

The canal smelled of rotten eggs and dustbins. Despite the heat, just looking at the water seemed to make my eyes feel cooler. I walked past rows of old men and young boys perched on foldaway chairs holding long metal poles extended across the water's width. Fishermen. Gaudy pink maggots squirmed blindly in Tupperware boxes at their sides.

I undid the blistering metal padlocks at my gate. As I walked up the garden my phone began to ring. Fumbling for my keys, I could see Job lying stretched out on the stone floor. He cocked his ears as I opened the door but otherwise he didn't move.

I got to the telephone just before my answering machine cut in.

'How was it?' It was Rob.

'Hold on a moment, I'm just in the door.' I pulled the phone across the room and collapsed on the sofa. The air inside the room was stifling. The door to the garden was still ajar and I kicked it wide open with my feet.

'I was just about to phone you. Hold on a second.' I put the phone down and stripped off my jeans and shirt. A line of dark sweat soaked the waist band of my jeans.

'Sorry, are you still there?' I said, picking up the receiver again. 'I met Judy Atkins and Grace Campbell and went with them to Angel Point. It was all right. Unpleasant, but all right. They still haven't ID'd the body. But listen, while I was there something else happened . .'

I ran through the events of the morning and my new idea. 'What do you reckon?' I asked when I'd finished.

'Possible. What are you thinking of?'

'Bracketing the film with the story of these two deaths. Exploring their lives, I don't know yet. Like you said, seeing what turns up.'

'Out of death comes life. The phoenix and all that.'

'Sort of.'

'Who was the dead man?'

'What was his name?'

'Yeah.'

'No idea.'

'So you have two dead men, and an identity for neither. The idea has potential, Karen, but if it is going to work, the first thing you need to do is find out who they are. And although that should be reasonably straightforward with the young labourer, if you don't know the identity of the vagrant, isn't it going to be impossible to follow up the story of his life?'

Rob was right. It would be impossible to give each man's story equal weight, if one of them were an unknown.

'Yeah. Perhaps I should drop it.'

'I didn't say that. I definitely think it's worth making a few enquiries. What's your plan for the rest of the day? Are you coming into town?'

'Why?'

'I was wondering if you fancied some lunch.'

'I wasn't planning to.'

'What about this evening?'

'What about it?'

'Can I see you?'

'Can we make it tomorrow? I'm going into the Finest Cut in the morning.'

He didn't answer immediately. That's the one problem with having an open relationship. Inevitably one of you ends up wanting more than the other. These days, I always seemed to be disappointing Rob. But the truth was, I didn't want to see him again this evening. He'd stayed over at my flat last night – I'd seen him less than three hours before. We'd had a good time. Today I had other things on my mind and I wanted to spend the night on my own.

'I thought you said your holiday had already started.' To disguise his disappointment his voice now sounded harsh.

'It has. I just thought I would check in and make sure everything is under control.'

'You're trying to keep your fingers in too many pies, Karen. You need to decide whether you want to be an editor or a film-maker.'

I decided not to rise to the bait. The one other dent in my otherwise smooth relationship with Rob was his tendency to try and boss me around, especially when he wasn't getting his own way. Why is it, if you're sleeping with someone, they seem to want to own all sorts of unconnected areas of your life? I started whistling a little tune in my head which always comes to mind in these situations. I think of it as Rob's theme tune. I call it 'The Revenge of the Wounded Pride'.

My silence made him change tack. 'Are you okay?'

'Of course I am. Why shouldn't I be?'

'Just, you know . . . Seeing that man fall might have made you—'

'I'm fine. I'm over it – really I am. See you tomorrow.' I hung up.

I didn't know whether I was over it or not. The best way was not to think of it. The best way was to lie here on the sofa and enjoy the faint movement of air across my skin. The best way was to think of something else.

What was I going to do about Rob? Our relationship was good, it was comfortable, but was it going anywhere? He had never suggested moving in with me; perhaps he knew I would say no. But there was always the feeling that he wanted more from me, more than I felt able to give. These days I had to tread so carefully.

Rob and I became lovers for three blissful squelching weeks last Valentine's. Bed, work, eat, bed, bed. More bed. But it's true what they say about sleeping with friends. It almost ruined a beautiful relationship.

I woke up one Saturday morning in early March, and realised that we hadn't talked since we had started to fuck. And when we talked, the only thing we could find in common was work. This project, other projects – that was it.

But we always used to talk about work, before we started sleeping together. Work worked, if you know what I mean. It was just the venue which had changed. Now we talked about work while drinking wine in bed. Except the conversation was more stilted and we failed to look one another in the eye. Wouldn't that tell you something? So, one morning I packed his dirty clothes in a pillow-case and sent him home.

Job was relieved. He doesn't like sharing me.

Rob was pissed off. He didn't answer my phone calls for

two months. But I persevered. Now we are working together, have a beautiful friendship, with sex as a shared recreational pastime.

I didn't mean to be flippant.

Well, maybe I did.

The truth is, I found the whole subject of Rob confusing, and now that we were going to be working together so closely for the next fortnight, confusion was non-productive. Perhaps I should suggest putting things on hold for a few weeks.

Things?

Us.

Damn.

To take my mind off Rob, I dialled the number of Hackney Town Hall. The sing-song voice of a switchboard operator answered. 'Hackney Town Hall, Angela speaking, how can I help you?'

I thought for a moment, apologised, then hung up. It was too early. I couldn't really follow up the lead of the young man who had just died. That would be ambulance chasing. There was no rush, we had over a week. Tomorrow would do.

Across the floor I saw Job looking at me.

'Walk?'

His ears twitched, but the expression in his eyes was sorrowful. I didn't blame him. I lay stripped to the skin while he sweltered under a fur coat that would have provided adequate protection for an Arctic winter. I'd tried to get his coat cut, but the woman who normally does him had a backlog of appointments and we'd have to wait two weeks.

I poured myself a long glass of water and then stuck my head under the cold tap to freshen up. Then I pulled on a T-shirt and shorts and a pair of open sandals.

'Hey, come on, you lazy dog. Up.'

Job gave me a disdainful look and lumbered gracelessly to his feet.

Outside, the sun beat down relentlessly. Some children were walking barefoot on the towpath. Each footstep was accompanied by a screech of, 'Ooh! Aah!'

Job planted all four paws on the hot concrete and looked at me. He sniffed the air half-heartedly. Then he turned towards the canal and plopped into the water before I could stop him. Visions of toxic blue algae breeding rampantly in the thick city soup crossed my mind. But it was too late. There was nothing I could do.

He stood motionless on a submerged step. The cool water came up to his neck. His long pink tongue lapped the surface. He didn't bother swimming. Too much effort.

When he was ready, I put my hand on his collar and helped him haul himself out. He made straight for home, showing no interest whatsoever in going for a walk.

He stood in the conservatory dripping one hundred years of industrial pollution all over my nice clean floor.

Chapter Three

'The temperature in Central London will reach twenty-six, twenty-seven today, with the current ridge of high pressure lasting over the weekend and well into next week.'

I turned off the radio and went outside to the garden.

It was seven-thirty in the morning. The dew on my feet felt fresh and cool. The traffic noise was still a distant hum. The daisies were asleep, each petal closed tight waiting for the light of the morning sun to reach them. Above me, the sky was a pale, pale blue, cloudless in every direction. The leaves of the eucalyptus tree rustled with the faintest of breezes.

Job came out to stand beside me. His great black nose twitched and sniffed, taking in all the different morning smells. Then he cocked his leg and pissed all over my favourite Hebe. He always does that. He knows I like that Hebe. Now one side of it is stained yellow with urine. The leaves fight a losing battle.

Home is Islington, London N1, north and very central. I live in a beautiful house backing onto the canal. Ordinarily this area would be way outside my income bracket, but the house belongs to a friend who lives in Brussels and rents out the top three floors to visiting European business people. I act as caretaker and pay a nominal rent. My basement flat consists of a bedroom and bathroom near the street, and a large kitchen with a wooden floor opening onto a living room/conservatory with French windows leading out to the best bit, my garden. Visiting European business people don't usually have much time for gardening. But for me it is my own private oasis.

Job finished his piss and lumbered back indoors. I followed reluctantly. Lying on the conservatory floor, I did some perfunctory stretches. Nothing too enthusiastic. I just couldn't seem to get going this morning.

A cold shower would help. The sharp needles of icy water bit into my skin, leaving me gasping for breath.

Wide awake now, I got dressed, while Job sat on the sofa and refused to look at me. He'd heard the weather forecast and was registering his protest. Normally I drive into work and take him with me. Not today. It was too hot to leave him in the car and with him in tow, lunch in a restaurant with Rob was out of the question.

Because I was on my own, I took the Tube, seeking relief from the heat in the bowels of the city. It was still fairly early. The train was packed but not crowded and I got a seat. I started making mental notes of things I needed to finish off at work and questions I wanted to ask Rob.

Just outside Kings Cross Station the train came to a lurching halt.

We all sat patiently for a few minutes. A couple of minutes became five minutes. Then seven minutes. Gradually the atmosphere changed. Perhaps, something was really wrong. People's eyes began to flicker warily from their books and newspapers. The penumbral gloom isolated us from our known world.

Suddenly there was light in the darkness as another train, travelling in the opposite direction, stopped alongside us. Through the windows, a young man's eye caught mine and he smiled. I felt my face twitch automatically in response. Then I froze. You can never be too careful. In embarrassment I looked away, scared to make even fleeting contact with this stranger. The trains started and moved on. The delay was never explained. Minutes later, a lift spilled me out into the bright morning sunshine on Tottenham Court Road.

Walking down to Soho, I couldn't shift the feeling of somehow having failed. I thought of the concentric circles of bodily fluids in a flat high over Hackney. Lonely lives, lonely deaths. To make up for it, I smiled at everyone. Newspaper-sellers, stall-holders, even a taxi driver who almost ran me over. Anything to make me feel connected.

I pushed open the door to the Finest Cut and was met by a refreshing blast of cool air. Our receptionist sat behind her desk looking fresh and immaculate. Her long blonde hair was tied at the back of her neck and her face was devoid of make-up. She wore a white linen shift which made me feel over-dressed in my skirt and shirt, another reason to resent her.

I still hadn't got used to not seeing Laura Lyle on reception. Laura was a good friend of mine, an American, who had been badly injured in a hit and run accident with a motor-bike. Her parents work in Paris and she is staying with them until she is better. Bob Wilkes, my boss, has kept her job open for her but her return isn't certain. With serious head injuries you can never tell. She's been gone almost six months now and we've had a series of temps from an agency – each one, in my opinion, more unsuitable than the last.

This latest girl seemed to have something wrong with her eyesight. Selective vision. She wasn't able to see women, or put another way, she could only see men. When I walked into the building, she didn't look up. When one of my male colleagues was around she was charming, energetic, efficient. She did manage to take my messages for me, but only just. I had to ask her if there were any. Then she would find them and hand them to me without making any visual contact.

I'd taken to provoking her with daily bonhomie.

'It's lovely in here,' I said. 'Just like living in a fridge. You must feel quite at home.'

No answer. I wasn't expecting one.

As I made my way to my edit suite I heard Bob Wilkes's

voice booming down the corridor after me. 'Can't keep away?'

I turned and waited for him to catch up. Three long strides and he stood towering above me.

'I shot some stuff yesterday. I just wanted to see what it looked like.'

Just out of Bob's vision the receptionist was twinkling. Shame. All that effort and Bob wasn't even looking her way.

'How's it going?'

'Early days.'

'I still think two weeks relaxing by a beach and drinking tequila would be a better idea. You've had a heavy year.'

'Yeah, well . . .' I shrugged. There was no point in arguing this through again. I *had* had a heavy year, but I didn't feel like going away on holiday. Making this film was more important to me. Besides, despite his opposition, Bob was letting us use all the editing facilities at Finest Cut for free.

'Make sure you don't enjoy it too much,' he said, striding on towards the lift.

'Don't worry, I'll be back – I like the regular money.'

As the lift doors opened he turned to me and winked. Bob owns the company and he's been good to me. He employed me on a hunch and trained me up. Then, earlier this year, he promoted me way beyond my experience in terms of responsibility and pay, when one of my colleagues suddenly had to leave. Naturally enough he didn't want to see all that time and energy deciding to walk out the door and become an independent film-maker.

I walked into my studio. The heavy door swung closed behind me. All was silent and still. I approached the console in the middle of the room with a familiar, pleasurable tingle of anticipation. With a flick of the switch an Anglepoise lamp created an island of light that was all I needed to find my way around the various keyboards and controls.

The sound-proofed room felt timeless and seasonless. I

inserted the cassette containing the footage I had shot so far, and with a detached eye I watched the pictures, alert for any camera shake or visually unpleasant framing. Not bad.

The footage of the Broadway Market contrast to the pictures taken inside the flat; life and vibrancy as opposed to the organised chaos of the building site and the desolation in the derelict flat. I played around with different juxtapositions of some of the sequences. Absorbed in my work, time sped by. A light flashed on the telephone and I picked it up.

'Rob for you,' said the receptionist.

'Put him through,' I said, mildly irritated by the interruption.

'Are you ready for lunch?'

I looked at the clock on my desk in surprise. It was 12.15. I'd been working for three hours without a break.

'Yes, I'm almost through.'

'I'll meet you in Mezzo's in half an hour. They've got air-conditioning. We'll eat at the bar.'

Everyone else seemed to have had the same idea – the bar was crowded. Rob had arrived before me and had saved us both a seat.

We kissed hello on the lips, smiled at one another and I relaxed with the pleasure of seeing him again. You see, this was the right way. I don't like being crowded. What we had remained fresh and enjoyable.

'So how's it going?'

I filled him in on everything I had done and seen.

'Shit. Poor bloke.'

'Which one?'

'Well, both of them, but I meant the one who fell to his death.'

'I know. It still hasn't sunk in. Perhaps when I have to give my statement to the police it will seem more real.'

'What's the next step?'

'I was thinking that I might try and find out his identity.'

'Ring the council?'

'The council, or the police. It shouldn't be too difficult.'

'What about trying to find some of the ex-residents waiting to move into the new accommodation?' We piled idea on top of idea. Our food arrived and was eaten unnoticed as we guessed our way through any scenarios we were likely to come up against.

Soon it was two o'clock and time for me to go. A cacophony of street sounds hit us as we walked out through the door of the restaurant. Taxi horns and bicycle bells. I had to screw my eyes up against the harsh brightness of the early afternoon sun. Sweltering heat clogged the air. We stood together on the pavement for a moment.

'Do you want to meet for a drink tomorrow night?' Rob asked unexpectedly. The tone of his voice was matter-of-fact, but he was standing too close. Something about his persistence irritated me.

'Why? I think we've covered everything.' My tone was equally matter-of-fact.

'I didn't want to discuss work. I just want to see you.'

He faced into the full glare of the sun so it was difficult to read the expression in his eyes. Damn! What was I going to do? I had to go with my gut instinct. I didn't want to sleep with him while we were setting up this project. There was no easy way to say it. Besides, it was too hot for sex.

'I can't, I have plans.'

We both knew I was lying.

I crossed the road and walked away. I put some distance between us and then I turned back. I could just make him out, a solitary figure walking slowly along Wardour Street, at odds with the rest of the world bustling by.

'There's a call for you on line one,' the receptionist told me as I walked through the door.

'Give me a minute to get there.' I hurried down the corridor and through my door into the enveloping black space. The light was already flashing on the console table.

'Hello?' A woman's voice floated down the line. The voice was mellow and rich and not one I recognised.

'Who is this?'

'Karen McDade?'

'Yes?'

'It's Grace Campbell. We just thought you would like to know, our man has been identified.'

'What? That's unusual, isn't it? Who is he?'

'His widow called us. His name is Ted O'Hagan. Aged eighty-four.'

'I thought you said he was in his seventies?'

'That was an informed guess, but we were wrong. Decay was so advanced we had very little to go on. He was much older than we thought. Mrs O'Hagan saw the advertisement we placed in the *Hackney Clarion*.'

'I didn't know the advertisement was still running.'

'It's not. Apparently she bought some vegetables in the market. They were wrapped in old newspaper. When she unwrapped them at home it caught her eye, she said. They'd been married for sixty-three years. She came in this morning and identified his effects.'

I felt a bubble of excitement. 'Where does she live? Can you give me her address?'

'Sorry, no. I can phone her though, and see if she's willing to see you. I'll let you know Monday.'

'Was he on the missing persons list?'

'Apparently not.'

'I wonder why she hadn't reported him as a missing person?'

'No idea. One thing you should know, the enquiry won't be under our jurisdiction for much longer. The man's been identified and from what his widow said, there is enough money available to bury him. No need for a parish funeral. Once the post-mortem results come through our involvement will finish.'

'When will that be?'

'Can't be definite about that. It's the holiday period and apparently the analysis laboratories are short-staffed.'

We hung up.

Yessss.

Ted O'Hagan, eighty-four years of age, married and living locally. What was he doing in an abandoned tower block? I thought back to the empty bottle of whisky found alongside his body. Probably an alcoholic. All I needed to do now was to find out the identity of the other man and we were in business. I decided to phone Rob and see if he wanted that drink after all.

He hadn't got back to work yet which was surprising as he had an office in a production company not very far away. I left a message on his machine and asked him to call me at home. I hailed a taxi on the street. The persistent heat had melted the roads, turning them to black treacle, and the traffic stuck fast. The taxi crawled towards Islington. It would have been quicker to walk.

'Too many people in London, that's what it is.' The cabby opened the partition to rail at me. 'It was all right before the blacks came. Now we've got too many people. Brought the weather with them and all.'

Sweat formed on my face and trickled down my neck, under my arms and down my cleavage. When I got out to pay the fare, a damp patch marked where I'd been sitting. I didn't leave a tip.

Job hauled himself off the wooden floor and stretched, wagging his tail. He was over his morning sulk and pleased to see me. I checked my machine. No messages. Rob hadn't got back to me. I opened the French windows onto the garden so Job could go out and have a sniff.

Collapsing on my sofa I made a few phone calls.

The first was to Hackney Press Office. I needed some names of people waiting to move from Angel Point into new accommodation. Predictably the woman wasn't willing to release the information over the telephone. She promised to ring around and call me back.

'By the way, what was the name of the young man who fell to his death yesterday?'

'I'm sorry?'

'A young man fell off some scaffolding yesterday morning at Angel Point and died. There were police all over the site, what was his name?'

'I'm sorry, I can't tell you that.'

'What do you mean, you can't tell me that? Surely that's information within the public domain. Why can't you say?'

'I've been instructed to release the information only when the next-of-kin have been informed.'

'This happened yesterday. How long does it take to let the family know?'

'I think I heard something about one of his close relatives being away on holiday.' The young woman's voice sounded awkward and tight.

Thwarted, I hung up. On impulse I dialled Directory Enquiries and asked for the number of the *Hackney Clarion*.

The telephone on the news desk rang and rang. Eventually it was picked up by a man whose voice sounded gruff with sleep.

'Are you running a story about the young man who fell to his death at Angel Point?'

'Yes, we did.'

'Oh.' I hadn't expected them to have been so quick off the

mark. 'Can you give me his name and an address if you have one?'

'I can't remember it off the top of my head. We run an archive service if you want to come in and have a look.'

'Where are you?'

He was explaining the directions to me when the significance of what he had said struck home.

'Surely it's in the current edition.'

'No. We're a weekly paper.'

'When did you run the story?'

'About six weeks ago.'

'Are you saying someone fell to his death six weeks ago?'

'Yes. Isn't that what you were asking about?'

'No, I was asking about the man who died yesterday.'

'I didn't know about him, what was his name?'

'That's what *I* wanted to find out.'

'Can't help you there. When did you say this happened?'

I told him. Funny, I'd rung him to ask for information, not to give it out. Now wasn't that strange? Two deaths on-site in six weeks. Nobody'd mentioned that to me. Didn't say an awful lot for their safety record.

Three dead men.

Perhaps I ought to follow up this earlier death instead. Besides, this man had died six weeks before. His family would have got over the immediate shock by now; they might be more amenable to talking to me.

I rang Rob to see what he thought. He still wasn't there. I didn't leave a message. Next I rang Hackney Council again. Switchboard transferred me to the Press Office. The phone rang and rang. And rang and rang. I looked at my watch. Four thirty-five. Of course. Local government. And the rest of us have to work for a living. I'd been on the phone for half an hour and found out precisely nothing.

Frustrated, I banged the phone down – nothing like punishing a piece of plastic. Job winced. There was only one thing to do. I would go into the archive department of the *Hackney Clarion* to see what I could find out for myself.

I spent a moment undoing the roof of my car before I set off. I drive a dark green Saab convertible. Although not new it goes like a dream. Together, we turn heads. Despite the oppressive, muggy heat I enjoyed the drive and found a place to park behind the newspaper offices. The Archive Department was a rather grand name for what was really a corner cabinet in a large, rundown and overcrowded office. A young woman showed me in and after explaining the somewhat antiquated filing system she left me to my own devices. It took me forty-five minutes to find the article.

CRUSHING BLOW — A man was crushed to death today in a tragic accident at Heaven's Gate. A bulldozer slipped its handbrake pinning the man against a pile of rubble. By the time the bulldozer could be moved the man was dead. He has been named as 23-year-old John Martin of Lytton Grove.

That was it, short and sweet. Two deaths. Three, if you counted the old man's body found in Angel Point. Building sites can be dangerous places.

I dug around under the debris beneath the passenger seat until I found the *A-Z*. Lytton Grove wasn't that far away, just east of Dalston. Now that I was already in the area, perhaps it would be worth a look.

It wasn't.

Lytton Grove turned out to be a long road of dilapidated three-storey Victorian semis. It stretched into the distance and curled out of sight around a corner. Most of the houses were split into two, even three flats. Without a house number it would be impossible to find where John Martin used to live.

Defeated, I fought my way home through the Friday afternoon traffic. There were no messages on my machine when I got home.

It was early evening and still sweltering. I stripped off my sweat-soaked clothes and lay down in the comparative shade of my bedroom . . .

I must have drifted off. The next thing I knew, Job's wet muzzle was nuzzling my ear. He'd had a drink and the water was streaming from his beard, down my neck, soaking my pillow.

'I know, boy. I'm sorry. Let's go out for a walk.' I looked at the clock. It was half-past seven. Although the heat of the day would be past its worst I was still feeling sluggish.

We pottered along the bank of the canal for half an hour. When I got back home there was still no message on my answering machine. Strange. I dialled Rob's home number. He answered straight away.

'Didn't you get my message?'

'Yes, I got your message.'

'Why didn't you ring me?'

'I was getting around to it.' He was still sulking. Ah well. I filled him in on everything I had found out – Ted O'Hagan, the nameless man who had fallen to his death, and John Martin aged twenty-three of Lytton Grove who'd died six weeks before.

'So, do you want to meet for a drink?'

'Why?'

This was hard work. 'So we can talk.'

'What about?'

'Rob, don't punish me! We agreed we'd be honest with one another. I'm doing my best.' I couldn't keep the exasperation out of my voice.

There was a silence. I was aware we were skating on very thin ice, if that were possible during an August heatwave.

'When?'

'What about this evening?'

'Obviously this evening. It has to be this evening, after all, you're busy tomorrow night. I wanted to know what time you wanted to meet.'

'Oh,' I said, momentarily thrown off-balance. 'Nine o'clock?'

'Okay. Nine o'clock at the Arundel. See you there.' And he was gone.

The Arundel is a five-minute walk from where I live. When we got there, Job and I, it was packed. Groups of people sat in clusters on the pavement. Rob was standing waiting for us by some railings. Job bounced up and down excitedly when he saw him. In victory he's been quite gracious.

'It's a nightmare in there, I thought I'd wait until you arrived before I fought my way through for a drink.'

'Let me. You look after Job. Pint?'

He nodded. Job cocked his ears, confused at being left behind.

Inside, people swarmed six deep round the bar. The Arundel's claim to fame is its decoration. Huge papier-mâché models of Punch and Judy hover over the bar painted in garish colours and smiling inanely.

I waved a ten-pound note in the air and shouted out my order. Minutes later I was slopping my way out of the bar clutching two pints of ice-cold lager with a packet of crisps between my teeth. We sat on the edge of the pavement with our feet stretched out between two parked cars. Job stuck his head over my shoulders and mugged me for the crisps.

'Well?' said Rob.

He was looking really good tonight, dressed in a plain white cotton T-shirt over a pair of dark indigo jeans. His skin glowed with a light tan. Despite previous resolutions, I leaned towards him and rested my head against his shoulder. In response, he put his arm lightly around me.

Curled up against him, I filled him in. 'I suppose there's no harm in asking a few questions, is there?'

'I suppose not. What about the widow? Her husband's dead, isn't he? She must have something to say.'

'I should find out about that Monday.'

Twilight slowly descended and we sat side by side on the pavement between two car fenders with the clink of glasses and the hum of affable conversation all around us. Rob finished his drink and stood up.

'Not yet, thanks,' I said. 'I'm fine. I haven't finished this one yet.'

'No, I wasn't going to the bar. I'm off. I'm supposed to be somewhere.'

'Oh! Where?' I tried to hide my surprise.

'Just meeting some friends in town.' He scratched Job behind the ears, kissed me on the forehead and turned away. I watched him walking up the street. The white T-shirt seemed to glow in the dark. He didn't look back.

After he left I didn't stay and finish my drink. I felt like a sad person sitting there by myself with no one but my dog to talk to. Rob was playing games and I couldn't blame him. I was sure he didn't really have anyone to meet. He was getting his own back.

I didn't know what was the matter with me these days. I did want to see him, I still wanted to sleep with him. Yet when we were together my level of irritation would rise and I'd want to get away. Job and I walked home.

I couldn't sleep that night.

'What about the widow? Her husband's dead, isn't he? She must have something to say.'

Words are discarded like so many pieces of litter and scatter to the winds in the constantly shifting, restlessly moving debris of the day.

It is only later as I drift over the deep water towards sleep that my mind sifts and sorts and finds and lingers on those words again.

'Her husband is dead.'

A daily occurrence. People get old and they die. People you love die. How does she feel, this faceless woman, now that her husband is dead?

Sixty-three years. I cannot imagine sixty-three years of intimacy.

Did he belch and fart and grate on her nerves? Or did their souls dance in rhythm?

How does she feel?

Lying here it is difficult to imagine her sense of loss.

Does she feel loss? Or does she feel free?

Does she feel a howling grief?

Now, in the still of the night, well-meaning neighbours having gone home to their complacent beds, now, at this moment, separated from me by a mile of streets and other lives, does she lie awake and whisper his name into the dark of the night?

Death's scythe wounds the living.

And what lies beyond?

Annihilation?

How can we live with that?

Human beings cannot bear too much emotion. Human beings cannot live with too much extremity of feeling. People get tired. Tired of crying. That's what they mean when they say that time heals. Time doesn't heal. Grief coagulates. Pain clots. The wound is scabbed over by daily routine. But underneath, the scar runs deep, ready to rip apart at the most trivial of recollections.

My mum used to bring me a cup of tea first thing in the morning. A cup of sugary tea on a saucer with a spoon. I could hear it rattling as she walked up the stairs to wake me for school. I would lie snuggled deep into my bed, holding the morning at bay until she turned back the blankets and stroked my hair. First thing every morning, that's how I would wake.

Daily routine.

Sometimes, on the edge of sleeping and waking I can still hear that spoon rattling on the saucer. I want to hear it.

Daily, a sense of loss.

I imagine her, this faceless old woman, this widow. Her gnarled fingers reach over to pick up a piece of mending. They hold the accustomed thread and darn and weave. Life does goes on. Doesn't it?

Her wedding ring catches my eye. It has moulded to the shape of the fourth finger of her left hand. Soft gold. The best he could afford.

Its warmth, the way it catches and holds the light, provides a tenuous hope of the promise of eternity.

Outside, a car passed by on the street. Its headlights travelled my bedroom wall and lit up the door peopled with dressing gowns and flung-over coats. Then the engine faded and all was quiet again.

Chapter Four

I awoke more tired than when I had gone to bed. From next door I could hear the sound of Job breathing. He was lying on my sofa, dribbling no doubt all over the cushions.

Job used to sleep with me. Then when Rob began to stay over I had to chuck him out into the living room. Eight and a half stone of jealous dog can be life-threatening. There are still scratchmarks on the outside of my bedroom door where the paint has been clawed away to the wood beneath. Now, even when Rob doesn't stay over, Job sleeps in the living room. He has decided he prefers it on the sofa. His sulk has become a habit. Men.

The more I tried to sleep, the more I tossed and turned. Thoughts crowded in on top of me. At 5.30 I stopped trying and got up. It was already light outside.

Job raised his head from my most comfortable cushion and looked at me hopefully. I pulled on my running clothes and let us both out onto the canal. Exercise would shake off this feeling of torpor. Job squeezed past me and in his eagerness, almost took the legs from under me. All was quiet. The air was pleasantly cool. A faint mist hovered over the surface of the grey water.

I ran east again, east from Islington towards Hackney. Concrete slabs on the towpath clunked under my pounding feet. Job ran beside me, a silent shadow at my heels.

Tower blocks rose either side of the canal. Sleeping people crammed in on top of one another, row upon row. Each home with a bird's-eye view of industrial wasteland.

At least now they were trying to change all that.

I was running too fast, working too hard. I steadied my breathing and slowed my pace. Job took this as a signal to start sniffing hopefully around the water's edge, ready to jump in. A swan in full armour sailed purposefully towards him, warning him off his patch.

'Come away, boy. Come away.'

That dog has no concept of personal safety. He ignored me. The swan began to hiss. Job still didn't get the message. He put his paw out undeterred, as if to test the water. I grabbed his collar and dragged him away.

We ran past Broadway Market and towards the gas towers, huge sculptural objects constructed from steel scaffolding. Overhead, an early morning jet wove its way through the metal bars leaving a stark white line on the virgin sky. A lone fisherman walked towards me with his day's kit packed into two bags.

We ran around the deserted park and Job delivered a personal wake-up call to the ducks and geese sleeping in the shallows of the central pond. I wanted to sit down and rest. I felt sluggish and out of condition. The journey home seemed miles away. I tried to forget about what I was doing, forget about the rasping breath and trembling legs. I set myself goals and promised myself rewards if I could only just get to that bridge and then the next and the next. But my body wasn't to be fooled; it demanded a break. I gave in and stood bent double on the bank of the canal, trying to catch my breath.

Opposite me, sitting on an inaccessible spot on the far bank, a young man was fishing. As I watched, his line went taut. I held onto Job's collar as he carefully played his catch home. The fish broke free from the water in a myriad of tiny drops, its silver skin sparkling in the morning sun. Gently he unhooked it, I watched him raise the fish to his face as if to speak to it. Strange. Then he released it. He threw it back into the canal where it dived swiftly leaving no ripples. Only then did he look up and see me.

'Lovely morning,' he said.

'Yes,' I said.

And suddenly it was.

I forgot about my complaining body and, conscious of his eyes on me, I began to run again. Stomach in, shoulders back, long legs, head held high until we were well out of his sight.

By eight o'clock, showered, fed and dressed, I was ready to leave the flat. I hoisted the camera bag over my shoulder and told Job what he already knew.

'You're staying here, boy. I won't be long.'

He stared at me disconsolately as I pulled the door behind me, double-locking it.

It was only ten minutes to Heaven's Gate. I drove down relatively empty streets and parked my car close to the site entrance. Seeing as it was a Saturday, I didn't expect the place to be very busy. But at only ten to eight, the area was humming.

Behind me, the first phase of houses had already been completed and were occupied. Neat little homes of honey-coloured brick with front gardens, net curtains and brass door-knockers. Satellite television receivers mushroomed from nearly every wall. The doors were painted alternate colours of red and green, and outside some homes stood pots of brightly coloured geraniums.

Out on the pavement, fledgling sycamores were planted in brown squares of dry earth. Each spindly tree wore a black metal jacket for protection. From what? Crashing cars or bands of bored, marauding teenagers? It wasn't quite clear. The newly planted communal flower borders already showed signs of neglect. Dock leaves had taken hold and straggly hollyhocks were turning to seed.

A green-painted wooden wall ran around the circumference

49

of the actual building site. A large sign welcomed you in bold type: MCLACHAN – BUILDING HOMES FOR YOUR FUTURE. I switched on the camera and busied myself filming the new homes. Then I followed the green-painted fence around until I came to a good vantage point. Angel Point dominated the background. Nineteen storeys high, it stood bleakly awaiting its fate.

Good. I had my contrasts. Old desolation, new promise. Rob would be pleased.

Perhaps I should have agreed to go out for dinner with him. I thought back to last night and the unexpected pang of loneliness I had felt as I watched him retreating into the distance.

I walked back round to the main entrance and in through the open gates. The door to the Site Office Portakabin was open. I climbed up the three steps and poked my nose around the corner. There was no one there. That was unexpected. Large plans of the Works Area covered each wall. They were flagged with different coloured dots and symbols. It was tempting to walk on in and have a look. Instead, I remembered my manners and hovered uncertainly on the doorstep. I didn't know where to go next. I needed to find the foreman.

All around the noise of drilling and hammering was deafening. The air was thick with dust. I felt as if I had moved from the city I knew into an alien environment.

As I stepped down from the Portakabin I almost fell straight into the path of a speeding digger. I had to flatten myself against the side of the hut. The driver snickered at my startled expression.

I walked on towards Angel Point, machinery continuing to trundle past me. There was still no one to talk to. Overhead, a giant crane swung slowly round bearing an unimaginable weight of concrete. I was becoming aware of the mammoth

Five Dead Men

effort of organisation and planning such a complex building project required.

Finally, at the foot of Angel Point I saw a man with a clipboard standing with his back to me. I headed towards him. He wore a yellow hard hat and a tartan workshirt. His faded jeans were thick with dust.

'Excuse me!' I shouted. I couldn't hear myself above the sound of the drilling, so he had no chance. '*Excuse me!*' I shouted much louder this time and reached out to touch him on the sleeve.

He turned round abruptly, shocked no doubt by the physical contact, the visor from his hard hat throwing his face into shade.

'Excuse me, my name is Karen McDade. I was looking for Jim Bryant.'

'Try the Site Office,' he bellowed in my ear.

'I've just come from there.'

His eyes scanned the horizon. 'He's never very far away.'

'Maybe you could help me?'

'I doubt it. But fire ahead.'

'I wanted to ask a few questions about the identity of the man who fell to his death yesterday.'

'I heard about that. Dreadful business. I'm afraid I can't help you.' He looked on past me over my shoulder. I turned. Jim Bryant, red-faced with anger, was storming towards us.

'What the hell do you think you are doing here without a hard hat on?' His harsh voice had no trouble in making itself heard.

Shit.

'Jim, the young lady was asking some questions about the accident yesterday.'

'What about it?'

'She wants to know the man's name.'

'Get off my site. I'll have you done for trespassing. Get off my site *now*!'

'Mr Bryant, we've met. I've been given access authorisation by Hackney Council to make a short film about your progress here.' My words aimed to appease; they didn't succeed.

'I don't care if you've been given access authorisation by God Almighty.'

The drilling stopped suddenly and his last few words sounded like a roar. Sometimes that happens to me at a party. The music is switched off suddenly and I find myself shouting. Whenever it happens to me, I feel embarrassed. This man didn't. He stared at me eyes bulging, fury foaming the sides of his mouth.

'What are you waiting for?' he roared again. His thick Northern-Irish brogue was unmistakable. I couldn't understand what I had done to cause such anger.

'I'm sorry about the hat,' I offered tentatively. 'I called in at the Site Office but there was no one there. I just wanted to ask a few questions.'

'So you were poking around the Site Office, were you?' He produced a handset from his pocket and flicked it open. 'Security to Section Three. Security to Section Three. We have an intruder.' He didn't bother looking at me to see what effect his words were having.

I didn't need telling again. I turned and, trying to maintain some dignity, I half-scampered, half-ran back the way I had come, past the car park and the open door of the Site Office which now revealed four or five men standing up and poring over some plans.

It wasn't fair. If only someone had been there five minutes before, I could have made a legitimate request for information and access. And I would have worn a bloody hat.

I got into my car and reversed back out onto the main road shaking with wounded pride, ignoring the angry horns and swearing voices of the drivers forced to let me through. A conflicting maelstrom of emotions ricocheted through my mind. Fear. Obviously fear. He was a frightening man. And embarrassment. I felt as if I'd had my feathers ruffled, or my fur ruffled, or whatever it is you get ruffled. Then there was fury. How dare he speak to me like that! I wasn't doing anything illegal, was I? I was there in broad daylight to ask questions I was entitled to ask.

I had put some distance between myself and the scene of my humiliation before I realised there was something on my windscreen. Something dark had been smeared over the glass restricting my vision. What the hell was it?

No. It couldn't be.

I pulled my car over on the Englefield Road and got out for a closer look.

Shit.

It was.

The smell hit me in the face. Some kids had smeared dog crap all over the glass. Strange – I didn't see any kids.

I didn't have anything I could clean it with. I hunted around in the car but all I could find was half a bottle of Evian. Getting back into the car, I sat in the driver's seat with my window open, trying to synchronise pouring the water over the window with switching on my windscreen wipers. Before I could jump out of the way, the filthy water sloshed over the windscreen, catching me on the arm. I closed my eyes and bit down firmly on my tongue to stop myself from retching.

Instead of cleaning the windscreen, I'd made things worse. A thin dark film of dog shit now covered the whole area. I drove slowly and carefully towards the Shell garage on the Essex Road. It was difficult to see anything through the glass. I found myself peering anxiously through a brown haze.

The man in the garage was unhelpful. There was no fresh water supply, he said. No hose. But there was a car-wash a mile away on the New North Road down towards Old Street. Thanks, I said. I had to buy four litres of Evian water which seemed a bit of a waste. I stood on the forecourt with some thick green paper towels and imagined all my favourite things as I poured the water slowly over the windscreen and cleaned off the excrement. Julie Andrews was right. Raindrops, roses, whiskers, kittens – they all kept my mind off what I was doing and it wasn't too bad. By the time I'd finished, the glass was sparkling. Perhaps whoever had covered my car in crap had actually done me a favour.

I disposed of all the disgusting paper towels and the empty plastic bottles, cleaned myself up as best I could, and went back into the shop to buy myself a coffee. Anything to take away the memory of that awful smell. Climbing back into the car with a Magnum ice cream and a cup of chemical cappuccino, I opened the roof, foraged for a tape and stuck whatever came to hand first into the cassette deck. I started the engine again and drove off down the Richmond Road. A cool breeze fanned my cheeks and the melancholy strains of Ibrahim Abdullah with his South African jazz filled the air.

I thought back to my encounter with Jim Bryant. Why react in such an over-the-top way? What was he protecting? Did I look like a vandal? It didn't make sense. People made documentaries in war zones, persuading murdering forces on either side to let them film. People made documentaries about corruption in high places, uncovering secrets and risking their own lives. And I couldn't even gain entrance to a local building site!

MCLACHAN – WORKING IN PARTNERSHIP WITH LOCAL PEOPLE. At a first encounter they certainly didn't live up to the image their billboards were trying to create.

Jim Bryant. Perhaps he just had a problem with women.

Perhaps it was me. We live in an age awash with information and I couldn't even get a simple answer to a simple question.

54

It was still only 9.30 a.m. I felt restless; I didn't want to go back home. Saturday stretched ahead of me, empty. I had no plans. Not one single plan for the entire weekend.

I could always phone Rob . . . No, that wouldn't be right. I couldn't just phone him up because I didn't have a better option. Pride prevented me from running to him with my tail between my legs just because I felt lonely.

It was true. I did feel lonely. I longed for the throng and bustle of a crowd. On impulse, I hung a left and turned east.

My mum always said never turn up at anyone's house empty-handed so I stopped at a flower stall at the top of the Broadway. All the flowers looked scratchy and past their best. I settled for two bunches of scraggly carnations, white with pink tips. The woman wrapped them in some colourful paper. At least the paper looked nice.

I parked on Albion Road at the foot of an eight-storey tower block. The local youth, all loud music and baseball caps, were hanging about the street corner doing nothing with menace. I wanted to leave the camera in the car but it wasn't worth the risk. So I took it with me.

Broadway Market was heaving. I pushed my way through and turned left towards the Poppingham Estate. I felt extremely nervous at the prospect of meeting my aunt and cousins again. Come to think of it, I had always been nervous about coming to see my aunt and my cousins. I think it was because there were two of them and only one of me. They always seemed to have secrets and games I knew nothing about, and my aunt had this loud booming laugh which I didn't like because I could see her teeth all the way back to her fillings. I used to hold on tight to my mum's hand and hide behind her tan mac. Funny, I hadn't thought of that mac in years.

'Give her half an hour and she'll warm up,' said Mum. 'She's always shy at first.'

Then I remember shrieks and laughter and hiding under the bedclothes and whispers.

'They like their secrets, those girls,' my aunt smiled indulgently. 'You can't get a word out of them these days.'

And cakes and lemonade and the bus trip home and snuggled up against Mum's warm body, falling asleep, smelling her perfume, I can't remember its name – she bought it from the Avon Lady. And the bus trundling up the Holloway Road and being carried indoors and put to bed.

'She's fine, the girls are well. They're all coping. You should go and see them, John. Family is family.'

Voices, sounds, smells, memories. Was that why I wanted to come and meet them again? So I could remember more about my mum?

I knocked on the door of No. 23. Seconds later a woman's voice sounded in the hall. 'About bloody time, Charlie,' she said. 'The tea's gone cold.' She finished the sentence just as she swung the door open to see me standing on her doorstep.

'Annie!' she said and gasped. Her face turned grey as I watched.

'No, Auntie Madge,' I said. 'It's me, Karen, Annie's daughter.'

Time stopped while she looked at me. In the distance a dog barked. Somewhere closer a tired child was crying, snivelling sobs that wanted attention. Then footsteps echoed up the concrete stairwell and I could hear someone whistling.

'Charlie, is that you?' A young woman with long blonde hair and skin-tight blue jeans appeared from inside the flat and raced to the door. The smile of delight died on her face when she saw me and she looked confused. Then she heard the whistling coming closer and she pushed past me.

'Charlie!' She ran down the walkway and flung her arms around a young man's neck.

He laughed and kissed her and half-carried her back along

56

the corridor towards where we were standing. They looked such a picture, I had to suppress a ridiculous urge to say, 'Aah . . .' – the way you do at the end of a Hollywood film when the couple get together for a final kiss and you know in your heart that schmaltz is schmaltz and that real life doesn't work like that but for a moment that knowledge is brushed aside.

'Got the milk, Mrs W,' he said, holding out two pints of semi-skimmed to my aunt and looking very pleased with himself.

'Oh Charlie, what kept you?' she said with fond exasperation.

'Been down the Dog and Duck and knocked Ron up to have a word about this evening. No problem, he says. There's a barbecue anyway. So you spread the word this morning, and I'll get on the phone, when I get back after my fishing. We should manage a fair crowd. Where's that tea then?'

Charlie and the woman, my cousin probably, but I didn't know which one, went on ahead into the flat. I still stood uncertainly on the doorstep.

'Sylvia's just got engaged,' said my aunt by way of explanation. 'You'd better come in.'

I stood in the centre of the living room feeling very unsure of myself. Noises off came from the kitchen. Laughing and screaming and the clinking of cups.

'Sit down, Karen.'

'Thanks, Auntie Madge.' The childish name was awkward to say and we both felt it.

'Maggie, love. It's Maggie really. Madge was your dad's name for me. No one has called me that for years.'

I sat down on a padded leather armchair and looked around me. There were roses, roses, everywhere. Patterned roses on the carpets, the curtains and the cushions. There was even a little basket of tiny china roses on a highly polished mahogany table. Apart from that, a huge television dominated the room. It was switched on with the sound turned down. The picture showed a pristine couple sitting on a sofa in some studio-based chat show; their eyes and hands gesticulated wide-eyed sincerity in some well-rehearsed and well-paid double act.

The door to the kitchen burst open and Charlie emerged carrying a tray loaded down with tea and biscuits. Sylvia was still glued to his neck like a child with a new toy she didn't plan on sharing.

'Here we are, Mrs W,' he said, giving my aunt a kiss before placing the tray on the table.

My aunt rubbed the cheek shyly and looked very pleased with herself.

'So who are you, then?' he said, looking at me.

'This is my brother's girl, Karen.' The introduction was brief. I nodded at Charlie and he smiled back at me.

Charlie looked to be in his late twenties. He had dark curly hair and warm honey-brown eyes. Yesterday's beard stubbled his chin. The skin on his hands and face was very deeply tanned, as if he had spent most of the summer outdoors. He wore faded jeans with torn patches on the knees and bum, and a white T-shirt with a sign reading *Gone Fishing* printed on the front. And that's when I knew who he was. Small world. I'd seen him this morning on the bank of the canal. Charlie. And he'd just got engaged. Shame.

'And this is your Cousin Sylvia.'

Sylvia looked at me for the first time. 'Yeah, I remember going on the bus to your house. Your mum gave us strawberry jelly for our pudding.' Her tone was off-hand. I could feel my eyes filling with tears. This stranger shared my intimate past.

Overhead there was a clunking sound of heavy feet on the stairs and the door to the living room opened.

'That's Carol – you remember Carol, don't you?'

Of course I remember Carol. We were the same age but she

always intimidated me she seemed so much older. Mum said when her dad left she had to do her growing up fast and that I should make allowances. At the time I didn't understand. I didn't see how someone could be the same age as you, yet they could grow up quicker than you.

Last time we met I had taken her up to my bedroom to show her my dolls while the adults downstairs talked, and she had laughed at me for still playing with dolls. We were ten. She had long blonde hair and a mischievous smile. And breasts. She pulled up her shirt to display them proudly. I didn't understand why breasts were meant to be good. I stared at her barely swelling chest dull-wittedly. I knew that she made me feel inadequate, somehow. We sneaked into my mum's bedroom and tried on her clothes and make-up and came clattering down the stairs in her high-heeled shoes, giggling together while Sylvia watched.

But this woman standing in front of me now bore no relation at all to the lithe little girl in my memory. This woman was eighteen stone. Obese. Huge. She was no longer a beautiful blonde. Mouse-brown hair fell limply to her shoulders, hiding her face.

I gawped at her in horror. What had happened? She was unrecognisable. Was she ill? I realised that I was staring and quickly looked away.

'Your cousin, Karen. She used to come and visit with her mum, Annie. The one who died. You remember?'

'Not really.' She squeezed past me to pour herself a cup of tea. Then she sank down into an armchair in the corner of the room in front of the television, hiding herself from view.

Maggie's brutal words hung suspended in the room. 'The one who died.' Family lore, gossiped about and handed on. Except she was talking about my mother. I shouldn't have come. I shouldn't have come. This was a mistake. I had to get out of here.

'So, Karen – play the violin, do you?' Charlie nodded at my camera case.

I looked at him in surprise, then recognising the life-line for what it was I grabbed hold of it with both hands.

'Saxophone.'

'In a band?'

'Now and again.'

'I'd like to hear you sometime.' His eyes twinkled at me.

'I'll let you know.' I looked at Sylvia guiltily, suddenly aware that I had been flirting with her fiancé. Luckily she didn't appear to have noticed. She was gazing at him in adoration. I glanced at my aunt. She looked similarly smitten.

'Are you coming to our party tonight? I won't hear no for an answer. You persuade her, Sylv. Mrs W? Family reunion and all that – it's a good omen. Now, I'd better go. Phil's saved me a place. But I'll have some catching up to do.'

'Where are you going?' The question came out in spite of myself.

'Fishing.' He sounded surprised, as if the answer were obvious.

'Good luck,' said Sylvia. She stood and stretched up to kiss him. Her legs moulded to his body and her white T-shirt rode up as she rubbed her tummy against his.

Carol sat on the armchair underneath them and munched through the plate of milk chocolate digestives.

'Steady,' he said, pulling away. 'Any more and I won't want to leave.'

'That's what I'm hoping.'

'You want me to win, don't you?'

'I want you to win but I don't want you to go.'

She followed him to the door and kissed him there long and slow. My stomach did a slow somersault. I thought of my own family, of my father and his attitude to affection and physical contact. I couldn't imagine him letting me kiss like that in his house. I looked across at my aunt. She didn't seem to mind. In fact, she had a surprising expression of calculated satisfaction on her face as she watched them leave the room.

The front door slammed, sending the net curtains in the living room billowing in the sudden breeze and Sylvia came whirling back into the living room.

'Oh Mum,' she laughed. 'Mum!' She flung herself into my aunt's lap and nuzzled her like a child, giggling and laughing. She couldn't keep still. She buzzed around the room alighting first on the arm of the sofa, then perching on the edge of the table.

'Mum, it's all turning out so well. I've got Charlie. And we're going to be getting our own flat.' She arched her back and the T-shirt rode up, exposing her flesh again, only this time I could see a diamanté stud glittering in her belly button. 'And my diamond,' she said, fingering it in wonderment. 'A real diamond!'

'Won't look so good with stretchmarks. You should be taking it easy.'

'Mu-um!' she said reproachfully. Then she draped her arms around my aunt's neck again. 'You know you're happy for me. You know you are. Go on, admit it!' She started tickling her.

Small giggles erupted from the pair of them. I looked away embarrassed. I shouldn't be here. No one, apart from Charlie, had spoken to me since I arrived. I looked at Carol. She was still munching her way through the plate of biscuits, oblivious to the world.

'I think I'd better go . . . Congratulations!' I stood up.

At once Sylvia was all over me. 'I'm sorry, Karen. We haven't spoken to you. But you will come tonight, won't you? Charlie said. He wants you to be there.'

'Yes,' said my aunt, 'you must come. This has all been a bit sudden. I don't know whether I'm coming or going. If you come tonight, we can have a chat. Please come. Will you come?'

I thought about the long and lonely weekend stretching ahead of me. I'd told Rob I was busy on Saturday night. Well, now I was. I couldn't miss my cousin's engagement party, could I? Family is family.

'I'd love to,' I said.

She showed me to the front door and as I turned to go, she smiled at me, a sad smile, full of regrets.

'You're the spit of your mum,' she said.

Chapter Five

I walked to the party.

Poppingham Estate was right next to the canal and the Dog and Duck was next to the estate. All these years I had gone running along the canal without realising that my aunt and cousins lived close enough to hear me shout 'Good Morning' as I ran past.

I brought Job with me. They hadn't said dogs were allowed, but they hadn't said no dogs either. If Job wasn't allowed it would be a good excuse to leave early.

The pub stood on the corner of a leafy triangle of grass near a little pocket of Victorian houses and trees that must have been about a hundred years old. The smell of slightly burnt sausages and barbecued chops hung appetisingly on the balmy air. A plastic banner hung across the front of the pub. It read *Happy Engagement*. Twinkling fairy lights decorated the two trees closest to the pub. A crowd of about eighty people stood outside. I could see no one I knew.

I tied Job to the leg of a metal table and told him to stay. That was fine by him. He was in sight of the sausages. He was drooling so badly, he hardly noticed me leave. Inside, the pub was almost empty, except for a group of overweight men who were jammed into the far corner concentrating hard on a small round board. Golden trophies lined the walls. Golden trophies glinted from inside locked glass cases. It was a darts pub. Team photographs took positions of pride behind the bar, wedged between rare flagons of rum and the prized bottles of single malt. *Dog and Duck Darts Team, 1997. Three years London Pub Champions.*

A heavy man in his early forties with a thick neck welded onto his massive shoulders pulled me a pint of bitter while still keeping one eye on the important action in the corner. Beside him on the bar sat a tiny little girl dressed like a doll wearing a pink frilly dress with golden studs in her ears.

'Hello,' I offered.

She stared curiously at me with a serious expression.

'Your daughter?' I asked.

'My granddaughter,' said the owner proudly. 'Me youngest's youngest.'

I took the pint and made my way back outside. Over the barbecue hung a notice. *As much as you can eat for £2.95.* Job would be pleased. The question was, one ticket or two?

I bought one ticket and grabbed two hot dogs. Then, when the woman was serving, I sneaked a couple of spare ribs inside my paper serviette. That should do us for starters.

We stood underneath the shady canopy of the large sycamore wolfing down the sausages, quite happy on our own. I nibbled the blackened pork off the ribs and then handed them over to Job. He crunched and cracked the bones, leaving not a sliver. The beer was mellow and slipped back easily.

It was 8.30 and although the sun had disappeared from the sky, it was still a fairly bright evening. With some food inside me and the warm glow of the beer I started to feel more comfortable and began to look around the group of people, noticing individuals.

I spotted my cousin Carol, sitting at a table. She was dressed in an unfortunate pair of waisted jeans and a T-shirt which showed her at her very worst. Well, maybe not her very worst – I hadn't seen her in a bikini. She was drinking a glass of Coke and talking to an old man wearing very thick glasses. When I noticed a lull in their conversation, I untied Job and we made our way over to them.

'Mum's over there,' she said as soon as she saw me, and

pointed towards the throng of people. I had wanted to talk to her. But after that remark it seemed impossible.

Suddenly there was a yelping, snarling, growling invasion. Five tiny Yorkshire Terriers, each one no bigger than Job's head, came charging towards us in strict battle formation. They sank their teeth into Job's fur. He dropped to the ground, protecting his eyes and nose with his huge paws.

'Henry, Ali, Frazier, Bruno, Tyson! Get back inside.' The man with the bull neck came towards us. 'Tyson! What did I tell you? Get out of there!' He picked up the leader, a wriggling and protesting bundle of red and silver fur and hurled him back into the pub. The others followed, still gamely snarling and yelping.

'Call that a dog?' asked our saviour.

'They weren't his fighting weight,' I replied.

'He's lovely, isn't he?' The publican bent down to ruffle Job's ears and popped a sausage into his mouth. Job rolled over and put his paws in the air. The way to that dog's heart couldn't be more clear. 'What kind is he then?' The man asked.

'He's a Bouvier des Flandres, a Belgian cattle dog.'

'A Boovy what? Look at the shoulders on him. Hey Charlie, look at the shoulders on this one!'

'Karen! How you doing?'

I looked up. Charlie was pushing his way towards us. He wore a clean white T-shirt printed with the words *Been Fishing*. Sylvia was still surgically attached to his neck.

'Karen, I see you've met Ron. Ron, this is Karen, my new cousin-in-law to be.'

'Nice one, Karen.' Ron shook my hand. The experience was surprisingly gentle. 'If you want another sausage for the big fella,' he said, 'feel free, just help yourself.'

'Thanks,' I said, remembering the hot dogs and the spare ribs and feeling slightly guilty.

Ron clapped Charlie on the back, turned away and began to gather up the glasses from a nearby table.

'Well, Sylvia, keeping her a secret, were you? You didn't tell me you had such a pretty cousin.' Sylvia looked daggers at me. Charlie bellowed with laughter. 'Don't worry, love, I'm a married man now.' He rubbed her stomach, his hand lingering possessively on her bare flesh. 'Good as.'

'Did you win?' I said, nodding at the sign on his chest.

'Almost – I came second. The fish were slow today. They were lurking at the bottom, keeping out of the heat. But I will do. You watch. Next weekend there's a competition for the Bank Holiday.' His eyes glazed over in sudden determination. Just as quickly he snapped himself out of it. 'What about you? Not brought your guitar with you then?' he joked. 'I was hoping you could give us all a bit of a sing-song.'

'It's a saxophone.'

'Sorry, saxophone.'

'Afraid not.' I smiled. 'It's my night off.'

'Seriously though, what is it you do? That was an expensive-looking piece of equipment you were carrying.'

'I'm making a film.'

'You're making a film?' He looked genuinely impressed. 'You didn't tell me I'd have such glamorous in-laws, Sylv.'

Sylvia had been nuzzling into his neck. Reluctantly she raised her head to look at me. 'I didn't know,' she said. 'We'd lost touch.'

'What's your film about?'

The onslaught of questions was now inevitable so I tried to explain in as low-key a fashion as possible what I was doing. I kept it vague and told him no details. The more off-hand I tried to be, the more impressed Charlie looked. Even Sylvia was taking it all in.

'Angel Point, know it well. I work for the same company.'

I was about to ask him what he did when out of the corner

of my eye I could see my Auntie Madge, Maggie, tottering towards us on stiletto sandals. I hardly recognised her.

'Don't look so surprised,' she said. 'I had to make a bit of an effort. It's my daughter's engagement party. Mother of the bride and all that.'

She was wearing a tightly fitting tailored top with a plunging neckline which lifted and separated to great effect. The skirt was white with huge black polka dots and a slit up the front. Her hair was piled on her head and her face was a painted mask of youth – pink lips, rosy cheeks and glittering eyes. She slid her arm around Charlie's waist and wriggled with pleasure as he pulled her to him.

'Did you hear that, Mrs W? We've got a new Steven Spielberg in the family. Our Karen's a film director. Here, Karen, what about making a film about us? You could have our wedding on the TV. How'd you like that, Sylvia girl? We'd be famous.'

Sylvia giggled suddenly and flashed me a coquettish look.

Maggie looked me up and down. 'You must have got your mum's brains then.' She made it sound as if I had inherited some dreadful bone-wasting disease. 'They certainly don't come from our side of the family, do they, Sylv?' Mother and daughter giggled in harmony. You could see their point. Brains in a woman, heaven forbid.

Conversation floundered. Charlie stepped in.

'You haven't got a glass, Mrs W, and yours is empty, Karen. We can't have that. This is meant to be a party. What are you drinking?'

'Just a half please this time. Half of ordinary.'

'Bacardi and Coke please, Charlie.'

'We'll be right back.'

As Charlie and Sylvia made their way towards the pub, they got swallowed by a group of loud laughing people. Maggie and I stood watching them. The silence between us was awkward and uncomfortable. I didn't know what to say. Everything that came to mind seemed too serious for such a happy occasion.

Job stood up and began to shift restlessly about. 'Sit!' I said. He ignored me.

'I bet your dad is proud of you.' Maggie's words were unexpected.

'He doesn't say.' The words that came out betrayed a bitterness I didn't know I felt.

Her eyes narrowed. 'That's just his way. He never was very talkative. He got worse after your mother died.'

There it was again.

'You said I looked like her,' I said quietly. I didn't have anything to hide behind. A drink is a convenient social prop but my hands were empty. My voice came out small, raw and vulnerable. Job sat down suddenly, his bottom on my feet, his back leaning into my legs.

'When I saw you on my doorstep this morning, I thought it was her ghost. I almost died myself.' She laughed raucously and then stopped abruptly when I did not join in. 'I'm sorry, love,' she said confidentially. 'I need a top up.' She leaned towards me and I could smell the sweet warm smell of alcohol on her breath. 'I'll just go and remind Charlie about those drinks. Be right back.'

I watched my aunt swaying towards the pub. A man reached over and grabbed her into a warm embrace and she laughed loudly at whatever he whispered into her ear.

'Ooh, he's lovely. Does he bite?' A young girl, maybe eleven, maybe twelve interrupted my thoughts. She had crouched down and was stretching out her hand tentatively towards Job. She wore tight jeans and a crop-top exposing her bare taut waist and outlining the beginnings of her breasts; long hair tied loosely in a pony-tail swung forward, masking her face. The sight of Job sniffing her outstretched fingertips was somehow unbearable.

'Only when I give him a secret sign,' I snapped.

She whipped her hand back and stood up. She was embarrassed and stood there with her shoulders slouching awkwardly. Then she wandered off, her movements gawky and angular. Despite her efforts she still looked very young.

I despised myself for the way I had spoken to her. There was something about seeing Maggie, about being here, that reminded me of myself when I was that age. Not a happy time. Still, that was no reason to take it out on a child. It was time to go before I did any more damage. I wasn't in the party mood: I shouldn't have come. I bent down to undo Job's lead. The chain had got tangled and twisted. I unhooked him and told him to stay. Job was in no hurry to move. His long pink tongue licked and licked at my wrist as I struggled to work it free.

'You're not off, are you?' I stood up to find Charlie standing there holding two pints of bitter. There was something odd about him. He looked different. It took me a moment to realise that he was on his own.

'Where's Sylvia?'

'Gone to freshen up, that's what she says. Me, I think she's gone to have a gossip with her mates in the loos.' He handed me my drink. 'Here you are. No point in doing things by halves, that's what I say.'

I hesitated. Job was still lying by my feet, showing not the slightest desire to leave. I let him make the decision for both of us.

'Thanks,' I said, and took the outstretched pint. 'So, when's the happy day?'

'Ten days away, Wednesday week.'

'You don't believe in long engagements, then?'

'What for? Once I knew about the baby, I wanted to do it there and then.'

There was no answer to that. I thought about my friend Sarah and wondered how she was getting on. Perhaps I should give her a ring.

'Been together long?'

'Long enough. Coming up to three months now.'

I was startled. 'Didn't take you long to get pregnant.'

'No. Amazing what you can do in five minutes.'

His remark was so unexpected I laughed, then choked; beer dribbled down my nostrils. 'I hadn't thought of it that way.'

Overhead, a random breeze rustled the leaves of the sycamore tree. The sudden chill made the hairs on my arms stand on end. All the people around us seemed to have melted away; the noise from the party receded into the distance. I felt suddenly, inexpressibly lonely.

'When did your mum die?'

His question took me aback. I had been thinking about my mum without even noticing it. I began to say something flippant but the expression in his eyes was genuine and concerned.

'When I was eleven,' I answered, flatly.

'Cancer?'

'No. She was knocked down by a bus.'

'That must have been hard for you.'

'It was.' Another breath of air sighed through the branches of the sycamore and the leaves murmured faintly in response. I rubbed my arms briskly and changed the subject. 'So what about you, Charlie? What do you do?'

He nodded. 'I'm a Contract Manager.'

'That sounds a bit grand.'

'Not really. It's my job to check all the work's been done and make sure the contractor doesn't get ripped off.'

'Whereabouts?'

'All over. I'm employed by McLachan Homes.'

' "Working in partnership with local people"?'

'That's us.'

'I'm impressed.'

'You needn't be. There's nothing to it. It's mostly routine.'

'Sylvia mentioned you were getting a flat.'

'Yeah, at Heaven's Gate as a matter of fact. What with the baby coming and us being local, PJ was able to pull a few strings.'

'PJ?'

'PJ Pickford, the locally elected councillor. Friend of Maggie's, friend of the family you might say. Talk of the devil, that's him now.'

A car was purring slowly past where we were standing. It was a Triumph 60, about twenty-five years old, bright red with gleaming chrome and polished hubcaps. You don't see many of those on the road these days. I caught sight of the pale, white face of a woman in the passenger seat who gazed towards us, at a party in full swing. The expression on her face was blank. The driver gave up trying to find a legitimate space and double parked a little further down the road. A man climbed out, hoiked up his trousers and adjusted his jacket before turning towards the Dog and Duck and the lights of the party.

'PJ!' Charlie shouted his greeting.

'Nice car,' I said. I noticed the passenger door remained shut.

'His wife's rich. Rumour is he could afford a lot better, but he doesn't – he's a good bloke. PJ's the Labour Councillor for Hackney East, has been since the year dot. Everyone round here knows him. He believes in the hands-on approach. If you've got a problem with your rent arrears or refuse collection, street-lighting or rehousing, PJ's your man.'

PJ drew level with us.

'You made it.'

'Course I made it, Charlie. It was only a dinner – I left as soon as the speeches were over. This is much more important. You've got a great girl there, son. I hope your new responsibilities aren't weighing too heavy. The way I look at it, it's good to know the tackle's in good working order.' He gave Charlie a playful punch then turned to me. 'Now, who are you?'

Charlie introduced me.

'Maggie's niece? Pleased to meet you. Me and Maggie go all the way back to the Flood.' I found myself shaking hands with a middle-aged man with smiling eyes and a firm, comfortable grip. 'Karen McDade . . . Now that name seems familiar. I've seen that written down somewhere.'

His eyes turned in on themselves and scanned his memory. 'A Karen McDade applied for permission to film the demolition of Angel Point. Anything to do with you?'

I nearly fell over in surprise. 'How did you know?'

'I'm closely involved in the Heaven's Gate project. It's in my constituency. Anything I can do, anything at all, just give me a call . . . Maggie!' He bellowed his greeting as Maggie and Sylvia walked towards us arm-in-arm. 'How's about a hug for an old man then?'

Sylvia coloured with pleasure and slipped easily into his arms. Her tiny body was enveloped in a large bear hug. Maggie looked on with pride; Charlie stood awkwardly to one side like a gauche adolescent, smiling fondly.

Just by chance I looked up and saw Carol. She was standing some distance away by the barbecue. The expression on her face was frightening. She was twisted up with hatred and jealousy. I wondered how many times this had happened. How many times the younger, prettier sister had so publicly received all the love and attention. She saw me watching her and made no attempt to hide her expression. Then she turned away and helped herself to another burger.

Sylvia wriggled free and transferred herself from one man to the other. Maybe there was something wrong with her, something wrong with her balance perhaps. I tried to remember if I'd seen her standing up straight and unsupported.

Charlie held her round the waist and pulled her to him.

'Congratulations again, son. And don't forget what I said – you take good care of her, or you'll have me to answer to.' With the practised ease of a career politician, PJ made his way through the crowd, warmly greeted by everyone he met. We watched him go.

'What's the story with his wife?' I whispered to Maggie.

'What do you mean?' Her words were slurred, her eyes glittered dangerously in the half-light.

'I presume that's his wife in the car?'

'You presume right,' she said, affecting a posh voice. Mimicking me? The unpleasantness of her tone took me completely by surprise.

'Stuck-up old cow! Thinks she's too good for the likes of us. She's lucky he's stayed with her all these years. Many's a one would have left her when they found she couldn't have any children. He's a good man, PJ. She just doesn't appreciate which side her bread is buttered.' She buried her face in her drink.

'So what about it then?' Charlie's voice was jovial.

'What about what?' He'd lost me.

'Filming our wedding. You'd like that, wouldn't you, Sylv?' Sylvia's eager eyes were huge round saucers in her face.

'I don't think I'd be any good at that,' I stuttered.

'Course you would,' said Charlie encouragingly.

'No, I mean it. There are people who specialise in that sort of thing. Someone like that would be much better.'

'Yeah, but someone like that is just who we *don't* want. We'd like a fly-on-the-wall sort of approach. You're family. We'd feel more comfortable if it was you. You know, following us around, watching us get ready, all that.'

'I don't think I could . . .'

Sylvia's gaze flitted from one face to another. 'Please, Karen!' she said.

'Can I think about it?'

'Come to tea on Monday night. Is it all right to invite Karen to tea on Monday night, Mrs W?'

'Not Monday, Charlie. Never on a Monday. It's my bingo.'

'Tuesday then?'

And it was agreed.

Chapter Six

On Monday morning, as arranged, I arrived at the Catherine Chorley building in Albion Street at 9.15. The sun was already beating down and the metal on the security buzzer was hot to the touch. A scrawny middle-aged black man with bored eyes insisted on making me open my camera case. I suppose at a pinch I could be mistaken for an international terrorist.

'You got a permit for that?'

'Carrying it or using it?'

'Filming with it.'

'I won't be filming with it in here. It's just for appearances.' I had a permit. The heat was making me bad-tempered and I didn't see what right he had to my life story.

Sullenly, he signed me in and gave me a visitor's pass. 'First floor. Room 107.' With one languid hand he directed me to the first floor and pointed me towards the lifts.

I pocketed the pass and took the stairs. Hot work. The fire doors at the top opened onto a long corridor of identical-looking doors. Room 107 was right at the end. I looked through the glass panel on the door into a room filled wall-to-wall with shabby grey metal cabinets.

When I walked in, Grace was on the phone; she raised one hand in greeting. Judy was leafing through a buff-coloured file, an expression of concentration on her face. 'Be right with you,' she mumbled.

The heat was stifling. I wandered over to the large grimy window at the end of the room and pushed and tugged at it before I noticed that it had been nailed closed from the inside. The window gave onto a small patch of city green. I watched an old man, still wearing his slippers, walking slowly, very slowly towards a park bench and lowering himself painfully down. When I turned back into the room, Grace was still on the telephone.

I caught Judy's eye. 'Do you mind if I make an internal call?' I asked.

'Not at all.' She shifted the file she was reading to the side of the desk to make room for me.

I pressed 'O' and asked the switchboard to put me through to the Press Office.

'A man called John Martin was accidentally killed on the Heaven's Gate development six weeks ago. Do you have an address for him?'

'Who is this?'

I identified myself and explained why I was ringing.

'I'll have to look it up. It'll take me five minutes. Can I call you back?'

'I should still be here. Much longer though and I will have left the building. I'm on extension 1070?' I looked at Judy for confirmation. She nodded. I hung up just as Grace was finishing her call.

'Right,' she said, standing up. 'The post-mortem results have finally come through. Everybody's very short-staffed because of the holidays – that was the reason for the delay.'

'And?'

'Mr O'Hagan had enough alcohol in his body to anaesthetise an elephant.'

'And there's no doubt that's what killed him?'

'None whatsoever. The verdict is alcohol poisoning. One thing is for sure, he would have died happy.'

'Does the widow know?'

'I've just spoken to her.'

'What did she say?'

'She said her husband didn't drink. I suppose it's only

natural, her desire to protect her own perfect picture of her dead husband, despite the evidence.'

'What happens next?'

'As we now have authorisation to release the body, the funeral will take place next Monday morning.'

'Fast work.'

'Undertakers are used to working at speed; they don't usually get advance bookings. By the way, I mentioned your name to Mrs O'Hagan and she's agreed to see you. Any time, she said. She's not going anywhere.'

'When did you do all this?'

'This morning.'

'What time did you get in?'

'Nine o'clock.' Grace grinned. 'I can't work once the heat of the day really gets going. Here's the address.'

I looked at the piece of paper she had given me. 'Eight, Albemarle Close E8. Where's that?'

'It's part of the Albemarle Estate at the east end of Richmond Road, near the railway line. About five minutes' drive from here. Used to be quite nice. That's part of the new development for Hackney 2000. The whole estate is due to come down. Several blocks have already been rehoused.'

Judy looked up from her file. 'You might want to check through these before you go. Grace mentioned you had offered to drop off the rest of his personal belongings. If you could, it would save us all a lot of time.' She reached under the table and pulled out a large see-through plastic bag. Inside was the same small tweed-coloured suitcase which I had last seen eleven storeys up at Angel Point.

'Let's just check the contents before you sign for them.' Deftly she eased open the lock. The bare little suitcase contained nothing but a few scraps of paper and the battered volume of poetry with the words *The Collected Works of John Donne* picked out on the front cover in black letters.

'No man is an island.' I remembered the words from my schooldays without even knowing that I knew them. 'Ask not for whom the bell tolls, it tolls for thee.' Cheerful stuff.

The phone rang. Judy answered it. 'For you.' She held out the receiver.

'I'm afraid I couldn't find the information you require,' said the woman from the Press Office.

'How come?'

'It's confidential.'

'What do you mean, confidential? I already have Lytton Grove, I just need—'

'Where did you get that from?' Her voice cut in.

'The *Hackney Clarion*. For goodness' sake, the man's dead and buried! That information should be in the public domain. Why the need for confidentiality?'

'I can't tell you that. It's not possible to access the file without the password and that is reserved for senior personnel. You'll need to put in an official request.'

I hung up, frustrated. Grace saw my expression and asked me what was the matter. I explained.

'Well, that's easy to deal with. You just didn't ask the right person.'

'What do you mean?'

'He's dead, isn't he?'

'Yes.'

'Dead people, that's what we do best. There will have to have been an inquest, therefore the coroner's office will have all the information.'

'How long will it take to find?'

'Watch these fingers do the walking.' She picked up the telephone again. Two minutes later she replaced the receiver. 'Number a hundred and twenty-nine. Top flat.'

I was impressed.

'When I move, I'm fast,' she winked at me.

'It only ever happens on a Monday,' Judy said dryly.

With the address in my pocket and the suitcase in my hand I went back down the stairs and out into the relentless sunshine. Too late, I remembered the visitor's badge in my pocket. Never mind, I could keep it as a souvenir.

Five minutes later I was driving down Mare Street on my way to Mabel O'Hagan's when I missed the turning to Richmond Road. The traffic was filtered on down to the left which more or less made my decision for me. I was on my way to Dalston by accident rather than design.

No. 129 Lytton Grove, top flat. I found it easily. In a street of seedy and rundown houses, No. 129 stood out. A wooden gate full of dry rot with peeling paintwork swung open on broken hinges and almost disintegrated to the touch. Three watermarked and illegible cards were fixed next to the bells for the three flats. I rang the top bell. There was no answer. I didn't hear the bell ring. I didn't even know if it was working.

I rang the bell again and peered through the grimy glass. I could see no movement. Next I tried the other bells. These too, brought no response. So that was that then.

As I made my way back onto the street, the front door of the house next door opened. A black girl with a sixties' hairstyle, a black knit crop-top and turn-up Levi's emerged holding a bin bag at arm's length, wafting the smell away from her nose with long, exquisitely manicured golden fingernails.

' 'kin' stinks, don't it? I made an omelette last night, I had beetles in me eggshells this morning. This weather's too much. You looking for someone?'

'John Martin.'

'He's dead.'

Just as well he wasn't my long lost brother. She didn't believe in letting you down easy. 'I know he's dead.'

'You're looking in the wrong place then, i'n't you?'

'I want to talk to his family.'

'They're not here.'

'I know. There's no answer.'

'No, I mean they've moved. What you want them for? Are you a social worker?'

'No!' I was indignant.

'Keep your hair on, I'm only asking. No, they've moved – lucky cow. Mind you, it might have been better if John was still here to share it. Then, seeing as how he ain't, she's lucky she got it.'

'Got what?'

'Her new flat. She's moved into one of them new flats down off Richmond Road.'

'What – Heaven's Gate?'

'Yeah, I think that's what it's called.'

'When was this?'

'Month ago.'

'Whereabouts? Have you got the address?'

'Yeah, yeah, I've always had a head for numbers, fat lot of good it's done me. Thirty-seven, Bay Walk. That's where she is.'

'Who's she?'

'Geri her name is, spelt G-E-R-I. And the kid's Lauren.'

'Kid?'

'Yeah, eighteen months. John adored her. Horrible way to go, being squashed like that. It gave me bad dreams for weeks.' She went back indoors and I went back to my car pleased with the new information, then indignant. Social worker indeed!

Should I drive straight to Bay Walk? Perhaps it would be better to wait until this afternoon. Time was moving on. I'd promised to be at Mabel O'Hagan's this morning. I looked up the address I had been given in the *A-Z* and found it easily. I parked down one of the quiet roads near London Fields and walked the rest of the way.

A footpath ran off Lothian Road down towards Albemarle Close and Albemarle Rise. As I followed it, it became a narrow walkway between two industrial buildings with windows far above ground level. Lichen grew in the crumbling brickwork; overhead I could hear the sound of a whirring saw.

The footpath was in shadow and despite the sweltering heat of the day it felt cool. A cat dodged down the alley between my feet and disappeared through a hole in the fence at the end. Seeing the cat made me think of Job. I felt guilty at leaving him at home again. But in this heat, what else could I do?

Albemarle Close was built in the shape of a horseshoe. The architecture was 1930s. Each house was two storeys tall. Each had their own gate and its own path up to the front door. Bay windows on the ground, and first-floor level promised plenty of light and there was a little patch of garden outside each home. At one time they would have been idyllic. Now they looked dreary and unkempt. Most of the houses were boarded up and abandoned. The little patches of garden were baked earth. Watermarks running down the sides of walls and flaking paintwork round the windows spoke of desolation and decay.

As I approached No. 8, I glanced up and thought I saw a face peering at me from a first-floor window. Then the face withdrew. Who was it? It looked like the face of a mournful child, wide eyes staring in mute misery.

I knocked on the door. In the distance, a dog barked. No one answered. Washing hung from an umbrella clothes-line in the garden next door – four grimy grey bras and various assorted outsized knickers were steaming dry in the morning sun. I sensed someone watching me. I looked around and saw a pigeon, one beady eye following my every move.

There was no reply. Maybe Mrs O'Hagan had gone out. Maybe she was asleep. I listened intently but no sound of movement came from inside the house. I knocked on the door again. Almost immediately it seemed I heard the scrabbling sound of a chain being pulled back.

'Don't you be in such a hurry, young woman, my old legs ain't what they used to be. Things take me a while.' The door opened and a woman stood there reprimanding me with a smile on her face.

Mabel O'Hagan was tiny, no more than five foot. As soon as I saw her, I wanted to put my arm around her and look after her. She seemed so ancient and very frail. Her body was slight, her legs and arms painfully thin. Despite the heat she wore a dress and a cardigan with a sleeveless housecoat on top, and on her legs were a pair of thick coffee-coloured tights. I remember wearing the same shade when I was at school and thinking I was so grown-up. American Tan, I think they were called. She peered at me from underneath a hood of overhanging wrinkles but the eyes that looked me up and down were young and bright.

'My name is . . .'

'Oh, I know who you are. That woman from the Council phoned me this morning. I've been expecting you. You're Karen McDade.'

I nodded and stretched out my hand. 'Mrs O'Hagan, I just want to tell you how sorry I am for your loss.'

Her hand slipped into mine in response. It was cool and dry and felt very, very delicate.

'That's all right, dear. Not your fault, is it?' Her tiny hand gripped mine tightly and she examined my face. 'You're sweating like a pig, love. Come down into my kitchen and I'll get you a drink. A cup of tea, mind. I don't hold with all those fizzy, bubbly things, they get right up my nose. The Chinese drink tea to cool them down and they should know.'

I put the camera down by a hall-stand inside the front door and followed her along the little corridor to the kitchen. Black and white photographs in simple wooden frames hung on the walls which were covered in embossed paper that had been painted white. The carpet underfoot was a dark, plain red, the kind that shows the dirt. It was spotlessly clean. In the small kitchen a floral blind was pulled down to keep the heat out and the air felt comfortable.

'I'll put the kettle on. Sit yourself down, it won't take a moment.'

'I've brought the suitcase,' I said, placing it on the kitchen table.

She ran her hands over the battered fabric, feeling it with her eyes shut. 'Yes, this belongs to Ted.'

'Do you want to check and see that everything is there?'

'What is there to check?' she was saying as she shrugged sadly. But I had already opened it. The papers meant nothing to her. But the book of poetry she picked up and held tightly in her hands. Not to read it, more to reach out to him.

'Now then, where's that tea?' She placed the book firmly on the table and moved the suitcase to the floor.

'That's a good idea.' I nodded over towards the blind. 'I can imagine the heat must get unbearable in here otherwise.'

She looked at me in surprise. 'It's because I've had a death in the family, love.'

I didn't know where to put myself. 'I'm sorry, of course. I'm really sorry. I wasn't thinking.'

'Don't worry. Death's so unusual these days, we forget how things are done.' She smiled reassuringly at me. 'Now, I'm sure I have some biscuits around here some place.'

I watched her stretch up to an overhead cupboard which seemed to be far too high for her.

'Here, let me!' I jumped up and reached past her with ease.

'No, I'm perfectly all right.' She shooed me away. 'If I have people doing things for me I'll stop being able to do them for myself.'

I watched her in silence as she warmed a china teapot, sloshing the water round and round before emptying it into the sink. Then she measured three teaspoons of loose tea into the pot, poured some milk into a jug and arranged the biscuits on a plate. I was beginning to find the silence disconcerting and I groped for something to say.

'Are you sure you don't mind talking to me?'

'Why should I mind?'

'Your husband has just died,' I floundered.

'I know that.'

'It must have come as a great shock.'

'Ted was eighty-four. I'm eighty-six. At my age, death doesn't come as a shock. It's more like an unwelcome interruption. Anyway, they say it's good to talk.' She set a cup and saucer in front of me and carried over the tea, milk, sugar and the biscuits, waving away my second offer of help.

'And the funeral is next Monday?'

At that, she stopped moving. She wiped her hands slowly up and down her apron. 'Yes. About time, I don't like thinking of him being cut up. I don't like thinking of him lying in a fridge somewhere. He should be in his resting place. He should be in the ground.' With a shake, she began to busy herself in the kitchen again.

'They're wrong about the drink,' I thought I heard her mutter under her breath.

'Sorry?'

'They are wrong about the drink. Ted didn't drink.'

I let her remark pass; I didn't know what to say.

Without using a tea strainer, Mabel poured out a hot stream of golden liquid and pushed the cup and saucer and the jug of milk towards me. The tea leaves resting at the bottom shifted grudgingly and then disappeared entirely as I poured in the thick, white creamy milk.

'No thanks,' I said when she offered me sugar.

'Go on, try a spoonful,' she urged. 'Especially in this heat, it keeps your energy up.'

I hesitated at the sugar bowl and then decided to put in half a spoon I stirred the sugar round and round, until a small whirlpool of tea battered a china cliff. And I searched for the words to explain why I was here and what I wanted to do.

'The film I'm making is about Angel Point, but it's difficult to make a film about a building. We have to make a film about people in relation to the building. So I wondered if I could talk to you about Ted's life. And his death. Why he died there. But, Mrs O'Hagan . . .'

'. . . Call me Mabel.'

'Mabel . . . don't you have things to do, things to organise? I quite understand if you want to leave this for another day.'

'I've organised what I have to. The priest's been and gone. My son Pete will be around later on this afternoon to sort out whatever else there is to do. I like the company. If you weren't here I'd be alone with my thoughts and there is time enough for that. Now, drink your tea up!'

We sat in silence apart from the occasional clink of a teaspoon against the side of a cup and the crunching of a biscuit which resonated loudly in my mouth. Outside, a police or ambulance siren wailed loudly, drawing closer and closer, then passed on by to some other distant emergency. I felt awkward, not knowing what to say, but Mabel seemed perfectly at ease, her eyes lighting in a small smile whenever they met mine. She was right about the tea, it was strong, sweet and very refreshing. I drained the dregs and felt tea leaves against my tongue. Discreetly I tried to spit them back into the cup.

Mabel finished her tea and set her cup back on its saucer. Then she reached for my cup and peered into it.

'Do you read the leaves?' I asked.

'Always have done – and my mother before me. They tell me more about someone than anything else can.'

'What do they say?' I don't believe in things like that, but it seemed polite to ask.

She held the cup close to her face and tilted it towards the light. 'They say you have a good heart, even if you don't always listen to it.'

Cheap fairground tricks. This could apply to anyone. I nodded. She angled the cup this way and that.

'I see sadness, great sadness . . . And I see Death.' Abruptly she banged the cup back on its saucer and raised her hand to cover her mouth. 'I'm sorry,' she said. 'Of course I see sadness and death. I'm sad that Ted died. The leaves are telling me my own story – that happens sometimes.' Her face was in shadow and I found it difficult to read her expression.

'Are you ready?' She reached out her hand and placed it on mine. It was cool and comforting.

I nodded. 'Are you sure you're all right?'

'No, but I'm ready. Come on then! This way!' she pushed her chair back with a sudden burst of energy.

She led me back down the corridor and into the front room. I followed her, noticing once more the black and white photographs on the wall. They seemed to be London street scenes. One in particular caught my eye. It was of a little girl aged maybe six or seven. She had a dirty face and was sitting on the front doorstep of a house. She wore a dress which was too small for her; white with puffed sleeves, it stretched tight across her shoulders. On her feet was a pair of lace-up boots worn with no socks. Her gaze into the camera was unflinching.

Mabel had come back into the corridor and saw me pausing in front of the picture. 'That's one of Ted's. These are all Ted's. That one was taken in 1947. He had a natural way with him. People forgot he was there. This one here is my favourite.' She gestured at a different picture.

The photograph was of three women in a pub. They would have been in their fifties. They were dressed for a celebration with hats and jackets and brooches pinned to their lapels. The shot was taken full-length. They stood with their arms around one another's waists and their glasses upraised. Their legs were up in the air. You could see their stocking tops. An old-fashioned knees-up frozen in time.

'That was at my niece's wedding. The one in the middle is my sister. It was taken in 1968, though you'd never guess it from the clothes. Maud never was one to keep up with the times. How she hated that photograph. She'd had a few that night and thought it made her look undignified. I said to her, if you can't let your hair down at your own daughter's wedding, when can you?'

'Your husband was a photographer?'

'He took photographs. I always thought he should do more with it. But there was never any telling Ted. Come in here.'

I fetched the camera and followed her into the sitting room. The curtains were drawn in here too. Mabel sat herself down in an armchair by the fireplace. I looked around wondering where to position myself.

The room was furnished with a three-piece suite; a round table stood in the bay window. A large spider plant, spawning hundreds of youngsters, squatted on a lace tablecloth on the centre of the table, dominating that end of the room. Two oil paintings hung on the walls. They were both paintings of park scenes, heavy on greens and browns and in a style which somehow spoke of the 1950s.

'None of your husband's photographs in here?'

'He would have thought that was the height of vanity. I couldn't persuade him to even put them in the hall. I just did it myself. And once it was done he never spoke of it. Never even mentioned it. I don't think he cared for the pictures themselves very much. He just enjoyed the taking of them.'

'Is that where you want to sit?'

'This is where I usually sit. I can move if you want me to.'

'No, that's fine. We don't have much light in here. Would you mind if I opened the curtains?'

'Yes, I would.'

I could have kicked myself. 'Sorry. Of course.'

'There's a lamp here.' She reached down to a plug by the fireplace and turned a switch. A standard lamp behind her chair lit up, casting a kind warm light on her face.

'That's much better.'

Mabel sat with her feet crossed at the ankle, her eyes staring into the distance and her hands folded demurely in her lap. And in an instant I recognised the mournful face of the child watching at the window.

'Mabel . . .' I interrupted her tentatively. Her eyes focused slowly on the present. 'You don't wear a wedding ring?'

'Ah, but I do,' she whispered. She unbuttoned her collar and reached into the front of her navy dress and pulled out a metal chain. Suspended on it was an old gold crucifix and a plain, round wedding ring.

'It got too big for me or rather, I got too small for it. I was frightened of losing it.' She smiled at me and slipped the ring onto the fourth finger of her left hand. It went on with ease despite the encumbrance of the chain. Her hand hung from her neck as if in a sling.

'Sometimes I sleep with it like this.' She leaned back in her chair and closed her eyes.

'You're not too tired for this?' I faltered.

'No, no, no. Don't mind me. I'm just saving my energy. These days it seems to come in fits and starts. Just tell me when you want me.'

I watched her through the viewfinder for a few minutes, taking in the almost imperceptible rise and fall of her chest. The featherlight breathing.

'What I'd like to do, Mabel, is to ask you a series of questions. If any of them are upsetting or difficult, please just say "Cut" and I will turn off the camera. Then you can have time to compose yourself and decide whether or not you want to continue.'

She nodded. I switched on the camera. Through the lens she looked as small and vulnerable as a child usurping her daddy's armchair.

On the mantelpiece was a selection of family photographs in cheap frames.

'Is this Ted?' I walked over to the mantelpiece and picked up a black and white picture of a man in his late twenties. Despite the fact that he looked ill at ease in a suit and tie, smiling rigidly for the camera, he was a handsome man. His dark hair was greased back in a side parting. His cheekbones were firm, his eyes dark and round. The mantelpiece contained their life in pictures. Snapshots of the passing years. Ted and Mabel. Mabel with a little boy. Ted, his arm round the shoulders of a gangly son.

'Let's do it,' she said softly.

I went back to the camera.

'Mabel: how did you discover your husband, Mr O'Hagan – Ted – was dead?'

'He'd been gone a few weeks. That wasn't very long so I wasn't worried. On Thursday I was out up the market and I bought a couple of pounds of fresh spinach. The man wrapped it up in the last week's copy of the *Hackney Clarion*. I had the spinach in the sink and the newspaper was on the draining board when it caught my eye.'

'What caught your eye, Mabel?'

'The story of a man's body found in Angel Point.' Her voice was low. 'Even then I don't know why I suspected it was Ted. I thought he'd just turn up – like he always does. But something made me call the number, and when I mentioned his suitcase, and they described the one they had found with his book of poetry, I knew it was him.'

'Did you have to identify the body?'

'Yes. Pete came with me. I didn't make him look at Ted. He's always been a bit squeamish.'

'And how was that?'

'Identifying Ted? I've seen him look better, if that's what you mean.'

I thought ahead to my next question.

'You said he had been missing for a few weeks. Why was he not reported as a missing person?'

'I didn't say he had been missing, I said he had been gone.' She must have looked into the unresponsive black eye of the camera and realised the need to explain further. 'That was Ted's way. He was always going off for a few weeks. I got used to it. The first time was at my own wedding reception. He left me a note. It said, *don't worry*. So I didn't. He came back two days later. He said he needed to see the sea. He'd been to Norfolk. People said I should have left him. Why? I don't hold with living in each other's pockets. He wanted to see the sea: I couldn't make him unwant it. Besides, there's plenty worse. It was never other women or drink or the back of his hand with Ted. I would have left him then.

'As he got older it became less frequent and he didn't stray so far away. Do you know, one time he got as far as Tangiers?' She laughed. 'He sent me a postcard. That was just after I lost the baby. That was the one time I could have done with having him around . . .' She trailed off.

'Can you tell me about when you and Ted met?'

Mabel's expression softened and her eyes seemed to turn in on themselves in search of some distant memory.

'1933. It was at my own parents' Silver Wedding anniversary. June. We all went on a picnic out onto the Hackney Downs. I'd been going steady with Albert for three years. I was working then at a milliners on Mare Street, mostly seeing to customers but also learning a little bit of hatmaking on the side. Me and Albert were saving up for a place of our own. My dad's brother brought his accordion and we had a bit of dancing. He never was much of a dancer, Albert. So there I was sitting on a picnic blanket with Albert and a couple of the old ones while the others were all up dancing. And Ted came over and asked me to dance. He'd been playing football into the twilight with some of his mates and he'd seen our campfire and come over to find out what was going on. I danced with him. I can still smell the smell of him now. He smelled of sweat and open air and the sea. After that, there was no going back. I told Albert that it was all over between us. He didn't take it well. Poor Albert. He's been dead this twenty-five years. And now Ted.' Her gaze was turned inwards. I didn't want to break the spell.

'And you had children,' I asked gently. 'You had a baby who died and a son. Were there any others?'

'I had no children.' Mabel's voice was suddenly bitter. 'I tried for eleven years and then I had a baby, a little girl, and I lost her. Pete was Albert's son. He was never mine. Albert finally got married during the war. I think with all those bombs dropping all around us, he decided it was now or never. But Betty died in childbirth, 1946 that was, when Pete was only one year old. Albert couldn't cope. He said he'd had his heart broken twice. He asked me to look after him. See, I couldn't have any more children after that one time and Ted, he knew that I longed for them. He said he didn't mind about Pete being Albert's son. He said he'd give him a good home. And he did. He was never the jealous type, Ted. Never one to hold a grudge . . .'

I left the camera running during the silence which followed. Mabel closed her eyes and leaned back in her chair. All was still. Perhaps she had fallen asleep. I pressed the Pause button. There was no movement. I switched off the camera and replaced the lens cap.

'I'm still awake, dear. But you're right. I think we've done enough for today.'

'One more question. What made you think that the dead man was Ted?'

'Simple. I couldn't hear his voice any more in my head. I've had that man's voice in my head every day since the day we met. Then I saw the bit in the paper about the man discovered on Angel Point and I got a bad feeling. Seeing how Ted used to work down there and everything, it all seemed to add up.'

'He used to work down there? I thought you said he was eighty-four?'

'And good for nothing?' she fired up. 'Pete, my son, he did us a favour. Ted wasn't as quick on his legs as he used to be and I couldn't stand him hanging around all day tripping me up. Pete used his influence to get him a job – sort of unofficial night-watchman. It gave him something to do.'

'So Ted O'Hagan was working for the council when he died?' Something in my tone must have displeased Mabel because she stared at me mutinously and for a moment she refused to answer.

'I didn't say that. I told you Pete was doing me a favour taking Ted off my hands and giving him something useful to do. It was all unofficial. I don't want anybody getting into trouble. If I know my boy he'll have been paying him out of his own pocket and no one any the wiser. Anyway, he's gone now.'

She sat up straight and winked at me. The wink couldn't disguise the sorrow deep in her eyes. 'How was I?'

'You were fine,' I said, smiling slowly. 'In fact, I think you were very, very good.'

'She's not just good, Karen, she's bloody brilliant. How on earth did you get her to open up like that?' It was later on that same day. Rob sat with his feet up in the privacy of my little third-floor edit suite at work. We'd had a working lunch. Sandwich wrappers and empty bottles of mineral water littered the table.

'I didn't do anything. It was all her.' To tell the truth I felt slightly awkward, watching it back. Mabel's suppressed grief was more apparent on camera; it felt like an intrusion.

'Well, it's absolutely magic. I think you should go with that.' Rob sat up, slapping both hands on his thighs. 'That's our documentary.'

'In what way?'

'People's lives. You think she's just a normal little old lady and then she comes out with all of that. She has a story to tell.'

'She is a normal little old lady.'

'Exactly.'

'Everyone has a story to tell.'

'Well, that's what I think you should go with. She's articulate, she's compelling, she would entrance any audience in the world.'

'So you think we should shift the focus of the documentary onto her?'

'Yes.'

'I'm not so sure.'

'I'm telling you, she's absolutely magic.'

'What about Angel Point?'

'Mabel, Ted, Angel Point . . . we can make it all tie together.'

'What about the young man's family?'

'Which one?'

'Either. Both.'

'Karen, thinking about it, we are focusing on three dead men here. Given our supposed subject matter, regeneration, don't you think that's a bit depressing? Perhaps we need to think about having a more upbeat emphasis. Besides, time's pressing.' What Rob said made perfect sense. Mabel's life spanned most of the century; there was plenty of material. We agreed, in theory, to concentrate on Mabel.

After he left, I sat mulling over everything we had discussed. He was right about one thing, time was pressing. But I still couldn't get away from the memory of those two lines in the *Hackney Clarion* and the terrified eyes of someone about to fall to his death. Mabel talked about death being an unwelcome interruption. The man I had seen die had been clinging to life with all the strength he possessed. There was a connection there. Obviously not a literal one, but there was a connection.

Youth, age, death.

I wanted to get home, and than get to Bay Walk and see what John Martin's girlfriend had to say. Heading towards Shaftesbury Avenue and the number 19 bus home, I walked past Mezzo's and, glancing in at the throngs of air-conditioned diners, I unexpectedly saw someone I knew. Just taking his seat at a table by the window was PJ Pickford. Yes, it was. He was a long way from Hackney.

Who was he with? Another man, so no tabloid scandal there. A well-dressed middle-aged man. For a moment I couldn't place him. But his face was so familiar . . . I paused a moment trying to work out who he was, without looking too conspicuous. I needn't have worried. Both men were concentrating on the difficult decision about what to have for lunch and were oblivious to the sweating rabble outside on the bustling pavements.

Then it came to me. He was Owen de Courtney, the Soho-based property developer. I recognised the man from his picture in the *Evening Standard*. Labour politicians and millionaire property men used to make strange lunch companions. Not any more. Good for PJ! He obviously believed in raising support and finance for Hackney 2000 from wherever he could. What had PJ said? He had offered assistance if I needed it. Surely the local councillor could open whatever doors necessary.

Once home I called Hackney Council and was told that he wasn't available. Of course he wasn't available, he was lunching the money. I asked to be put through to his secretary. The woman on the switchboard informed me that he didn't have a secretary but that she could put me through to somebody who would take a message for me.

'I thought PJ was a full-time councillor. Surely all councillors have a permanent office and secretary?'

'Oh no. Councillors are elected, but their positions are largely voluntary. We don't have the money to fund full-time back-up.'

'But PJ works for Hackney Council, doesn't he?'

'Mr Pickford is an elected councillor, and has been for many years. He represents Hackney East as a councillor but he is *not* an employee of the council.'

'So they are not like Members of Parliament with a full-time salary?'

'Oh no, not at all. Some councils pay their councillors an allowance of between five and twelve thousand pounds. Hackney pays an annual allowance of one thousand pounds plus reimbursement of expenses for all council meetings attended.'

'So someone like PJ would need to have some other form of income or employment.'

'I really couldn't comment on the financial arrangements of individual councillors, I can just repeat that the position of councillor is largely voluntary. Do you wish to leave a message?'

I did. I left my name and number and asked him to call me.

Afterwards I drove to 37, Bay Walk. The dinky little door-knocker with the brass finish was already beginning to show signs of wear and tear in the form of spots of rust appearing at the joints. Despite the millions of pounds being poured into the Heaven's Gate development, the contractors obviously didn't believe in wasting their money on quality fripperies.

No one answered the door. Thinking about it, in this weather, Geri and Lauren were probably among those paddling in the pool in the park.

I knocked just once more for luck. As I turned to go I became aware of the sound of subdued snivelling. I put my ear to the rippled glass panel on the door and listened carefully. It came from inside. I knocked harder, then banged on the wood with my fist. The crying escalated. Was the little girl here on her own? Was something wrong?

I opened the letterbox and shouted through. 'Geri! Geri! Geri!' Then I turned and scanned the walkway. What should I do? Should I phone the police? Knock on a neighbour's door? I was about to shout through the letterbox again when I saw someone standing there.

'Geri?'

'Who are you?'

'Can you open the door?'

'Not likely. Tell me who you are.' Somewhere behind her in the flat the child was still crying.

'I will if you open the door. I've come to speak to you about John.'

There was the sound of a chain being pulled back and the door opened abruptly. A pale young woman with short dyed blonde hair stood there blinking in the light. 'They've found out?' She spoke the words eagerly.

'Found out what?'

'That he's been murdered.'

Not what I expected to hear. 'John died in an accident on the building site.'

Her watery blue eyes were bloodshot with grief. 'John was

murdered,' she said with desperation.

'Can I come in and talk to you? Is that Lauren crying? Please – can I come in, Geri?' The expression in her eyes wavered between uncertainty and anguish. Finally, she held the door open wide and I walked on in.

A little girl in a grubby yellow T-shirt sat in the middle of a pile of coloured plastic in a corner of the living room. Tears and snot streaked her dirt-smeared face. When she saw me, a stranger, she got up and ran arms outstretched to her mother. Geri brushed her away without seeming to notice her distress, distractedly, the way you would a pesky fly.

Appalled, I noted the child's sodden disposable nappy, gaping and sagging to her knees. It looked as if she hadn't been changed all day.

Her mother sank into a corner of the sofa, lit a cigarette and stared blankly ahead of her. There was something habitual about this pose. The sofa seemed to close in around her. I was sure she had been sitting like this all the time I was knocking at the unanswered door.

'What were you saying about John?'

'He knew too much, didn't he? He told me we was going to have some real money. He told me he was going to take me and her away. Then the next thing, he was dead.'

'He died in an accident.'

'That's what they said.'

I listened to her words in horror. 'Are you really saying someone killed him?'

Her face twisted in mute misery. She nodded.

'Who killed him?'

'I don't know.'

'You said he knew too much. What did he know?'

'Stupid bastard wasn't saying. He liked to have his secrets, John.' I noticed the telltale piece of silver paper folded obsessively neatly in the ash-tray and looked again at those watery blue eyes. A junkie's eyes. Never trust the word of a junkie.

'Geri, have you got anyone to help you? Do you have family living round and about?'

It was as if she didn't hear me. Behind one of the armchairs, hiding from me and her mother, the little girl, Lauren, was still crying. I couldn't just leave her. I got up and rummaged around in the kitchen. There was some bread, some milk, some jam. I made up a plate of sandwiches and left them on the mat in the middle of the floor.

'Thanks.' I looked round, surprised to hear her voice.

'Thanks – I'm having a bad day today. I'm not normally this bad. It's just today.' Geri's voice trailed off.

'Are you sure you're all right?'

She nodded. Then she stumbled off the sofa and onto the floor. Little Lauren scrambled onto her lap and carried on eating the sandwiches I had made, the very picture of domestic bliss. I didn't know what else to do, so I left and shut the front door behind me feeling very disturbed. *Had* John Martin been killed? Highly unlikely. Anyway, if she were so free with her suspicions, surely Geri would have told the police.

Poor woman. Was anyone keeping an eye on her? Whoever moved her into this flat must be aware of her situation.

I snorted to myself. That black girl with the nails was right – I *was* turning into a ruddy social worker.

Chapter Seven

The following day was Tuesday. I forced myself out of bed at 6.30 and let myself out the back gate with an eager Job.

The towpath was almost deserted – the surface of the canal so still it provided a perfect reflection of the buildings lining the banks. A moorhen was foraging for food close on the bank, Job gave her a cursory glance and decided not to bother. He was too pleased with the exhilaration of this early morning run to break his stride.

I passed the spot where I had seen Charlie fishing on Saturday morning and involuntarily turned my head hoping to see him. He wasn't there. Of course he wasn't there. This was a weekday morning; no time for fishing, he would be at work.

I ran on around Victoria Park enjoying the best of the day and then headed for home. My stride was long and evenly paced. Breath flowed in and out easily, life felt good. On the long open stretch, past the gas towers but before Kingsland Basin. I saw him. He was standing gazing into the depths of the murky water. I saw him before he saw me. Should I stop and say hello? Should I just carry on running?

Job made my mind up for me. Without warning he leaped into the water, displacing half the canal all over Charlie's shoes. Charlie didn't have time to jump out of the way.

'You!'

'Sorry,' I said lamely. My heart was pounding, my chest was heaving; it took me a moment to catch my breath.

'It wasn't your fault.' There was a twinkle in his eye.

'Sorry about your shoes.'

'It's not my shoes I'm worried about. I was having a quiet word with those fish, striking a bargain with them about the competition on Saturday. Now they'll think they can't trust me.'

I was conscious of him looking at me, aware of my naked thighs and the flush on my skin.

'You coming around this evening then?'

'Planning to.'

'I might see you then.'

'Yeah.'

He watched me haul Job out of the water. I had to put my hand on his chain and wedge it against his neck to lever him out. For a moment I thought he was going to refuse. He splayed his two front paws wide apart on the bank and looked at us, daring us to come into the water and join him. Then, straining forward on his huge shoulders, he pulled himself out of the water, and recognising Charlie leaped up and bunted him affectionately on the shoulder. Charlie lost his balance and began to topple backwards. For a moment time paused. But only for a moment. Frantically Charlie's arms sliced the air like the blades on a helicopter. Then he fell backwards into the water with a huge splash. Job paused for a moment, astonished and then jumped joyously back into the water to join his new friend.

I stared at them both in horror. 'Job!'

He didn't even look my way.

Charlie's expression was priceless. He was treading water, trying to come to terms with what had just happened to him. Job was whimpering with excitement and in his enthusiasm was paddling over to lick his face. At the end of those big paws are long, strong claws. I had to get Charlie out quick. I turned around to look for a lifebuoy. Vandals had nicked it.

'Swim!' I shouted. Charlie made his way to the bank. I reached out my hand and somehow managed to pull him out.

He was soaked through; his wet T-shirt and jeans clung to his body as he bent forward and coughed up the dirty water from his lungs.

I turned back to haul Job out for the second time. I had a good mind to leave him there, permanently. He clambered back onto the towpath with no sense of having done anything wrong. In fact, he added insult to injury by wagging his tail and going up to smell Charlie's arse in a friendly doggy sort of a way.

'Job!' I sounded like an indignant maiden aunt.

Charlie looked at me, and quite suddenly I couldn't help but laugh. I laughed and laughed till the tears ran down my face. 'Sorry!'

'That's the second time you've said sorry.' I think he was trying to sound cross. But there can be no true anger without a sense of power or dignity and there was certainly no dignity left in this situation.

'He's never done anything like this before.'

And quite suddenly Charlie was laughing too. Job bounced gaily from one to the other of us, licking our faces, barking short happy barks. We laughed and laughed until the laughter had run out and then we stood looking at one another on the empty towpath.

Job was perplexed. The short stump of his tail continued to wag as he waited for the fun to begin all over again.

'I'll have to go back home and change.'

'Yeah.'

The silence was awkward now. The physical distance between us seemed to concertina. His eyes were warm deep brown pools and I wanted to jump in.

This man is going to marry your cousin, I had to keep repeating it over and over.

'I'd better go.'

'Me too.'

'See you this evening.'

'See you.' I ran on, with Job dripping by my side. I didn't look back: I didn't let myself.

It was still only ten past seven when we got home. I showered and dressed and thought of Charlie. Then I tried not to think of Charlie and only succeeded in thinking about him some more.

It was a long time since I had responded to someone in quite such an immediate way. Years before I'd ended up in bed with Jack the first night we met. That had been a disaster. This was bound to be a disaster too.

Yeah but when I slept with Jack we were both pissed. By the time I sobered up I realised what a mistake I'd made.

Trouble was, I'd met Charlie three times now, and each time I was stone cold sober.

At half-past nine the traffic by the Angel was very congested. Buses, taxis, trucks and cyclists were trying to change lanes only to get stuck behind cars turning right at the traffic-lights. Job was so pleased at this unexpected trip into town that he leaned over and gave me a Bouvier lick all over my face.

'Thanks, Job,' I said, wiping my mouth dry with the back of my hand. I don't think he picked up on the sarcasm. There was nothing to do but relax. I let my mind go into free-fall, sliding up and down with the haunting melody of the saxophone playing on Jazz FM.

What if Geri were right? Why would John Martin have been murdered? I needed access to more information, that's why I was driving into Town. *McLachan – Working in Partnership with Local People*. They must have a company spokesman I could talk to. Someone a little more forthcoming than Jim Bryant.

Soho Square was relatively quiet. Media London had made its annual exodus to places tropical – whitewater rafting on the Galapagos Islands seemed to be the 'in' thing this year. I pulled into an empty parking space and bought myself two hours of time. Job leaped over the side of the car and onto the pavement, making sure that now he'd got this far, he wasn't going to be left behind.

I was starving. We walked down the shady side of Wardour Street and stopped at a takeaway franchise for something to eat. I tied Job to the railings outside the entrance. He stood there licking his lips in anticipation. I came out clutching a styrofoam cup of tea with half a spoon of sugar and smiling to myself. I also had a croissant for me and a sausage roll for Job.

Bob Wilkes was talking to the receptionist when I walked into the building. She was virtually prostrate over the desk trying to boost her non-existent cleavage.

'Karen!' Bob greeted me warmly when he saw me. The receptionist looked as if she had just taken a bite on a piece of sour lemon. That pleased me.

In the past Bob and I have had words about Job. Now it is a subject we don't discuss. When I'm working I try to keep Job out of sight of the clients as much as possible. Then if we do bump into one another, Bob just pretends that Job isn't there, which with an eight-stone dog shows a remarkable gift for self-deception.

'So, how's the filming going?'

I made a wry face.

'I knew you wouldn't be able to live without us for long.'

'Don't worry, I've said I'll be back after the Bank Holiday weekend.'

I walked down the corridor and into Edit Suite Two. Home sweet home. The outer door whooshed slowly shut. I felt that familiar moment of aural disorientation in the soundproofed room. A halo of light shone over the control panel. Tiny red dots glowed in the dark on the wall behind to show the equipment was turned off. The rest of the room was in inky blackness. I heard Job snuffling out the best place to lie, and saw his large shadow climbing up onto the soft leather sofa in the observation area.

I turned on my PC and logged onto the Net. Within a minute and a half I was staring at the home page of McLachan Construction plc: Established 1968. Annual turnover £200 million. Nice. General construction work in the British Isles and France. Combination of public works, housing developments and Private Finance Initiatives, whatever they were. Head Office – a postal box in Berkeley Square. No address. Just a telephone number. Several subsidiary companies listed, but no names of any people. No Managing Director, no PR company. No one to approach.

I dialled the telephone number for the Head Office. 'I'd like to be put through to the Managing Director's office.' Might as well go all the way to the top.

'May I ask what this is regarding?' The well-groomed voice belonged to a middle-aged woman.

'I'd prefer to explain that to him,' I said.

'I'm afraid there's no one in that office today,' she continued. Her voice didn't sound afraid. At least, not that I could detect. 'May I take a message?'

'I'm ringing about the Heaven's Gate Development in Hackney.'

'Ye-es?'

'I have some questions regarding the discovery of a body in one of the buildings due for demolition and I would like to know whom to approach for answers. Do you, for example, have a PR agency?' By now my voice sounded almost as well-groomed as her own.

'Who is this calling?'

'Karen McDade, from Terminator Films.' God, how I hated that name. Rob said he christened the production company years before as a drunken joke, but he still refused to change it. He said that as the company had begun to build up an industry profile, changing the name would be like starting all over again.

'We don't have a PR agency. Any enquiries should go through Heaven's Gate Site Office.'

'I've tried that. Your foreman wasn't exactly welcoming.'

'I'm sorry to hear that. In that case, you should contact the local lawyer dealing with that particular site.'

'And that is . . .?'

'Hold the line one moment, please.'

I waited on the line. She must have been gone for over a minute. There was no music played to distract me, to make sure I didn't get bored and hang up. Perhaps she didn't care if I did. Then I heard her voice again.

'Any enquiries are handled by Graham, Sacks and Kennedy, on the Kingsland Road.'

I jotted the name down on my pad.

'What did you say your name was again?'

I severed the connection. I didn't mean to be rude. Well, maybe I did.

Before I left work I dialled Mabel's number.

Her clear old voice answered the phone, each word enunciated and articulated in such a way as to avoid any misunderstanding.

'May I come and see you again later on today? We loved what you gave us yesterday.' She agreed and I left the West End with a clear conscience.

On my way to Hackney I dropped Job back at the flat and picked up my camera bag. There was a message on the machine from PJ Pickford returning my call. To give the man his due he lived up to his reputation as someone who was on the nail. I called him back but he was busy. Telephone tag is growing more and more popular as a solitary sport.

As I left, Job offered me his usual doleful look. Give him an inch and he wants a mile. After all, he hadn't done too badly today.

Graham, Sacks & Kennedy, McLachan's local lawyers. I found the office wedged in between a Turkish food store and a disused wet fish shop which had been turned into an immigration advice bureau. Telephones and ledgers with multi-lingual leaflets were piled up on the old white marble counter. A drainage furrow bisected the white tiled floor. Apart from immigration advice the shop offered a cheap satellite telephone link to countries such as Nigeria, India and Vietnam. The late-twentieth-century equivalent of the long-awaited letter home. The prices were so reasonable I was tempted to ring someone myself but I didn't have anybody to call.

I went into the Turkish food store and bought myself some Coca-Cola brewed in Lagos and stood swigging it on the pavement trying to figure out an approach. In the end I couldn't think of anything more plausible than the truth.

The blinds were drawn on the windows of Graham, Sacks & Kennedy, but a sign said *Open for Business*. I pushed open the door. The office was small and dingy. Not exactly the representation I would have expected for a business with an annual turnover of £200 million.

A woman sat at a desk-top computer typing away and didn't look up when I came in. Two fans bracketed either side of her desk rotated the warm air as she worked.

'Take a seat. I'll be right with you,' she called.

Four black plastic chairs were lined up against one wall. Two of them were taken. On one sat a young Asian woman in a pink and green sari cradling a sleeping toddler. In the other sat a tall and bony middle-aged black man. Neither of them acknowledged my arrival. They stared blankly into space as if resigned to an indeterminate wait. I plonked myself down next to them. In front of me was a coffee-table with this week's issue of the *Hackney Clarion* and a couple of out-of-date copies of *Woman's Own*. It was like being in a down-market dentist's.

After ten minutes – it seemed like an hour and a half but I say ten minutes because I know that in these situations I have a tendency to exaggerate – the woman still hadn't looked up from her computer screen.

Reluctantly I turned away from a very absorbing article about the best way to get rid of wine stains on antique lace tablecloths and approached her desk.

'Excuse me,' I began politely.

'Take a seat. I'll be right with you.'

'You said that already.'

She looked at me in surprise. She was a middle-aged white woman. Her face was caked in what must have been an inch of powder to prevent her foundation from running in this heat. She wore glasses which magnified the uncertain blue of her eyes and her lips were stained bright red. Whatever she saw when she looked at me wasn't what she was expecting to see.

'Can I help you?' she asked.

'I understand you are the lawyers acting for McLachan plc on the Heaven's Gate site.'

Her eyes grew wary. 'Mr Sacks has that pleasure,' she said.

'May I speak to Mr Sacks?' I asked in my most charming voice.

'He's a very busy man.'

I looked around at the shabby office and its waiting clients and nodded in understanding. 'Please. I will only take up a few minutes of his time.'

'Who may I say you are?'

'My name is Karen McDade. I work for a – um – film company.' I extracted a card from my purse and handed it to her. Perhaps it didn't look so bad written down.

Miss Moneypenny began to look impressed. She reached her hand towards her telephone.

'I'm making a documentary about the life of a man who was discovered dead there a few weeks ago,' I went on. 'My questions to Mr Sacks are purely background research.' There. I sounded so professional I could almost believe I did this every day.

'Mr Sacks?' said Miss Moneypenny. 'There's a television director here . . .'

I basked.

'. . . from Terminator Films . . .'

I cringed.

'. . . who would like a few words with you . . . No, it's a she, Mr Sacks and she wants to ask you a few questions about McLachan plc . . . He says you are to go right up.'

I turned apologetically to my fellows in waiting, but they gave no sign of having paid attention to any of this. They both continued to stare blankly ahead of them.

I went through the door at the back of the room. It led onto a narrow corridor with two closed doors to my left and a flight of stairs leading off on my right. From behind one of the doors I though I could hear the low murmur of conversation.

It was now apparent that much of their decorating resources had gone into the reception area. The corridor was gloomy and dank. It smelled. The smell was a combination of rotting fish and damp. I had been told 'to go right up', so I climbed the narrow stairs. There was one door when I reached the top. I knocked.

'Come in!'

I opened the door and walked into the most delicious cool.

A large air-conditioning unit pumped out freezing air into the small room.

'How can I help you?' A small man in his early forties with a black beard and wearing a skullcap had risen from behind his desk and was walking forward to greet me.

'I think you already have,' I said, relaxing into the cool.

'Ah, the air-conditioning unit,' he said, a wide grin splitting his face. 'So much more enjoyable when you remember all the others sweltering in the heat down below. Please!' He ushered me to a chair and then retreated once more behind his desk. He folded his hands and stared at me for a long moment, continuing to smile and nod his head. 'So. You are a television director.'

I could feel the denial welling up inside of me. I almost started to say, 'Well, no, actually . . .' And then I stopped myself. I crossed my legs and clasped my hands.

'Yes,' I agreed, pleasantly.

'And what can I do for you?'

'It's regarding McLachan plc and their site at Heaven's Gate.'

'Yes, a wonderful company. Working together with local people. Transforming the face of Hackney. These immigrants are lucky people to have come to live in such a Borough.'

'Yes, I agree,' I said, looking at his Jewish skullcap and remembering my Irish origins. 'London has become home to so many of us.'

'Indeed.' His smile didn't falter. 'So how can I help you?'

'I'm making a documentary about the development for Hackney Council. There have been several deaths on-site. I tried to speak to the site foreman yesterday morning but he wasn't very helpful and one way or another, I have been referred to you.'

'And how can I be of help?'

'I was wondering if you could confirm the circumstances surrounding each death.'

'And why would you need to know this? Is this within your brief from the council?'

'My brief from the council is wide and I'm trying to build up a picture of how exactly the site operates. For example, Ted O'Hagan. I understand he was actually employed as a night-watchman at the time of his death.'

'I am afraid it would be impossible for me to give you the information you require. You see, I don't have it. Working on a construction site, Miss McDade, is a notoriously fickle business. Some employees, especially labourers, are paid in cash on a casual basis and frequently there is no list at any one time of who precisely is working on-site.'

'Mr O'Hagan was eighty-four. I don't think he would have been working as a labourer. Surely there is someone who would know whether or not he was employed there.'

He tilted his head to one side. The gesture was non-committal.

'There was another man killed on-site.'

'Killed? Really, Miss McDade, you mustn't use such emotive language.'

'Another man who died, John Martin. The verdict was Accidental Death. What were the circumstances surrounding the accident?'

'Do you have a card, Miss McDade?'

I produced another card from my purse and handed it to him. He reached out one elegant manicured hand to take it and looked at it carefully. 'There is no address on this card.'

'Someone mans the phone during office hours. Outside that time there is an answering machine.'

'I understand. Times are hard, overheads high. Leave this with me. I will see what I can do.'

'Thank you for your time.'

'The pleasure has been mine.' He showed me out. Afterwards I remembered that he even managed not to shake my hand.

Downstairs the waiting room was empty apart from Miss Moneypenny who was still typing away, still guarding the entrance to the inner sanctum.

'Did you get what you were after, dear?'

'No, I didn't,' I said, realising in surprise that I hadn't learned anything at all.

I rang Mabel from the car expecting to go around and see her straight away. There was no answer. The heat was sweltering: it was too hot to be alive. I didn't fancy sitting outside Albemarle Close waiting for Mabel to come back. There was no telling when that might be. I wound the roof down and headed for home.

With the blind down in the conservatory and the doors wide open I stretched out on the sofa with a cold flannel on my face. Job had begun by licking my feet but his pleasure at seeing me was soon defeated by the sheer effort of movement. Instead we surfed the daytime talkshows. Adultery, incest, sheep-fucking – people would confess to anything in order to get their fifteen minutes. Their chance to explain to, to be liked by, to connect with the faceless millions. It was all so depressing. Especially if you were a sheep.

I rolled over and reached for the telephone. 'Rob? Do you think it's possible to run some kind of company search for me?'

'To find out what?'

'I'd like you to run a search on McLachan plc. They are the people who manage the site where Ted O'Hagan was found dead. And it needs to be a proper search. I've looked them up on the Internet. Their home page gives very little concrete information.'

'What are you looking for?'

'A name. Any name. I want to find out if Ted really was working on the site when he died.'

'Karen, a search will cost money and I don't really understand the relevance of this.'

'How much money?'

'A hundred pounds, at least.'

'Money well spent.'

'In your opinion.'

'In my opinion.'

'I thought we'd agreed to go with Mabel.'

'No. You suggested we go with Mabel.'

'Look!' Exasperation coloured his voice. 'I really think Mabel is a much better bet. She's obviously a rich and vibrant source of oral history and she's got the added attraction of being alive. I think you should go and see her again.'

'I tell you what,' I bartered. 'I'll go and see Mabel again this afternoon if you agree to run the company search and find out what I want to know.'

'Good. You're seeing sense.'

I smiled and said goodbye; no need to tell him I'd already spoken to her that morning. The lunch time news came on. Lunchtime. It was too hot to eat. I dozed through the obscure and desperate items gleaned from the world of international politics. Everyone was on holiday. There was nothing happening . . . I drifted off and then came to suddenly as something caught my attention – the sound of the voice or the subject-matter, I don't know which. I opened my eyes and saw PJ Pickford in close-up, in my living room.

'The money is vitally needed,' he was saying. 'Not just because of the homes it will provide. This new initiative takes us into the millennium with a boost to the morale of the people of this Borough.' He came across well. Caring, committed and dynamic.

Just at that moment the phone rang. 'Can I speak to Karen McDade, please?'

'Talk of the devil, or rather think of the devil.'

'Sorry?'

'I was just watching you on the TV.'

'And how was it?'

'The words caring, committed and dynamic spring to mind.'

'Fancy making an investment in a sure-win local community project?'

'I didn't know there was such a thing; besides, I don't have any money.'

'So what can I do for you?'

'I'm having difficulty finding out anything about the young man who died the other day.'

'Micky Holman? That was an awful business. He's an only son. I've known the family since before he was born.'

'PJ, you're amazing. You wouldn't happen to have an address for him?'

'I would. Why do you want it?'

I explained.

'I'll need to see what I can do, but I wouldn't hold out much hope. The mother's very cut up. I don't think she'll want to see you.'

'Come to think of it, PJ, the police were supposed to contact us regarding witness statements and they haven't done so.'

'I've read the report on that incident. There were no suspicious circumstances. That could well be the reason. Let me get back to you.'

I waited on the sofa until the scorching heat of the day had abated, then took Job outside along the towpath for a quick sniff around. He climbed down some steps and lowered himself into the canal. He didn't even bother to swim, he just stood there enjoying the cool water lapping at his skin. Back indoors, I covered the sofa with a black plastic bin bag and a dark-coloured towel and just to be sure I closed my bedroom door giving him only one choice of bed. I know the way that dog thinks.

At four o'clock I headed back to Hackney. A woman in a nurse's uniform was coming down Mabel's path as I arrived. Mabel was waving to her from the front door.

'Are you all right?' I asked, concerned.

'Yes. Social Services. Checks up on us twice a month.' She faltered. 'Checks up on me, now. Tea?' she finished, brusquely.

'I'd love some.' We went into her little house and I shut the door behind us. I followed her down to the kitchen. 'Rob and I loved what you did.'

'Who's Rob?'

'My partner.'

'Been with him long?' She looked at me shrewdly.

'My business partner,' I corrected. Judas.

Ted's suitcase was wedged between the cooker and a cupboard. Mabel pulled it free.

'I forgot to take this up the stairs with me. You wouldn't be a dear and save my legs? I've been sorting out some of Ted's clothes to take down to Oxfam. No point in leaving them for the moths this winter. Put the case on the bed beside his jackets. I'll see to it later.'

Upstairs all was quiet. Too quiet. The noise of Mabel pottering in the kitchen receded and it felt as if I were alone in the house. The curtains were still closed blocking out the harsh sunshine, bathing the rooms instead in a somnolent half-light. The air was still and heavy. Mabel had given me permission to go upstairs; indeed, she had asked me to put the case away, but still it felt as if I were trespassing.

At the top of the stairs a huge spider was weaving a web from light-fitting to the door lintel. As I approached she stopped and we looked at one another.

114

I found Mabel and Ted's bedroom at the front of the house. The room was simply furnished. There was a double bed covered in a white towelling counterpane. A dressing-table from the 1930s, vaguely Deco in style, and a large wardrobe. Ted's clothes were on the bed, almost as if he were packing to go away somewhere. Three jackets, a winter coat, several pairs of trousers and a pile of socks. It felt somehow heartless of Mabel to be going through his belongings, getting rid of them so soon and I felt a sharp spasm of distaste for her pragmatism.

Once, with the lorries thundering past outside, I sneaked into my mum and dad's room after school. Mum was vanishing from me, her shape, her smell, the way her lips used to crinkle together before she smiled. I had to recite these things to keep them fresh. Even her smell was going from me. So I sneaked into her room and opened the door to her wardrobe ready to bury my face in the scent of her, press her clothes to my skin and inhale. Feel for her, search for her warmth. The wardrobe was empty. Completely empty. Almost as if she had come back to pack up her things and move out. Shoes, hats, coats, cardigans. Everything. Gone. Bundled away. Two wire coat hangers jangled together in the empty cupboard like wind chimes.

For a fleeting moment I felt as if she had done it. I imagined that she had come back and packed everything up herself and moved out. Why didn't you wait for me, Mum? If you couldn't take me with you, at least you could have waited to say goodbye.

My dad must have done it. One day when I was at school he must have taken everything she had ever owned and thrown it all away.

Memories. Funny how one death brings back memories of another. Time stood as still as the motionless air. I sat down on the corner of Mabel and Ted's bed and remembered my mother's dancing dresses, the ones she had made herself.

She used to take me in on the bus to Oxford Street. She'd choose the pattern and then I'd go round with her, feeling all the different materials, watching her while she held the bolts of fabric up against herself in front of a mirror to see which one suited her best. Together we'd try and imagine the finished dress.

Then in the evenings, after I finished my tea, when I was bathed and in my pyjamas, sometimes she used to let me sit and watch her working away, her mouth full of pins. When she had finished, she'd try it on. She'd tie her hair back, put on some make-up and her earrings and slip the dress carefully over her head. I always thought she looked so beautiful. She laughed to see me watching her with my mouth wide open.

'One day very soon, we'll be dressing *you* up to go out,' she'd say. She put one of her dresses over my head, gathering it in at the back with her hand to make it fit better. 'You can borrow one of these when you're bigger,' she promised, and looking at myself in the mirror, I'd glow with pleasure and anticipation.

Instead my dad had bundled them up and thrown them away.

The feeling of loss was overwhelming. I was frightened by the intensity of my own grief. I had nothing to keep. Nothing to hold on to which belonged to her. Nothing to grow up into. No clothes to borrow, to sneak out of the house in. To mark my transition from girl to woman.

I didn't ask him what had happened to them. How could I? We never mentioned Mum's name. For months afterwards I scoured the secondhand shops looking for them. Searching for a fragment of familiar fabric.

I was going through the party dresses in the Oxfam in Highgate one day when some snotty-nosed cow made me jump.

'Leave those dresses alone. They're all too old for you. You might get them dirty.'

My well-scrubbed hand shot guiltily back into my pocket.

'That's the trouble with girls these days. They're all trying to grow up too young,' she said to her assistant.

Snotty-nosed cow.

I was only eleven when she died, not yet old enough for my mother to embarrass me. In my memory she always looks beautiful. You see, everyone has a story to tell. If only there is someone to listen.

When I came to I was sitting on the side of Mabel's bed. I stood up hurriedly. At the sudden movement, the little suitcase fell to the floor. I bent down to pick it up and to my surprise, I noticed a small scrap of blue and white paper protruding from the battered cover. Something had fallen out of the lining – a printed piece of paper with a perforated edge. On it was the name and address of a chemist on the Queensbridge Road, not far from Angel Point. It looked like a receipt for thirty-six colour photographs. It must have slipped down into the lining and lain there undiscovered by Grace. Curious. I slipped it into my pocket and went back downstairs.

'Kettle's boiled,' Mabel said as I walked back into the kitchen.

'I'm sorry I was so long. I hope you don't think I was snooping.'

'I don't mind. In a way, that's what you are here to do, isn't it?'

'Yes. I mean no. What you said yesterday about one death leading to memories of another . . .'

Mabel looked at me quizzically.

'I was thinking of my mother.'

'She's dead?'

I nodded. 'I was eleven.'

Mabel looked at me and I couldn't read the expression in

her eyes. Then she poured out the tea, a golden stream of hot liquid arching from teapot to cup. She didn't say anything. For a moment I was resentful: I wanted to be asked. And then I realised she was right. It was my story. I could tell it if I wanted.

'Why are you getting rid of Ted's clothes so soon?'

If she was surprised at the abrupt change of subject and my hostile tone, she didn't show it.

'Because he's not coming back,' she answered simply. 'It will be winter soon. No need to leave them there in the wardrobe while someone else could be making use of them.'

'But don't you want something to remember him by?' I asked, again aware of the aggression in my voice.

'Ted is a part of me. I will never forget him,' she responded.

'You think that now,' I said crossly. 'But time wipes things out and you find one day that you can only remember memories of memories. And even those are vague.' I trailed off, biting my tongue to hold in the pain.

'I'm eighty-six. I don't have that kind of time left, Karen.' Her voice was kind and gentle. She sensed that my fury was not directed towards her.

I took a sip of the hot tea, grateful for the distraction. Outside there was the sound of a fractious baby coming closer and closer and then being wheeled on past and into the distance.

'This heat is difficult for little ones,' said Mabel.

'It's difficult for everybody,' I replied, wiping beads of sweat off my forehead. 'Do you mind if we do some more filming today?'

'Of course not.'

After we had finished our tea, I followed Mabel down the corridor, wading through the stifling air towards the living room. I picked up my camera case from the hall. When I entered the living room I was just in time to see her pick up a bottle of pills from the coffee-table and hide it behind the clock on the mantelpiece. The pills rattled in the bottle as they were set down on the hard stone. She sat and waited patiently as I set up the camera. I turned on the light, checked the reading and adjusted things accordingly.

On camera Mabel told me about the great literacy drive after the war and about how she'd gone to college and got her diploma and then gone on to teach evening classes in English Literacy at the Adult Education Institute on Hackney High Street in the forties and fifties. She spoke about working alongside Ted, who taught art and photography in the same building, giving working men and women the chance to experiment in clay and oils and watercolour. Giving them a chance to be children again, these people whose lives had been bisected by the hardships of the war. She spoke about instilling people with a sense of pride in their achievements. She spoke of optimism and hard work. She brought the past alive.

I said that to her. 'You bring the past alive, Mabel.'

She looked at me sadly. 'I'm not talking about the past, Karen. I'm talking about my life.'

She told me about bringing up another woman's son as her own. She told me about how she loved him. She spoke of him fiercely, protectively, sorrowfully.

'Sometimes I worried if I was the right person to be bringing him up. I wondered if he could feel my disappointment in him. Not in him exactly, but in the fact that he reminded me I couldn't have my own. You see, I could feel all along there was nothing of me or Ted in him.'

'Do you still see him?'

'All the time. He works for the council round the corner, so he often pops in. He doesn't live round here though. He's done very well for himself. His wife's got money – they live out in Essex. We get on better now. He never had children of his own either. Sometimes I wonder what would have happened if Ted hadn't swept me off my feet that night. Me and Albert . . . sometimes I wonder.'

'Do you have any regrets?'

'No,' she laughed. 'I loved Ted. I can never regret that.'

Long after I'd run out of tape and been forced to stop filming we chatted on over cups of tea and a packet of digestive biscuits.

'Karen, one thing really confuses me. They keep saying that Ted had a lethal amount of alcohol in his blood.'

'Yes?'

'Ted didn't drink. I've told you that before, Karen, but I don't think you believed me. Ted didn't drink.'

I kept my eyes glued to the kitchen table. You can't argue with facts.

'He'd say it was the black Irish in him. There was the Irish that was the good bit of him, and then there was his dark side, like we all have a dark side. His was the drink. He'd say it came from the dark bit of his tribe.'

'So he did drink?'

'No. But he had been drunk twice in his life. The first time was when he was fifteen. He drank with a group of his friends, some other boys. Then he got into a fight and broke someone's nose. He had to be pulled off the boy by his friends. He says he could remember nothing about it except this overwhelming feeling of rage. Ted grew up in a small village, so everyone got to hear about it. He was so ashamed by what had happened that he left Ireland and never went back.

'The second time he got drunk was with some fellows after work who'd egged him on. He tried to turn his fists on me. He was legless, I got away easy enough. But I told him that if it ever happened again, I'd leave him. No question. No going back. So he swore to me that he wouldn't drink again. "I'll

120

save up my drinking till my old age," that's what he used to say.'

'But Mabel, don't you think that's why he went away on his own, so he could drink in private without hurting you, without hurting anyone?'

'No, I don't.'

My disbelieving expression angered her and she began to harangue me. 'I was married to the man! Why do people believe that because I was married to him, I knew him less well than those who never met him?'

'But he used to go away.'

'You are right to think the two were connected. He needed to go away because he had the soul of a poet and sometimes he couldn't bear to be caged.'

'Are you saying that poets need to drink?'

'No, don't twist my words, I'm not saying that. I'm just saying that there was a wildness at the heart of him and I loved him for it. I feel sorry for you if you can't understand that. Let's leave it there for today.'

'I'm sorry,' I said.

She shook her head. 'Don't be,' she said. 'It's you I'm sorry for.'

She showed me to the front door. 'I like you being here, Karen,' she said as I was leaving. 'Come again.'

For a moment I felt the gulf of years which separated us drop away and I said goodbye to her as I would to a close friend.

Chapter Eight

After leaving Mabel's, I drove back to the flat to fetch Job. I felt the need to escape the city and so did the next best thing. Together we headed north up the Holloway Road and climbed Highgate Hill towards Hampstead Heath. With the roof down and Job sitting beside me in the passenger seat I attracted amused glances from other drivers. I kept thinking I must buy him a pair of World War One aviator's goggles to complete the look.

We parked in the shade of Kenwood car park. Job was so filled with joie de bouvier that he jumped over the side of the stationary car and almost strangled himself on his choke chain. With his head twisted back, he gave me a desperate if somewhat foolish look for help.

The Heath was beautiful. Dried-out grass had turned the golden colour of sun-ripened wheat. We walked down through the oak meadow and sat in the shade of a great tree. Overhead the wind rustled through the dry leaves of late summer, a papery breeze.

On the way home I took a detour down the Archway Road past the house where I grew up.

No reason.

That's not true.

When I go to Hampstead Heath or if I am up by the North Circular Road driving home that way is something I sometimes do. I know why, too.

My dad still lives there.

After my mum died, we didn't just drift apart, our relationship snapped in two. He didn't know how to cope with me.

He didn't know what to say to an eleven-year-old girl. He didn't have the words and there was no longer anyone there to teach him. Maybe he'd never been any good at it. Maybe Mum had been our bridge.

When I was sixteen I left home. Nowadays we see very little of each other. Christmas and birthdays, if that. We still have nothing much to say. But I drive down the Archway Road whenever I can, hoping to see him. I'm like an adolescent, longing to catch a secret glimpse of my boyfriend. I know that. I know I want something from him. I just don't know what it is. I also know that even if I did, he wouldn't be able to give it.

Driving home that evening I saw him. For the first time ever, I saw him. I watched him come out of a newsagent's with a newspaper tucked under his arm and shuffle slowly towards home in his slippers. Although barely sixty, he walked like an old man. Prematurely old. He stopped living his life more than twenty years ago and since then he has just been waiting to die. Not waiting to die, no. That implies an activity of the will and really he is a man who has made no decisions; he has just stopped living. He lives his life with blinkers on, looking neither to the right nor to the left.

I slowed down and crawled behind him on the inside lane. A driver stuck behind me blared his horn in frustration, unable to swing out past me into the fast lane and the heavy moving traffic.

My dad shambled down the road, oblivious to his surroundings. I pulled up beside him in my car with the roof off and my dog tethered beside me on the seat, both visible signs that I am getting on in the world, that my life is different from his.

I tooted my horn. Still he didn't look up. Perhaps he thought I was going to ask him directions and if he ignored me long enough I would drive away. Perhaps in a way that's what I have always done.

'Dad!' I shouted his name awkwardly. He didn't hear me above the loud thunder of the heavy lorries.

'*Dad!*' I shouted louder.

He looked up and for a moment I saw the strangest thing. I saw the beginnings of a pleased smile flash across his eyes. He shuffled towards me.

'I was just passing.' The words hung there between us.

'Are you coming in for a cup of tea?'

'Please.'

'You'll have to bring him with you. You can't go leaving him in there on a day like today.'

'Give me a minute. I'll park up.'

'I'll go on ahead and put the kettle on.'

It took me ten minutes to find a space down one of the side streets, long enough to regret my impulse and to begin to worry about what we could possibly find to say. I walked back towards the main road with a well-exercised Job padding contentedly by my side.

I still had a key to the front door. The hall was cool. The interior was unchanged for twenty-five years; the floral wallpaper had long gone grimy and grey with the heavy pollution.

'Through here,' called my dad. 'I thought you'd changed your mind.'

'No.'

We sat almost side by side in two armchairs which faced the television and were not positioned for conversation. Job made himself into a small dog and curled in behind my legs.

'Doesn't take up much space, does he?'

'No,' I said.

We sat in silence. I listened to the distant rumbling of the heavy traffic vibrating this little house all day every day, year in, year out. I looked at the photographs on the wall. A grainy picture of me and my mum on holiday squinting into the camera, difficult to see our faces properly.

A studio portrait of Maggie and her two daughters. Sylvia sat on her mother's knee. Carol stood against Maggie, resting her body up against her mother's shoulder. Both children were laughing freely. Sylvia I could recognise easily. But it was impossible to associate the other laughing child with the heavy woman with the bloated face and the hostile eyes she had now become.

Typical of my dad that those pictures were there. He probably never looked at them. They were not there because he wanted them there. They were there because he had never bothered to take them down.

'So how's tricks?' he asked.

'Fine,' I said. Then I told him about Madge, Maggie. I gestured at the picture as if it were a thought that had only just occurred to me. I told him carefully, cautiously. We both knew that after Mum died he had tried to persuade Maggie to have me. In her letter Maggie had said no. I was not supposed to have seen that letter. We both knew that I had.

I told him everything and he listened in silence. I surprised myself. I told him about Maggie, dressed up and enjoying herself. I told him about Sylvia, pregnant and engaged. I even told him about Carol, unpleasant and obese.

'Why did you and Auntie Madge lose touch?'

'Your mum and Madge had a row.'

I held my breath, not believing my ears. It was as if a wild bird had flown down and unexpectedly landed on my outstretched hand. He had mentioned Mum's name. Silently I willed him to continue.

'She mentioned to Madge that Carol had gone a bit odd and come over all tearful and clingy, begging her not to leave the last couple of times Annie took you down to visit.' He paused. He looked perhaps as if he had nothing left to say. He looked perhaps as if he were thinking of stretching his wings and flying away.

'Then what happened?' I whispered, trying to make my voice small and inconspicuous.

'Madge gave Carol a good smack across the knees and sent her to her room. Never was good at trying to understand anyone else's feelings, that sister of mine.' He said the words bitterly. 'After your mum . . . afterwards . . . Madge never bothered with us, so I never bothered with her.'

'Sylvia's getting married soon.'

'No doubt she is.'

'They've asked me to do the video of the wedding.'

'I'd have thought you had enough on your plate. More fool you if you've said yes. She'll take what she can get for free, Madge.' There was an abrupt change of tone. 'I never did like weddings.' The bird had stretched its wings and taken off.

'Would he like a drink of water, that dog of yours?'

I watched it soar high into the pale blue evening sky.

'I'm sure he would.'

'Never known an August so hot,' he said as he led the way into the kitchen.

I was at home and sitting at my kitchen table eating some supper, thinking over what Dad had said when I remembered my promise to go and see Maggie that evening. My broken promise. Shit.

I pulled on shorts and sandals and in the comparative cool of the evening Job and I let ourselves out through the back gate. It was eight o'clock. The whole world had moved outdoors. Children, mothers, office-workers with ties loosened and sleeves rolled up, sat chatting on the grassy banks.

I saw a fat yellow double-decker bus squeeze itself over a tiny metal bridge which looked as if it could barely take the weight. Underneath the throbbing bridge a group of teenage boys sat smoking and slurping cans of Energy Fast nutrition drinks.

'Smell your cunt, love?' one of them suggested, safe in the anonymity of his sniggering mates.

I walked past the new canalside developments and saw couples sitting on white plastic furniture on their balconies decorated with tubs of pink hydrangeas. The smell of barbecued sausages hung heavy on the still air. Job stared wistfully across the water and looked back at me reproachfully.

By Kingsland Basin a middle-aged man hung over the parapet, vomiting into the canal twenty feet below. The scum floated on the water. A duck with six ducklings swam over to investigate. As I walked past I smelled the hoppy scent of beer.

Mabel didn't want to admit that Ted was a secret drinker. Still, try as I might, I couldn't think of her as the kind of woman you could get one over on for sixty years.

Maybe she deliberately chose not to see? No. That didn't ring true either.

Bees buzzed in the buddleia along the bank oblivious to the school of fishermen who were arriving and setting up their gear. They carried extending fishing rods which reached the full width of the canal, along with green rucksacks laden with Thermos flasks and white Tupperware lunchboxes – containing sandwiches, I assumed, until I saw the squirming maggots dyed attractive shades of pink and yellow.

I found myself looking out for Charlie. By the time I reached No. 23 I was fighting to suppress the silly girlish excitement at the prospect of seeing him again.

Carol answered the door when I knocked. 'They're not in,' she said. My heart sank. 'Nobody's here but me and I'm on my way out.'

She didn't look as if she was on her way out. She was wearing a large baggy T-shirt and a pair of flip-flops. In one hand she held a large bag of popcorn and with the other she scooped out handfuls of toffee-covered Butterkist and shoved them in her mouth. She didn't bother to offer me any.

'Where have they gone?'

'Out.'

She'd already said that. We looked at one another in silence. The expression in her eyes was one of blank hostility. I struggled to find something to say.

'I was supposed to call round earlier, only I was working late.' That wasn't really a lie. I was working and then I forgot.

'Really? Mum said you hadn't bothered because you thought you was too good for us. Mum said it was always the same with your mother, she was always putting on airs and graces and trying to show that she was better than the rest of us.'

And suddenly I remembered travelling down here on the bus with my mum bringing a home-made Victoria sponge with jam and cream in a tin, because that was a cake I could help her to make. She'd made me wear my old coat which didn't fit me any more.

'It's not fair if you go flaunting your new clothes in front of your cousins, Karen. Since your uncle died, Madge hasn't had it easy.'

She didn't put on airs and graces, I wanted to protest. And then I saw Carol's face. She was watching me intently for my response. A mean little smile lurked in her eyes. She wanted to see my pain.

I wasn't going to let that happen. I dropped my eyes and swallowed hard to clear the lump in my throat. 'Do you know when they'll be back, Carol?'

'No.'

And Charlie? I stopped myself from saying the words out loud.

My cousin started to close the door.

'Can you tell them that I called around? Will you say I'm sorry to Sylvia, and that of course I'd love to do the video for her wedding? Will you tell them I'll call around again tomorrow?'

I think she mumbled okay or maybe it was no. Anyway, she shut the door in my face. With Job at my heels I walked back to the canal and then decided to make the most of my trip by carrying on down the road towards Victoria Park.

'Bet you he costs a few bob to feed,' an old man said, nodding at Job as we walked past. He was sitting on a deckchair in his tiny red brick garden taking the air. Beside him, three potted sunflowers strained their faces towards the last rays of the dying sun.

I nodded in return, not bothering to pause to speak to him. Instead I thought back to those bus journeys down the hill with Mum. It was all such a long time ago. I remember eating jelly and ice cream – party food. I remember bouncing and jumping on my cousins' bunk beds and banging my head on the ceiling and crying. I remember Carol and me ganging up on Sylvia and not letting her play with us because we were older and she was still such a baby. I remember feeling awkward and not wanting to come.

Why? When did I start feeling awkward? I couldn't remember that. I just remember wanting to stay down beside my mum and her telling me to run along and play.

'Honestly, Madge, I don't know what's got into her.'

I remember feeling shy but even so, I always used to look forward to coming to visit them. I didn't remember that we hadn't got on.

Standing there and feeling the venom behind Carol's words I had wanted to ask her what I had done. But there seemed no way to say it. The woman who stood in front of me had been too much of a stranger.

It was beginning to get dark and the park was almost empty.

I wandered slowly round as Job paused to sniff the strong scents on the gradually cooling air. Above me a breeze played in the uppermost branches of the trees. An airplane twinkled like a shooting star in the night sky, heading east, on its slow descent towards Stansted.

I meandered in the gloaming until I heard the bell ring. No point in getting stuck in the park and having to climb the fence back to the canal towpath. I turned on my heel and hurried towards the gate with Job jangling along in my wake.

There was a message on my machine when I got in. It was Rob.

'Okay Karen, I've done what you asked. So from one timewaster to another, here it is. I ran a search on Lexus. I couldn't get the names of any individuals who actually run the company. Instead I found two other companies, Orion Holdings and PloughShare Ltd. They are listed as holding companies. They both share a lawyer, which I thought might interest you – Dibble and May. Their offices are in the City, just off Chancery Lane. Don't ever say I wouldn't make a good secretary. How did you get on today? Give me a call when you get in.'

I rang him straight away, but once again he was out. Where? If he'd been there I would have asked him round that evening. Instead I left a message. Our answering machines have a great relationship.

On impulse I dialled Sarah's number. My fingers tapped it out automatically I am as familiar with that number as I am with my own. The phone rang only twice before it was answered by Sarah herself. She sounded out of breath.

'Hello?'

'Sarah, it's me. You sound as if you've been running.'

'No, I always sound like that at the moment. It's a design fault. I seem to have run out of lung space.'

'When's the baby due?'

'Two weeks, and in this heat not a moment too soon. Quiet, you two, I'll only be a minute.'

'How are you feeling?'

'Fed up. Heavy. As if two is more than enough and I'm mad to want more. But being fed up is usually a good sign. It usually means I won't have long to wait.'

'Do you fancy some company?'

'Not really, Karen. John's due home any minute.'

'I've missed seeing you.'

'You're on our list of people to call after the birth. Give us a couple of months to settle down and then it would be lovely to see you after that.'

'Mu-um!' The noises off were reaching a new peak.

'I've got to go.'

'Yeah . . . Good luck!'

'Thanks.'

After I spoke to Sarah I felt too restless to stay indoors so Job and I went out and walked the streets. People were emerging from their bunkers into the cool of the evening looking slightly dazed and dishevelled.

All along Upper Street where every second shop is a restaurant, the transition was taking place from day to evening. I walked along, curious as a tourist with Job padding by my side. Bright lights, big city and this was less than a mile away from the desolation of Heaven's Gate.

An old woman, dressed despite the heat in a heavy overcoat and a woollen cardigan tied around her waist with a length of string, was foraging in a rubbish bin by Islington Green. Job's ears flattened and he gave her a wide berth as we passed by. She didn't notice.

The night was close and clammy. Sleep was elusive. I tossed and turned and turned and tossed, trying to get comfortable. I could hear Job padding around the kitchen changing position, the clinking chain of his collar tinkling and jangling like a bell every time he sank down on a new, cool piece of floor.

All the following day I thought about what my dad had said, about Madge taking what she could get for free.

I thought about it when I rang the lawyers to Orion Holdings, and was told that the partner in charge of the file was diving in the Maldives. I thought about it as I tried in vain to contact Grace. I thought about it and thought about it and the thing was, I realised I didn't mind. I liked being needed; I liked having something to offer. I even quite liked being the glamorous cousin who was making a film. I liked the way they were impressed, the way Charlie was impressed. Despite what Carol said, they *were* impressed. I knew they were.

So the next evening, Wednesday, I called round again. Job came with me. I thought if all else failed and we had nothing to talk about, then we could talk about what a nice dog he was. I brought my camera with me. I thought it might appease them if I were to offer to record our discussion of the wedding plans. I could edit it into the final video, a kind of 'before and after' sequence.

As I walked along the canal, a memory whispered at the back of my mind, the whisper was as fleeting as the summer's breeze. I tried to grab hold of it but it slipped between my fingers. Something about my mum and my dad.

It was all so long ago.

But there it was again.

'She's your sister, why don't you come with us?' Mum was saying to Dad. 'All right then, at least I'll take Karen. If we run out of things to say, we can always talk about how they are all growing up so quick. You know that song, don't you, Karen, the one you've been learning at school? You could sing it for your cousins.'

And there I am, standing in the centre of Auntie Madge's living room with my socks pulled up tight to my knees, singing something. And my aunt and my cousins are watching me, politely saying, 'Very nice,' at the end when I am finished. And yes, we are all growing up so quick.

Maggie answered the door when I knocked. She was surprised to see me. The expression on her face had to readjust itself several times in a few seconds. First she wore a fixed expression of pleasure and welcome. Then she saw it was me and she looked momentarily confused. Then she began to smile again, but this time it was one of forced politeness.

'Karen!' She said brightly. 'And you've brought your dog.' She motioned me into the hall.

I hesitated on the doorstep. Maybe this wasn't a good time. 'I can take him home and come back later.'

'Not at all, you're here now. Carol gave me your message. Is that your camera you've brought with you?'

'I'm really sorry about last night.'

'Not to worry, you must be very busy. Come on in, we were just discussing the wedding. Charlie is expected any minute.'

I followed her into the living room. 'That's why I brought the camera – I thought we could record the preparations.'

'You know PJ, don't you?'

PJ Pickford was standing by the fireplace.

'Of course,' he answered for me and stretched out his arm. We shook hands. 'Sorry I haven't got back to you yet, I've been very stretched this week.'

There was something wrong with the atmosphere in the room and I couldn't put my finger on what it was. Maggie was standing there smiling at me, PJ was standing there smiling at me. Carol was sitting in an armchair eating her way through a box of Black Magic and watching athletics with the sound turned down. She wasn't smiling at anyone.

She didn't even look up when I walked in.

It wasn't the fact that Carol ignored me; there was something else wrong. Had I interrupted something? Or perhaps they'd found somebody else to do the video and didn't know how to tell me.

'Sylv, it's your Cousin Karen, she's come to talk about the wedding.' Maggie's voice was high-pitched and artificial.

Sylvia came out of the kitchen. There were splashes of cold water on her face and she was wiping it dry with a towel. She looked as if she had been crying.

'Is there anything the matter?' The words popped out before I could bite them back. Everyone froze.

'Just a few pre-wedding nerves.' Maggie bustled over and put her arm around her youngest daughter's shoulders.

Sylvia smiled bravely at me.

'That and her hormones,' added Carol, holding a strawberry fondant high in the air and dribbling the cream onto her outstretched tongue.

No one looked at Carol. PJ and Maggie smiled relentlessly at me. Sylvia's face began to twist and turn to tears again.

'That's a great dog you have,' PJ said.

We all looked at Job. He was looking at the box of chocolates. He knew better than to drool publicly but the self-restraint was killing him. Poor dog. I didn't think he was going to get any joy out of Carol.

There was a knock at the door.

'I'll get it,' Maggie trilled musically and fluttered to the door.

'That'll be Charlie,' said Carol. Her tone was spiteful. She didn't look away from the television.

'Have you had your medicine, Carol? We wouldn't want you having a fit on us,' PJ's voice was low and insidious. Carol affected not to notice but I saw her face blanch.

What medicine? What was going on? I had no idea.

'It's Charlie,' sang Maggie.

Charlie walked into the room like a breath of fresh air. It was as if the Allies had landed. Before, I had felt awkward and alone. Now there were two of us. The atmosphere changed instantly. Job began to bounce around excitedly.

'Down, boy, down.' I forced him to lie at my feet.

Charlie looked as if he'd come straight from the site. His face and clothes were impregnated with dust and grime. Going straight to Sylvia, he gave her a kiss on the forehead and presented her with a bunch of orange gladioli wrapped in pink and white flower-printed paper.

'Flowers for the bride. I got these down the Broadway.' Warm brown eyes glowed in his dirt-streaked face and he grinned at everyone.

'Oh Charlie!' Sylvia flung her arms around his neck and buried her head in his shoulder.

'Hey,' he stroked her hair. 'What's this? Anyone would think I'd been gone for weeks, instead of just out doing an honest day's work.' She remained nestled into him. Cynics amongst us might think that being this close, he wouldn't be able to see that she'd been crying. 'Let's get these flowers in water then. They're dying of thirst.'

We all looked around the room, searching for a vase. It was then that I noticed a bunch of roses in a vase on the dining table. They were large perfect blossoms, white with a streak of red in the centre of each petal.

'What beautiful roses!' I exclaimed.

'Yes, they are, aren't they?' bustled Maggie, snatching the bunch of flowers from Charlie's hand and heading for the kitchen door. 'Tea, anyone?'

'I'd kill for a cup,' said Charlie. 'Brought your saxophone then, I see, Karen.'

'Go on – set it up!' PJ urged. 'You're very lucky to have a professional in the family.'

I felt very foolish.

'Go on!'

I started to take the camera out of the case, aware that everyone's eyes were upon me.

'Tea, PJ?' Maggie called from the kitchen.

'Not for me, thanks,' he said. 'I was just leaving.'

'I'll help you make it, Mum.' Sylvia flitted after her to the kitchen.

Carol smirked.

'Is it all right if I take a shower, Mrs W, make myself a bit more presentable?'

'Go right ahead, Charlie.'

He squeezed past me, pausing to give Job a good scratch behind the ears. 'Won't be a minute.' He winked at me. Impulsively I winked back.

He stomped off, his footsteps resounding on the flimsy staircase. We heard him whistling and then the sound of running water.

It was PJ who managed to pick up the thread of conversation. 'I haven't spoken to the Holman family yet,' he told me quietly. 'It's a delicate time. You understand.'

'I understand.' I did understand; that didn't mean I wasn't disappointed.

'Is there anything else I can do, anything else you'd like to know?'

'One of the other subjects of my documentary – an old man – was found dead at Angel Point a week or so ago. There aren't any suspicious circumstances, but there is a rumour that he may have been employed on-site. When I went there to find out more, I was ejected by the foreman, which is not surprising as I had no authorisation. But I can't work out who I need to speak to, to get the authorisation.'

'What is it you need to know?'

'Nothing specific. I'm just trying to build up a picture of

the last days in the life of this old man. The more detail we
can get, the more we can flesh him out, humanise him. At the
moment the picture I have is very two-dimensional, as I've
only been able to speak to his widow.'

'Mabel O'Hagan,' PJ murmured.

'Yes.' The man was more and more remarkable. 'You know
her?'

'Yes.'

'How?' He didn't respond. 'Don't tell me you go way back.'

'Something like that.' He refused to volunteer anything
more about Mabel. Never mind, I could always ask him
another time.

'So do you know anyone I can talk to about Heaven's
Gate?'

'Yes, I do.' He was laughing openly now.

'Can I talk to them?'

'You already are.'

I was confused.

He explained. 'Angel Point comes under my PR brief. It
just so happens I'm giving a guided tour to the local press in
advance of next Saturday's blowdown. It's taking place
tomorrow morning at eleven o'clock – you can come along if
you want.'

'I want.'

'Great. I'll make sure you're well looked after. Just turn up
before eleven tomorrow. I'll have your name on the gate.'

'Brilliant.'

'Do you have a card?'

I grimaced. 'Not with me. Why do you need one?'

'Just in case arrangements change. But it doesn't matter. I
don't suppose there will be any changes.'

'I could give you my home address and telephone number.'
I felt inefficient and obstructive, all the more so because PJ
was bending over backwards to be helpful.

'That would do.'

I patted my pockets half-heartedly, knowing they were empty. 'Carol, have you got a pen?'

Carol ignored me. She didn't even bother to shrug.

'There'll be one in the hall by the telephone.' PJ certainly knew his way around. I followed him out through the living-room door and sat on the stairs obediently writing down my address and phone number.

Just then the bathroom door opened. I craned my neck around. Charlie emerged in a cloud of steam, towel drying his hair. He was dressed only in a pair of jeans, his feet and chest were bare. 'Sorry.' He came down and pushed past us in the narrow hallway. 'I left my clean shirt in the kitchen.' He looked over my shoulder 'Noel Street – that where you live, then?'

'Yes,' I said and blushed. Why did I blush? At least I hadn't written 'Terminator Films'.

'Nice area.'

PJ pocketed the piece of paper with my telephone number and address. 'Now I do have to go. Have to go, Maggie!' he shouted through to the kitchen.

'I really appreciate your helping me out in this way,' I stuttered.

'Not at all. I think it's great, your coming along to video the wedding. Maggie and her daughters, they are like family to me.'

'Are you coming to the wedding?'

'Of course I am – I'm giving away the bride.'

He left and shut the door behind him. Job and I wandered back into the living room where Carol was still glued to the television. Job decided to try the direct approach and pulled me over to stand by her chair.

'Did I interrupt anything when I arrived?' I asked her.

'Nothing unusual,' she said. That was all. But at least she spoke.

I'd gone off Carol in a big way. She sat in the corner of the room like a fat, greasy spider. The bad feeling in the room probably emanated from her. I could imagine the hurtful things she would say to her younger, prettier sister.

It was so hot. A small fan churned round stale air. Perhaps that was it. Perhaps I had just felt uncomfortable in the close atmosphere, and had imagined everything else.

'Do you mind if I open the window?'

'If you've got a brick handy.'

I looked at the windows to see what she was talking about and saw that the aluminium frames were painted shut. There was no way you could open them. Tiny air vents were positioned at the top of each pane of glass, but in this weather they were useless. Design for living.

'I suppose it makes them burglar-proof.'

Carol ignored me again.

When Maggie came into the room carrying a tray of tea and biscuits, I rushed to clear the little coffee-table of newspapers and magazines. The table was Job-height. He was obviously torn between the plate of biscuits and the box of chocolates. I tugged sharply at his lead and pointed firmly to the carpet. The look he gave me was priceless. He flumped himself down and rested his head in his paws with that owner-transfer wish still visible in his eyes.

'I'm so pleased you came to see us, Karen.'

'Are you?' I almost choked on my first sip of tea.

'Yes. It will be good to talk through next Wednesday. We thought you were too busy to spare us any of your time.'

'I'm terribly sorry,' I waffled. 'I got involved in something and I forgot—'

'Are you sure you want her to do a video of this wedding? You know about these fly-on-the-wall documentaries, Mum. They reveal everything, warts and all.'

This was the longest speech I'd heard Carol make.

'We don't have any warts, Carol. I don't know what you are talking about.' Maggie giggled; the sound jarred. 'Go ahead Karen, feel free. Why don't you film something now?'

Sylvia and Charlie came out from the kitchen. Charlie was carrying the vase of gladioli, which he put on the dining table next to the roses. Fully dressed, Charlie was less of a distraction. He and Sylvia sat side by side on the sofa, while I positioned myself in the corner of the room, raised the camera to my eye and switched it on. To begin with, everyone was very stilted and self-conscious, then they began to relax and forget that I was there. For the next half hour we went through all their plans for Wednesday afternoon. The wedding was booked in Hackney Town Hall for one o'clock.

'Everybody's got to be prompt because there's one at twelve-thirty and another one at half-past one.'

'That's a bit rushed.'

'They were lucky to get it. The Saturday was completely booked. People like a summer wedding.'

'Just as well, really, I'd have had to miss my competition.'

'Charlie!'

'It's the main competition of the year, Mum,' Sylvia reminded her. 'The first prize is five-hundred pounds. Me and Charlie could have a holiday on that.'

'It's a fishing competition,' Maggie explained.

I'd gathered.

'I'll need to get some practice in before then, love.'

A hairdresser was going to come round to Poppingham Gardens at ten in the morning to see to Sylvia, Maggie and Carol. It was agreed that I would show up at about eleven o'clock and film the final preparations up to the point when they left for the Register Office.

'How are you getting to the Town Hall?'

'We've booked a white taxi.'

'Do you want me to be here to film your departure or there to catch your arrival?'

'There, I think.'

'Right.' I made a mental note to leave ten minutes before the taxi was due and walk through the park. That would give me plenty of time.

'What are you wearing, Sylvia?' I asked.

Charlie looked interested. Sylvia looked coy. 'You'll see,' she whispered.

I'm not into weddings but even I started to get excited as we discussed logistics and locations. The party was going to be at the Dog and Duck. I hoped the weather would hold.

It was Charlie who finally broke up the discussion. 'Right, that's it, I'm starving.' The plate of biscuits was long empty and a disgusted Job lay motionless at my feet.

Charlie stood up and rubbed his hands together. 'Who's for fish and chips?' Sylvia turned green, 'Sorry, love, I forgot.'

'Not me,' said Maggie. 'I'm watching my weight for Saturday.'

He looked at me.

'No thanks, it's gone ten. I'd better get a move on – I've still got work to do. Do you want me to come around next Tuesday evening again, just in case you've thought of anything specific you might like me to include?'

'Can't keep away, can she?' No one acknowledged what Carol said. I began to think of her malign little comments as some form of insanity which everyone else in the family had got used to.

Maggie replied as if Carol had not spoken. 'That would be lovely, if you've got the time.'

'I'll walk down with you. The chip shop's out on the Broadway.' Charlie shifted his weight from foot to foot, keen to get going.

I said goodbye. Maggie kissed me on the cheek. Sylvia

squeezed my hand. Only Carol remained engrossed in the television. She'd left the box of chocolates on the floor beside her chair; there was one left. Amid the activity of our departure, Job sneaked across and swiped it. He wolfed it down, licked his lips and gave me a guilty sideways look. I wasn't saying anything. As far as I was concerned, it served her right.

Maggie saw us out to the front door. 'Will you be long, Charlie?'

'Twenty minutes? I'll eat out on the canal bank. I don't want Sylvia throwing up on me with the smell.'

Outside it was already dark. A cool breeze coursed along the narrow walkway, banging the door shut behind us. Once Charlie and I were alone, I couldn't think of a thing to say.

Now, isn't that a bad sign?

We walked side by side down the narrow stairwell to the ground floor, with Job trotting behind us. The atmosphere was electric. At least, I thought the atmosphere was electric; I don't know what he felt. The hairs on my arms were tingling alarmingly. Breath pulsed hot and heavy in my nose and ears. At the bottom of the stairs we stopped and looked at one another. The silence went on and on.

'Good luck with your fishing competition!' Why did I say that? Where did that come from?

'I'm seeing you before then. The competition isn't until after the wedding.'

'Of course.'

'And you. I hope your filming goes well this evening.'

'No, I'm not filming this evening,' I rushed to correct him. 'I'm going home to do prep work for tomorrow.'

'Oh. Well, good luck anyway.'

'Thanks.'

We said goodbye on the corner of the Broadway. Charlie turned left and I turned right towards the canal, only to find that the gates to the towpath were locked. I could have found a way to jump over, but it was late and even with Job at my side, I didn't want to take any risks. You hear about people being ambushed and mugged in the shadows. You even hear about cyclists being thrown in the water along with their bikes. All sorts.

Instead, I walked home along the streets bordering the canal. From time to time I could hear voices echoing underneath the low hanging bridges, lads calling to one another. The night was clear and mellow; all was quiet and calm. I felt good. I'd enjoyed the companionship and the warmth of my family, despite Carol. Quite simply, I had begun to feel at home. And then there was Charlie. Charlie.

I drifted slowly home, savouring the memory of the electricity which had passed between us. Tell me I should have known better, tell me he was my cousin's fiancé, but I've never thought there was anything wrong with a bit of window-shopping. Besides, this one had a bright red SOLD sticker on him. Nothing would come of it.

The bridge on Bagshot Street was traffic-free. I paused for a moment. Overhead a dusky moon smiled in secret pleasure at its companion in the deep dark water. Then suddenly, as a gentle breeze caressed my skin, the still, smooth surface of the dark water changed into kaleidoscopic, dancing patterns of reflected light: orange, red and silvery white roused to excitement, rippling, melting, shifting and finally coming to rest.

I quickened my pace and felt Job do the same. By the time I got home, my clothes were sticky from the fast walk. I went into my bedroom and stripped off. The night air was exhilarating against my bare skin. Although it was late, I didn't feel tired. I was too restless to go to sleep.

Naked, I walked back into the kitchen and fed Job his dinner. While he was eating I sprawled on the sofa, channel surfing, but could find nothing I wanted to watch. The lights from the television were jarring and garish. Sweat collected in the folds of my skin.

I remembered reading somewhere that cotton was cool and refreshing next to your skin so I walked back into the bedroom and pulled on a simple white nightdress bought for some holiday in Greece or Tenerife. Bought and never worn.

I turned off the television and opened the conservatory doors again. Then I moved the sofa round to face the garden. The balmy air of summer filled my nostrils, sweet-scented jasmine undercut by the sharper smell of rosemary. I lay stretched out, staring at the moon and listening to all the sounds of the night.

The air was very still. When Job finished his meal he came and sat by my side. We rested there somewhere between waking and sleeping, utterly at peace, utterly calm.

A little after midnight I heard the buzzer on my intercom. And I knew.

There is always a choice. Remember that. There is always a choice in everything you do. And I could have chosen not to answer the door. I could have pretended to be in a deep sleep, had I not been waiting.

Waiting?

I picked up the handset. 'Yes?'

'It's me.' His voice was a low, determined whisper.

'Hold on.' I went into my bedroom and pulled on my jeans. The harsh material chafed my bare skin. I put on a sweatshirt on top of my nightdress and went back into the living room and turned on one of the lights. The light was harsh and unreal, out of keeping with the tranquillity of the evening. I turned it off again.

I lifted up the handset again. 'Come on down.' I pressed the buzzer and opened the door to my flat and there I stood. Waiting.

His tall figure walked down the dark hallway. 'You aren't surprised to see me?'

'Not very.'

'I shouldn't be here.'

'Go home then.'

'I wanted to see where you lived.'

'Generally it looks better in daylight.'

'Do you want me to go?'

'That would be a shame. You've only just arrived. Come in.' I held the door open wide. He walked into the flat and stood there, the outline of his body silhouetted against the moonlight.

'You've been sitting in the dark?'

'Yes. It's a beautiful evening.' I walked to the open door leading out towards the garden. He followed. I felt suddenly awkward. 'Would you like a drink?' I asked abruptly, inhospitably.

'Sure,' he answered.

'What would you like?'

'Beer?'

'I don't have beer.'

'What do you have?'

'I have white wine.'

'I'll have white wine then.' I could feel him smiling at me.

I crossed the floor to the kitchen and opened the fridge. White light flooded the room. Pints of milk, broccoli, ham and pasta. Normal things. Too normal. I didn't want to be touched by normality. I took out a bottle of wine and shut the door. My hand fumbled in the cutlery drawer for a corkscrew.

'Do you want to turn the light on?' His voice was calm and considerate.

'No,' I barked, 'I can see perfectly.' I carried two glasses and the open bottle back to the sofa and poured out our drinks by moonlight.

146

'What were you doing?'

'Before you arrived? Just drifting.' I plonked myself down on the sofa. The harsh material on my jeans cut into my naked skin. Charlie sat down at the other end of the sofa. I took a sip of my wine, for something to do. Its dry sweetness stung my taste buds and flooded my mouth with saliva.

'It was a good evening, wasn't it?' I said, breaking the silence with small talk. Why was I making small talk?

'Yeah.'

'How did you get here?'

Not how did you get here, but why are you here? You don't need to answer that. I know why you are here. I know why you are here.

'I walked. Karen, I shouldn't be . . .' His voice was uncertain, confused.

'Don't say that,' I interrupted him. 'If you don't think you should, then I think you should go.'

We sat in a silence which was broken only by the distant clunking of the houseboats against the canal wall, a deep harmonious sound. I could hear him breathing beside me.

'I need to kiss you.'

I nodded, inexplicably close to tears. This was not a joke. This was no simple bit of fun.

He reached across and gently took the wine glass from my hand. He placed the glass on the floor. I turned my face towards him and looked deep into his eyes. They say that if someone is attracted to you their pupils dilate. The deep pool of liquid black in Charlie's eyes went on for ever and ever.

My mouth met his. Softly, gently at first. Dry lips, light as a butterfly's wings. They say that chaos begins with the distant flapping of a butterfly's wings.

Kissing him, breathing in the smell of him. Wine and warmth and hair and skin. Then, locking my mouth to his with a cry that came from somewhere outside me, somewhere inside me. Teeth crashing together in our awkwardness. Twisting, turning to one side. Trying to find a comfortable angle. A way to join. A way in.

Our rigid bodies still schooled by good manners remained upright sitting side by side, ignoring the longing exploration of lips and teeth and tongues. I closed my eyes, hiding from the intensity of his gaze and used my fingers to explore his face. Tracing my touch over his mouth, his nose, the edges of his eyes. Touching as if for the first time.

He pulled away, forcing me to look at him. I opened my eyes, scared of what I might see. And I found him . . . smiling the warm, accepting smile of my oldest friend.

'Take off that sweatshirt.'

I pulled it up over my head.

The thin cotton shift made me feel exposed and I shivered in the night air. My eyes stayed locked into his own. Charlie reached over and ran his hand from my chin down the line of my neck and slowly on down my nightdress until his hand cupped my breast. Then he leaned towards me and retraced his journey, this time using his tongue. My nipple rose to meet him. He sucked at me tentatively through the thin fabric.

My body was painfully alive. I felt dizzy and light-headed; a pulse throbbed between my legs. It resounded in my ears driving every other thought from my head. My body took over. I pulled down the straps and raised my arms until I had fought free of the nightdress. It fell towards my waist, but was stopped by his face still sucking at my nipple through the material.

'Please!' My voice came out in a harsh whisper. He raised his face to mine and the fabric dropped away. My skin glowed in the moonlight. My nipples were painfully erect.

'Kiss me,' I said, hungry for the feel of his tongue on mine.

'Of course.' He bent to my other breast and licked it. A

sharp, single dart of his tongue. A taste. He moved back and looked at me again. 'I knew,' he whispered. 'From that first evening I knew.'

I knelt on the floor beside him and started to unbutton his shirt.

'Not yet.' He tried to pull my hand away.

'Yes, now,' I said. I undid the shirt one button at a time and pulled it down over his shoulders. He knelt there proud and unresisting. Without pausing I reached for the button on his jeans. I pulled the zip down gently over his hard erection.

'Stand up and help me,' I said.

He stood and pulled the jeans down over his strong thighs. When he was naked he reached for me and pulled me up to him. I unbuttoned the top button of my jeans and stepped out of them. Warm skin met as one and for a long moment we touched and smelled and breathed in each other. The hair under his arms smelled a little of dry sweat and an evening walk on a summer's night. I ran my nose and tongue over his smooth chest. I took each nipple in my mouth and circled it with my tongue.

His erection was hard against my stomach and my body strained to greet him.

He sank to his knees in front of me and smelled my fur.

Then he pulled me down beside him. My knees enclosed his body. Firm hips. Strong thighs. He placed his hands under me and lifted me up. I felt his penis nuzzling against me. And then he was in. And everything was all right.

'Who's Rob?' he asked afterwards.

'What do you mean?'

'You said his name?'

'Did I?'

'Yes.'

'I suppose he must be the last person I slept with.'

'He must have made quite an impression.'

'Not really.'

'If you say so.'

'Sorry. I didn't mean to say his name. I wasn't thinking of him.'

'Don't worry, love. I don't mind. I shouldn't be here either.'

'I told you if you felt that, you should go.'

'I felt it. But not very strongly. And I'm glad I stayed.' He pulled me to him and started kissing my hair, warm tender kisses.

'Are you going to marry her?' The words slipped out when I next came up for air. Quickly I moved on to kiss his cheeks, the lobes of his ears.

'Of course.' He breathed in sharply through his nose and pulled back to look at me closely. I had spoiled the feeling of innocent intimacy. Other people crowded into the room. Job got up from his corner and began to pace. I wanted to bite back the question, to pretend that it had never been asked. 'Why do you ask?'

'Nothing. I just wondered. I mean, you're here with me, aren't you?'

He pulled my head down on his shoulders. I felt so at home and comfortable on the warm firm pillow of his chest. We lay in silence for a while. His hand cupped my chin and his thumb caressed and caressed my cheek.

Overhead, the moon, small and high, watched us through the grimy glass of the conservatory roof.

'Why are you going to marry her?' I couldn't stop myself from probing further, although I didn't really want to know. I could hear the rhythmic thudding of his heart beating deep within his chest.

'Because she is carrying my baby,' he replied simply.

I wanted to jerk away, to jump up, make tea, change the subject. Instead I forced myself to lie quietly, I forced myself to ignore the sound of the sea rushing in my ears, to search instead for the sounds of traffic and dogs barking and voices on the still, summer's night.

'What is this then, a last little crop of wild oats?' I fought to keep the hurt out of my voice.

'I don't sleep around, Karen. I don't enjoy it.'

'You looked as if you were enjoying yourself a moment ago.'

He ignored my flippancy. 'It's more than the baby. Me and Sylvia, we'll be all right for each other. It'll work out. She's got her mum and her mates. I've got my mates and my fishing. We're both happy. But you're something else. We couldn't be together, you and me, Karen. It would eat me up. It would eat us up. You'd need more and I'd need to give you more. I'd *want* to give you more.'

'So why are you here?' I asked bitterly.

'Because I find you irresistible.'

After that I had the sense to ask no more questions, enjoy what I had, live in the moment. We played and tussled and fucked until midnight, when he went home like a good little boy, so he would be fresh and bright for a hard day's work the next morning.

Job came out from hiding behind the sofa. I had forgotten all about him. When Rob stayed we used to lock him in the bathroom. So this time, when he sensed what was coming, he must have slunk off quietly, finding more dignity in a discreet departure than enforced banishment.

After Charlie left, I went into the bedroom and found him lying on my bed. Just to prove he wasn't sulking he gave my proffered hand a few dainty little licks.

I curled up next to him and slept a blissful, satiated sleep.

Chapter Nine

I had a shower when I got up but I still smelled of sex. Rich and ripe it leaked out through my pores. Thursday was another sweltering day which didn't help. I was walking around in a cloud of heavily scented pheromones, or so it seemed to me.

I turned up for my appointment just before ten to eleven. Somewhat apprehensively I stated my name and business to the man at the Site Office, but this time I didn't have any difficulty. I was issued with a yellow hard hat and given an identity badge proclaiming my name and the day's date. One more to add to the collection.

'Where is the Press Conference taking place?' I asked, putting on a crisp and efficient voice and flashing him a toothpaste smile.

Press Conference. The words had such a grand ring to them.

'I'll take you round.' The man scraped back his chair and led the way towards Angel Point.

Outside, a mechanical digger with huge metal jaws chewed its way through a pile of rubble, spewing dust into the already oppressive atmosphere. I breathed in at the wrong moment and a thin film of dry concrete particles covered my teeth and tongue. It was an hour before midday and overhead the hot summer sun beat relentlessly down, casting little shadow anywhere, offering no refuge. My guide strode ahead of me and I struggled to keep up on the uneven ground.

Two men came walking towards us. One of them was Jim Bryant. The other was a middle-aged man wearing an expensive suit, a yellow hard hat and dark sunglasses. As they drew level, my heart began to beat faster. I dropped my eyes to the ground, expecting to hear a harsh voice and renewed anger when Jim Bryant saw me here again. But he was so deep in conversation with his companion that he didn't notice me. We passed one another by and I exhaled slowly with relief. Perhaps he had not thought to look at me closely because today was Press Day and he was expecting to see strangers.

My guide and I drew closer to the empty tower block. Shading my eyes, I could see PJ in the centre of a small group of people. He was in his shirt-sleeves, fiddling with his tie and smoothing down his hair. Everyone was wearing name badges so I was able to work out quite easily who was who. There were three officials from Hackney Council, and of course, PJ. Then there was the Press Corps which consisted of two representatives from the *Hackney Clarion* – a reporter and a photographer – one freelance journalist, a tired and jaded-looking man in his late forties who appeared as if drink or drugs had got the better of him many years ago, and a tall, spotty teenager with a tape-recorder whose badge told me that he came from London East Independent Radio, a station I'd never heard of.

So useful, these badges. After a quick glance round I was on first-name terms with everyone.

PJ was working hard, keeping up the banter and making people laugh.

'Karen!' He saluted my arrival and glanced at his watch. It was five past eleven. 'Are we ready?' he asked one of the local government officials. She consulted her list and shrugged. He made the decision for her. 'I think it's time to begin.'

Everyone got into position. Notebooks were poised, microphones checked for level; the photographer took a last pull on his cigarette, before stubbing it out underfoot. I hoisted the camera onto my shoulder and turned it on. The picture flickered to life. PJ put on his suit jacket and smoothed down his hair one final time. Then he cleared his throat, clasped his hands in front of his chest and began to speak.

'As you all know, on Saturday week we will be bringing this area of London to a standstill. Saturday is Blasting Day. Saturday is Blowdown. Not only in practical terms will we be destroying this old building which for almost three decades has contained the lives, heartaches and hopes of so many people, but also we will be clearing the way for the final phase of development of this housing project which, with its emphasis on people and community, will represent the best of Hackney's vision for the future.'

I found myself charmed by PJ's mellifluous voice and his polished performance. His face in close-up was sincere and direct. Here was a man who had built his career and his public reputation on this gift of an open and honest nature. I pulled back as far as I could, framing his small figure against the huge, empty tower block.

'Two hundred kilos of high explosive are waiting to be put into position once the final checks have been completed. Saturday will be an exciting day. We will be having the biggest street-party seen in this area since the end of the war.'

Just then another man walked into the frame beside him. It was Jim Bryant. My heart stopped.

'Jim! Just in time for the guided tour,' PJ welcomed him heartily. 'This is Jim Bryant, our site foreman. He is the man with the overall responsibility of running the project on a day-to-day basis.' Jim nodded at us, but the muscles in his face did not twitch into a welcoming smile. Jim was someone who might benefit from a few lessons in how best to deal with the public. I didn't think I'd make the suggestion.

'Ladies and gentlemen, this way, please.'

PJ led the way through the heavy doors to Angel Point. Squeezing through the narrow entrance I was jostled and pushed by the other journalists. In fact, it was next to impossible to film in the small hallway. I kept the camera clamped to my face, however, as camouflage. The air inside was cool and musty. At first it felt like a welcome relief from the intense midday sun, but before long the unpleasant stench of rotting rubbish and stale urine made me long to be outside again.

We traipsed down the stairs and into the basement. This had been the heart of this massive building. Huge load-bearing concrete columns supported its weight. But now the pulse had stopped, the generators were silent. The lifts no longer hummed up and down the deep shafts. Rubbish spilled out uncollected from the disused rubbish chutes. The abandoned building had been given over to the unseen forces of nature – rats, cockroaches, mice and ants. I imagined a squeaking and a scampering, unseen, in dark corners just beyond where we were standing.

Because there was no longer any electricity down here. We were dependent on small windows at ceiling height to let in the daylight. Through the black and white viewfinder of my camera, dramatic shafts of sunlight lit up areas of the large underground space, and particles of dust sparkled in the still air. Like the good showman he was, PJ positioned himself in one of these areas of light to continue his briefing and his voice echoed in the empty cavern.

'Ladies and gentlemen, if you look around you I will be able to explain in layman's terms just how complex an operation the destruction of this building will be – Jim, correct me if I go completely wrong.' He gave a self-deprecating smile towards the foreman who was standing to his left just out of shot.

'For the past few weeks, skilled workmen have been cutting away the supports of the building with acetylene torches. Although it looks as if we are standing beneath a solid structure, the building has in fact already been considerably weakened.'

I glanced up nervously despite myself.

'The workmen have been making notches where the explosives will go. The trick is to weaken the building just enough in advance and then to use the minimum amount of explosives to finish the job. Sometime next Friday, when we are absolutely sure the site has been completely cleared – we're even serving eviction orders on the cockroaches . . .'

We all laughed politely.

'. . . the explosives will be brought in and put in position. These will be long, copper-shaped charges. Large ones for the foundations of the building, smaller ones as they go up. The charges are calibrated with great precision. In order to make sure the timing is perfect, the operatives use a detonating cord which burns at incredibly high speed. If you look around you will see that this has already been put in place.'

I looked around me and noticed a spider's web of interconnecting detonating cord linking each and every column.

Someone behind me asked a question. 'How far away will you be able to hear the explosion?'

'Strictly speaking it's not an explosion. This will be an implosion. The building will implode on itself, minimising the risks to those coming to watch this clearance and join in the celebration.'

'And what are the risks?' The voice came from my left. It was the man from the *Hackney Clarion*.

'Yes, Brian, you are right to ask. There are always risks with such an operation. Any mistake could be fatal. But the team in charge of the demolition has international expertise. Every detail will be carefully monitored.'

'Are you running on schedule?'

'Absolutely.'

'Any chance you will start to fall behind?'

'None. A delay would cost the tax-payer money. You should know me by now, Brian. After twenty-three years associated with Hackney Council, my reputation precedes me. I am as careful with the public purse as I am with my own. This building will come down on Saturday – the thirty-first. You have my word for it.'

I stared around me in wonder as we began to make our way back up the stairs, the import of such a calculated and complex piece of planned destruction finally sinking in on me. In ten days' time, these solid, timeless walls would no longer exist.

Passing through the swing doors and outside into the open air again, I swung the camera sharply up the huge height of the tower block to look at the bright blue sky. From this angle of diminishing perspective the building felt as if it were falling on top of me.

When I turned around it seemed the briefing was over; the little group was breaking up. PJ flung his arm around Jim Bryant's shoulder and motioned to the photographer from the *Hackney Clarion* to take a picture of the two of them together. They stood on the wasteground with the imposing but soon-to-be defeated structure of Angel Point dominating the background. I kept the camera running. Behind me, someone asked another question. It was a man's voice. I couldn't see who was speaking.

'I understand the body of an old man was discovered here a couple of weeks ago?'

My ears pricked up and I zoomed in on PJ's face, curious to see his response.

'Regrettably so.'

The next question took me completely unawares.

'I understand that the old man was your stepfather.'

The camera almost slipped off my shoulder. I tightened my grip and stared through the viewfinder at PJ's face. As far as I could see, he didn't even blink.

158

'That is correct,' he replied slowly, sadly.

I was speechless.

'How does that make you feel?'

'In what way?' asked PJ, buying time.

'Your old man dying here.'

I risked a quick look over my shoulder. The person asking the questions was the spotty youth from LEIR.

But PJ had collected his thoughts and was master of the situation once again.

'Obviously, to lose a close relative in any circumstances is extremely distressing. My stepfather was old and his mind wandered. He'd had a drink problem for many years. Unfortunately, the two were a lethal combination. All families need to be left alone with their grief. His death only serves as an added incentive to proceed with the demolition of this dangerous old structure and to make way for the future. Thank you. No further questions?' He paused for the briefest of moments. 'Good.'

Then he turned his back on us and moved away to stand behind the protective shelter of the local government officials. He appeared not to notice me or if he did, to have forgotten his promise to show me around. I switched off the camera and put it back in its case still reeling from the news.

Ted was PJ's stepfather. PJ was Mabel's adopted son. Why hadn't he said?

The young radio reporter was packing away his tape-recorder, betraying a clumsy unfamiliarity with the equipment, something I recognised in myself. Perhaps he was a kindred spirit. I wandered over to speak to him.

'How did you know that Ted O'Hagan was PJ's stepfather?'

He carried on packing up his equipment and when he had finished, he gave me a cautious, cagey look. 'Rule Number One, don't give away your story to the competition.'

Yeah, right. I was going to take his story and sell it to

Reuters. Rule Number One, if you need to quote from the rules you are a sad and incompetent arsehole. Still, he was an arsehole with information and all's fair in love and research.

'I'm not competition,' I assured him. 'You're obviously hard news. I'm just making a little low-budget documentary. It's my first time, actually.'

Karen McDade, virgin film-maker. I laid on the naiveté so heavily – too heavily. Surely, he would notice. But no, he just smirked, hoisted his tape-recorder onto his shoulder and gangled down at me with a smug look of superiority.

Some kindred spirit.

I put on my little-girl, extremely impressed face, opening my eyes wide and staring up at him from underneath my eyelashes. After that, he couldn't help boasting. He told me that his father had worked with Ted years before and thought there might be a connection.

'I made a few phone calls to my contacts and he was right. It's my lucky break. I'm going to use it as a human interest story. You know, *Stepson Seeks Revenge on Stepfather's Tomb*.' By now he was carried away by his own enthusiasm, painting the headline in the air as he spoke. Personally, I didn't think it had much of a ring to it and I told him so. I broke the news gently to him, searching for a kind and supportive way to let down a fellow hack.

'Sounds crap to me,' I said and left him to it.

I turned around to talk to PJ but he was gone, swallowed up by the group of officials from the council. It felt as if he had been spirited away. I trailed behind the group of local reporters as they made their way to the exit. Everyone was happy with their copy and the feeling of a good morning's work well done. Everyone except for me. I had come along as a time-filler, sure that I would find nothing of much interest. And now I had discovered that Ted O'Hagan had been PJ's stepfather. I couldn't let this go. I *had* to find out why he hadn't mentioned it to me before.

When the others went into the Site Office to return their hard hats and identity badges, I sneaked a look around the back where the cars were parked. And there, next to the sign saying *Site Traffic Only – No Unauthorised Vehicles* – was PJ's red Triumph. The power of contacts.

As far as I could remember, there was only one exit. I could catch him as he left. Quickly, I ran around the corner and went to find my own car. Parked on the road was a black Mercedes with tinted windows. The engine was running even though the car wasn't moving. Never mind the people on the streets who were choking with the pollution from too many cars, whoever was sitting inside was doubtless enjoying the pleasures of his mobile air-conditioning, air-filtration system.

I was loading the camera into the car when PJ appeared on foot. Before I could shout to him he went over to the black Mercedes. A window slid open. PJ poked his head inside and emerged a few minutes later, smiling. He walked back through the gates of the site and turned to give the Mercedes a final thumbs-up and a smile.

The car moved off and purred past me, the window slowly sliding closed again, but as it went by I caught a brief glimpse of the man in the back. It was the same expensively dressed man who I had seen with Jim Bryant. There was something about his face, it looked vaguely familiar.

Of course, it was Owen de Courtney! I was surprised to see *him* here. He was the kind of person who wouldn't dream of coming to Hackney without his passport and vaccination certificate. Normally, he would be way out of Hackney's league. Still, Private Finance Initiatives involving private money in public projects were part of the New Way Forward in terms of infrastructure investment, that's what we are always being told, and de Courtney was known to have his finger on the pulse.

161

You had to admire PJ for encouraging such heavyweight players to take a gamble on a public housing scheme in an area more renowned for unemployment and petty crime than stable growth. It was very hard to see how there could be a guaranteed return on his money.

As I sat in my car, waiting for PJ to appear again, my face and hands felt clammy and uncomfortable despite opening all the windows. I wound down the roof and took a swig from a bottle of lukewarm Evian which I found fermenting beneath a pile of rubbish on the passenger seat.

Five minutes later, Ace Ventura from LEIR drove past in a little brown Mini. I raised the bottle to him in fond farewell. He pretended not to see me.

The next car out was PJ's red Triumph, its polished fenders glinted like reflecting mirrors in the bright sunshine. I opened my door, stepped out onto the road and flagged him down. His car pulled up beside me.

'Karen!' His greeting was formal. Beside him in the passenger seat sat the young woman from Hackney Council. Damn. I could hardly ask him intimate questions about his recent bereavement standing in the street with a council official looking on.

'Sorry I had to rush off,' he continued. 'There were a couple of forms which needed my signature. Did you enjoy the tour? It's impressive, isn't it?' He was still working hard. Fine by me. I rose to the challenge.

'Very. Though I do still have a few questions that need answers.'

'I'm afraid now isn't a very good time. We're late for a meeting at the Town Hall.'

'What about after that? Are you free for lunch?'

He squirmed and looked as if he would like to say no. Then something made him change his mind. Perhaps the witty and attractive company on offer was just too tantalising to resist.

'There's a Vietnamese Canteen on the Englefield Road – it's in the old Public Bath House,' he said. 'I'll meet you there at one-fifteen.'

I drove home and flopped on my bed for an hour. The sheets still smelled of sex, warm and sweet with that slight tang of decay. It was hard not to think about Charlie. I tried, but it was hard. I remembered his tongue playing with me and then had to push away the memories of moans which began deep in my belly and escaped unguarded from my throat. Across the room Job was looking at me reproachfully. Out on the street there were children playing. The window was open. I could hear the sounds of their laughing voices.

It had been open last night.

Shit. Double shit. Had we been broadcasting an evening's entertainment to the neighbours? Not that I knew my neighbours.

I leaped out of bed and went into the living room. On the floor were two empty wine glasses. I tidied them away. I tidied everything away. I vacuumed the flat, stripped the bed, mopped the kitchen floor and emptied the rubbish. It was when I found myself scrubbing the grill pan that I realised I'd got it bad.

I wanted him to phone. He wasn't going to phone; he'd said that. We both knew where we stood. Anyway, he was right – me and him would never last. If there's one thing I've learned it's that passionate flings have a very short shelf-life. Still, it couldn't just be that once, could it?

God, I wanted to call him. I wanted to know if he was thinking of me too. He had to be. That was great sex. I mean, it wasn't just your average run-of-the-mill one-night-stand sort of sex. It was great sex. For me.

Uncertainty began to set in. Stop it, I said to myself. I don't do married men, remember? It is my Number One Rule, written in blood.

Charlie isn't married, he's engaged.

That is hair-splitting.

He is getting married in less than a week.

I thought of Sylvia, I didn't know how I was going to be able to look her in the face.

It was one o'clock. I looked around my pristine flat; amazing what you can achieve in half an hour. I should start my own cleaning company.

I walked outside onto the street. The baking heat of the afternoon sun sapped all my energy. I drove reluctantly back to Hackney, arriving dead on 1.15. PJ was there before me, already ensconced in a corner table.

'I've ordered,' he said. 'I have to be somewhere else by two. There are a lot of things to co-ordinate before next weekend.'

'One of them being a funeral?'

'One of them being a funeral.'

'Why didn't you say?'

'There didn't seem to be an appropriate moment. I knew you'd find out soon enough.'

'Well I have. But I still don't understand why you didn't say anything. You knew I had an interest in Ted. Was your grief too raw?'

'Grief?' He snorted with laughter. 'Irritation, more like.'

I waited for him to explain himself.

Just then lunch arrived. We were both given a steaming bowl of clear soup with noodles, green vegetables, grey slices of meat and what looked to be suspiciously like red chillies floating on top – just the thing to eat during a heatwave. I nodded an unconvincing thank you at the young waitress.

PJ unwrapped his chopsticks and tucked into his food. After a few minutes I realised the conversation was on hold. Bereavement is an awkward subject to force. I let him eat, sure that he would explain himself when he was ready.

The soup was spicy and hot, the flavour amazing. There was garlic and ginger and soy and several other tastes I could not name. My tongue began to tingle with the heat. PJ himself was breaking out into a sweat. He took out a pocket handkerchief and mopped his forehead. I used my serviette to do the same. Then something surprising happened. The more I ate, the cooler I felt. Overhead, a helicopter fan provided a faint breeze. I felt more comfortable than I had done all day.

When he had finished he wiped his lips and started to speak. 'You might as well know the truth. Ted was an idle bastard, a drunken ne'er do well, isn't that the phrase? I know Mabel loved him and all my life, even as a tiny child, I tried to respect that. But he was a bastard. She saw a poet and an artist. I saw a selfish old bugger who left her in the lurch more times than I could count.'

'In what way?'

'In every way that you could imagine. For most of his life he never held down a job. Working for a living made him feel trapped, he said. So it was Mabel who supported us until I was old enough to go out and start to earn some money. Even then he had the cheek to bum off me. He was in his forties, I was fourteen and I was giving *him* pocket money.'

'Why did you?'

'If I didn't give it to him, he'd take it out of her purse. Mabel would never ask me for anything: she'd never ask anyone for anything. She'd just go without herself. Once I saw her walking down the road with two bags of exercise books to mark. I asked her why she didn't take the bus. She said she didn't feel like it. Turned out she'd been doing that walk twice a day for a month. Ted had been off on a bender and bled her dry.'

'Mabel said he didn't drink.'

'Mabel never saw him drink. Anything that didn't fit in with her image of him, Ted did privately. When he was pissed,

165

he stayed away. Slept rough. Then he'd come back with a few scribbles of poetry and tell her he'd been off on some kind of artistic retreat.'

'Mabel said Ted was working at Heaven's Gate.'

'Working? Ted?' He snorted.

'At Heaven's Gate,' I repeated.

'Ted and a bottle of whisky used to keep one another company at Heaven's Gate from time to time, is more like the truth. Mabel had been worried about him. She said he was depressed. She said that Ted needed to feel like a useful member of society and could I get him a little job. Useful member of society, that's a bloody joke. Every time I helped him out, I always swore it would be the last time. I knew no good would come of it.'

'So Ted was working for McLachan plc?'

'No. Ted was working for nobody. He used to go over there in the evenings, "to keep an eye on things". It was a place he could drink privately. I'd give him thirty quid a week. And Mabel was happy.'

'Then what happened?'

'One morning he had disappeared. When I was told, I thought he had gone walkabout. He'd done that so many times before. The rest you know.'

'Why didn't you say any of this before?'

'Why should I? There was no reason to. Anyway, there was no love lost between me and Ted. A death is a death and he should be mourned, but my own father, Albert, was worth ten thousand of him. I never liked Ted.'

'Mabel said Ted took you into his home. He made you welcome,' I protested.

'Mabel was the one who turned that house into a home. She was the one who gave me a home. She gave me a home because once, long before, she had loved Albert, my real father. Then Ted came along and blinded her with his lies and his false charm. Me and Ted tolerated one another.'

'So why did you stay there?'

'I didn't. As soon as I was sixteen, I left.'

'And you are going to the funeral?'

'Of course – I'm organising it.'

'If you disliked him so much, why are you bothering?'

'If it was up to me he'd be off on the nine o'clock trot. It's for Mabel. They do say a funeral is for the living, not the dead; she likes to see things done proper.'

'What's the nine o'clock trot?'

'That's what we used to call a pauper's funeral – despatch them early before the respectable world is up and going about its business. That's what I'd do if it was up to me. Now, is there anything else you want to know?'

Disconcerted by the abrupt change of subject, it took me a moment to collect my thoughts. 'Would you be prepared to repeat what you have just told me on camera?'

'About Ted?'

I nodded.

'What do you think?'

'I think you might.'

'No chance, Karen. It wouldn't sit well with PJ Pickford's public image, would it, the fact that he hated his stepfather?'

'You don't mince your words.'

'I didn't intend to. Now, if there's nothing else . . .'

'About Micky Holman . . .'

'I've told you – the family don't want to be disturbed in their hour of grief.' He stood up and I felt him slipping away from me.

'Is there any chance he might have been murdered?'

'What an extraordinary thing to say!'

Extraordinary yes, but I had his attention.

'If I'm not mistaken, you were one of the people who saw young Micky slip and fall. How can that be murder?'

'What about John Martin?'

'Who?'

'The other dead man, six weeks ago. His girlfriend said . . .' But here my voice trailed off as I remembered her doped-up eyes.

'That crackhead – what has she been saying?' PJ sounded angry.

I shook my head. It wasn't worth repeating. PJ sat down again. His voice dropped to a whisper but he spoke each word with deadly seriousness.

'Karen, let me tell you a few facts of life here. Hundreds of jobs and the livelihood of thousands depend on that development at Heaven's Gate. At the moment Heaven's Gate is a building site, new houses, new homes – as subject-matter for a film I can imagine it's like watching paint dry, but you chose it. Trying to find something to spice it up is understandable, but it won't work – and if you start spreading any nasty rumours around, some of those West End fiancés I have spent so much time and effort wooing may decide not to come up the altar with me – and that won't be any good for anybody.'

I changed tack. 'It's very good of you to work so hard for so little return.'

His eyes narrowed. 'I'm not with you.'

'I understand your position with the council is largely voluntary.'

He mopped the spicy gravy off his lips with a clean white napkin. 'I'm an elected councillor.'

'The pay hardly justifies the effort.'

'Congratulations, you've been doing your research.'

'It's very public-minded of you. A man of your obvious capabilities could receive large remunerative rewards in the private sector.'

'As I think I've already mentioned, my wife has a private

income, so I don't need the money. Besides, it is a privilege to be able to serve the people of Hackney this way. There can be no greater reward than getting a project such as this off the ground, since it will regenerate the entire area. Heaven's Gate is the result of over ten years' work. Heaven's Gate is my baby. Now, if you'll excuse me?'

He left abruptly. It took me a moment to realise that he'd gone without paying. I finished off my meal and signalled to the waitress.

'Can I help you?'

'The bill, please.'

'Mr Pickford has already paid. He said you were to eat what you wanted and take your time.'

Chapter Ten

'Okay, it's time to recap. What exactly have we got?'

It was Thursday afternoon, an hour or so after my lunch with PJ. Rob and I were upstairs on the third floor of the Finest Cut in a little old-fashioned editing suite. We were both so familiar with this room. This was where we had edited Rob's first two films. Night after night we used to sit here together, alone in the empty building. It was only natural that at some point we would want to go to bed. But there had never been anything like the jolt of electricity I had experienced with Charlie. I thought of this with a tinge of sadness. Really it would have been so much better if things had turned out differently with Rob. What was it Charlie said? We could have been all right for each other, me and Rob.

I wondered if Rob could tell. Could he smell the sex on my skin? Would he mind?

Unbidden, an image of Charlie suckling my nipple in the moonlight came into my mind and my stomach gave a little leap – the way it does when you drive too fast over a hump-back bridge. Down, girl, down.

Why had I said Rob's name aloud when we were making love?

'So, you go first. What exactly have we got?'

I flicked through my notes on structure and forced myself to concentrate on Rob's question. 'Right. We start off with the sound of flies buzzing, children playing, distant traffic. Then we have a shot from the window of the eleventh floor. Then we cut to the caption *Angel Point*. That's where we have a shot of Angel Point dominating the landscape. Then we cut to the shot of the room in which Ted died. Dead silence. Except for a distant, very faint sound of a buzzing fly, so faint that it is probably only registered in the subconscious. The camera pans around the room. The narrator announces the facts of the discovery of Ted's body. The sound of the fly buzzing gets louder and louder. Then we cut to a shot of the morgue and a refrigeration unit being slammed shut.'

'Possible reverb on the metal door shutting?'

'Great.'

'What next?'

'I've tried to track down the families of the two labourers who died.'

'Any luck?'

'No.'

'Karen, I really don't think we need them, we have more than enough material here. Especially when we culminate with some spectacular footage of the blowdown. I've arranged for us to have access to an eighth-storey flat a few hundred yards away. That should give us what we need. They'll be well pleased. So, where are we with Mabel? Where do you envisage introducing her?'

'I thought we could begin with that spell-binding section of footage where she talks about how Ted swept her off her feet on Hackney Marshes. Campfires in the twilight, picnics on the grass and the sound of accordion music . . .'

For the next three hours we swapped ideas back and forth, weaving existing themes and coming up with new suggestions. By the time we finished it was 7.30. We walked down the back stairs and out onto the streets of Soho. The area was packed. The streets had a holiday feel to them – loud laughter and pints of lager, people spilling over onto the pavements outside pubs and restaurants, flirting and having a good time.

'Do you fancy a drink?' Rob asked.

I hesitated. A drink would be nice – then I caught sight of

Rob's face. He was looking at me mutinously, almost daring me to say no. I thought again of whispering his name while making love to Charlie. Things were still too fresh. Best leave well alone.

'Not tonight, thanks.'

'Why not?'

'Do I need a reason?'

'Not normally. Karen, if we're finished, just say it. Say we're finished.'

I couldn't look him in the eyes. Yet I couldn't bring myself to say the words. 'I'm sorry, Rob. I just don't know. I feel very crowded at the moment.'

We said goodbye. No tingle of electricity, just mutual irritation. I should have told him about Charlie, but I couldn't face it.

As I drove back to Islington I turned on the radio. Jazz FM was playing Piaf, just the thing for a sultry summer's evening. The world-weary bitterness in her tone fitted my mood which was one of specific recrimination and self-doubt. Nimble fingers played the accordion and summoned up a feeling of days and nights long gone, Paris in the fifties, London in the thirties, Mabel and Ted.

I didn't want to go home. I couldn't stay in alone and think about last night and Charlie and this evening and Rob. I needed company, but the company I wanted wasn't on offer. It was an evening to be out and about. An evening for picnics and campfires and falling in love. I decided to go to Hackney Marshes while the light was still good and film some footage. We could run it with Mabel's voice talking about how Ted swept her off her feet all those years ago.

I stopped off at the flat to pick up the camera. Job was lying asleep on the sofa when I opened the front door. Moments later, when he realised I was going out again, he leaped up and out of the door, almost bowling me over with his enthusiasm. Anyway, there was no reason to leave him behind and every reason to bring him along. With him at my side, no one would try and nick my camera.

I checked the answering machine before I left. You never know, Charlie might have decided he couldn't live without me.

There were no messages.

I drove to Hackney Marshes with the roof down. We got there at dusk, but there were still plenty of people about. I positioned myself with my back to a tree for support and set up the camera. Job lay Sphinx-like, on guard at my feet. I needed to be quick. The light was fading fast.

I just let the camera run for a few minutes, zooming in and out of whatever I could find.

The scene was timeless. Teenagers sat in circles drinking illicit beer and practising smoking. Mothers with young children gossiped in the long grass. Older couples sat sedately on benches by the paths. A group of teenage boys idly kicked a football around. There was a casual feeling of London at play.

In the distance, I spied a young couple lying on a picnic blanket. I zoomed in to have a closer look. She was kneeling, staring down into her boyfriend's face. He rested his head in her lap. It looked as if he were pretending to be asleep. She tickled his nose with a stem of long grass. He kept his eyes resolutely shut although a huge smile cracked open his face. When he could bear it no longer he jumped up and began to chase her until they both fell over laughing and rolling on the ground. I was so far away that I could watch them unobserved. Their play was private and special and universal. There was something haunting about the scene. The sound of accordion music continued to play over and over in my mind. It felt as if I were looking down a long lens and into their future.

The visibility light came on in the camera. The sun had gone down and it was suddenly and unexpectedly chilly. Here and there, the odd illegal campfire glowed in the twilight. For the first time I could feel a hint of autumn in the air. It was time to go. All around me people were packing up to go home. Job and I joined the exodus.

I headed back to Islington, turning left and right down deserted streets, automatically finding the quickest way home, but once I pulled up outside my flat I knew I was reluctant to go inside. I felt restless and ill at ease. It was early and a solitary evening held no appeal. I knew that if I went into the flat, I would only sit there willing and willing and willing Charlie to ring me.

I closed up the roof on the car and locked up, going through the motions. And still I couldn't bring myself to go inside. I walked to the end of the street with Job. The air was muggy, the heat oppressive. A couple were arguing outside a pub, their two unhappy children trying not to listen to words of blame and hatred being shouted over their heads.

So I walked back again away from them towards my flat, but instead of going inside I lingered on the doorstep listening to the sounds of the evening, breathing in the smell of burning paraffin from a thousand barbecues wafting on the night air. Job couldn't work out what I was up to. He snuffled my hand, trying to encourage me to open our front door. I stroked his muzzle absent-mindedly. If I didn't do something to burn off some energy, there was no way I was going to be able to sleep later.

Suddenly, I had an idea. I knew what to do. Hackney Downs was where my story began. Angel Point was where it ended. At night, each place has a different atmosphere. So far I had only seen Angel Point by day. It was worth another look. I wouldn't be able to do any filming because of the lack of light but what the hell, it was something to do. Job jumped up at me and snuffled my ear, sensing adventure. We were on.

I phoned Rob from the car. Think of it as bridge building.

Perhaps I could persuade him to join me on my outing. It would be exciting. I mean, I knew I was breaking the law, but it wasn't like real crime. I wasn't going to nick anything. I just wanted to have a look around in my own time without someone looking over my shoulder and hurrying me away. I wanted to soak up the atmosphere, imagine what it would be like to be in the dark and alone.

Rob wasn't there. I didn't leave a message. There didn't seem much point.

Job and I drove with the windows down enjoying the cool air.

All along the Essex Road, pubs and restaurants spilled out onto the streets. Swarms of young men clustered twenty deep outside each pub. Gangs of girls linked arms five abreast and strode down the centre of the road, forcing cars to slow to a crawl. They all wore the same uniform – hair scraped back, eyes lined with black, tattoos on an arm, or a shoulder, or the top of a breast. With their short, crotch-length dresses, stiletto heels and heads held high, they wove their way in and out of the stationary traffic looking as if they owned the road.

I thought briefly of my friend Sarah and the times we cruised the pubs together. Those days are long gone. I've never really found anyone to replace her.

I thought of Charlie and wondered where he was. He might be in some pub with his mates. The Dog and Duck? I could just drop by . . . I was in the area.

No. No.

He might be lying stretched out on the sofa, his head in Sylvia's lap . . . Stop it. I had to stop this.

I thought of Rob again and wondered what he was up to. No, that wasn't fair. In fact, it was pathetic, trying to think of Rob to stop myself from thinking about Charlie. It wasn't fair to use Rob like that.

I reached out and ruffled Job's fur. He gave my arm little gentle licks.

By this time we were halfway there, on the Islington-Hackney borders. Speed-bumps stretch out across the first half of the Englefield Road, slowing down the traffic, preventing it from speeding through the residential streets. At the junction with Southgate Road you enter the nuclear-free zone of the London Borough of Hackney and the speed-bumps disappear. I accelerated to forty miles an hour, crossed the Kingsland Road on an amber light, drove up over the railway bridge, down the Richmond Road – concentrate on the driving, don't think of Charlie – and a couple of minutes later we arrived at Heaven's Gate.

The streets around Angel Point were deserted. I parked as near as I could to the site entrance but as far away as possible from the orange glare of the overhead street-lamps. Leaving Job in the car, I closed the windows, got out and locked the door. The contrast between the crowds and activity on the Essex Road and these empty streets couldn't have been more extreme. The silence was eerie.

I walked along the perimeter of hoarding surrounding the site. Everything was locked up securely for the night. The wooden fencing was too high to climb; there was nowhere to get a foothold. At the entrance to the site I peered through the gap in the metal gates. No lights. No noise. No activity. In the shadows huge pieces of machinery squatted silently in the dark.

I was glad I had come. By night the place was very different. It looked like a ghost city. But I didn't know whether it was the ghost of time past or of time future. Angel Point loomed above, empty, failed and desolate. Underneath, in its gloomy shadow, half-completed houses lurked in the darkness. No glass in their windows, no roofs to shield them in.

The Site Office was dark. I shifted to get a better look

through the gap in the gates. Strange, there was no night-watchman on duty. If Ted had really been working as a night-watchman, wouldn't they have found someone to replace him?

I thought of Ted coming here at night just to drink. A solitary drinker, coming to this lonely place to drown his demons.

All of a sudden I heard the sound of voices coming from the other side of the fence.

'Is that it then?'

'That's it.'

'Let's be off then. If we get a move on we'll be finished before last orders.'

'That's all you ever think about.'

'No, not all.'

Their voices travelled clear across the night air. As I peered through I could make out nothing.

'Here – don't forget to let them out, otherwise there'll be hell to pay.'

'You're right'

I could make out the sound of a metal chain rattling. Then there was the loud slamming of a heavy metal door, once, twice and the chugging roar of a large engine coming to life. They had forgotten to turn the headlights on. I felt rather than saw one of the lorries parked by the Site Office begin to move. Its heavy black shape loomed closer and closer. On impulse, I ducked between two parked cars as one man jumped down from the cab of the lorry and swung open the gates to the site.

The truck pulled out into the street and the gates were bolted and locked behind it. Then there was the heavy clunk of the cab door closing and they rolled off down the street, still in darkness. That was odd. They were working very late. I wondered what they had been doing. Mind you, from what I could gather, the pressure was on to keep the job moving, the schedule was tight, no wonder people were working through the night.

As I walked back to the car, my hand trailed along the hoarding. A section of the wooden panelling moved beneath my fingertips. I stopped and pushed at it, gently at first, then harder as I felt it give way. Noiselessly I worked at it, pushing and pulling, pulling and pushing. I turned round nervously, hoping that no one was watching me. Only Job. I could see his large shadow in the car standing bolt upright, head turned to one side, ears alert, trying to work out what I was doing.

Eventually the hoarding gave way. Not much. But enough for me to twist my body and squeeze through. Victory! This time there was no one here to warn me off and chase me away. I could go where I pleased.

I looked around me. All was silent. I walked across the empty space towards the Site Office with a sense of achievement, passing in the shadow of a huge, silent bulldozer.

I retraced the path of the lorry I had just seen leaving. Behind the Site Office I found nothing more interesting than a large stack of bricks covered with a makeshift plastic tarpaulin which fluttered and flapped in the faint breeze.

Suddenly the hairs on the back of my neck stood on end. What was that noise? I could hear a scuffling sound somewhere in the distance. Rats? Whatever it was I didn't like it. I turned to run, to get back to the car, the blood pounding in my ears. I couldn't hear beyond the sound of my own fear.

Was that really a noise? Or was I imagining things? I didn't want to stop and look. Out on the empty expanse, I was exposed and helpless in the bleak, cold gaze of the watching moon. There was something behind me and it was getting closer and closer. I ran. Where was the hole in the fence? In my panic I couldn't remember. Instead I headed for the gates.

Where was the gate? Where was the gate?

179

There.

I flung myself on the gates and began to climb. Up and up, towards safety.

Not quite.

A sharp, hot pain seared into my ankle. I turned and saw yellow eyes gleaming malevolently in the darkness. A large Rottweiler gripped me tight, his teeth locked into my running shoe. He was swinging from my foot, his hind legs only partially on the ground and was pulling me steadily down from my place of safety. Another dog stood just next to him, waiting silently on the ground. Too late I made sense of the rattling chain before the departure of the truck. They had freed the dogs.

The pain in my ankle was intense. I hung on tight to the fence and tried to haul myself higher away from his reach. But the weight of his body dragged me down. I couldn't scream; I couldn't cry out. Instead, with every atom of my strength, I willed myself to hold on. Just to hold on and try to pull myself up.

I looked down into the dog's cold, yellow eyes. And at the other dog standing silently in the background. I remembered everything I had heard about dogs in packs. I thought of those teeth and how they would tear me to shreds. There would be no one here to help. There would be no one to pull them off me.

The muscles in my arms were shrieking in agony. Still I held on.

Please God. Please God. Just give me strength.

It was no use. I was weakening. My sweaty hands were slipping. I couldn't hold out for much longer. Yes, I could. Try. Just try.

And then . . . Suddenly the pressure on my ankle miraculously disappeared. The dog was no longer dragging me down. Quickly my tired hands scrabbled further up, and gasping, I

180

heaved myself out of reach. Ragged breaths saved me from slipping into unconsciousness. I could hear something happening below, but I didn't want to look. I didn't know how I had been saved, but I didn't want to look. I rested on my plateau of pain, weeping tired, silent tears.

As the minutes passed, the sounds began to separate themselves. I could hear scuffling, a deep-throated yelping and a low growling. Now I did look down. Three large shadows had merged into one seething mass of fur and bared teeth.

'Job!' I called out in terror. He was no match for these two killers. 'Job! No!'

I flung myself off the fence and landed on the ground, almost fainting with the pain in my ankle. The dogs were locked to the death and ignored me utterly. Job had one dog by the neck and was holding him in a paralysing grip. The other dog had his teeth locked into the thick fur on Job's back and was mauling him from behind. None of them were able to move.

What could I do?

'Job!' I screamed again. The dogs paid me no attention.

I limped around looking for something, anything I could use as a weapon. How do you stop a dogfight? Water. A bucket of water. There was no water. No bucket. No hosepipe. Not anything. There had to be something. Job couldn't hold them both for much longer. I stumbled over some tarpaulin and fell sprawling in the dust. My hands could make out something hard and solid beneath the canvas cover. Frantically I pulled back the sheet. Scaffolding poles. They were too long and too heavy. Come on, blast you. Damn. I couldn't move them.

Behind me, there was ferocious growling. I turned. Job had not been able to keep his hold on the other dog's neck. The animal had twisted himself around and grabbed Job by the muzzle. Now, it was only a matter of time. Those killers would finish with Job and then they would come after me again.

Desperately I kicked and pulled at the metal scaffolding. I could feel it moving. One bar seemed to be shifting. It was much shorter than the others. It came away in my hand.

I ran back towards the dogs, raised the pole above my hand and brought it down hard, unsure of my aim. In the dark it was difficult to make anything out. I flailed around wildly. There was a sickening thud and the shock reverberated up through my arms. No time to stop and think. I raised the pole over my head again and brought it down hard again. This time there was a loud crack and the dog on top of Job went limp.

Freed from the heavy weight, Job and the other Rottweiler rolled over and over in the dust.

But the limp dog wasn't dead. I could see it trying to struggle to its feet.

No, you don't.

I went over and raised the metal bar again and this time with more deliberation, I swung it hard on the dog's skull.

Bone splintered. All movement stopped.

Job had the first Rottweiler by the throat again. The two dogs rose to their hind feet and circled each other, locked in mortal combat like two great grizzly bears. I watched them as if in a dream. There was something unreal about their size and the deadly seriousness of this fight.

Panting, I limped towards them and struggled to lift the pole over my head. It was difficult to get a clear aim. I didn't want to hit Job by mistake. I swung the pole but had to deflect the blow at the last second as the dogs shifted position. I raised the pole again and stood staring at the heaving shoulders of the huge dog until I was sure of my aim.

Crack.

The force of the blow stung my fingers and the pole clattered to the ground, leaving me defenceless. There was no need to worry: I had broken his spine. The dog lay writhing in the dust. He tried to struggle back to his feet but gave up and lay there, his panting gradually growing more ragged and uneven until at last it stopped.

Everything was still.

I turned to Job. He stood unsteadily on all fours, his head bowed.

'Good dog,' I whispered in the sudden silence. 'Come here!'

He didn't move. Instead he raised his head to me and I could see the exhaustion in the depths of his eyes. I staggered towards him and put my arm around his shoulder. He leaned his full body weight into me and I could feel compulsive shuddering convulsing his muscles.

'Good dog!' I whispered again and caressed his mane. Something felt sticky. My hand jerked away. I held it up to the light of the moon. The skin glistened a reddish brown.

'Job?' I put my hand back to his neck and tried to part the thick fur to see the extent of his wounds. His body spasmed twice. Then he sank to his knees.

'Job, get up!' I said desperately.

He didn't move. I put my hands around his muzzle and raised his face to mine. 'Get up, boy. We have to get out of here.'

Still, he didn't move. His eyes looked at me and in their expression I read warmth and tiredness and a deep, deep sadness. He was slipping away.

'No!' I said firmly. 'No, you are not leaving me, you are not going to give up.' I took my hands away from the side of his face. They were covered in blood. The soft skin around his mouth was mangled and torn.

'Come on, Job.' I stood up, all thought of my own pain and distress vanished. I pulled at his collar. He wouldn't, or couldn't budge. 'You're going to be all right, Job. You are going to be all right.'

I managed to get my arms underneath his front legs and half-dragged, half-carried his body towards the fence, all eight stone of him. I don't know how we succeeded. Job feebly tried to support some of his weight on his back paws and shuffled along with me.

I had to drop him onto the ground again when we reached the gap in the hoarding. Job must have followed me in through here, but there was no way it was big enough for us to squeeze through together.

I kicked and pulled at the wood, oblivious to the damage I was causing until we could both get through. I pushed and pulled him through the hole and then hauled him along the street towards the car. Underneath a street-light I stopped to examine his injuries. His fur was so dark it was difficult to see. His mouth was foaming with exertion and he was panting heavily, his ribs shuddering with each breath.

'Good dog. Good dog.' I took my hand away and was shocked to see the sticky river of blood coating the bare skin; it looked brown in this orange light.

By the time I reached the car, I was carrying him. I opened the door and climbed in the back seat, then turned round and hauled him in after me, wedging my feet under the seat so I could use my weight to lever him in. Then I climbed out the other side and walked round to where he still lay half in, half out of the car and pushed him from behind.

'Good dog, good dog!' My voice was singsong, the intonation reassuring. But inside I was so frightened for him I wanted to cry.

When he was in the car, I put my head close to his ear. 'Please don't die on me,' I begged.

I got in and dialled Directory Enquiries and started the car. 'The RSPCA emergency number, please.'

My fingers fumbled with the numbers as I punched them in and I realised how badly I was shaking. The emergency vet on twenty-four-hour duty in my area was in Hampton Terrace, Islington. I dialled the number and spoke to the vet as I put my foot down and headed that way fast. As I drove along I became aware that a cool breeze was blowing on my face. Looking up I saw that the roof had been ripped to shreds. Job had fought his way out of the car so that he could get out to rescue me.

'Good dog, good dog,' I said, desperately trying to keep him conscious.

We waited to turn right on the Essex Road. I tooted my horn at the delay and the driver in front of me raised a two-finger salute. I looked at Job lying on the back seat of the car. His breathing was becoming more and more shallow. What could I do to get his attention?

'Cats!' I said.

His ears twitched.

'Biscuits!' I said.

His eyes gleamed faintly.

The pubs on the Essex Road still spilled out onto the pavements. For me a lifetime had passed, and here the same people were still out enjoying themselves. The traffic crawled as drivers ogled the girls in their short skirts and skin-tight jeans. I wanted to stand on the horn of my car with frustration but stopped myself in case it made the wanker in front drive even slower.

'Good dog, I'll take you for a walk tomorrow.'

A walk. That word always produced a response. But this time nothing. Job lay motionless. No. It was not going to happen. He couldn't be bleeding to death on the back seat of my car! I turned right up Hampton Terrace. The vet stood waiting for me outside his surgery. He was a young man, in his late twenties with blond hair and a strong-looking build.

Australian. I remembered he'd sounded Australian on the phone. What irrelevant details we notice.

I flung the car door open and jumped out onto the pavement. Come on, Job. You're here.'

Together we pulled him out of the car. The vet picked him up bodily and carried him like a baby into the surgery.

The bright fluorescent light was momentarily blinding. Disorientated, I was no help whatsoever. I followed meekly behind as the vet kicked open the door to the examination room and placed Job on the table.

Under the harsh glare of the spotlight, the extent of Job's wounds was brutally apparent. He was bleeding from the muzzle, the soft flesh on his lips and nose had been torn to shreds. He was haemorrhaging from his throat and bleeding badly from the back of his neck. The vet's hands probed his wounds gently, while I stood there rigid with horror.

'He's lost an awful lot of blood. I'm afraid I don't hold out much hope for him.'

'Don't say that, he might hear you.'

'We'll do what we can. In the meantime I suggest you talk to him. Say anything that might stop him from losing consciousness.'

I cradled Job's head and spoke to him softly. I talked to him about all the stupid things he'd done as a pup and how he'd made me laugh. I told him that if he got better I'd take him for lots of walks and feed him lots of biscuits and allow him to chase after all the cats he desired – all the trigger words that usually produced a response. This time however he just lay there limp in my arms. Still, he was alive and I was sure he was listening to me. Tears streamed down my face.

'Please be well, Job. Please be well.'

'Right, I'm giving him a transfusion. And I've just given him an injection to alleviate the shock and to help him sleep.

I think you should leave him now. See to yourself. You've done all you can.'

'I'm not going anywhere.'

'There's nothing you can do here.'

'You don't understand. I'm not going anywhere.'

'I need to sew him back together. It's involved work and I need to concentrate. I'd prefer it if you weren't here.'

'But you don't understand. He saved my life.'

'And you may have saved his by getting him here so quickly. Now you need to go and get yourself seen to.'

'I'm fine.'

'You don't look fine. There's blood all over my floor. Look!'

I looked down, surprised.

'Have you been hurt as well?'

'Um.' I paused to think, trying to remember.

'It's difficult to know if the blood on your clothes belongs to you or to your dog.'

My body felt numb and distant.

'Have you been bitten as well?'

'Yes, I . . . think I was bitten on the ankle.' I was distracted. My mind wandered. He was saying something, but I couldn't concentrate. I didn't hear him.

He said it again. 'Which ankle?'

I recognised that sing-song tone and I didn't like it. I didn't need it. I wanted him to look after Job.

'This ankle,' I replied, looking down at my jeans. Both legs were saturated in blood. I stared at them in surprise. They felt as if they didn't belong to me. 'This ankle, I think.' I raised the fabric of my trousers. Blood stained my sock scarlet. The heel of my shoe was lacerated. I felt a strong hand on my arm.

'You have to go to a hospital. Do you understand? Promise me you'll go!'

'I promise.'

'Shall I ring an ambulance for you?'

187

'No, I'm fine, I'll drive . . .' My voice tailed off. 'I don't want to leave Job.' The words came out as a mangled cry.

'Please, you've done everything you can.'

'Will you?' I choked back sobs of desperation.

'What?'

'Will you promise you will do everything you can? He's not just a dog, you know.'

'I promise,' said the Australian, and as I looked into his kind, grey eyes I believed him.

'Give me one minute.' I went over to Job. 'Job?' I whispered. He was unconscious. The tranquilliser had already taken effect. I leaned closer to him. 'Job? Can you hear me? Thank you . . . Thank you.'

'Are you sure you'll be all right?'

I nodded through my tears.

'What's your telephone number? I'll leave a message on your machine when I've finished with him in half an hour or so. You'll probably still be in Casualty.'

I recited my telephone number automatically.

'There's a drinks machine in reception,' he continued in a slow, calming voice. 'It takes 20p coins. You'll find a basket with some change in it behind the counter. Buy yourself a drink – something with sugar in it. Call me in the morning, but not before eight o'clock. When I've finished with him I want to try and get some shut-eye.'

I helped myself to a cup of hot chocolate and took it outside to drink in the car. Sitting in the driver's seat I noticed that my glove compartment was open. While I was in the vet's surgery, someone had walked past and nicked all my cassettes. I was too dazed to care. I drank the hot liquid and felt the sugary chocolate clear my mind and sharpen my senses. When it was finished, I put the key in the ignition and started the car.

'Please Job, please, please be all right!'

I swung out into traffic and almost hit an oncoming car. The driver slammed on his brakes and beeped wildly. I waved feebly in apology. My whole body seemed to be shaking. My hands trembled and I gripped the steering wheel tightly to steady them. I was minutes from home. I wanted to sleep. Perhaps I should just go home? Then I remembered my promise. If I wanted Job to live, I had to keep faith with that promise.

I headed towards the West End, the A and E department of University College Hospital.

In Casualty a nurse was arguing with a drunk man, trying to persuade him to put out a cigarette. The unforgiving glare of the overhead lights made my fellow patients look an unappetising lot. Drunks, hookers and winos, they all seemed to be staring at me. Perhaps it was the fate of every newcomer to be the momentary object of attention.

I gave my name at reception.

'Have you been to this hospital before?' The professional voice was crisp and detached.

'Once. A long time ago.'

'What's the problem?'

I peered over the top of the reception desk. The stern woman on duty seemed to be fading in and out. I used my arms to steady myself and hold myself upright. I couldn't think of the right words.

'Have you been in an accident?' she prompted.

I shook my head.

'A fight?'

I nodded. 'A dog fight,' I managed to whisper. 'But I'm all right, I think. I think it's just shock.'

'Take a seat.'

People continued to stare as I found myself a seat. It was disconcerting. I stared back and one by one they dropped their eyes. As I sat there I realised how dirty and dusty I was.

My jacket was covered with sand and my hands and finger-nails were stained with Job's blood. Please let him be all right.

'Karen McDade?'

My name was the first to be called. That was surprising. I had settled myself in for a long wait. I stumbled over to the waiting nurse. As she led me through the double doors towards the examination rooms I caught sight of my face in a mirror and realised why people had been looking at me and why I had been seen straight away. Black glassy eyes stared out of a hollow white face which was streaked with blood. I hardly knew myself.

'Which bit of you hurts?' The doctor's voice was brisk and cheery.

I sat on the side of an examination bed. 'My ankle,' I mumbled.

A nurse helped me off with my shoe. The ankle was swollen; my shoe was sticky with blood. Together we peeled back the saturated sock. Huge teethmarks perforated the heel. Already the bruising had turned my foot blue.

'Nasty, nasty! Still, you were lucky the dog got you by the heel and not on the bone of the ankle itself. Big dog, by the looks of it. If he'd bitten your ankle he'd have crushed it. What kind of dog was it?'

I told him. He examined me closely as the nurse washed my foot in lukewarm water. I flinched away. It stung at first but her hands were gentle and I began to find it soothing.

'Bleeding's almost stopped. I'll give you a few stitches here just to draw the skin together. It'll hurt for a few days, but there's no major damage. We'll dress it for you and then you can have a tetanus. Now, which leg would you like to volunteer for this injection?'

I chose the left leg. The right one had suffered enough.

I drove home, shivering despite the balmy air. All adrenaline had drained from my body. My foot had seized up and was very painful to walk on despite the painkillers I had been given. I was very, very, very tired. I heaved myself out of the car and locked it behind me. No need to bother, really. The roof was torn to shreds and anything nickable had already been nicked.

There was one message on my machine. The vet had called to say that Job was holding his own. 'Good dog!' I smiled into the darkness.

Chapter Eleven

I woke at half-past seven. I lay licking my lips, tasting the foul taste in my mouth, trying to figure out why I had the feeling that something was wrong. The flat felt silent and empty. I sat up. Pain screamed in my upper arms and between my shoulder blades. My fingers were stiff and swollen.

Memories came crowding back.

Job swaying precariously on all four legs looking at me with an expression of fatigue and defeat. Job lying lifeless on the examination table in Hampton Terrace. I panicked and leaped out of bed, crumpling to a heap on the floor in agony. Putting weight on that ankle wasn't such a good idea.

I needed to know how he was, but just as I was about to punch in the vet's number, I remembered what he had said. Not before eight o'clock. It was twenty five to. As good as. That would do.

Maybe not.

I forced myself to put the phone back on the receiver. If he'd saved Job's life he deserved his sleep. If Job was dead . . . Well, I didn't want to hear those words anyway.

I made a cup of lethally strong black coffee and ran a hot bath. My difficulties in manoeuvring myself into it, without getting the bandage wet, would have been comical in any other circumstances. The hot water eased my tired muscles. By the time I'd got out and dried myself it was five past eight. I limped experimentally into the kitchen and swigged back some painkillers with the cold remnants of my coffee.

The phone rang, causing me to jump out of my skin. 'Yes?'

'Karen? Are you all right?'

'Rob?'

'Yes. Are you all right?'

'I'm fine.'

'You don't sound fine.'

'It's just I thought you were someone else.'

'Sorry to disappoint.'

'No, I didn't mean it like that.'

'You rang.'

'Did I?'

'Last night. I dialled 1471 when I came home.'

'Yes, I did.'

'Did you want something?'

'Rob, I have to go.'

'Karen, are you sure you're all right?'

'Why?'

'You sound strained.'

Strained? That was putting it mildly. 'I have to go. I'll call you back.'

'When?'

'This afternoon.'

I hung up and rang the vet's. It couldn't wait a moment longer. A sleepy Australian voice answered after ten long rings.

'It's Karen McDade here. How's Job?'

'Hi. I was just on the point of ringing you.'

'How is he?'

'Not the most frisky-looking dog I've ever seen, but he's alive.'

Yesss! Inside my head, I shouted with joy. 'Can I come and see him?'

'We're not open.'

'Please?'

'All right. But Karen, he's not out of danger. He needs to be kept very quiet.'

'I'll be there in fifteen minutes.'

Getting myself dressed took longer than fifteen minutes. When I stretched my arms above my head the pain was excruciating. Where each muscle hurt, I stretched it a little further and breathed into the stretch until the pain began to subside. The pain was a kind of punishment. Self-inflicted because of what I had done to Job.

I drove to Hampton Terrace and parked outside the door just as the vet was raising the blind on the surgery window.

'How are you?'

'How's Job?'

'He's all right. He's awake but only barely.'

He led the way into the examination room. Job still lay on the table which had been pushed against the wall. His eyes were partly open but they were unfocused. Huge sections of his fur had been shaved away and I could see the cruel, jagged teethmarks scarring his creamy blue skin. Stitches held the tears together, so many of them, to begin with I didn't know which was thread and which was dried blood. A drip monitored his fluid level and a computer screen showed the regular undulations of his beating heart.

'Job?' I whispered gently. The pupils in his eyes showed a faint glimmer of awareness but that was it. 'Good dog,' I said, stroking him gently. His normally healthy coal-black muzzle looked dehydrated and grey.

'How long will he be like this?'

'I told you, he's not out of danger yet. The next twenty-four hours are crucial. If he survives that long, he should pull through.'

'Will you keep him here?'

'No alternative. If you moved him now, it could prove fatal.'

I watched him roll up an exercise mat on the floor and put it in a corner beside a small pile of neatly folded blankets.

'Did you sleep in here?' I asked, surprised.

'I wanted to keep an eye on him.'

I felt such a surge of gratitude towards this stranger that I almost flung my arms around him. Instead I lowered my head and thanked him in a small voice.

I went over to Job and hugged him carefully. 'I'll be back this afternoon. You just stay here for me. Good dog. I'll see you later.' Again his eyes flickered. At least he knew I was there.

At reception I gave the vet my name, address and Visa card number.

'Do you want an idea of the bill so far?'

'No. That's not necessary.' My credit limit was reasonably high and in these circumstances, money wasn't a consideration.

'And what about you? Are you all right?' he asked as I left.

'I'm fine,' I answered, buoyant on painkillers.

Outside, a white parking ticket stared smugly from my windscreen. It was tucked behind the wipers. 'No!' I yelled out loud in frustration. It wasn't even 8.30 yet. Parking restrictions didn't exist until 8.30. This was too much.

I looked at the time written on the ticket. It read 8.36. Then I looked at the time on my dashboard clock: 8.40. I scanned the street. No uniform in sight. I swear the wardens hang from underneath my car, travelling around with me, waiting to catch me out.

Back home, I collapsed on the bed. I wanted to phone Charlie. When he became my lover, he suddenly moved to the status of new best friend. I wanted to call him and have him come round, and tell him all about it. I wanted to relax in his arms and feel the pain in my foot and my useless, ceaseless worrying over Job float away.

It was odd that he was out of bounds – unnatural, somehow. After one night together, he had become part of me. Or was I

196

kidding myself? Perhaps it was just the attraction of the unobtainable. Once upon a time I had got engaged on the strength of one night's drunken sex. That little fiasco had ended in rape and four years of sleepless nights before the memories began to lose their hold on me. If that experience had taught me anything, it was to be suspicious of my own motives. Still I continued to think about Charlie. At unexpected moments the memory of his caress was there and I was feeling very sorry for myself.

I spent the weekend indoors, checking in with Job every few hours. He continued to hold his own. The days passed in a haze of pain, painkillers and lots and lots of bed rest. Too much. I downed a couple of pills on Sunday evening and didn't hear a thing until the phone rang on Monday morning at 8.15. Fearing the worst, I answered straight away. It was Rob.

'You were going to call me.'

Shit.

'I meant to.'

'Well?'

'Something came up, I'm sorry.'

'Can't you tell me what it is?'

'Not at the moment. I'm sorry, Rob. I've just woken up and I have a splitting headache. Can I ring you in about an hour? Where will you be? Home?'

I didn't wait for his answer. I hobbled into the bathroom and showered. The limp was getting better.

I had washed and dried and was drinking some strong black coffee when the doorbell rang. I ignored it. Few people know where I live and those who do would be unlikely callers. It was probably a double-glazing salesman or someone with the wrong address. After a few minutes the bell rang again. Persistently mistaken or mistakenly persistent, whoever it was I continued to ignore them.

A few minutes later I heard my name. Someone was shouting my name in the street. I limped into my bedroom and pulled down the sash window. 'Yes?'

It was Rob. He was standing in the middle of the road.

'What are you doing here?'

'You didn't sound well on the phone. What happened to your car?'

'Job ripped the roof in order to get out.'

'Finally decided he would get a better quality of dog food elsewhere?'

'Something like that.'

'Can I come in?'

'Why?'

'Cup of tea, you know, general hospitality – that sort of thing.'

I buzzed him in. The intercom was jamming for some reason and it didn't work properly. I had to go and open the front door myself. By biting hard on my inside lip I managed to keep from limping. Something told me that Rob wasn't going to be particularly receptive to my night-time adventure.

'So where is Job?' asked Rob.

'He's at the vet's,' I answered nonchalantly.

'Oh?'

'Yes,' I said, heading towards the kettle, buying myself time so that I could think of an innocuous reason. 'He's . . . um . . . having his teeth done today. You know, they have to give him a general anaesthetic before he lets anyone clean his mouth.'

To my relief Rob asked no further questions. When I turned around again he had made himself at home on the sofa. He was looking very respectable in a lightweight grey linen suit with a white shirt and a black and white geometric tie. His responsibilities as producer were obviously affecting his dress sense.

198

'I was worried about you on the telephone.'

'I can't imagine why. You take sugar, don't you?'

'No.'

'Sorry, I forgot.'

I walked carefully across the room balancing the two cups of tea.

'This is the morning of Ted's funeral, isn't it?' Rob carried on. 'I thought I'd come along as an observer. It might be helpful to have someone you can bounce ideas off.'

I looked at him blankly.

'You haven't forgotten, have you? Why do you think I'm dressed like this?'

Shit. Ted's funeral. Of course I'd bloody forgotten all about Ted's funeral – what time was it? I spun round to look at the clock and lost my balance. Scalding tea slopped all over me. As it burned into my trousers I hopped around on my one good leg. I put the weight on my bad ankle to try to regain my balance and yelped in agony. The cups bounced on the hard floor and I fell forward, powerless to help myself.

'Quick, Karen. Get those trousers off.'

I rolled onto my back and fumbled with the zip. Rob reached his arms under mine and lifted me up. I hobbled over to the sofa whimpering in pain. With difficulty, I managed to pull the jeans over my thighs. The skin was bright red. Rob disappeared into the bathroom and reemerged carrying a soaking flannel.

'Put this on it. I'll get some ice.'

I clamped the cold cloth to my thigh. Rob went to the kitchen and opened the fridge. Then he banged the contents of the ice tray out onto a tea towel and with a wooden spoon he crushed the ice to pieces.

'Take those trousers right off. They're soaking.'

I tried. First I had to take off my shoes. Gingerly I undid the shoe on my right foot and pulled it off. Then I tried to pull the trouser leg over the bandage. The pain made me whimper. Half-naked with my sometime lover. I wanted to think up some kind of witticism but just couldn't manage it.

Rob handed me the tea towel filled with crushed ice. 'That should do the trick.'

I placed the ice over my scalded skin and finally I eased the trouser leg over my foot.

'What happened your ankle?' Rob's voice was concerned.

I looked at him defensively. 'I got bitten by a dog.'

'Karen, that's terrible.' He sat on the sofa and put his arm around me. My shoulders tensed at his touch. I hoped he didn't notice. 'Have you been to see someone?'

'Yes, I went to hospital on Thursday night.'

'It must have been some dog. Where did this happen?'

I was dreading this question. 'At Angel Point,' I answered defensively.

'On Thursday night?'

'Yes.'

'In the dark?'

'Yes.'

'On your own?' Rob withdrew the arm from my shoulder. 'What were you doing at Angel Point?'

'I was having a look around.'

'On your own, in the dark?'

I nodded defiantly.

'Karen, where's Job?'

I had to tell him then. I ended up telling him everything. Rob was furious.

'What the hell do you think you were playing at?'

'I wasn't playing. I was doing research.'

'Research? I've had it, Karen. You don't consult me . . .'

'What do you mean, I don't consult you. You're not my doctor or my parent or my teacher.'

'No, I'm your bloody partner. Well, not any more. If you

200

want to work on your own, you bloody well can.' He stormed out of the flat and banged the door.

I sat on the sofa shaking with fury. Well fine, I thought, I bloody well will.

It was a quarter to ten. The funeral procession was supposed to leave from Mabel's house at twelve noon. Time to get a move on. Spurred by my anger, I limped to the bedroom to find something to wear. One thing was sure, high heels were out.

Damn Rob! I was going to tell him. I had intended to invite him along. If he'd been at home when I phoned then he'd have known all about it. He might even have been able to talk me out of it. I thought back to his comforting arm on my shoulder and then shrugged off the memory. Where had he been anyway? He was always bloody well out these days. We were supposed to be doing this project together and yet he was always off enjoying some mystery social life.

I struggled into a pair of black trousers and a white cotton short-sleeved shirt. Over that I wore a purple cotton jacket. Not very suitable for a funeral, but I don't usually kit my wardrobe out with funerals in mind. People don't die very often these days.

As I left the flat I took one last look at the sofa where Job normally lay and sent him silent good wishes. Surely there was something more I could do for him. When people are ill in hospital you can send them flowers to show you care. Somehow I didn't think a bunch of the florist's best would mean much to Job. Suddenly I had a better idea.

Outside, the sunshine was dazzling. I screwed my eyes up against the glare, having difficulty adjusting to the bright light, so at first I didn't see him.

'Sorry I was so angry.' Rob was leaning against the bonnet of my car.

'What are you doing here?'

'I want to come with you.'

'I don't need you.'

'Obviously. You do so well on your own. I still want to come.'

'You're crowding me, Rob.'

'Sorry about that, but we're making a film together, remember?'

I got into the driver's seat without another word. Rob clambered into the passenger seat, uninvited. 'Why have you got that cushion with you?'

I gave him a look. Rob was here on sufferance. I didn't have to explain myself. 'You'll see.'

I drove down the Essex Road and hung a left up Hampton Terrace.

'This isn't the way.'

'There's something I have to do first.' I pulled up outside the vet's, went inside and asked after Job.

The receptionist told me that he was still heavily sedated, but holding his own.

'I brought him a cushion. It's one he sleeps on at home. I thought perhaps it might make him feel more secure, you know.' Frightened of sounding foolish, I was relieved when she smiled and took the cushion from me.

'I'll put it beside him straight away,' she said.

'How's Job?' asked Rob when I got back into the car.

'He's fine – you know, like the weather, fine.'

We drove to Hackney sharing a wary truce and parked on Lothian Road. My ankle was painful but bearable, and with close attention I could control the limp. The sun was already high in the sky and the heat was unrelenting. Parched weeds shrivelled in the cracked pavement.

In the shade of an overhanging warehouse stood a carriage drawn by four jet-black geldings, their coats brushed and gleaming, their hooves oiled and shining. They wore polished harness of leather and shining silver. Large black ostrich feathers crested their heads. The carriage was a nineteenth-century ebony and glass hearse. It was lined with flowers. Ted's name was spelled out in yellow and white carnations. On the central podium lay a bouquet of white lilies. No coffin.

The undertaker stood in the shade by his patient horses. He wore a top hat, a dark grey overcoat over a black suit, a white shirt and a black cravat and a pair of black leather gloves.

'Is this the hearse for Ted O'Hagan?' I asked.

With his top hat, the man seemed impossibly tall. He nodded.

'No coffin?' I asked.

'We pick it up from the morgue on the way through. The body's too far gone. It wouldn't be pleasant in this heat.'

I didn't need to know that. Graphic images of decay danced before my eyes, my imagination probably worse than the reality.

A small crowd of about a dozen people clustered outside Mabel's front door. They were mostly onlookers. Only two or three people were dressed in mourning as far as I could see. On the door hung a large black-ribboned wreath.

Rob and I pushed our way through into the gloomy interior. I found Mabel in the living room. She wasn't alone. Two old women comforted one another on the sofa, cooing softly like wood pigeons. Another woman dressed in a floating grey lace suit sat opposite Mabel on the other armchair, sipping tea from a china cup and saucer.

Mabel was not alone. But she might as well have been. There she perched, a tiny figure in the huge armchair. There was something remote and untouchable about her. I called her name and her eyes came back from wherever they had been. She smiled at me. I introduced Rob briefly and respectfully. She gave him a shrewd and appraising look.

'Are you all right, Mother?' Someone had come into the

room behind us. I turned around and saw PJ.

'I'm fine, son,' she replied, smoothing the hair back from his forehead. 'Karen, have you met my son, Pete?'

'Yes I have, several times.'

PJ and I shook hands, then I introduced Rob. I was relieved to find PJ his usual charming self. Mabel accepted my answer without asking any questions.

'What happened to your foot?' she asked.

A momentary lapse in concentration and I had limped. 'Nothing much. I got bitten by a dog.' I muttered, sending silent good wishes to Job.

PJ stiffened.

'And this is Tilly Pickford,' Mabel informed us. 'My daughter-in-law.'

The shy woman in the floating grey lace shrunk under the gaze directed at her by everyone in the room.

'Ah – yes,' she said and went back to her tea, watching us all nervously over the rim of the cup. I remembered the white face I had seen in the passenger seat staring straight ahead of her as the car drove away. There was an embarrassed silence, which I didn't quite understand, then the two old women sitting on the sofa fluttered off to make some more tea.

Rob and I tucked ourselves into a corner and got to work, setting up the equipment. When we were ready I turned on the camera and told Mabel quietly to take her own time. When she began to speak, her voice was scarcely louder than a whisper.

'I feel that it is final now,' she said, 'that he is really dead. But I also feel relieved in a way. It is right to bury a dead man. Decent. He belongs in the ground. Not in a deep freeze. These past few nights I've been lying awake, worrying in case I die before I've done my duty.'

'Your duty?'

'Seeing to a respectful burial.'

'I saw the undertaker outside. You've chosen a horse-drawn hearse.'

'I like to see things done right.' For several moments she said nothing.

'Are there any other thoughts going through your mind?' I probed.

'Not really,' she smiled. 'Just that sixty years can be a very short time.'

The phone rang, its bell a violent assault on the silence. Mabel answered it.

'Yes?' she said, and listened for a few moments.

Suddenly she bent forwards and let out an anguished cry. 'No-o-o-o-o!'

She began to sob. It was a sound of anger and loss, high-pitched and piteous to hear.

PJ raced back into the room; others swarmed to her aid.

Through the gathering vultures I could just make out Mabel doubled forward on her chair. She was clutching the telephone receiver as though she had forgotten that she still held it in her hand. She moaned and squirmed, trying to fight something away, trying to rip some pain out of her body. I didn't want to go in. Such naked grief was unbearable to witness.

Tilly Pickford stood beside her armchair, her hand placed ineffectually on Mabel's shoulder, a look of panic on her face.

'Karen . . . Karen! . . . Where's Karen?'

She called my name again.

'Karen!'

'I'm here, Mabel.'

I knelt in front of her.

'They won't release his body,' she wailed. 'They say they can't release his body, not today. T-ed!' She lifted her head and yelled his name as if calling to him somewhere far, far away.

I rose to my feet. Two birdlike hands grabbed my own with unexpected strength. 'Stay with me!' she pleaded.

'Mother . . . I think you should lie down. I think you should go upstairs and have a rest. Come with me.' PJ reached forward to lift her out from the chair. She flinched away from him in fury. 'It's not you I want!' she hissed. 'Leave me alone!'

His jaw went slack, all the air went out of him. He stood beside her, his arms dangling uselessly by his side.

'You should try and have a rest,' said Tilly, ineffectually.

'Time enough to rest. What do I want rest for?' Mabel spat at her.

'Mother, what did they say? Why won't they release Ted's body today?'

'They didn't tell me.'

'Surely they must have given you a reason. You can't just cancel a funeral at the last minute without a reason.'

'What do you care? You never liked him anyway. Leave me alone, Pete. I don't need your fake sympathy.' She wrapped her thin, bony arms around her body and, hugging herself tight, she rocked back and forth trying to calm herself down.

After a few minutes she was able to speak again. 'Send the sightseers away,' she said in a much calmer voice. 'All of them. I just want Karen to stay.'

'I think that it would be a good idea if today was just family.' PJ tried again, he was insistent. 'We can ring them, find out what the problem is.'

'What's the point? It's very kind of you. I don't mean to hurt you, son. But I want everyone to leave, including you and your wife. I just want Karen. That is, if she doesn't mind.'

I offered my hands to her again and she held them tight. I nodded my head. I had questions I wanted to ask but now wasn't the time.

The house emptied of people. When Rob came in to speak to me, I was still kneeling at Mabel's feet.

'What do you want me to do, Karen?' he whispered.

'Go on back to the office. I'll phone you this afternoon. You should be able to pick up a taxi on the Richmond Road. Leave the equipment here if you want. I'll pack it up and take it with me later.'

Mabel's hands rested in mine. She sat with her eyes shut, her head bent forward on her chest.

PJ was last to leave. 'I'll phone you later.' He kissed her on the cheek. 'Take care of her!' he said to me. His words were somewhere between pleading and warning. Tilly Pickford floated out in his wake without saying anything.

Finally the house was silent and it was then I noticed the telephone. She was still clutching the receiver. The dialling tone had given way to a continuous high-pitched beep. I replaced the handset and called Mabel's name gently.

She opened her eyes. The expression I saw there was vacant, lost. But it was not that which worried me. The skin around her lips had turned pale blue.

'You have a bad heart, don't you?'

She nodded feebly towards the mantelpiece.

I stood up and reached for the bottle of pills hidden behind the photograph. Following the instructions, I shook two pills out onto the palm of my hand and gave them to her. She swallowed them with the help of some cold tea.

'Shall I get a doctor?'

She shook her head. 'They'll just tell me to keep taking the tablets.' She smiled faintly.

'Would you like a fresh cup of tea?'

'No, thank you.'

'Would you like something to eat?'

'No.'

'How much have you eaten today?'

'Enough.'

'Mabel, you've got to eat.'

'No, I don't love. I don't have to do anything.'

'I felt awkward in the silence which followed. 'What did they say on the phone? Why didn't they release the body?'

'They said that some of the tests they had done in the laboratory had yielded unexpected results, and that they needed to run further tests. The man was no more specific than that.'

'How are you feeling now?'

· 'I'll live.' She leaned back and rested her head in the wing of the chair. Gradually, as I watched, and listened, her breathing steadied and deepened. The colour of her skin returned to normal. Tension eased out of the lines on her face. She was asleep.

I stood up. She didn't stir.

The kitchen sink was filled with unwashed cups; on the table were plates of cakes and sandwiches covered in cling-film. I set to work washing, drying and clearing away, trying not to make too much noise. When I'd finished, I dialled Grace's private line.

'So you know?' she said when she heard my voice.

'I know that you've refused to release the body and that you are planning on running further tests. I don't know why.'

'It's the strangest thing – completely unexpected. Ted O'Hagan had his skull bashed in with a blunt instrument some time before he died. In fact, you might say the two were connected.'

'Murder?'

'We're not sure. But yes, there is a strong possibility.'

'Why did it take such a long time to discover that it may be murder?'

'Can't say for sure. He had really thick hair for a man of his age. That, coupled with the fact that the body was in such an advanced state of decay when he was found. Even so, we should have known before this. There was an error in procedure. The body was X-rayed during post-mortem as usual. The X-ray for the right side of the skull was mislaid, put in the wrong file. It's because of the holiday period, everyone is short-staffed. It was finally traced this morning when the chief lab technician came back from leave.'

'So it was nothing to do with the toxicology tests?'

'Nothing whatsoever. Except we were lucky. If it hadn't have been for that delay, Ted O'Hagan would be in the ground by now and we'd have had to order an exhumation.'

'So what happens now?'

'Now it's a police investigation. Normal rules apply.'

'Which are?'

'You'd need to ask them.'

'Grace, one more thing. That man who died the other day, his name was Micky Holman. See what you can find out about him.'

'What do you want to know?'

'Anything and everything. Dead people's what you do best, remember?'

I went back in to see Mabel. For a moment I considered telling her the news on camera. Then I dismissed the idea, angry with myself on two counts. Firstly, for thinking of it, for thinking of recording her grief and her reaction to the news of her husband's murder with the detached, clinical eye of the scientist. And secondly, for not doing it, for coming to make a documentary and then imposing limits on what I would and wouldn't film.

I pushed open the door to the sitting room. Mabel was awake. She sat bolt upright in the chair, her body wracked with silent sobs. It was as if she had been holding herself together until the funeral. And now that the funeral had been postponed the dam had burst, and all her pent-up grief poured forth unchecked.

She turned her head away as I came into the room.

'They think Ted might have been murdered. That's why they wouldn't release the body,' I said softly.

The sobbing ceased abruptly and she looked at me in disbelief. For a moment I thought she was going to faint. She clutched on tight to the arms of her chair and her body shuddered.

'I knew something was wrong. He would never have left me for ever without saying goodbye.' She smiled to herself, as if in memory of some whispered promise.

As I watched, her expression changed to one of acceptance and then she said something odd. 'I told you Ted didn't drink!' she said.

I couldn't see the relevance. Ted had still had an abnormally high level of alcohol in his blood at the time of his death. I didn't know what to say. Now was hardly the time to go into graphic details about him having his skull bashed in.

Mabel's body began to shake and tremble as if from cold. 'Pete was right, I do need to lie down. Help me up the stairs, Karen. I can't take all of this in. I need to rest.'

We squeezed up the narrow stairs together. She leaned on me, insubstantial as a ghost. The air at the top of the house was warm and heavy and still. Brown cardboard boxes were stacked neatly in each corner.

I looked at them in surprise. 'What's all this?'

'Have you forgotten?' Mabel said. 'I am due to be rehoused next week. I was getting myself organised.'

'This is all too much for you, Mabel. You could ask them to postpone your move.'

'No. I want to go. This place is no longer a home for me.'

'Have you had someone to help you?'

'No need.'

The bedroom was sparse and bare. Everything had been cleared off the dressing table and Ted's side of the wardrobe was empty. The room felt abandoned.

210

'Will you be all right?' I asked.

She nodded, then sighed. 'Now you leave me, Karen. I really do want to be on my own. I am so tired.' She leaned back on the bed and closed her eyes.

'Shall I come and check on you later?'

'Please,' she whispered with a faint smile. 'Later.' She was almost asleep.

'Whatever you say, you're the star.' I went over and kissed her on the forehead. Her skin was dry and papery. She didn't open her eyes.

'Sweet dreams,' I whispered, and gave her folded hands a comforting squeeze. They felt cold to the touch.

I left, glad to get away. If Ted had been murdered, then why? The question buzzed around inside my head like an angry fly.

Our documentary would be dynamite. Angel Point, the slow-burning fuse of the background to our investigation, Ted O'Hagan, the man he was, the woman who married him and the void left by the explosive violence of his end. Perhaps we could even sell it to a terrestrial channel . . .

It was as I dug around in my purse for my car key that I noticed the forgotten receipt for photographs I had found secreted inside the lining of Ted's case. A receipt for photographs . . . Ted had been a photographer; he spoke out of time through his pictures. It had to be relevant!

It never occurred to me to take what I had to the police. In my excitement, all I could think of was my investigation, the thrill of the chase and some naive idea I had about avenging Ted's death by exposing his murderer on film.

Chapter Twelve

The chemist on the Broadway was a smiling Asian man with a round face and a bald head. I handed the slip of paper to him.

'I am surprised that Ted did not pick these up himself before now.'

'You knew him?'

'Knew him?' His face fell.

'I'm sorry. Mr O'Hagan is dead. He died two weeks ago. Is there any charge for the photographs?'

'No,' he said, blankly. 'There's no charge.'

Outside, the sun was blinding. I tore open the envelope, impatient to see its contents. What I found, however, took the edge off my excitement. Inside was a series of photographs of what looked to be a building site. In fact, they looked to be photographs of Angel Point. But they were nothing special. They weren't even particularly good photographs. The light was dim and the composition was uninteresting. I could see nothing remarkable, only pictures of cars and machinery and piles of bricks. They were the work of an old man idling away the time.

The sun had dipped lower in the sky. I drove straight to Hampton Terrace. It was half past four, the vet's would still be open. I didn't want to call them on the telephone – I wanted to see Job face to face.

The receptionist buzzed through to the surgery when she saw me appear and asked me to take a seat.

'How is he?'

We were interrupted by a telephone call. She answered it quickly. Too quickly?

'The vet will be with you right away,' she said brightly before becoming involved in another conversation.

I waited. The minutes ticked slowly by. By the time the vet appeared I had convinced myself that Job was dead.

'He's dead, isn't he?' I said, rising slowly to my feet.

'No.' The Australian's response was cautious. 'He's not dead, but as I told you before, his injuries are severe. He has been sleeping all day. Animals do that. They have the sense to try and recover their strength.'

'Can I see him?'

'Of course.' He led me to a room at the back of the surgery where Job lay in a cage, his head resting on our cushion. It broke my heart to see him in a cage.

'I want to take him home,' I said.

'I wouldn't advise that. Some of his wounds are deep. Moving him might cause them to open up again. He can't afford to lose any more blood.'

'How long will he have to stay here?'

'Tomorrow we should have a better idea of how he's doing. In three days we'll be sure. In four days you may even be able to take him home.'

I nodded.

'Do you want some time alone with him?'

'Please.'

The little room was silent after he had left. Then, as my ears adjusted I was aware of the sound of Job's breathing. He breathed fast and shallow. I knelt on the floor by his cage. The door wasn't locked. I opened it and reached my hand out carefully to him. It was difficult to know where to touch him. The most serious injuries had been sustained to his head. I stroked his paw very gently and called his name. He didn't open his eyes, but his ears twitched and I knew that he could hear me. I sat with him for some time. Resting my head beside his. Breathing in and out with him, in time

214

with him, whispering his name over and over.

There was a gentle tap at the door and the vet stuck his head round the corner. 'We're shutting the surgery now.'

'He's going to be left alone?' I was horrified.

'No. I'm on night duty all this week, but I think it would be better if you left. After last night I want to try and catch up on my sleep while I can. Call me in the morning.'

It would have been unfair to insist on staying. I left reluctantly. The smell of a Thai takeaway coming from a white plastic carrier bag on the counter reminded me that I hadn't eaten all day. I began to head for home and then realised that I couldn't face the overwhelming silence of the empty flat.

I bought a bag of fish and chips from the Upper Street fish bar and drove to Highbury Fields to eat them. I sat with the roof down watching children playing and city workers released from their day cooped up in the office, gambolling in the grass with their equally relieved dogs. Hot, scalding, steaming cod burned my mouth. I devoured my food greedily as I watched them play. Soon I realised that the portion of food was too much for one. I couldn't remember the last time I had eaten alone.

I bundled up the battered skin of cod and the leftover chips and chucked them in a litter bin. I was tempted to save them for Job, as a silent mark of good faith in his recovery. Then I recognised my attempt to do a deal with Fate and decided that it might backfire on me.

I decided to drive over and check on Mabel. This time, I was going as a friend. Remembering what she said, I left my camera behind.

She was up and about when I knocked at her front door. I had been scared to waken her, but she answered immediately, as if she had been standing there waiting for me.

'Come on in, I'm upstairs.' She led the way with such

energy that I had difficulty keeping up with her. 'I'm sorting out some more things in the bedroom.'

'Don't you think you should be taking it easy?'

'Time enough for all that. There are things to be done.'

'You've had a terrible shock.'

'This keeps my mind from dwelling on it.'

I followed her into the bedroom. The bed was covered in piles of papers, costume jewellery, underwear and thick brown stockings. Such a frenzy of activity had me worried.

'Mabel, sit down. You'll make yourself ill. I don't want you dying on me next.'

She sat suddenly in a chair by the side of the bed, her hands clasped, her feet tucked underneath her, her face the face of a haunted child.

'What's wrong?'

'I just can't stand the thought of him lying there in a fridge somewhere. Ted would have hated it. He should be in the ground. I feel as if I'm betraying him by letting it happen.'

'There's nothing you can do.'

'I know that. It makes it worse. Now that he's been murdered, they could keep him in there for months.'

'It probably won't come to that.'

'Who says? I wanted to see things done right.'

'And you will.'

'Will I?'

'Yes.'

I began to tidy things away unbidden. She didn't stop me, just watched what I was doing. I sorted them into neat piles on top of the dressing table. When the bed was clear I helped her to lie down.

'Just rest, I'll come and see you again tomorrow.'

'Can you do something for me?'

'Of course.'

'I've written a letter. After I'd written it, I realised that I didn't have a stamp.' She withdrew an envelope from the pocket of her cardigan. I glanced at the handwriting. It was addressed to Pete Pickford. 'I shouldn't have spoken to him like that', she went on. 'I didn't mean to say those things.'

'He won't take them seriously.'

'Ah, but he will. All his life he has been over-sensitive. He thinks that I didn't really want to bring him up, that I only did it because I couldn't say no. But that's not true. I couldn't have another baby and he was a godsend.'

'I'm sure he knows that.'

'And then when he is trying to help me, I say those things to him. He is a proud man, my Pete. I should never have spoken to him like that in front of other people. Please post it for me. Make sure it goes this evening.'

I promised. Mabel smiled at me faintly. For a moment there was something really special in the room, a heightened awareness I can only describe as being like falling in love.

'My daughter would be in her fifties if she had lived – old enough to be your mother. And yet when I look at you, sometimes I imagine . . .' She broke off and shook her head. 'Old woman's fancies, you mustn't mind me.'

I held Mabel's hand until she went to sleep. It rested featherlight in mine. When I was sure her breathing was deep and regular I gently disengaged myself and went downstairs. Mabel had been so anxious, and PJ had been so helpful to me that I decided to drop the letter off at his house this evening; it was the least I could do. But perhaps it would be polite to phone first. I hunted around for an address book and found it in Mabel's handbag. I dialled the number. It was engaged. I pressed five and waited for the automatic call back.

Ten minutes went by.

I dialled it again. It was still engaged. I could always just post the letter and go home. But to catch the post I'd have to leave now and I didn't want to leave her. She seemed so weak, so frail.

I tiptoed back upstairs and sat on the floor outside her bedroom door to keep vigil, I could hear her regular shallow breathing. I found myself listening like a mother might listen to a newborn, following each breath. In. Pause. And out.

Once I thought she'd stopped breathing; the pause was too long. I began to panic and crossed into the room rapidly to shake her awake. Before I reached her, she breathed again, a deep, stuttering inhalation.

Half an hour passed and the phone still hadn't rung. I went back downstairs and dialled the number again. Engaged. According to the envelope, PJ lived in Waltham Abbey, out by Epping Forest. Not that far. And it wasn't as if my evening was packed full of alternative plans. I decided to go regardless. Mabel had been so very anxious. Besides, I was curious. I wanted to see what living with a rich wife could buy.

One other thing, the camera was still in the boot of my car. Now that there was a possibility Ted had been murdered, perhaps PJ would agree to be interviewed.

I drove through the high-density housing of London's East End and out towards the A10. A new road had carved its way through large swathes of local housing, swallowing homes and protesters alike, and tearing apart long-established communities. Whatever your politics, you have to admit the traffic now is much lighter than it used to be.

Epping Forest began at the city limits. Stretches of green trees and parkland gave way periodically to solidly built red brick Edwardian houses with turrets and gables. I found the street and the house without any difficulty. PJ Pickford had done all right for himself. Twenty-five minutes from his office in Hackney Town Hall and he lived in a different world. I turned into the gravel drive, feeling shabbier than was justified.

As I got out of the car my ankle almost gave way beneath me. I was tired. It had been a long day. I paused a moment to catch my breath before opening the boot to lift out the camera.

The door was answered by Tilly Pickford herself. Funny, I hadn't expected to see her and the sight of her irritated me in some way. The door opened just a crack and the face that peered out at me was taut and pale. Her appearance came as a bit of a shock. I hadn't really noticed her at Mabel's, I hadn't looked at her properly. I had just been aware of her hovering somewhere behind PJ.

Heat had settled on the city for so many weeks, that I had grown used to sunburned faces wherever I looked. But Tilly Pickford's face was white. Then, as I looked, I realised that what I had mistaken for natural pallor was actually a mask of make-up.

'Yes?'

'It's Karen McDade. I'm a friend of Mabel's.'

Recognition dawned, but not in any welcoming way. Her body blocked the doorway to the house. 'He's not here.'

That was a blow. I hadn't expected any social engagements on the night of his adoptive father's funeral.

'Can I come in?'

She looked as if she would like to say no, but the effort was too much for her. Despite the oppressive heat she was still dressed in her funeral outfit of grey woollen dress and tights, with grey leather T-bar shoes, each fastened with a tiny golden buckle. A crocheted cardigan was draped across her shoulders like fine cobweb, and her dark hair was swept back into a French knot giving her face a look of vapid innocence that I found irritating in a woman of her age.

She looked me up and down and her expression said I didn't quite come up to scratch. Then she turned on her heel and led me down the hall. She tiptoed her way through her own house, noiselessly, carefully, as if she were trespassing.

The house smelt of furniture polish – a heavy, saturated overbearing scent. It was extremely expensively furnished with lots of shining pieces of brown furniture. It looked like an immaculate example of interior design which was just waiting for the photographers to come and immortalise it for the pages of some glossy magazine. And yet it also looked as if no one lived there. Everything was too perfect.

Our eyes met by surprise in the reflection of a gilt-framed mirror as we walked along the corridor and we both looked away quickly as if stung. I had surprised an expression of fear in those eyes. Why on earth would Tilly Pickford find my visit frightening? I must have been mistaken.

She ushered me into a large sitting room with high ceilings. The walls were hung with English watercolours of pastoral scenes. The furniture was Victorian, the carpets Persian, there was even a crystal chandelier. Through the open French windows I could see a lush green garden and hear a garden sprinkler, or was it a fountain?

Tilly Pickford positioned herself on a red velvet settee protected by white lace antimacassars. She gestured me gracefully towards a matching armchair, looking for all the world as though she too were ready to pose for the photographers. There was something unreal about her. She sat in front of me, hands clasped on her lap, feet tucked daintily underneath her. She wore her assumed gentility like the latest fashion and the whole picture gave the impression of artificiality and insincerity.

Then I noticed a large plaster on the back of her hand. It looked fresh and new; I was certain it hadn't been there that morning.

'What happened to your hand?'

'I burned it on the kettle.' She didn't look down, just turned the hand over to hide the bandage from view. She sat there passively and neither asked me my business nor volunteered any information about when PJ was likely to return.

'Stuck-up old cow!' Maggie's words rang in my ears and for once I agreed with her. I was aware of the silence. Here among the plush furniture and fittings, the cushioning of wealth, there was no sound except the delicate tinkling of the garden sprinkler.

'Is PJ due back soon?'

'I'm afraid it's always difficult to say.'

'I did try ringing. The phone was engaged for a very long time.'

'I take it off the hook when I don't want to be disturbed.'

Tinkle, tinkle, tinkle.

'Mabel was very upset this morning.'

'Yes.'

'She was ashamed of what she said. She asked me to bring this letter for PJ.'

'Did she?' I nodded, while at the same time remembering that Mabel had asked me to do no such thing. 'How kind of you.'

Tinkle, tinkle.

'This is a nice house. How long have you lived here?'

'About three years.'

Tinkle.

The more unresponsive she was, the more unnerved I became. I started to babble on. 'It must be nice to inherit so much money. My family has never had any money . . . never any to speak of . . . really.'

'What do you mean?'

'I was told you inherited the money.'

'Were you?' She looked at me with those infuriating eyes which looked permanently startled. 'I'm afraid you were misinformed. PJ had some business deals that worked out rather well. The house is mostly his. May I see the letter?' She held out her hand. I surrendered it reluctantly. She tore open the envelope, extracted a folded sheet of paper and with an air of disdain, read through the contents. 'Touching.'

I didn't like anything about this woman. I didn't like the way she spoke, I didn't like the way she dressed, I didn't like the way she sat, I didn't like the way she held Mabel's piece of paper. She soiled what, I was sure, had been a heartfelt letter.

The heavy smell of polish was overpowering in this room. It made me feel light-headed.

'Roses,' she volunteered unexpectedly. 'The smell is roses. PJ loves roses.'

I walked over to the open French windows and looked out. She was right. The smell I had taken to be furniture polish was in fact the scent of a huge rose garden. Roses of every colour and size bloomed in glorious profusion. There were rose borders, rose beds and climbing varieties of wild roses which twisted high up into the branches of surrounding trees. The sight was breathtaking. At the end of the garden I caught sight of a man sharpening up the edges of one of the borders. A rich wife and hired help – can't be bad.

'Lovely garden,' I said.

'You like it?' She cocked her head quizzically to one side and looked at it dispassionately. I floundered, not sure if I had said the right thing.

'And you have only lived here for three years?' I looked out at the rose garden in surprise. It was a garden that had been there for years. She followed my gaze.

'PJ wanted to buy the house because of the garden,' she explained.

'My Aunt Maggie likes roses.'

'Maggie?'

'Maggie Wilkins.'

'Maggie Wilkins is your aunt?'

'You know her? Of course you do. I forgot – Charlie says

PJ knows everybody and everybody knows him.' Babble, babble, babble. I was babbling.

'Charlie?'

'Charlie Hammond. My Cousin Sylvia's boyfriend . . . well, fiancé. They are getting married the day after tomorrow. I'm doing the video. The whole thing's a bit of a rush job. I think Sylvia wants to do it before she starts to show.'

'Show what?'

'Show. She's pregnant.'

'Sylvia Wilkins is pregnant?'

'Yes.'

'And that will make Maggie a grandmother.' She began to laugh and laugh. Her laughter was eerie, jarring. I didn't know what she meant by it. I just wanted her to stop.

'And who's the father?' The tone of her voice changed abruptly, slicing through any lingering echoes of her off-key mirth.

'Charlie, of course. That's what I said. They are getting married on Wednesday.'

'Of course.'

We watched the man in the garden doing his edges.

'Would you like some tea?' She disappeared abruptly from the room. Moments later she came back. 'Actually, I'm afraid we don't have any milk.'

'Don't worry.'

'So I was wondering if you wouldn't mind leaving?'

I was startled.

'I'm getting one of my headaches, you see. They do tend to come on rather suddenly. It must be the humidity. I wouldn't be surprised if there weren't a thunderstorm before long. Never mind, I suppose the rain will be good for the garden.' As she was speaking she was leading me back along the corridor to the front door, the protective hand which massaged her temple masking her face. She talked and talked me to the door and all the time her voice never rose above a well-bred, well-modulated whisper.

Before I knew it, I was back out on the drive, and the front door had been shut in my face. I stood there feeling confused. Never before had I been got rid of quite so efficiently. She couldn't have done it better if she had got someone to lift me up and eject me bodily.

I looked at the ivy-clad façade of the red brick house, the epitome of middle-class respectability. It stared back at me, blankly. All I could hear was the twitter of early evening birdsong and the distant sound of a motorised lawnmower. The sweet scent of freshly cut grass filled the air. It was all so different from the rough and ready housing estates of the inner city.

There was nothing for it but to get back into my car and drive to London. I felt humiliated by the way I'd been treated. I tried to rationalise her behaviour and couldn't. As I drove, I replayed our conversation, but could find nothing I'd said which would have given offence.

Then I remembered what Mabel had said about her not being able to have any children. I bet that was the reason. We were doing fine until I'd mentioned that Sylvia was pregnant.

Mind you, it wasn't something I liked to think about very much either.

Chapter Thirteen

Charlie was sitting on my doorstep when I got home. His face was hidden in deep shadow. All day I had been willing and willing and willing him to call. So when I saw him there it was a shock. I thought my imagination was playing a trick on me. Then, for a second, I thought that it was Rob, I began to feel cagey and defensive, a thousand excuses and explanations sprang to my lips. When I accepted it was Charlie, my heart turned a somersault. He looked even better than I remembered.

He grinned when he saw me. I sat down beside him on the front doorstep and rested my head on his shoulder. He slid his hand into mine. Overhead the swallows swooped for flies and a faint star twinkled in the evening sky.

'Aren't you going to invite me in?'

'I'm thinking about it.' I stood up and a bubble of joy rose in my throat. With one hand I fumbled for my keys to open the door, with the other I grabbed his arm and slid it around my waist.

'I've been thinking about you all day,' he murmured. His lips tickled and teased at my ear. 'I had to come.'

We stumbled down the stairs towards my flat together, almost tripping over one another on the steps. I was so happy to see him that a stupid smile seemed to be permanently plastered to my face. Then the high-pitched noise of my alarm reminded me of my empty flat and Job spending his fifth night alone in the vet's recovery room. At once my smile vanished.

Charlie looked at me then looked around the flat. He whistled a low whistle and patted his thigh. There was no response. 'Where is he?' he asked, beginning to look alarmed.

I told him what had happened.

'And what about you, are you all right?'

'Almost.'

'Karen, what were you doing there after dark?'

'I just wanted to have a look around.'

'But you must know that all buildings have security measures in place.'

'Not those kind of measures. I was imagining a night-watchman or something like that. Not a pack of wild dogs. I only wanted to look.'

'You madwoman. On building sites things walk. On building sites things get nicked.'

'I know that.'

'And Angel Point is being prepared for Blowdown. There are tons of explosives on-site. Those dogs were there to protect all that equipment. It's a highly sensitive area.'

'I wasn't thinking.'

'Why did you go?'

'I was doing it to take my mind off things.'

'What things?' He knew. He just wanted to hear me say it.

'I was doing it to take my mind off you.'

For a while, Charlie said nothing. Daylight was fading. Standing barely a few feet from him, I could hardly make out his face. I began to get worried, in case I had been too direct. I worried that he might turn on his heel and get out fast. But he didn't. When he spoke again his voice was ragged, urgent.

'I had to come and see you again. I know I shouldn't be here but I couldn't let it rest. I keep seeing your face.' He moved hesitantly towards me. Looking up into his eyes I could see a hollow expression of hurt and indecision.

I reached up to him and put my hands round his neck feeling his strength, stroking the crinkly hairs on his neck with my fingertips before sliding my hands through his rich

226

luxuriant hair. I pulled his head down towards me until his forehead rested on mine. Our noses touched and we each looked deep and unflinchingly into the other's eyes, nervously at first, then our smiles returned as we each found expressions of comfort and welcome. I turned my head gently to one side as my lips sought his.

Okay, so we both knew it was wrong. It was wrong and it was good. How often do those two go together?

Gently we kissed and held and caressed one another. My hips arched to meet him and when he entered me it was as true and natural as a summer's sunrise.

Afterwards, my head rested on his shoulder and we lay in each other's arms. The light faded slowly, until we lay together in darkness, lit only by the orange glow of the lamp on the street.

Gradually the timbre of the silence changed. Instead of being satiated, content and at ease, it became wary and anxious. Charlie was here when he should be elsewhere, and the day after tomorrow he was getting married.

Eventually I sat up, switched on the beside light and turned to face him. Although I didn't say a word, he could read the unspoken challenge in my eyes.

'I wouldn't make you happy,' he said. He said the words softly, sadly.

'How do you know?'

'Believe me, I know.' He reached up and brushed the hair out of my eyes. The gesture was intimate but curiously asexual. He didn't touch me like a lover, he touched me like a father.

I didn't want to feel like a child. But I do. Sometimes.

I leaped out of bed and wrapped a robe around my naked, sex-smelling body and made us a cup of tea. Wearing something made me feel less vulnerable and more in control.

'Here, you're in the trade.' Changing the subject, I tossed Ted's photographs onto the bed, 'What do you make of those?'

'What are they? Where did you get them?'

'Ted O'Hagan took them – the old man who was murdered, the subject of our documentary. PJ Pickford's stepfather.'

'PJ's old man? *Murdered*?'

'Looks that way. Someone bashed him over the back of his head with a blunt object when he was stociously drunk.'

'Where did this happen?'

'At Angel Point.'

He flicked through the pictures.

'What can you see?'

'Nothing much.'

'That's what I thought. I don't understand it. Ted was quite a keen amateur photographer – he knew what he was doing. Any reason why he should take photographs like these?'

'Not that I can see. Perhaps he was just running off the film.'

'Perhaps. But if that was the case, why go to the expense of developing them? These are the only pictures on the film.'

Charlie flicked through them again. Something caught his eye. He paused to look at one picture more carefully, then went back and looked at the other pictures again.

'Have you seen something?'

'N-no. Karen, do you mind if I borrow them for a while?'

'Are you holding out on me?'

'No. Can I?'

'Not until you tell me why.'

'I don't want to do that. It may mean nothing.'

'I don't want to let the whole roll go. You can borrow one, if you need to.'

'One is all I need.'

I was just about to climb back into bed when Charlie jumped up. 'Can I have a shower?'

'You're not leaving?'

228

'I have to.' He came over and stood behind me and wrapping his strong arms around my body, he held me close. I wanted to hold onto him and say no you don't, but I kept my mouth shut. I didn't want to come across as the clingy type; he had one of those already.

'Where were you this evening?' he called from the shower. 'Were you filming?'

'Not exactly. I went to PJ's.'

'PJ's house?'

'Yeah.'

'Why?'

I told him about Mabel, how close we'd become and how worried she'd been about hurting PJ's feelings. 'Besides, I wanted to see how the other half lives.'

'You mean, what having a rich wife could buy?'

'A little bit and then some, believe me. You should see the place.'

'Us poor working men, eh?'

'What about me, Charlie? Is that what it would take – would you stay with me if I were rich?' The remark came out flippantly, but as soon as the words were out of my mouth I wished I could call them back.

He said nothing. I was hoping that he had decided to ignore that comment. He was right to. I back-pedalled furiously.

'Strike that, I didn't mean to say that. It was supposed to be a joke.'

There was still no response. I started to babble on about green trees in Epping, Tilly Pickford, anything to cover up my spiteful little attempt at humour.

'Anyway, Mrs PJ denies all that. She says the money is his and that he's made it through various business dealings. Mind you, Maggie is right, she is a bitter old cow. When I told her about you and Sylvia and the baby she asked if that made Maggie a grandmother and then she laughed and laughed.

The way she laughed was eerie. I couldn't work out what she meant by it.'

Charlie came back into the room, towel-drying his hair. His face was like thunder. He hardly noticed I was there.

'Charlie, I'm sorry – it was a bad joke. I shouldn't have said what I said.'

He didn't appear to hear me.

'Charlie!'

He was miles away. I stood and waited for him to come back. Eventually he saw me and forced a smile. 'I have to go.'

'You've said that already.'

I watched him get dressed. He put on his jeans and then sat down on my bed to put on his shoes, turning his back towards me. I felt helpless and slightly desperate. It was only a joke. Why had the atmosphere between us changed so completely?

He reached over to the bedside table and pocketed the photograph I had shown him. Feeling my eyes on him he turned around. 'You say he was murdered?'

'They think so. He had a kind of part-time temporary job as a night-watchman on Angel Point. They think someone bashed him over the back of his head with a blunt object when he was very drunk. What are you thinking?'

'Nothing concrete. Leave it with me for a couple of days, I'll ask around.'

I showed him to the door. Will I see you again? The words reverberated in my head. I didn't say them out loud. 'See you around then.'

'See you.' He turned to go, then spun back to face me again. He bent his head to kiss me, soft lips suckled mine. I broke contact before the tears came. A girl's got to have some dignity.

After he left I paced the flat, exhausted, lonely but unable to sleep. I was filled with a terrible sense of loss. The day after tomorrow Charlie was getting married. If he went ahead with it I must never see him again. Having an affair with a married man turns a relationship between two people into a triangle. And with a threesome, someone is going to get hurt. Invariably that person would be me.

Strike the conditional. Inevitably that person was going to be me. God, why was I thinking like this? I was in far deeper than I ever intended.

I couldn't just sit here. I dialled the vet's in Hampton Terrace. The Australian answered the phone.

'Hi, it's me, Job's . . . owner.' What do you say? I don't own Job. 'I can't sleep, I was wondering if I could come and see him.'

'It's very late.'

'But you're awake.'

'I'm on duty.'

'Need anything to help you make it through the night? Shit, that sounds like I'm flirting, I'm not flirting. I just meant a bar of milk chocolate or something.'

'Well, since I'm gay I think I find the offer of chocolate more tempting. Make it dark chocolate and I'll meet you in reception in ten minutes.'

I drove to the all-night garage and then to Hampton Terrace. After letting me in and fleecing me of my booty the vet showed me into the recuperation suite and very tactfully left me to it.

Job was doing fine, no better than that. He tried to lift his head to greet me, but I could see the pain in his eyes, and leaned into him instead. His muzzle was dry and his breathing was irregular; his normally healthy coat had lost its shine.

I sat with him for half an hour and willed him to get better. Then I stood up. It was time to go. Staying here was helping nobody. I said goodbye to the vet on the way out.

'Better?'

'Yes. Thanks.'

'No, thank *you*.' He held up the remains of the chocolate bar wrapper and we both smiled.

I drove sadly home. It was late and I was lonely. I parked right outside my front door and was taking the keys out of the ignition when a blow to the back of my head careered me forwards, slamming my forehead onto the steering wheel. An explosion of colour ignited behind my eyes.

Close to my ear came a harsh whisper. 'Stay away from Angel Point, bitch.'

By the time I was sufficiently recovered to do anything, I was alone. I turned around. There was no one there. The streets were empty.

Chapter Fourteen

I awoke the following morning with a mild headache and feeling slightly sick. For a moment I thought I was coming down with something and then I remembered the hazy events of the night before.

After being struck, I vaguely remembered coming indoors and lying down. That was it. Nothing else. I must have passed out. With difficulty I sat up, waited for the world to stop spinning and then staggered still fully dressed into the kitchen to get a drink.

In the bright light of day, it seemed like a dream. The only proof that it had happened was a feeling of excruciating tenderness at the base of my skull.

Perhaps I should phone the police. And say what? That I had been trespassing at Angel Point and that some nice man had come along and asked me to stop? It was bound to come out. They would ask me about my attacker and why he would have told me to stay away. I was still feeling very dazed and I didn't know why he would have told me to stay away. I decided not to phone the police until I had done some thinking.

With hindsight I'm sure that I was mildly concussed. At the time it seemed to me that the most sensible thing to do was to have a shower and get into work. I needed to be doing something. I felt twitchy and unsettled. I could put together a rough assembly of the footage I had shot so far.

I got myself ready on automatic pilot and phoned Rob to arrange to meet him at lunchtime.

Soho Square was as close as Central London ever gets to being deserted. For once there was no difficulty in finding somewhere to park. Tourists wandered around enjoying the sunshine and snapping the sites. Groups of chattering foreign students lolled on the grass in the centre of the square.

I sat in my car thinking things through, trying to decide whether it would be best to wait and see if I heard from Charlie, or whether I should phone him and tell him what happened to me after he left. I decided to leave it. If he had a lead on the photograph which would prove helpful, I was sure he would get back to me.

I dug out the envelope of photographs again. Thankfully, my head was beginning to clear, but the photographs still meant nothing to me. A series of pictures of a building site with several vehicles parked in the distance.

I held the negatives up to the light and tried to see if there was anything special in the picture that Charlie had borrowed. It was impossible to tell. They would need to be blown up quite considerably and if I tried to do that, all clarity would go.

Suddenly, I had an idea. Pony Labs on Dean Street. They were a specialist processing lab who were experts at digital enhancement. I had a contact there, a female rollerblader called Lexi Dee who spent her working day on her skates and was the fastest operator around. She'd done some work for me before. She was the only person I've ever met who can run up the stairs with her wheels on.

The only problem was the time of year; she was probably burning the sidewalk down in Monte Carlo or wherever it is that cool bladers hang out. But my luck was in.

I leaned over the counter and called her name. 'Lexi Dee.'

She skated the breadth of the building, braids swinging, spun twice and came to a perfect stop in front of me.

'Karen, girl. How are they hanging?'

It wasn't hard to communicate with Lexi once you took the lead from her.

'They're bouncing on the airwaves.'

'A pair like that should be speaking to the nation.' She looked down at her own flat chest ruefully. I looked down at her long, long legs and felt not a twinge of sympathy.

'You look well fucked.'

'Well, thanks,' I said, bristling. I didn't think I looked that bad.

'Don't mention it,' she said. 'So who is he?'

'Oh!' I said, blushing now I realised what she meant. 'I can't say.'

'Like that, is it? Well, make sure you return him to his rightful owner when you're finished with him. What can I do for you?'

I explained what I wanted. She looked at the pictures then held the negatives up to the light, all flippancy gone.

'What do you think?'

'Pity the light's so poor.'

'Exactly. It's strange, the man was a photographer. I'm surprised he under-exposed the film as much as he did.'

'Maybe he was using one of those little throwaway cameras. He might not have had any choice.'

'They come equipped with a flash though, don't they?'

'He might not have wanted to draw attention to himself.' Lexi Dee rolled her eyes. The eyeballs made two perfect circles – a party trick you needed to practise to get right. I didn't laugh. She only imagined intrigue but what she said had to be true. Charlie had seen something in the pictures which made sense to him. What could it be?

'When can you do something with them?' I asked with renewed urgency.

'When do you need them?'

'Now?'

'No, it'll take me a while. I'll have to print them up large before I try to enhance the image and I may need to run them through twice. Where can I reach you?'

I gave her my numbers, work, home, car mobile and Rob's mobile. How lucky I am to be so digitally blessed. 'Let me know as soon as they are ready.'

'I should have something for you by tomorrow afternoon. If I don't, I'll call you.'

'I'll pick them up towards the end of the day, about five o'clock?'

'Perfect. And listen, about the other – if you want a second opinion I'll be prepared to give him a road test before you send him back.' And she winked at me.

When I pushed through the doors of the Finest Cut into the magnificent chill of the air-conditioning, it felt so civilised. The doors of my edit suite whooshed comfortingly closed behind me. It was so good to be back. All the banks of sophisticated equipment lining each wall lay silent waiting for my touch. I went to the console in the middle of the room and activated several of the switches. At once the machines hummed into life and a pool of light lit the central island where I was standing.

I worked for a couple of hours playing around with putting scenes in different orders and re-recording Mabel's voice so that I could use it over different scenes that I had filmed. And suddenly there was Charlie, filmed at Maggie's house, when I went around to discuss the wedding.

I froze his picture on the screen, then magnified it so that his eyes filled the screen. Watching him now, I felt that I could look at him in a way I could not when he was in the room with me. I could drink in every feature and enjoy the sensation of going hot all over.

The door opened and I was startled by Rob's sudden appearance. Quickly I hit a button and Charlie's image returned to its normal size and the picture began to fast forward. Jerky figures flitted about the screen, moving at four times the normal speed. I stood up hurriedly to greet him as the film ran out and the screen was filled with white rain.

'Are you all right?' Rob was looking at me strangely.

'Yeah.' I felt like a guilty teenager. 'Coffee?' I offered.

'Please.'

Filling up the machine with coffee and turning it on bought me enough time to regain my composure.

'Are you sure you're all right?'

'Of course.'

'You look very pale.'

'Pale is in this year.' I wanted to tell Rob what had happened and get him to feel the soft bruising at the base of my skull, but after the way he had responded to the incident with Job I didn't want to risk further condemnation. I was sure he would think it was all my fault. Besides, I didn't think I could bear it if he touched me. I wanted to be touched, I wanted to be hugged and held, friend to friend. But that would open up a whole can of worms that I wasn't ready to deal with yet.

'Have you eaten?' Rob asked.

I shook my head.

'I thought not.'

'I'll grab something later.'

'No need. Look what I've brought.'

We picnicked on ciabatta and olives, sundried tomatoes and crumbly goat's cheese washed down with strong black coffee as we concentrated on the rough assembly I had been working on all morning.

The film had begun to take on a life of its own. Mabel's voice had become the dominant one, with the other stories echoing faintly in her shadow. But that was fine. The viewer would be entranced by this candid old woman. There was a sense of the past running through the present and stretching out into the future, into all our futures. That point was well made without being overdone. Especially in the sequence I'd shot that night at dusk of the young lovers on Hackney Marshes.

'So where do we go from here?' I asked.

'Blowdown, that's what we agreed.'

'But Ted was murdered – doesn't that change things?'

'I don't see how,' he objected.

'*I* do – it changes everything! We need to stick with that and follow through with the possible murder investigation, maybe as seen through Mabel's eyes – the effect that the investigation will have on her.'

'Come on, Karen, that's too open-ended; it could take for ever. Have you any idea how many unsolved murders there are in London each year?'

'N-not exactly. Look, we've alighted upon something which takes this documentary out of the ordinary. The fact of Ted's murder will be a selling point, and I don't think you can just ignore it.'

What could I say? As so often with Rob, I ended up absolutely frustrated with him. I wanted to tell him about all my other suspicions, about Tilly, about the photographs, about the harsh whisper in my ear warning me to stay away. Images whirled in my head, but as I sought to put them into words they felt nebulous and intangible, even to me. The base of my skull began to pulse with pain.

'I think we'll have to agree to differ over our approach to this.'

'Up to a point, Karen. We're in this together, remember? We gave ourselves a specific time-frame to shoot this film and that time runs out this weekend. After that I want to get on with editing and selling the finished piece. My money finances fifty per cent of this project and I want to complete our commission and get paid. I don't mind if you want to explore the circumstances around Ted's death for the rest of the week. But I think you need to work on a final interview with Mabel which we can fall back on if you don't come up with your alternative.'

I did go to see Mabel that afternoon, but not because Rob had told me to. Reaching for the tea in the cabinet above her kitchen sink I realised how intimate I had become with this woman who in the natural order of things was separated from me by several generations.

Mabel sat at the table in the middle of the room, uncomplaining and unheeding. I was worried about her. She seemed so withdrawn, insubstantial, as if she were fading away in front of me. I set the tray the way I had seen her do it, wanting to please her.

'I should be doing that.'

'There's no rule to say so. Just you sit there.'

'I don't seem to have any energy.'

'I expect it's the shock.'

'That's very kind of you. I just think it's life catching up with me.'

'Sugar?'

She pursed her lips as if to say she didn't really care one way or the other

'I went to see PJ yesterday at his home,' I said, hoping to jog her out of her apathy.

'Did you?' She answered me listlessly.

'I took round your letter.'

'And?'

'He wasn't there.'

'He's a busy man.'

'I spoke to Tilly.'

'And what did you make of her?'

'Not a lot.'

'Don't be too hard on her. She's had a lot to put up with.'

'In what way?'

'Not worth going into. Old history – water under the bridge, to use a cliché. I'm not very fond of clichés, but sometimes they do.'

'She's had a lot to put up with from whom – PJ?'

'Let's just say I didn't marry Albert for more reasons than just Ted. Albert could be a bit domineering, he always thought he knew what was right. Did you bring your camera?'

I was startled. 'It's in the boot of my car.'

'Will you get it?'

When I returned to the house Mabel was already settled in her armchair. Her dress was smoothed down, her hands folded in her lap and her legs crossed demurely to one side, like a well-behaved child waiting for Teacher. On her face, however, was the expression of a sad, wise old monkey.

'You don't have to do this, you know.'

'Ah, but I want to.'

I set up the camera with reluctance. As I checked the lighting, framed, focused and pressed the record button, she spoke.

'I've got something I want to talk about.'

'What?'

'You.'

'Me?' I jerked in surprise and my hand came up automatically to switch the camera to Pause.

Mabel was smiling at me. 'If you switch that camera off now, you are no longer welcome to return to my house. You're good at asking prying questions, not so good at answering them.'

'I didn't mean to pry, Mabel.'

'Yes, you did. You've made it your job and you're good at it. You made me want to answer you and explain my life to you because you've got a good heart. I told you that already. So, now it's your turn.'

240

'What do you want to ask?'

'Will you get married?'

'I don't think so.'

'Why not?'

'It's not so important these days.'

'Who says?'

I shrugged.

'Just remember this, there's nothing so lonely as a fifty-year-old woman, who didn't apply her mind to the right questions at the right time.'

'That's a very sexist attitude.'

'Or man. A woman or a man. But you're a woman and it's you I'm talking to. As the years roll by, the trick is to keep up with them, not ignore them. There's no point in thinking like a twenty-year-old when you're fifty-five. What a waste!'

'Is that what was wrong with Tilly Pickford?' Something made me want to probe.

She looked at me sharply. 'In what way?'

'When I told her Sylvia was having a baby, she reacted very oddly.'

'Sylvia?'

'Sylvia Wilkins. She's my Aunt Maggie's daughter. You might know them – PJ is a close friend of the family.'

'Which one is Sylvia – the fat one?'

'No, the younger one.'

'The pretty little girl with the long blonde hair and the laughing blue eyes.'

'I think that's the one but she's older now. She's twenty-six.'

'Of course. Twenty-six, she would be.' Mabel paused. 'And who's the baby's father?'

'Charlie.' I spoke his name reluctantly. 'Charlie Hammond. They're getting married tomorrow.' Saying the words out loud I was struck by their finality, so for a moment I didn't realise that Mabel had also lapsed into silence. I stuck my head around the side of the camera to try and get her attention. She looked up.

'That'll do now, Karen. I'm tired, love. This weather's pressing me down. It's got to rain soon. We need something to wash the streets and clean the air up a bit.'

I switched the camera off and went through the by-now familiar routine of putting it away.

'Help me up the stairs when you've finished, there's a dear.'

I put my arm around her waist and took her weight as we climbed the stairs. I was shocked and frightened by how light she felt. I could have carried her easily. Upstairs in the soft half-light of the shaded bedroom I helped her onto the bed and loosened the laces of her sensible, old lady's shoes.

'When did you say they were getting married?' Her question startled me. It seemed to come from a long way off.

'Tomorrow.' And suddenly I wanted to tell her everything. I wanted to tell her all about Charlie and how I was being grown-up and sophisticated about this because that was the done thing, but how I really wanted to say to him that he was mine. And then there was always the fact of the child, which made me hold my tongue.

I caught her looking at me oddly, an expression of almost maternal concern on her ancient face. 'Be careful with yourself.'

'Me?' I laughed off her concern, as always. 'What could possibly happen to me?'

She reached out towards me and her old, withered hand gently stroked my skin. 'Go on now, Karen. Leave me, I want to make a phone call.'

I left her sitting up in bed. As she reached out to the telephone it seemed as if she had already forgotten I was there. By the time I had reached the front door I could hear the muffled sound of her voice. I let myself out and strolled back across the park to where I had left the car.

I meant to go home. I had no intention of calling round but was too close and the temptation was just too great. I knew I should have resisted it but I just couldn't help myself. I justified it by convincing myself that Charlie would be there and he would have some news about the photograph by now.

He wasn't.

Carol answered the door. When she saw who it was, she went to shut it in my face again. I wedged my foot in the door and almost got it broken. That hurt. It was my bad foot too. With a rush of temper I confronted her.

'Carol, why are you so fucking rude all the time?'

'To you? That's obvious.'

'It's not to me.'

'Don't pretend you don't remember.'

'I don't remember. What should I remember?'

She looked as if she was going to ignore my question. She turned away from me and folded her arms, staring stubbornly at the ground.

'Please tell me,' I said, sensing a softening.

She turned to me and in her eyes flashed a look of anguish. 'That last time we came to see you, I told you something. You said you were going to speak to your mum. And that's the last I ever saw of you.'

The years rolled away and we were children again. Except we weren't. I still didn't know what she was talking about.

'What did you tell me?'

The shutters came down again, not angrily but with resignation. 'It no longer matters. It mattered then, but it no longer matters now.'

'My mum died. Maybe that's what happened, maybe I never got round to telling her before she died. Tell me now.'

'Fat chance. Get out of here.'

'Please tell me. I'm sure this is a misunderstanding.'

She changed tack. 'Are you hanging around hoping to see Charlie?'

'What do you mean?' I felt my face flame red.

'I've seen the way you look at him, don't think I haven't.'

She snickered at my dismay. I didn't have a leg to stand on. My desire to befriend her was genuine but I knew she wouldn't believe me if I said as much. The gleam of malice in her eye was like a suit of armour she had put on and there was no getting through.

Shamefaced, I turned on my heel and made my way down the stairs with the sound of her snide laughter following closely behind me.

The phone rang at eleven o'clock that night.

I wasn't asleep. I was curled up in my bed trying not to think about Charlie. Without success. When the phone rang I thought it was him. I raced into the living room to answer it.

'Charlie?' There was a silence on the other end of the phone.

'Charlie, is that you?' There was no reply.

Once upon a time I would have played along, now I have no patience with that kind of nonsense. Charlie or not, I hung up. Five minutes later the phone rang again. This time I answered it without speaking. Again there was a silence but this time it was broken by a hesitant voice. A woman's voice.

'Is that Karen McDade?'

'Y-yes.'

'It's Tilly Pickford here, you came round to my house yesterday.'

I was amazed. Whoever I had been expecting, it wasn't Tilly Pickford. After identifying herself she seemed reluctant to go any further. I sensed an enormous struggle taking place at the other end of the phone.

'It's very late,' I said finally.

'I know. I want you to come and see me.'

'Tonight?' I was incredulous.

'No, not tonight,' she said hurriedly. 'He may come back. I doubt it, but you never know. Tomorrow morning would be better.'

'I have another appointment tomorrow.'

'I know. That's why I want to see you.' Her words sounded strangled as if she were trying to hold them in, but anger and misery were forcing her to speak. 'Come round at ten o'clock. Even if he does come home, he'll be gone by then.'

'That's cutting it very fine.'

'I can't let him get away with it any longer.'

'Get away with what?'

There was another long silence. So long that I thought she had gone away leaving the phone unattended, dangling in space.

'The bastard . . .' she hissed finally. The line went dead.

I stared at the receiver in surprise. That wasn't the kind of language I'd come to expect from Tilly Pickford. What could she want to tell me? Obviously it was about PJ. At least, I assumed it was about PJ.

I couldn't guess why she wanted to see me. But one thing was for sure, she wasn't a happy woman.

Chapter Fifteen

On Wednesday morning, the day of the wedding, my alarm clock interrupted a dream of Sylvia, the size of a house, her diamond engagement stud twinkling in her huge, distended belly. I struggled out of bed and made myself a cup of tea. The milk in the fridge had gone sour. I discovered this when I poured it into the tea and half of it blobbed around on the surface, big congealed lumps of yellow curd.

I drank black tea with some sugar and sat clutching the cup in front of early morning television, slowly waiting to come round. There was nothing appealing about the day. The very thought of it made me want to go straight back to bed and stay there till tomorrow.

First of all I had to drive to Epping to see what was up with Tilly Pickford. In order to fit everything in, I needed to get a move on. It was Sylvia's big day. In a few hours' time, wedding bells would be tolling.

If I got to Tilly's dead on ten, we could have a quick chat and I'd still be back in Town in time to go round to Maggie's house to film some of the final preparations.

I wasn't going to the wedding reception, I'd already made my mind up about that. I would plead the demands of work. My plan for the afternoon was to go back and do one last interview with Judy and Grace. I needed them to explain on camera what was going to happen next in the case of Ted O'Hagan. Perhaps they could give me an introduction to the police officer in charge of the case. If nothing else, I could have a chat with him about form and procedure in these situations.

I sat there in the relative cool of the early morning and felt a vague tickle of unease – a crawling on my skin which I put down to the forecast for thunder. The weather forecaster spoke of a ridge of high pressure building. She spoke of storms in the not too distant future and before that at least a couple more days of heat and discomfort.

My head felt thick and groggy and after a second cup of tea didn't work, I decided to have a cold shower. The white tiles were covered by a huge, thick, black cloud. It took me a moment to work out what it was. A swarm of winged ants had appeared from nowhere; perhaps they had been hatching and growing under the floorboards and had crawled through a crack in the tiles, possibly driven to the surface by the mounting air pressure. They clustered motionless on the bathroom wall: hundreds and hundreds of ants. Not one moved. There was something unnerving about their stillness. Some part of me wanted to scream in terror at the sight.

I didn't know what to do, I only knew that I wanted them gone.

I plugged in the vacuum cleaner in my bedroom and pointed the long nozzle attachment through the bathroom door. I expected them to swarm into the air as soon as I switched it on. I was prepared to slam the door to prevent them from invading the rest of my flat. But at the sound of the machine, not one moved. I sucked them all, ant by ant, into the body of the cleaner and still, not one moved. That was even more unnerving than an attempted escape.

After I had captured every one, I put on a pair of rubber gloves and with a plastic bag in one hand I carefully removed the dustbag from the vacuum cleaner and even more carefully manoeuvred it into the plastic bag and sealed it tight. Victorious and relieved, I carried the bag out of my front door and up the stairs to the street where I placed it at the bottom

248

of the dustbin with all the other black bin bags of rubbish on top.

There was a rank smell coming from the dustbins. The week's rubbish was fermenting in the continual heat.

Back in the bathroom, no sign remained of the ants. Still, to make myself feel better, I poured bleach down every tiny suspicion of a crack I could find. I didn't let myself dwell on the thought of a huge fat queen and a silent seething swarm somewhere just beyond my reach.

I had my shower but it didn't make me feel fresh and it didn't make me feel clean. It was only eight o'clock in the morning and already the air was beginning to feel muggy, the heat oppressive. I decided to go out for a walk. Time was tight, but I couldn't pass up my chance of seeing Charlie before he tied the knot.

Just a quick stroll. I'd be home in ten minutes and then I'd be off.

I phoned the vet's before I left the flat.

'He's doing well.'

'How did you know it was me?'

'It's five past eight in the morning, I made an informed guess.'

'Define well.'

'He could have a relapse, I must tell you that. But I have to say that your dog had a good night. He even managed to pass urine this morning without straining anything open. If he keeps this up, you should have him home for the weekend.'

Yesss. Buoyant with the good news I walked faster than I intended until the pain in my ankle forced me to slow down.

Outside the feeling of pressure was overbearing. A maw of polluted smog hung over the city; sweat beaded my brow. There were few people about and those I saw were feeling as anti-social as I was. No one met my eye.

I walked east. Just a little bit further. What would I say if he was there? What could I say to him? Hello. Don't get married. Stay and play with me.

The thing was, Charlie was still new. Two more weeks of sex and laughter and we might have burned ourselves out. That had happened to me before, and not just once. So you could say Charlie was right, that he had his head screwed on. Better to stick with contentment, than to take a chance on an uncertain passion.

And then, of course, there was the child. Best not to think of the child.

I got nearer and nearer his special place. Just ahead was the hump-backed bridge and beyond was the quiet corner from which Charlie watched the world and talked to the fish. Talking to fish, I ask you. Proof positive the man was a nutter. We couldn't last.

As I walked over the hump-backed bridge my stomach did a slow somersault and my breath caught in my throat. Surreptitiously I glanced to the right.

He wasn't there.

Of course he wasn't there! He was getting married today. He would be busy. What did I expect?

All pretence of taking the air vanished. I didn't want to walk any further. There didn't seem to be much point. I sank down on the grassy bank and stared at nothing. A heavy depression settled on me and I felt as if I couldn't move.

I didn't know if I could bear being behind a camera while he and Sylvia said 'I do'. At least the camera would shield my face. Not that anyone would be looking at my face anyway, I wasn't the one getting married. Mind you, you never know, Carol seemed to have a sixth sense for pain. I was sure she could guess exactly what was going through my mind.

The rising sun cast long shadows westwards. Water lapped at the bank, a whisper of a breeze caressed my cheek and ruffled my hair; overhead came the sharp cry of a seagull. I followed its flight, mirrored in the still calm of the murky water over to where Charlie normally sat. Something gleamed in the sunshine and I stood up for a closer look. His stool was there. And I could just make out a fishing rod propped against the wall of the bridge. Where was he? Perhaps he had left his gear while he went to the café or a shop or something. Would he have done that? It didn't seem likely.

I turned, and with my heart in my throat I ran up the steps and over the bridge. There was no pathway down to the bank that I could see. I clambered over the wall with a sick feeling of dread in my stomach that I couldn't explain. A makeshift scaffold of rattling planks wobbled underfoot as I scrambled down onto the bank. Nettles rose high around me stinging my calves, my knees and my thighs. I was oblivious to the pain. Something was wrong. I had to get to the bank.

I fought free of the undergrowth and emerged onto a small patch of grass. From here the world seemed very far away. There was no sign of anyone, just the empty stool sitting at the edge of the water and a bucket of blind, squirming, orange maggots.

'Charlie?' I called his name tentatively.

There was no one around. Opposite me the towpath was empty. There was nothing to do but wait for him here. He would be back soon. He wouldn't leave all his gear just lying here for anyone to nick. I sat down at his secret vantage point and looked out at the world. I could understand now why he chose this spot; surrounded by all the greenery, it felt like a little island paradise remote from the grey tower blocks and the ramshackle industrial buildings all around us.

A swan swam past, followed by her seven cygnets. They were almost the same size as she was, except their juvenile feathers were still a muddy brown. If Job were here, there would be no holding him.

I watched them sail past and into the deep shadows under

the bridge. A large white plastic bag floated on the surface of the murky gloom. The birds broke rank to pass around it and out into the sunlight on the other side.

I looked at the huge plastic bag suspended just beneath the surface of the water. Who would do that? Why do people jettison their rubbish in such a careless manner? And as I looked I saw that it wasn't plastic, it was cloth – white cotton. A billowing white cotton parachute. Strange. Some unknown underwater current swayed the object; it bobbed and submerged and when it floated back to the surface I could see . . .

At this point no clear thought had formulated itself in my head. Afterwards, I tried to think back to when I realised what I was looking at. The truth was, I didn't realise until the very end. And when I did, it seemed, of course, as if I had always known.

At the time, I was just responding to the urge to have a closer look at the strange sack. It was too far from the bank for me to reach. There was no path or ledge going under the bridge on my side of the bank, so there was no way I could go alongside to have a closer look. I'd have to bring it to me. I hunted round for a stick I could hook through the cloth, or a pole. Of course – one of Charlie's rods. I was sure he wouldn't mind.

I reached for the rod and extended the pole. Then carefully with one hand holding onto a crevice in the brickwork I tentatively stretched myself out over the water. The pole hooked and twisted itself around the white cloth and I pulled it back in towards me. Whatever it was floated easy and free.

I guided it to the bank and that was when I realised what it was. Who it was. I couldn't see his face. His face was turned away from me. But I could see his neck, the swarthy skin from having worked outdoors in the summer sun, the short dark curls, the raw bloody wound at the base of his skull washed clean by the canal's foul waters.

252

'Stay away from Angel Point, bitch.'

In the distance I heard the sound of a siren blaring. For a moment I thought I'd called them and they were coming to help me, help him. I tugged and tugged at him, trying to get him up onto the bank, trying not to fall into the water myself. In the water he had floated easily but trying to pull him onto land, he was a dead weight. 'Come on, come on!' I grunted, hauling and heaving with all my strength. It was no use.

'Oy you two, it's a bit early for that sort of thing.' A man stuck his head over the wall to jeer down at us. Then: 'Bloody hell! Are you all right? Help! Help!'

Within seconds, the small island paradise was full of people. Three men hauled Charlie out of the water. They laid him on the grass while they waited for an ambulance to arrive. Someone tried to give him the kiss of life, holding his nostrils and forcing air through his mouth and into his unresponsive lungs.

When the man had finished, or rather given up, I went over and sat down on the ground and lifted Charlie's head to cradle it in my lap. His skin was smooth and pale and clear and perfect and so, so cold.

I thought his blood might run onto my clothes – I didn't care if it did. But it didn't. My clothes stayed clean.

'Know him, do you love?'

Love him, do you know? Oh yes, I know him.

Before the ambulancemen took him away, I kissed him. Just once. On the lips. And rested my head on his cheek.

I imagined a pulse. A faint, faint pulse.

No, there wasn't a pulse. That was wishful thinking; the faint warmth I felt came from the heat of the summer's morning.

There *was* a pulse. I could feel it! I sat up abruptly and put my hand on his neck. There was a pulse.

'He's alive! He's alive!' I screamed. And taking in a huge

gulp of life-giving air, I forced it between his motionless lips, again and again, until a paramedic pulled me off and took over.

He worked and worked and worked at Charlie, filling him full of breath, then turning to watch his unresponsive lungs deflate. It seemed hopeless. Then, imperceptibly, his colour began to change and before my eyes he coughed, choked and vomited a trickle of canal bilge.

He was alive.

The police wanted to know what had happened. I told them what I knew. I told them who he was. In a daze I climbed into the back of a rickety transit van and went with them to Hackney Station. After a wait, an interview room became free, if you could call it a room. In reality it was a small, grey cubicle. The window was a tall slit high in the wall from which it was possible to catch a brief glimpse of the blue sky. The ugly grey furniture was bleak and comfortless, the airless room was stifling. I began to feel faint and had to put my hand on the table to support myself.

'Can I have something to drink?'

The plainclothes policeman, middle-aged and balding, wearing a jacket and trousers which would have made him look over-dressed for April, left the room wordlessly and returned shortly after with a small plastic cup of chilled water. I swallowed it in one long draught and felt the cold liquid glug down my throat, work its way through my intestines and gather in an icy pool at the pit of my stomach. I felt no better.

Was this connected with the photograph Charlie had borrowed from me? I wanted to tell the policeman everything I knew, but I didn't know where to begin.

Instead the policeman took the lead and produced a pen and paper. 'What is your relationship with the injured man?'

'He is my cousin's fiancé.'

'You a very close family?'

'Not especially.'

'I can see that you're in shock but I want you to answer my questions to the best of your ability. When I arrived, you were kissing the injured man – why?'

'He was, is my lover.' There. It was out. And for me anyway it gave me a legitimacy that I would not get elsewhere. For this brief time, I was distraught next-of-kin. Not Sylvia.

'Cosy,' said the officer.

With one hand he wrote down what I was saying. With the other he kneaded away the beginnings of a headache. Sweat filmed his forehead and his thick jowly cheeks.

'What were you doing on the canal this morning?'

'Just out for a walk.'

'Did you know Mr Hammond – Charlie – would be there?'

'No, but I hoped he would be.'

'Had you planned a rendezvous?'

'No,' I said sadly.

The policeman looked at me sharply. 'When did you last see him?'

'The night before last.'

'How did you know where to find him?'

'I didn't.'

'In your own words, tell me what happened.'

I struggled to remember and to describe what had happened clearly.

'I saw some of his gear in his usual fishing spot. He wasn't there, so I went to have a look. That's when I saw something floating under the bridge.'

'Any idea what happened to him?'

'I thought that was your job.'

'Most attacks on people's lives are committed by people they know.' There was a question in his statement.

'I didn't do that.'

'You had an unusual domestic set-up. Was there no jealousy?'

'There might have been jealousy, but I didn't do that.'

'What about the other one, your cousin?' he continued before I could speak.

'What about my cousin?'

'What does she think about your relationship with her fiancé?'

'She doesn't know.'

He raised one eyebrow.

'You're barking up the wrong tree.'

'Maybe. We rule nothing out at this stage.'

'How is he?'

'The doctors aren't saying.'

'They were due to get married today.' I said this almost to myself.

The detective pushed back his chair, stood up and walked around the room. His sweat-soaked shirt was stuck to his back and his belly sagged. He asked me to finalise my statement by signing my name at the bottom. I went through the motions still aware that I had said nothing to him about anything that had happened. I didn't know where to begin. Did I start with the man who had warned me off Angel Point with a blow to the base of my head, did I mention the photographs, or Mabel or the two men who were dead? Three. Almost four.

Before I knew it, I had been ushered out of the police station and I was standing on Mare Street in an utter daze. The bright glare of sunlight, the thundering traffic, the sweltering heat and mass of people, the activity, all this made me feel totally disorientated. I needed to go home and think. Spotting a mini-cab firm just across the road, I made straight for it and almost got myself killed. Horns blared and someone shouted at me angrily. I scarcely noticed.

Inside the tiny cubicle of an office, four black men in

neatly pressed trousers and mock-croc shoes made me wait until they had finished telling one another a long and involved story in some unidentifiable language. I sat on a chair. Normally being ignored in such a blatant way would make me angry and impatient. That day I was grateful for the hiatus in time when I could just drift. Finally I was shown to a battered orange car with torn upholstery and no seat belts in the back. Keeping the window open during the jerky ride home made no difference. The air was so heavy you could touch it. I paid off the driver and let myself into the empty flat. Still nothing, no emotion, no tears. Just a hollowness inside.

I phoned Homerton Hospital to ask for news.

'And what's your relationship to the patient?'

'Ummm, friend.'

'I'm afraid we can't give out information to anyone other than his immediate family.'

'Has he died?' I asked, immediately fearing the worst.

'No,' the voice at the other end of the phone conceded. 'He's not dead.'

I hung up, emotionally drained and completely at a loss. Who could have done this? Was it connected to Angel Point? Or was it a nutter? There are plenty of nutters wandering the streets who should be either in hospital or in prison.

No. There were too many deaths associated with this project. Ted, John, Micky Holman. Three dead men. And now Charlie. Almost.

I had to phone my cousins and tell them. The police would have told them already. Still, I ought to say that I was there. The phone rang and rang. No one answered.

I wandered from room to room growing angrier and angrier. There was the sofa where we had lain together, there was my bedroom, here was my fridge from which I had taken the bottle of wine, and here the two glasses. I was angry with myself for letting him into my bed. I was angry with myself for making myself vulnerable to loss. I picked up a glass from the work surface and hurled it into the living room. It exploded against the wall, the sharp fragments scattering all over the floor.

I wanted to bury my head in Job's fur, feel his huge body pressed into mine, wrap my arms around his powerful shoulders, feel that he was there for me. It was the absence of Job which triggered the tears and when they came, huge hysterical racking sobs echoed back to me in the empty flat. I cried for everything that had ever mattered. Job was the trigger, Charlie was the reason.

And then there was my mum – that grief that nestles deep in my heart and poisons my outlook on everything. Few people have ever made me forget that it is there. Charlie was one of them. And now he was lying in a hospital bed fighting for his life.

The photographs had to be relevant. They had to be the key. Lexi Dee would have the enlargements ready for me later on today. Once I had them back in my possession I would take them straight to the police. They would find whoever was behind all of this.

In the meantime, I could ask a few questions of my own. The thought of action made me feel better. I went into the bathroom to wash my tear-swollen face with cool water. I had to make myself presentable.

I banged on the door of No. 37 Bay Walk for the second time and still didn't get an answer I opened the letterbox and shouted Geri's name. I needed her to tell me again. I needed her to tell me everything she knew.

The door to the living room opened and a shaft of light from the window beyond flooded the hall. 'Who is it?' The voice was defiant.

I told her.

She moved her body close to the glass. I thought she was going to open the door, but instead she started swearing at me. 'Fuck off!' she said. 'Fuck off! Fuck off!' She repeated the words over and over like a mantra until they stopped making any kind of sense. It was impossible to speak to her, to explain my presence, which I was sure was her intention.

'Fuck off! Fuck off! Fuck off!'

I waited until she had finished. 'Geri, open the door!'

'Why?'

'I want to talk to you.'

'You've done enough.'

'What do you mean?'

The door swung open abruptly. I blinked in shock at the sight of her face. She had two black eyes which were swollen and puffed up so much that she was barely able to see. Already the bruising had begun to turn green, yellow, purple and black.

I gulped. 'What happened to you?'

'I walked into a door.'

'Where's Lauren?'

'The Social took her.'

'I'm so sorry.'

'I love my little girl. She's mine. I love her.'

'I'm so sorry,' I said again, aware of my own insincerity, aware of my own desire to get the platitudes over and done with and move on. 'Geri, I've come to talk to you about what you said about John being murdered.'

'I've no idea what you mean.'

'You told me that John was murdered.'

'Did I? Have I even met you before? I took some really good smack the other day. Funny, it always does strange things to my memory.'

'Geri, please try to remember, this is really important.'

'So is my little girl.' At that she swung the door closed in my face, walked down the hall, into the living room and slammed that door behind her.

Still spurred on by the need to do something, I drove to Homerton Hospital.

As soon as I walked into the small reception area of the huge hospital I knew that coming here had been a mistake. Sylvia sat on a plastic chair in the foyer hugging her own body and rocking back and forth. My aunt sat beside her with her arms around her. Carol watched them both with what looked like a malevolent gleam of triumph in her eye.

Despite everything I felt sorry for Sylvia. What a dreadful thing to happen on your wedding day. I paused, uncertain what to say. In the end, I didn't get a chance to say anything. Sylvia realised I was there and flew at me, her grief transformed into a raging fury.

'Bitch!' she screamed. Her hands flailed at me, sharp nails ripping the skin on my face. I put up my arms to defend myself. No one made a move to stop her – not Maggie, not Carol, not the passers-by avidly drinking in this soap opera of emotion, not PJ, who I registered standing on the sidelines.

'You're not wanted here,' he said gravely.

At the sound of his voice Sylvia ceased to flail and batter at me. 'You're not wanted here,' she echoed, breathing harshly.

'Sylvia, sit down, think of the baby!'

'In a minute,' she snapped at Maggie, before turning the full force of her anger on me. 'You think you're so high and mighty coming round with all your airs and graces, just like you did when we were children, always better than us. Well, we knew what you were after. Carol twigged you straight away. You couldn't keep your eyes off of him. You couldn't keep your hands to yourself. Why did you ever come here in the first place? Why couldn't you just stay away? We were doing fine until you came along. Just fine.'

260

'Sylvia, I told you. Sit down.'

She did what she was told without once taking her eyes off me, and what I saw in her unrelenting gaze was scathing contempt. I was staggered by the transformation in Sylvia. I had thought of her as a non-person, a simpering, weak-minded, child-woman. And now here I was, wilting under the heat of her justified rage.

'I'm sorry,' I muttered.

'For what? You don't even know what you've bloody done. For sleeping with Charlie? Did you? I don't bloody care about that.'

'What else have I done? What else is there?'

'So you did. Ah well, nothing like keeping it in the family.'

'Must run in the genes.'

'Shut up, Carol – shut up, you stupid cow! I've had fucking well enough of you. Shut up!' Maggie slapped her daughter hard across the face. Again no one moved to stop any of this. A silent ring of bystanders enclosed this theatre of emotions.

Carol's hand lifted to her cheek, then like a sleepwalker she took one step towards her mother and raising her hands, grabbed her by the throat and squeezed. Maggie tried to fight her off but she was no match for her big, overweight daughter. Carol's face was impassive, showing no emotion or awareness of what she was doing, and no exertion either, apart from a bead of sweat which trickled down her temple.

It was Sylvia who stopped her. 'Carol!' she said. 'Leave it girl!'

With a cry Carol released her grip and her hands flew to her own head. Maggie collapsed onto the ground, breathing raggedly. Carol was groaning from deep inside, as if from a tunnel of pain. She lumbered around squeezing her fat cheeks together and screwing up her eyes as if to block out the light. Then she fell to the ground, her eyes rolled back in her head, her limbs rigid.

Sylvia, Maggie and PJ rushed to help her. 'Quick, PJ, she's choking.'

PJ put his hand into her mouth to pull her tongue free. 'Aaagh!' he screamed, trying to tug his hand away from the strong grip of her sharp teeth. He backed off, holding his hand underneath his armpit.

Two paramedics fought through the crowd to bring assistance, manipulating Carol's body into the recovery position and pulling her head back until her tongue was clear. I could see the whites of her eyes; it looked as if she was having a fit. In the rush of activity I was ignored.

'It's epilepsy,' I heard Maggie saying to the paramedic. 'She's had it since she was a teenager.'

'What's she on Rohypnol?' he asked.

Maggie nodded.

'Did she take it this morning?'

My aunt looked at Sylvia and Sylvia shrugged. I backed away from them. Why had I come here in the first place? Why didn't I just stay away? My relationship with Maggie and Sylvia and Carol was old history that should never have been revived.

Only one thing was important now. I had to see Charlie. I had to find out how he was, no matter what it took. I was going to pretend to be his long-lost sister, if that got me in through the door to see him.

I pushed my way through the crowd and walked off down the corridor – unobserved, or so I thought.

'You sneaking off to see Charlie?' Sylvia's voice lashed out strong and cruel above the general hubbub of the hospital.

I didn't turn around.

'You can save yourself the bloody bother. He's bloody dead!'

No.

I turned around and marched up to Sylvia and grabbed her

by the arms. 'Why did you say that? Why did you say that? Why did you say that?' I was shaking her and shaking her but I couldn't shake those words unsaid.

Someone wrested me from her. It was PJ. With my arms pinned behind my back I was powerless. Sylvia walked up to me and stuck her face into mine

'He's fucking dead,' she said. 'Didn't recover consciousness. Dead.'

PJ let go of me. 'Now get out of here!' he said coldly. 'We don't want you here. You've done enough.'

I didn't need telling twice. I turned on my heel and fled.

Chapter Sixteen

I fled back down the unfamiliar streets, got into my car and drove, putting as much distance between myself and their contemptuous faces as quickly as I could.

My car seemed to have a mind of its own. Up I climbed, up the Holloway Road, up Highgate Hill, through the village and left towards Kenwood and Hampstead Heath.

I found a parking space beneath a shady tree. The tree stood at the edge of the wood and was permanently in shade, so that beneath its branches the air felt cool and the faintest of breezes freshened my hot, stricken face.

Up here it was a different world. The heat although intense was not overpowering in the way it had been far below in the clammy streets of Islington and Hackney. This was a pleasant heat, the relaxing warmth of a late summer's afternoon, and all around me people were enjoying themselves. The Heath was crowded with picnicking families, children playing games and lovers of all ages. I walked through the long grass feeling out of place. It was not that I envied people, or resented them, I was too far gone for that. I just needed something more. I needed to be away from everyone.

Charlie was dead.

I made my way into the wood and found a secluded spot beneath a great oak tree looking out onto the towers of the City and the peak of Canary Wharf shimmering in the distance. Once I was sure I was unobserved I gave way to tears for the second time that day. I felt the tension well up and release; tears poured down my face. I sobbed and I sobbed and I sobbed. At one point I was aware of the crack of a dried-up branch behind me. Out of the corner of my eye I saw two mothers walking, each with a young child in a backpack. They gave me a wide berth, unwilling to risk a confrontation with someone so obviously distraught.

While I cried I couldn't think. It was as if my sorrow acted as a jamming device permitting no recollection or analysis of my situation. The worst thing about this black hole of grief was that the only person who could make it better, who could ease the pain, was the one person who would never return.

But I had to stop crying. I had to stop crying. Crying was no use to anyone. I was missing something. What? What was I missing?

I made my way back to the car, drove down the Archway Road and parked up by my old house. What made me seek comfort there? I associated grief with this house. Was that it?

My dad answered the door in his slippers; he was wearing a pair of shabby old trousers and a T-shirt. He looked surprised and then pleased to see me.

'Come in, come in,' he said. 'I'm just out the back.' He didn't ask any questions. He never asked any questions, Dad, about me or my life. And for once I was grateful for his lack of interest. I followed him into the house and left the outside world behind.

We walked through the dark hall, through the living room and out into the little backyard. It was tiny. Not much bigger than a central drain, a place to put the bins and a washing line. However, owing to a gap in the buildings opposite it always caught the sun, and for as long as I remember, first my mum, and then my dad had two window boxes with a colourful display of pink and white pelargoniums which continued to bloom throughout the year.

I perched on top of a dustbin and watched him as he wandered in and out of the kitchen filling up a glass milk bottle with water time and time again. He had got old. Beneath his shirt the flesh at his breast was sagging, under his upper arms the skin was loose. Knotted blue veins stood out against the white skin of his forearms. Gently he tended to his plants, lifting up the variegated leaves and directing the water to the needy roots.

'They are very like the ones Mum used to grow,' I said as another memory came to the surface. Her name was out of my mouth before I realised that I had spoken aloud and I wanted to bite the words back, sure that they would provoke the usual sullen atmosphere which accompanied most of our communications.

'These *are* the ones your mother grew,' he replied without looking at me. 'Or at least they are cuttings of the original. I've kept them going. It helps me to feel that she is still there, somewhere.'

I was so surprised by what he said I felt my jaw drop open and my eyes pop out in amazement.

I stared steadfastly at the ground trying to process what he had said.

'Where's that dog then?'

The question caught me unawares. I told him, sketching in the bare bones of what had happened, trying to keep the catch out of my voice as I spoke. Dad carried on tending and watering and made no comment. I waited for him to say something – words of blame, words of criticism – but he didn't. The silence was restful.

I used to think my love of plants was entirely my own hobby, that it came from me, that it was something I discovered. Watching him I realised that gardening, in a small way, was something which had surrounded me from early childhood. There had been a time when thinking I was like my parents in any way would have caused me to rebel, close my mind off, change what I was doing. Now, watching my father I felt comforted by this sign of continuity.

'I have a garden too,' I offered shyly.

'Do you?' He looked at me with interest. 'It's been a tough summer for the plants, what with the hosepipe ban.'

For once we stood on common ground. 'I haven't always stuck to it, I must admit.'

We were searching our way to one another.

'That's the one advantage of having such a small patch, you can always keep it going, no matter what the weather. Mind you, it'll rain soon.'

'How can you tell?'

'The pressure. Can't you feel it building? Sooner or later it's got to burst.'

I looked up into the never-ending blue haze. It was hard to believe it would ever rain again.

'Would you like a cutting?'

'From one of the pelargoniums?'

He nodded.

'I'd love one.'

In the kitchen, as he packed it in some damp tissue paper and a plastic bag, I asked him a question. 'Dad, did Mum ever say something about Carol?'

There. We had mentioned her name twice in one day. This was unheard-of. I expected him to clam up, change the subject. He handed me the bag with the pelargonium cutting and sighed. In such a small space it was difficult to avoid eye contact, but we managed it.

'She did mention something. I'd forgotten all about it until the other day when you said that Sylvia was getting married. It brought it all back.'

'What?'

He reddened. I waited in silence for his answer and eventually he told me, the words tumbling out on top of one another.

'Carol told Annie that she had a boyfriend but that she

didn't like him any more. She wanted to know how to make him go away. But she made Annie swear not to mention it to Maggie. I told her it meant nothing, that children were always having these little secrets. Especially Carol. She reminded me of Maggie at that age. Carol was always a difficult child. She took it very hard when her dad died, she used to try and attach herself to any man around. Understandable in a way. She was always wanting to have a boyfriend, to grow up before her time. That's when she started with the epilepsy. I never had those worries with you. I thought I'd never cope raising a teenage girl without her mother, but you never seemed interested in things like that. That was the one thing which surprised me about Maggie. I thought she'd get married again after she lost Ned. I never thought she was one to survive for long without a man. What Carol said worried your mother for some reason, more than it should. That was the week she got knocked down. It wasn't like your mum to run out in front of a bus without looking where she was going. At the time I remember thinking she must have had something on her mind. And the only thing I could think of was Maggie's problems. That's the thing about other people's problems. They suck you in.'

'Did you say anything to Maggie?'

'She never bothered herself with coming to the funeral. I wrote to her once to ask her to give me some help with you. It's not right, a young girl not having an older woman in her life. She wrote back to tell me she wasn't interested. So, I put her and them out of my mind. I don't think I even thought about them again till the other day.'

'But Dad, you've got their photographs up on the wall in the other room.'

'Have I?' He poked his head through the door and looked at the picture with genuine surprise.

I wanted to rewind the conversation and play it back. I

269

wanted to count the number of words he had spoken, sure that
he had said more to me in those few moments than in all of
the last twenty years combined. And what he had said tugged
away at some buried memory. What was it?

'I'm going to put the kettle on, are you staying?'

I nodded. 'Dad, do you mind if I go upstairs?'

He narrowed his eyes, but asked me no questions. 'Go
ahead.'

It was years since I had trodden these narrow stairs. As I
climbed the two flights to my bedroom my sense of self split
into two. Part of me became again that sad, lonely teenager.
Inevitably things looked smaller.

My bedroom faced out front. The net curtains which
covered the windows were a uniform grey. The room was
dark and gloomy and steeped in sadness. I switched on the
light, my hand flicking down the black Bakelite switch
unchanged since the war. The flood of light was too bright.
The room seemed to blink in shock. Quickly I turned it off
again and the room relaxed back to its habitual gloom but not
before I had seen that everything was unchanged. Nothing
had been moved since the day I left home.

I sank down onto the edge of my old bed and felt a spring
twang in protest. The bedding smelt musty. It had probably
been unchanged for fifteen years. I caught sight of my
reflection in the dressing-table mirror and was surprised to
see my adult face.

I felt sorry for my dad. What was he waiting for? He knew
I was never coming back. Why had he kept this shrine for me?
When Mum died he got rid of her things so quickly, I had
expected him to have done the same after I moved out. I had
expected to open the door and see at the very most packing
cases containing some of my old gear.

Sitting here listening to the old familiar noises, the pounding traffic on the road outside, the gurgling of the ancient

water tank in the roof, it was easy to be transported back. I heard again the muffled voices of adults talking downstairs, the chink of cup against saucer – Mum always used her wedding china whenever Auntie Madge came to call. I heard again the sound of their voices downstairs and our giddy laughter as Carol and I bounced up and down on my bed.

Again the feeling that I was missing something tugged at a corner of my mind. What was it? What was it?

She had asked me for help, Carol. I did remember something. I remembered us bouncing and bouncing and bouncing on the bed, laughing and giggling. Then I remember we stopped. And in the sudden silence it felt as if we were alone in the house, as if the grown-ups had left and there was no one else about. Carol looked at me oddly. Then she began to whisper her secrets into my ear. She told me that she had a boyfriend. She told me what he did with her. She told me that her boyfriend had hurt her down there and she showed me the blood. She said she didn't know how to make it stop. She had a wodge of rolled-up toilet paper stuffed down her knickers.

I understood nothing of what she was saying.

After she left I told my mum. That was it – I had asked her to explain. I remembered her, thin-lipped and cross – I had thought she was cross with me. She said there was time enough for all that. That I'd know soon enough, when I was ready.

I told her that someone was hurting Carol and had made her bleed down there. She told me not to be silly. That Carol was a naughty girl for making up such stories. And that I'd know all about it soon when it happened to me. And she told me, in a roundabout way, about blood and monthlies and the curse, in words that still made no sense, but did much later, when she was dead and I was on my own. She said that if I heard Carol talking that kind of nonsense again, I was to tell her and she'd have a word with my Auntie Madge.

'Tea's ready!' my dad shouted from the bottom of the stairs and I came to with a start. I left the bedroom closing the door behind me gently, and made my way back down the stairs.

Dad and I sat in the parlour and drank our tea in silence. Our newfound equanimity hovered between us, a fragile butterfly on gossamer wings. Neither of us wanted to say another word lest we damage it for ever. But there was a question I needed to ask.

'Dad, why was Mum so worried?'

He hesitated, reluctant to voice his thoughts. 'I think your mum got the impression Maggie knew all about Carol's boyfriend.'

'So.?'

'I think your mum thought Maggie knew what was going on.' His voice tailed away. I'd known my dad long enough to recognise the silence which followed as prohibitive. He would say nothing more.

'I'll be off then,' I said as I drained the last of the sugary dregs.

'Good to see you, Karen.'

We stood awkwardly in the hall, unsure of how to part.

'Don't forget to see to that cutting when you get indoors.'

'I won't.'

'See you then.'

'Yeah.'

Chapter Seventeen

Going back home was unbearable. Everything reminded me of Charlie. The scent of his body still impregnated my bed. For a time I curled into the sheets and used them as a comfort, reliving our brief time together. But that was no good. At midnight I got up and stripped the bed. Then I loaded the washing machine, turned it on and watched as it began to turn round and round, washing his smell away. After that I had a shower, put on fresh sheets and went back into bed. Still I tossed and turned. In the silence, I heard him whisper.

I dragged the duvet into the conservatory and attempted to sleep on the sofa. That was no good either. I closed my eyes and saw our bodies together, my knees riding his strong firm thighs. Above me a hoary moon gazed down with pity. I can't stand anybody's pity.

At two in the morning I got up and wrenched open the fridge door and took out a bottle of Pinot Grigio, filled a large glass to the brim and drained it in one draught without pausing to savour the crisp, clean taste on my tongue. As I lay on the sofa my head began to spin, thoughts whirled in my head but the wine dulled their pain. Next thing I knew it was morning.

I awoke, one hand numb with pins and needles. It was already ten o'clock. My temples were pounding and my mouth was dry. My thick head subsided under a cold shower and I had a couple of paracetamols for breakfast. This was good. The discomfort of a hangover prevented me from thinking too clearly about Charlie's death. The worst thing about it was that I could acknowledge my grief to no one. He was not mine to lose.

The phone rang as I was getting dressed.

'I thought you were coming to see me.'

It was Tilly.

'Something came up.' I didn't want to go into detail.

'Can you come this morning?'

I could see no reason why I should. I hadn't warmed to the woman in the first place and nothing had happened since to make me change my mind.

'Mrs Pickford, can you give me some idea of why you want to see me?'

'Not over the phone.' Again she paused and her anguish was apparent. 'This is very difficult for me,' she said. 'You don't understand. I have held my tongue for years now.' She lapsed into silence.

'All right. Give me an hour.' I was curious, impatient to hear what she had to say.

I hung up and tried to ring Job. The number of the vet's was engaged, so I drove to Hampton Terrace. The surgery was crowded with people. There were two scared-looking cats in cat boxes and a couple of small dogs with a couple of small owners. The receptionist was trying to calm people down, saying that the vet was in emergency theatre operating on a Siamese cat which had been run over by a motorcycle. The din was chaotic.

'How's Job?' I mouthed when she caught my eye.

'He's doing fine,' she told me distractedly.

'Shall I come back later?' The look in her eyes said yes, please.

I drove out to Epping feeling both frustrated and disloyal at not seeing Job, but pleasantly insulated from thinking about Charlie and other stronger emotions by the fluffy remains of my hangover. Going against the traffic, it didn't take me long to reach PJ's house. Turning into the drive in daylight I was able to appreciate the immaculate perfection of his garden with its precision-cut borders and edges. The flower beds looked as if any debris was vacuumed away at first light.

I rang the doorbell. There was no answer. I rang it again. I could hear it echoing far away in the bowels of the house. She was in, I knew it. She wouldn't have rung me and then gone out. Her need to talk was too great. I peered through the rippled pane of stained glass on the door and as I looked a shadow seemed to detach itself from the wall and move towards me.

Tilly Pickford opened the door and I gasped in shock.

When we had met before her attention to her own appearance had been meticulous. Today she wore a dirty old housecoat and no make-up. Her sallow skin was a mass of tiny purple lines where little blood vessels had broken on the surface. The shadows under her eyes were so dark they looked like bruises. And her right arm was in a sling. Its pristine bandage mocked the rest of her haggard appearance.

I didn't know what to say, where to begin. 'How did you do that?'

She held the door open wide and gestured me in. 'How do you think? I fell down the stairs.'

As I walked over the threshold I could smell stale alcohol on her sour breath. She led the way down the hall and into the same room I had been in before. We sat down but only for a moment.

'Not in here,' she said. 'I don't want to be in here.'

She stood up, swayed then stumbled. I put out a hand to steady her but she pushed me away. I followed her out through the door, down another corridor and into a kitchen filled with rows of immaculate white units and sophisticated cooking aids which looked as if they had never been used.

Next to the window, overlooking a small dark corner of the

garden was a sofa which was entirely out of keeping with the rest of the surroundings. It was grubby and old and floral, piled high with cushions. Tilly made straight for it and plonked herself down.

'Pull up a chair,' she said expansively.

Warily I fetched a chair from the other end of the room and carried it to where she was sitting. This self-neglect told an obvious story. I didn't know whether I could bear to listen to the rambling malice of a drunk.

'You wanted to see me?' She must have seen the expression of disgust in my eyes.

'I've not been drinking,' she hissed, thrusting her face into mine. 'At least not today.'

'Why did you want to see me?' I persisted.

She twisted and turned her hands. 'What happened yesterday?'

'What do you mean?' I was stalling for time. I didn't want to talk about what had happened to Charlie with this stranger.

'The wedding, why did the wedding not take place?'

'How did you know the wedding didn't take place?'

'I went there.'

'Where?'

'The Town Hall. No one showed. PJ hasn't been home since. Tell me what happened.'

'The groom met with an accident.' I didn't want to go into detail, not here, not with her.

'What happened?' Her voice was urgent.

'The groom died.' I kept it brief and impersonal.

'Oh my God.'

I pushed the conversation forward, unwilling to listen to any fake expressions of sympathy from this woman about people she hardly knew, unwilling to dwell on this private tragedy with someone I could barely tolerate.

'Is this about PJ?' I said, trying to steer her back to the

276

reason she asked me here in the first place.

'Yes,' she said. When she finally started speaking, her voice was frantic. The words came out tripping over one another. 'I've said nothing for years. Who could I say it to? Who would believe me? But when you told me he was going to marry her off, I knew I had to say something. That's why I went there. I was going to confront him. I was going to say it in front of everyone.'

'Mrs Pickford,' I said. 'Can you tell me what this is all about?' I was impatient to hear what she had to say and then get going.

'This is very difficult for me. PJ always wanted to have children. You see, he was an only child.'

I nodded. I knew this already.

'Wanting to have children, that was PJ's charm. Most men I knew didn't seem to want them, you see.' The words squeezed and twisted themselves out with difficulty, forcing themselves through her tight little mouth. 'That's why I married him.'

I wished she would just hurry up and say what she wanted to say.

'We tried for children for two years. At the beginning it was such fun. I'd lived at home until I was married. I found it so . . . romantic, being . . . with the man you love. But as the months wore on, as each month came to a close, the fun went out of it. I could feel him slipping away from me.'

This story was no different from the stories of thousands of infertile couples across the land.

'Please, Mrs Pickford, I have come all the way here. What is it you want to tell me?'

'PJ stopped coming home every night. He started to stay away. I tried to pretend there was nothing wrong and then a year later, when I could bear it no longer, I confronted him. He laughed in my face and told me he was now the proud father of a little girl.'

'He was having an affair?'

'Yes.'

'Why didn't he leave you? Why didn't he divorce you and marry the mother of his child?'

'I owned our house. My father had left it in trust for me. There was a provision in his will stating that if I ever divorced, my husband would have no claim to the property.'

'And?'

'You don't understand my husband. Ever since I have known him, PJ has carefully cultivated his image. He likes to be seen as a Lord of the Manor with a common touch. It wouldn't suit him to be living in a council flat with two screaming children.'

'Two?'

'They had two children. Daughters.'

'Maggie!' I breathed.

She nodded, tersely.

'Why did Maggie put up with it?'

'PJ never offered her an alternative.'

'So, let me get this straight: PJ has been maintaining two households for the last thirty years. Or rather, you have been maintaining this house and PJ has been maintaining the other house.'

'No, not this house. Our first house. I told you before, this house belongs to PJ. He bought this one. We both put money into it.'

'What did you ask me here for, Mrs Pickford? So far, all you have told me about is a failed marriage and ongoing affair. All very difficult I know, but not really worth the trip, I'm sorry to say.'

My unfeeling words galvanised her.

'That's why I went there – I couldn't let him just marry her off!' All hesitancy had vanished, her voice built to a crescendo. 'Sylvia Wilkins is carrying Pete's child.' The words shot out

278

and in the ensuing silence we both looked at one another appalled.

'But you've just told me that . . .' I was adding two and two together but I kept reaching five and Tilly Pickford was looking at me as if five were the right answer.

'How do you know?' I stammered.

'I know.'

'How do you know?' I repeated.

'The doctors never could find anything wrong with me. PJ likes to humiliate me with proof. He told me. He told me the baby was his! It was the last straw. All these years I've kept my mouth shut. I was scared of him, but I loved him too. You won't understand that. I'm still scared of him but I don't love him any more. That's worn away. Finished.'

I was hardly listening to what she said. I felt sick to the stomach. Charlie had been going to marry Sylvia because of the baby.

I moaned aloud. 'Did Mabel know this?'

'There are things which Mabel knows and chooses not to see.'

'What you are talking about is the systematic and knowing abuse of two little girls.'

'Most of the time it was just one. The eldest spilled the beans on him to someone. After that he refused to touch her, as a punishment.' Her eyes were pinning me down, searching for absolution, but there was none that I could offer.

'And you stayed with him even though you knew about this? Why didn't you leave him?'

'If I left him, what would there have been for me? A childless divorcee, condemned to live alone somewhere for the rest of my life.' Her eyes were bitter, distant.

'Yeah. That sounds about right,' I said cruelly.

I stumbled out of the house, wrenched open the car door

and drove blindly back towards Town. What Tilly Pickford had told me was too fantastical to be true. But if she were right? If she were right, what did that mean?

PJ. The omnipresent PJ. Everywhere I looked, he was there. Arrogant bastard, having sex with his daughters and running the area like it was his own private fiefdom.

PJ. He was Mabel's adopted son and Ted was dead. He knew Micky Holman's family and Micky Holman was dead. When I had mentioned Geri, John's girlfriend to him, he'd called her a crackhead. So he knew them as well. John was dead and Lauren had been taken away by the Social Services. Was that done to keep Geri's mouth shut?

He knew Charlie and now Charlie was dead.

Were these deaths, in fact, all connected? Driving back to London, thoughts whirring, the idea no longer seemed so far-fetched.

PJ. He'd been so helpful to me, offering to open doors. But then when the doors had opened, I was allowed to see so far, and no further. He'd been helpful to me with all my queries about Heaven's Gate, but if I were to think about it, I'd actually learned nothing from him. Instead, he'd been able to keep tabs on everything I was doing.

But why?

And how?

I thought of Owen de Courtney and the limousine with darkened windows. I thought of the house in the country with the roses, the lawn sprinkler and the paid gardener. I thought of the wife with the separate life, who wouldn't be around to contradict the story he put about, telling people that the money belonged to her and that he was a kept man. I thought of his association with Hackney Council, not employed by them, nothing directly to do with them, but privy to many decisions regarding construction contracts throughout the many years of his so-called public service.

The more I thought of it, the less plausible the whole set-up began to seem.

And now, if Tilly were to be believed, he was into a touch of child abuse and incest in his spare time.

The photographs. What had Ted seen? Those photographs were crucial.

I was going straight to see Mabel – she had some explaining to do.

One image kept trying to force itself to my consciousness. Eventually I wasn't able to prevent it from breaking through.

I saw my mother that day, her preoccupied face as she was running for a bus. Days before, Carol had confided in me and I had told my mother everything. Was it playing on her mind, so much so perhaps, that she wasn't looking where she was going?

Did I have PJ to thank for that?

Shaking, I left the car in the shade down a side street by London Fields and pushed my way through a line of children snaked along the pavement clutching their money waiting in line at an ice-cream van. The power for the refrigeration unit pumped out noxious fumes into the static air.

I half-walked, half ran down the shady passageway towards Mabel's house. To my surprise, the house next door was boarded up, there was no washing on the line and wooden planks were nailed across the windows. Up and down the crescent, the picture was the same. The only house which still looked occupied belonged to Mabel. After she moved, this little enclave would be empty and then the bulldozers would come in and erase all trace of the lives that had been lived here.

I rang the bell to Mabel's house and waited. I remembered what she had said the first time I called around. If she was upstairs, it could take her a few minutes to get to the door. Overhead came the high-pitched cry of a bird. I looked up and saw two gulls mid-air fighting over some scrap of carrion.

I rang the bell again and waited. And waited. I rang the bell one last time; perhaps she was asleep upstairs. I felt faint and nauseous; I had questions which needed answers. As I rang the bell, I leaned against the front door for support. To my surprise it gave a little. I stood up and pushed it gently – it was open. The door was on the latch. Mabel had forgotten to shut it properly.

It didn't feel right being inside the house without Mabel's knowledge. 'Hello!'

In this dead atmosphere, my voice sounded muffled, sucked up by the silence and the gloom, and ignored. The door to the parlour was ajar but I went upstairs first, sure that I would find her asleep on the bed. Careful not to frighten her, I tapped gently on the bedroom door. She wasn't there. On the pillow was the faint indentation of her head as if she had only just arisen and the bed had not had time to adjust to her absence. The coverlet was uncreased; Mabel's weight was so light and insubstantial that it left no trace.

I went downstairs and into the kitchen. No one there. She wasn't outside in the yard either. On the kitchen table was a pot of tea with two used cups. Without thinking my hand went to the teapot. It felt cold to the touch.

Remembering my first visit, I looked at the dirty dregs in the tea cups. In both cups the leaves clustered like black ants down one side of the white porcelain. I shuddered at the memory of the motionless cloud of black ants on my bathroom wall.

Mabel had seen death in the leaves of my tea and she hadn't been mistaken. I could still feel the weight of the dying Charlie heavy in my arms like a pain, the way they say you still feel pain in a limb long after it has been amputated.

Where was she? Wherever she was, she wouldn't be long. I was sure that she wouldn't be long. So sure that for something to do, I rinsed the tea cups out, laid a tray and put the kettle on in anticipation of her return.

In order to pass the time I went out to study the photographs in the hall. He was good, Ted. He had a good eye. This one of the middle-aged women having a knees up – that woman in the middle particularly, the one who has lifted her leg highest, so high that you catch a glimpse of her matronly suspender belt under the dark shadows of her skirt – she would not like to see this picture. The following morning she would wake and, in the recollection of last night, self-hatred would stare back at her bleary-eyed from her dressing-table mirror. A mask of make-up would be applied, her conventional appearance a comforting buffet from an uncomfortable world.

And this one of the chubby young girl wearing a dress that was too tight and too small for her. A dress which was straining at the sleeves and over the bodice. Adult eyes stared out from a child's face. Eyes that have already seen too much. Sad eyes. The picture of a mutinous, abused, sad little girl. A mutinous, abused, overweight woman. Carol. So much to think about. Too much to think about.

Where was PJ now? What was he doing? What did I have to give to the police?

Slow down. Slow down. Think.

In truth I had nothing to give to the police. There had to be something concrete in those photographs. They were my only hope.

Charlie, Charlie, how much did you know?

At least now I had a better idea of what I was looking for. No, I didn't. I still had absolutely no idea what I was looking for. Sylvia, Heaven's Gate – I still didn't see the connection.

I went back into the kitchen and drained two glasses of tap water in an effort to get rid of the headache which was intensifying steadily behind my eyes. The weather had to change. It had to break soon.

I decided to wait for Mabel in her parlour. I could phone Rob and arrange to meet him, tell him everything I knew. I walked along the hall with no immediate sense of foreboding, through the open door and into the front room.

Mabel was lying stretched out, face down on the carpet. I rushed to her side. She was still breathing although the skin around her thin lips had turned blue. With all the stress, her heart had given out.

All this time I had been in her house while she lay here, desperate for help.

I picked up the telephone to dial 999 and give all the details.

'No, Karen.' She enunciated the words on the faintest exhalation of breath.

I replaced the receiver in surprise and rushed to her side.

'Upstairs. In the drawer by my bed.'

I took the steps two at a time, wrenched open the drawer and found the pills. Then I ran back down, fetched a glass of water, pulled her gently to a sitting position, placed two of the pills into her mouth, gave her a sip of water and with my hand shut her mouth. She was almost too weak to swallow.

'Don't die on me, Mabel. Don't die on me, Mabel.'

She managed to swallow the medicine. I reached across her to phone an ambulance for medical back up.

'No!' Her voice was still a faint whisper, but her will was implacable.

For the second time I hung up. 'You need help, Mabel.'

She shook her head. 'Give me a minute!' she said, and closed her eyes. I sat on the floor with her cradled in my arms and felt her breathing begin to gain in strength.

What about the bottle of pills I had seen the other day on the mantelpiece?

There it was, on the floor, by a corner of the fireplace. I was able to reach over and pick it up. The cap was sealed, but the bottle was empty. Mabel must have felt the pains in her heart beginning and known what they meant. She had reached for the bottle of pills which she kept close to hand, but it was empty. She had forgotten to get her prescription.

Hold on a moment – that wasn't true. When I was here, only days ago, that bottle was full. I had seen it with my own eyes. Perhaps there were two bottles in this room. Perhaps she had got confused. I propped Mabel against the armchair for a moment, got up and searched behind the photographs on the mantelpiece. Nothing. But I had seen a full bottle of pills, in this room with my own eyes. It must have been the same bottle I now held in my hand. And it was empty.

My own heart was thudding as ominous possibilities began to crowd and jostle for consideration. There were two obvious explanations and neither of them were pleasant. The first was that Mabel had emptied the bottle of pills herself because she no longer wanted to live. The shock of Ted's possible murder had been so great, she no longer had any will to live. She emptied the pills out knowing that some day soon, the pains in her heart would overpower her and kill her. A suicide attempt.

I had not known Mabel for long. Who can know the depths of pain and sorrow in the heart of any other human being? Suicide was possible but even so it seemed unlikely. And if she had emptied the pills away, why keep the bottle? Why reach for the bottle when the familiar pains began to tighten her chest? It didn't make sense.

I thought about the alternative explanation. If Mabel hadn't emptied the bottle then someone else had emptied it for her. By accident? It's not the kind of thing you do by accident. On purpose?

'Mabel! Mabel, are you okay?' I wanted her to speak to me. I thought of the two cups and saucers sitting on the kitchen table which I had helpfully washed and dried and put on the tray. Who would be with Mabel in the middle of the day, in her kitchen, drinking tea? The answer was all too obvious.

'Mabel!'

She didn't respond. I began to feel frightened and trapped. Lost in my own thoughts, it took me a moment to realise that her eyes were open and that she was looking at me.

'Better?'

She nodded.

'What happened, Mabel? Was PJ here?'

She dropped her gaze.

'Tell me, please. What is PJ up to?'

She closed her eyes.

'Did PJ do this?'

Her eyes remained shut.

'Mabel, Charlie's dead – Sylvia's Charlie. My Charlie. I don't understand any of this. Please. You've got to speak to me.'

For a split second, I thought that something had happened to her, that her heart had seized again. But her breathing was strong and regular and when I mentioned Charlie's name, behind her paper-thin eyelids I saw her wince.

'Right, I'm going to phone for some help.'

This time my words brought no reaction. Perhaps she had passed out.

I dialled 999 and requested an ambulance. While waiting for it to arrive, I began to worry. What could I say to the ambulance crew? What could I say to the police? I had been in this house for over half an hour, the house of a woman I did not know very well, and all the while she had been lying dying in the front room.

Meanwhile I had systematically set about destroying any evidence which would identify the person who might possibly prove to be the last person, apart from myself, to have seen

Mabel alive. And the tampered-with bottle of pills was now covered in fingerprints from my hot and sweaty little hand. I had to get out of here. I had to think.

I wanted to leave straight away, but I couldn't leave Mabel like this. Her hands were beginning to get cold. I chafed the skin gently and pulled a throw from the sofa to cover her body.

'Hang on in there,' I whispered, 'help's on its way. Everything will be all right.' The words were meaningless, because I didn't know what was wrong in the first place. Something. Everything.

I heard a siren outside. It was getting louder and louder and closer. The instinct for self-preservation overtook me. Any second they would be here. I made sure the front door was still unlocked and then dashed down the passage, through the kitchen, out the back door and over the fence. The garden backed onto a small communal area with a passageway leading back out onto the Richmond Road.

Sure enough, the ambulance was parked out on the main road. I made myself slow down, I made myself stand and watch from a safe distance and ten minutes later I was rewarded with the sight of a stretcher bearing Mabel being loaded into the back of the van. I could see her face. The paramedic was bending over her. She was alive.

As I got back into the car the phone began to ring and I nearly jumped out of my skin. Who would be on the other end? PJ? The police? I couldn't bring myself to answer it, nor to decide to leave it be. Eventually it stopped.

I pulled out into traffic again and went with the flow. The phone began to ring again; I ignored it. Fifteen minutes later it rang again. I was stationary in a long stream of traffic heading north. It rang and it rang and this time I picked it up.

'Karen McDade,' I stated aggressively.

'Karen, I've been trying to reach you for hours.'

It was the vet. Oh no, this was the last straw. With a strangled sob, I felt my stomach turn to water. Not Job. How could I have forgotten all about Job? I should have insisted on seeing him this morning, if only to say goodbye.

'Karen, are you all right? Are you still there? I'm just phoning to say that Job is on the mend. In fact he's ready to go home, if you want to stop by and pick him up.'

I hung up and began to giggle nervously. I laughed and laughed, uncertain of the reason why. I caught the startled looks of other drivers and choked back the jerky, staccato machine-gun eruptions of mirth. The last thing I needed at this moment in time was to be stopped by the police. I pulled myself together and drove straight to Hampton Terrace.

When I saw Job standing upright waiting for me, trying feebly to wag his tail, I almost cried. Instead, scared of hurting Job, I hugged the vet. He looked both shy and pleased at the same time.

'I never thought he'd pull through. He's some dog.'

I signed a bill well into four figures without a twinge. It looked like we'd be having a frugal Christmas this year. Who cared? I listened carefully to all the instructions about which tablets to give and when. There was still a real danger of post-operative infection. Apart from the medication the vet also gave me some tranquillisers.

'You'll need to be careful with him to begin with; he might think he's better than he is. We don't want him to over-exert himself until he's had a chance to mend properly. These will keep him calm for a few days. Only use them if you have to.'

And then it was time to go home. Job stood at the door to the street, blinking in the sunshine. He sniffed the air tentatively, as if he did not trust the signals he was receiving.

I walked with him to the car. The vet stood at the doorway watching us leave.

'Do you need any help?'

288

'We'll be all right.'

'Keep a close eye on him for the next few days. After that, just let him take things at his own pace for a few weeks. I think he'll be fine.'

'Thanks,' I shouted back. 'I don't even know your name. What is it?'

'Mike.'

'Thanks, Mike.'

I brought Job home. His legs were still very wobbly, and I had to help him climb out of the car. When he stood, his legs were splayed wide apart like a puppy learning to walk. I kept a steadying hand on his collar while I locked the car. He twisted his head to the side and kept giving me little grateful licks. I squatted down on the pavement and looked deep into his eyes. Then I hugged him. It was good to have him back. We went slowly and carefully into the house and down the stairs. I turned off my alarm and took us into my flat.

The first thing Job did was walk to his bowl of water, lie down Sphinx-like on the floor and lap and lap his fill. Normally excess water streams down his beard, but the hair around his mouth had been shaved away and I could see the black stitches holding together his mangled flesh. After he had finished he limped to the conservatory door. I opened it and went out with him to the garden. He wasn't able to cock his leg properly. Instead he squatted like a bitch in the centre of our small patch of lawn.

He sniffed each usual place and, satisfied there had been no intruders during his involuntary absence, he hobbled back indoors, climbed on the sofa and went to sleep. His stertorous breathing had a comforting sound. The message light on my machine was blinking. There were two messages. I stared at it uncertainly for a moment and then pressed play.

The first message was from Rob. It was so good to hear his voice.

'Karen, what's going on? Why haven't you been in touch? I'm worried about you. Is Job all right?'

I called him straight away. 'Job's fine. He's home. Listen, Rob, can you meet me at the Finest Cut in an hour? I'm in over my neck here and I need your help.'

'What are you up to, Karen?'

'Don't ask. I'll explain when I see you. Please be there, Rob. I know I've been vague this last week or so, but I'll tell you everything when I get there.'

The second message was from Lexi Dee. I rang Pony Labs and got put through to her immediately.

'I'm never going to work my tits off again for you, woman. Those photographs have been sitting here, done and ready, since yesterday afternoon.'

'I'm sorry, Lexi. Something came up.' How could I even begin to explain?

'I hope he was good.'

'He wasn't good. He's dead.'

'Karen, baby, are you serious? I'm sorry. I didn't mean to . . .'

'You weren't to know. Listen, I'll be into town in the next hour to pick up the pictures. Have you looked at them?'

'Sure. There's nothing much to see. Just a whole bunch of people shaking hands and some cars and vans parked in a building site.'

Of course – that was the connection! I had been so stupid. I thought back to the truck leaving the site in the dead of night with its lights switched off. There was a fraud here somewhere and the photographs would provide the proof.

'I'm just on my way into town now. I'll be there within the hour. Promise.'

'I'll hold you to that.'

I replaced the receiver and hung up. Job's eyes followed me mournfully around the flat as I got ready to leave. He knew I was going out. I hated to leave him so soon, but it couldn't be helped. He tried to struggle to his feet, as if he wanted to come with me.

'No, boy, you stay here!' I gave him a couple of the tranquillisers, gently prising open his huge jaws, being very careful of his healing wounds. I placed the pills at the back of his throat and held his mouth firmly closed while I waited for him to swallow them. He stared at me mutinously, I stared back.

'Good dog,' I said encouragingly.

Job didn't have the energy to hold out for long. He swallowed the medicine and rested his head on his paws.

I filled up his water bowl before I left.

Just as I was on my way out the door, the phone rang again. Absent-mindedly I punched a button. 'Yes?'

'Karen, it's Grace Campbell. I'm sorry it's taken so long to get back to you. I've tried to call you a couple of times. You asked me about Micky Holman. The reason I'm calling is that it's his funeral today. Now, in fact. It starts at two-fifteen.'

I looked at my watch. It was ten past two. 'Where?'

'Our Lady and St Joseph's Roman Catholic Church. It's on the Balls Pond Road. That's just north of Dalston. It shouldn't be difficult to find.'

My thoughts were whirring. If I went along to the funeral, I might unearth something concrete. The downside was that I would be late for Lexi and late for Rob.

'Grace, was there anything suspicious about his death? Did anything show up on his post-mortem?' I asked.

'Not a thing. Clean as a whistle.'

'Thanks, Grace. I appreciate this.' I looked at my watch again. All going well, I could be there in ten minutes. You never know, I might discover something really useful . . .

The funeral service was in midflow by the time I got to the church. I slipped into the end pew and the organ played 'Abide with Me'. An old Irish priest talked about the mysterious will

291

of God and a life cut short in its prime. Then he recited the achievements of Micky's short life. These seemed to consist of being a good son and making his parents proud.

Even in this cavernous space, the air felt muggy and oppressive. Still, it gave me time to review what I knew. If PJ was the father of Sylvia's child, then who was I to report him? If he was the one who had abused Carol and sent my worried mother under a bus, then how could I grass him up without Carol's testimony? And for one reason or another, Carol had chosen to say nothing over the years. These things were wrong, but as crimes they would be hard to prove.

How did that link in with Charlie?

And what about Mabel? I must have been mistaken about that. PJ wouldn't have deliberately thrown Mabel's drugs away. And even if he had, it was my fingerprints on the tea cup and my fingerprints on the empty bottle of pills. Besides, why would he want her dead? If she had said nothing about his incestuous abuse of the Wilkins' girls over the years, why would she blow the whistle on him now?

At the end of the short service, a grieving family walked out behind the coffin, while the organ played 'Amazing Grace'. Once the family had passed by, the rest of the mourners began to leave their pews, old men, young men in ill-fitting hired suits, plump matrons in buttoned-up overcoats, a young girl with red eyes and long blonde hair.

From high up in the church tower a bell began to toll. A cold shiver ran up and down my spine, the hairs rose on my arms, the sound was unbearably poignant.

Shit!

There was PJ. I pretended to drop something and threw myself under a bench attempting to search for it.

Double shit! There was no getting away from him, he was everywhere. I scrambled about the floor for a few minutes and when I emerged, he had passed on by without noticing me. Thank God. But how was I going to get out of here?

I walked away from the exit, up to the front of the church near the altar, and pushed open one of the Fire Doors. Walking carefully along the outside of the church, I soon discovered it was impossible to make a quick getaway. There was no way out but through the crowd. I would have no chance of remaining unobserved.

I hid myself behind a cluster of young men who had gathered outside for a quiet smoke. From here, I could see the coffin being loaded onto the hearse.

'Shame.'

'Shame.'

'Bad luck.'

'Yeah.'

'Just as things were going right for him with that promotion and all.'

Stubby, red, workworn hands cupped cigarettes in silent comradeship. Five minutes later and most of the young men had dispersed, leaving only one boy behind. He looked to be about fifteen. He watched proceedings with glassy concentration.

'Are you family?' I asked, using his body to shelter behind.

'Micky was my cousin,' he replied without looking at me.

'I'm sorry.'

He shrugged.

'Can you tell me about the promotion?'

He looked at me curiously. 'Who's asking?'

'*Hackney Clarion*,' I lied. 'What was his promotion?'

He looked impressed. 'It's no big secret. He'd been appointed Site Foreman on Stage Three of that big new development he was working on. Pleased as punch he was. He bought himself a new car and all.'

'When was this?'

'About six weeks ago.'

The hearse was beginning to move, and the boy I was talking to jogged off to get into one of the waiting cars of mourners. The door slammed shut and the cars moved off in convoy on Micky Holman's final journey to the city boundaries and a grave dug from arid earth.

I wondered what had happened to his new car.

Both the men killed on the building site had just come into good fortune. And with that good fortune had come a death sentence. For the life of me, I still couldn't see how all that connected with Sylvia's baby.

I waited where I was until the churchyard had cleared. Then I walked, with purpose and with relief, out of the gates and right towards where I had parked my car.

PJ was leaning against the wall with his hands in his pockets. 'I was wondering where you'd got to, I thought perhaps I'd missed you.'

My first impulse was to run, except his voice was good-natured and he seemed positively pleased to see me.

'Karen . . .' The brash, self-confident PJ Pickford seemed hesitant, embarrassed. 'Karen, I've been wanting to speak to you. I'm sorry for the way I spoke to you at the hospital yesterday.'

I shrugged.

'You've been to see Tilly, haven't you? Look, you and me need to have a little chat. There's things I need to explain. How's about we have a drink?'

'When?' I could feel my eyes narrow.

'Now. There's a pub across the road.'

'Now?'

'It'll only take ten minutes.'

I looked at my watch. Three o'clock. I needed to be in the West End. I would be late for Rob and Lexi Dee would go through the roof. But I had to get my facts straight and here was PJ offering to explain everything. No use making a fool of myself by rushing to Rob and to the police with a cock and bull story which turned out to be all wrong.

Besides, it was broad daylight.

What could possibly go wrong in broad daylight?

We were the only people in the pub. Standing beside PJ at the bar I felt ill at ease. Despite his bluff good nature, I couldn't get over what Tilly had told me, or the sight of Mabel stretched out, almost dead on her living-room floor. And that was just for starters.

PJ asked me what I wanted to drink and I ordered half a lager. The barman bestirred himself reluctantly, put down his crossword, and poured us our drinks whilst obviously still trying to work out the clue to seven across. Customers were the bane of his day.

It took a moment to register that, for once, PJ hadn't been recognised. He paid for the drinks and carried them to a seat in the window. I followed on behind.

'Dykes and queers drink in here, it's not on my patch,' he said with a grimace as if he'd read my mind, and made a gesture with his shoulders that reminded me of Job shaking himself clean.

'What did you want to tell me, PJ?' I was aware of the minutes ticking by and my appointment with Rob.

'Give me a minute to settle myself. Drink your drink,' he said. 'I hate funerals. Funny that, go to a funeral, and the feeling stays with me all day.'

I knew what he meant. I took a sip of my beer and felt the acrid, fizzy liquid immediately quench a thirst I didn't even know I had. I enjoyed one sip. Then another. Then another.

Overhead, a helicopter fan moved stale air around the room. With each slow revolution, the rotary blades caught the light, painting silver circles in the air. Just watching it made me feel dizzy.

'I called round to see Mabel, this morning.'

'Did you now? And how is she? I haven't spoken to her today.'

'She wasn't very well. I had to call an ambulance for her. They took her to hospital.'

'And how is she?'

'I think she'll be all right.'

'Do you now? Looks like you showed up just in the nick of time. That was lucky.' Whatever I could detect in his voice, it wasn't sincerity.

For some reason, I was beginning to feel very, very light-headed. I looked at PJ. He appeared to be looking back at me with an expression of malign satisfaction. I had to get out of here. Something was very wrong. I tried to stand up, but my legs wouldn't take my weight. I tried to push myself up on my arms. They seemed not to obey me. The sensation would have been almost pleasurable, if I didn't know that I was in danger.

'My, my. You've got me into a *lot* of trouble.' PJ's voice came from far, far away. 'The drug is called Rohypnol. Carol gets it for her epilepsy. I find it very useful. It makes people . . . malleable, conscious but malleable. They call it the date-rape drug. A pharmaceutical leg-opener. But don't worry your little head about that – I'm well looked after in that department. The best thing about Rohypnol for my purposes is that no trace remains in the body afterwards. Time to go, I think.'

He slid an arm under mine and helped me to my feet. I was powerless to resist. As we left, I managed to throw one desperate look towards the barman. He had to help me. He had to stop this.

'Pregnant. Hormonal. She's come over all faint. You know how it is.' I heard PJ's voice floating down a long tunnel.

The barman looked away in disgust.

Chapter Eighteen

PJ walked me around the corner to his car. Once we were moving, my legs knew what to do. I could walk freely, on my own. No, not freely. I was unable to run away. We got into the car and drove and drove. Time went on a loop. It seemed as if we were driving for hours but that can't have been the case.

Next thing I knew, I was out of the car and walking again, down the passage and into a deserted Albemarle Close, up the stairs of No. 8 and into Mabel's empty bedroom. I recognised the soft, subdued yellow light; the curtains were still drawn. If Mabel had been taken to hospital and the street had been cleared all ready for demolition, no one would find me here.

Crack!

Safe from prying eyes, PJ permitted himself to do what he really wanted to do. The blow hurled me across the room and onto Mabel's bed. Pain exploded in my jaw, but even the pain seemed to come from a long way away.

'Where are the photographs?'

'What photographs?'

He slapped me twice, hard. 'Now, let's start again,' he said. 'Charlie said you had some photographs. Where are they?'

Drugged out of my brains, one small instinct of self-preservation remained. 'I gave them all to him,' I said.

Dead men can't tell tales.

Confusion clouded his features. He said nothing in reply. Instead, he prised open my teeth and poured a small capsule of powder into my mouth. My tongue rasped like sandpaper over the roof of my mouth. I refused to swallow.

Next, I felt hot liquid trickling, burning down my throat.

'I'll be back for you later.'

I heard those words and slipped away into dreamless, drugged oblivion.

It was dark when next I came to, jerked roughly to my feet.

I say that I came to, but it was still nothing like true consciousness. I was aware of sights and sounds and some movement. My body was half-supported, propelled down the stairs and out into the dark of night. Rainbow halos surrounded each street-lamp; I stared at them in wonder as I drifted along on pavements made of cotton wool.

The next thing I knew I was somewhere deep, dark, dank and silent as a tomb. Someone was shining a beam of light directly into my face, blinding me.

'I thought I warned you to stay away. Now, where the fuck are the photographs?'

The harsh new voice was familiar. A fist crunched into my face, slamming me into a concrete pillar.

'I gave them to Charlie.' I held onto the lie, almost believing it myself.

Displeased with my answer, the fist punished me again. Somewhere inside of me, I was very, very frightened. But even that emotion felt remote, as if in truth it had nothing to do with me.

'That's not true, Jim. Charlie told me she had the pictures.' I recognised PJ's voice but it contained a tone I had not heard before. He was whining and wheedling.

'You've made too many mistakes on this job, PJ. Maybe you're losing your touch. You choose two lads – good families, you tell me. And what happens? Both boys get greedy and have to be sorted. Next, your old man fancies a bit of blackmail. And then we have Charlie Hammond. Like a son to you, that's what you said. Four dead men, it looks careless. Fuck up again PJ, and you can answer to de Courtney yourself.'

I scarcely heard the words the man was saying; I was too busy trying to place his voice. The wheels in my brain turned slowly. Simple thoughts wouldn't connect. And then I had it.

Jim Bryant.

Jim Bryant and the surprising look of satisfaction on his face after Micky Holman had fallen to his death.

'What shall I do with her?'

I struggled to focus on what they were saying.

'Tie her up and stick her upstairs. In twenty-four hours, they'll need a microscope to find her. Do it properly this time.'

After that, my memory goes again. I have no idea if I climbed the eleven storeys myself or had to be dragged up. I have no idea whether or not I was drugged again. Maybe I just blacked out. The next sound I heard was birds, the twittering and chirruping of what sounded like thousands and thousands of birds.

I thought I was with my mum. She had taken me to London Zoo. It was my birthday. I was five or six, maybe, and I was holding her hand. We'd been to see the giraffes and we were standing by the aviary, a huge wire-net construction on a steel beam frame. Suddenly there was a loud bang. I don't know what it was, but at the sound all the birds took fright. Hundreds and thousands of birds flew up into the air blackening the sky. The sound of their squawking and twittering frightened me, the panic of their beating wings was infectious and I cowered behind my mum with my eyes closed.

My eyes were closed now and for some reason that I couldn't quite understand, I was frightened. Gradually I was coming to. The sound of the birds receded into the background. I tried to open my eyes, but they were crusty with sleep. I went to wipe the sleep away and found I couldn't move my hand. I couldn't find my hand. I could feel my arms but my hands were numb. I had to blink the sleep out of my eyes. Finally I opened them.

Where was I?

It was dark. No, not quite dark. Through the large window I could see the faint glimmer of light in an eastern sky. The birds still sang and now I knew what I was hearing. It was the dawn chorus. They no longer sounded anxious, they were just birds welcoming in the dawn of a new day.

But where was I?

I tried to move. Everything hurt. There was a throbbing pain behind my eyes. Pain seared through my ankle and my arms were immobile. My arms were joined together behind my back. I tried to separate them. I couldn't. My arms were tied behind my back. Of course they were. It felt so natural, to be lying here in this strange room. So natural, I felt myself drifting back to sleep.

No! I had to wake up! There was something wrong. A distant, oh so distant memory teased at my brain.

I am in a church and the organ is playing 'Abide with Me'. A bell starts ringing, the deep, relentless toll of a church bell. *Dong. Dong. Dong.* The bell frightens me. The funeral is mine. No – I am still alive. Next I am walking to my car. That's it. That's all.

That was as far as I got. I pressed the play button, but the film stopped there.

What happened next? Where was I now? I had to wake up. There was something terribly wrong. I forced my eyes open. Okay, I was in a large room. My body was in a sitting position. I was on a mattress propped up against a wall. Opposite me were two large windows and through the windows I could see the sky. I seemed to be very close to the sky. I seemed to be high up. I remembered having been here before. Had I?

All at once everything made sense. And I remembered everything. I knew where I was and I moaned aloud in fear. This was Angel Point. I was lying in the room where Ted's body had been found. I was lying on a mattress impregnated with the stench of his decaying body.

I struggled to stand up. I had to stand up. I had to get out of here. The effort triggered a blinding pain behind my eyes. That's all I remember.

The next time I came to, the sun was high in the sky. The pain in my head hadn't receded; if anything, it was more intense. My lips were parched, my swollen tongue rubbed against the roof of my mouth. Ahead of me I could see the deep, unfathomable blue of the unobstructed sky.

PJ was standing staring down at me. 'Not long to go now,' he seemed to be saying.

What do you mean? I struggled to form the words but my mouth would not obey me.

'I never thought that Ted would be found. That was the mistake. But this time things will go to plan.'

'You did kill Ted?' Did I say those words or merely think them? I tried again. 'Four dead men.'

This time I managed to speak but even to my ears my voice sounded very weak. It didn't seem to matter. Was PJ talking to me? I tried to concentrate.

'At first he refused when I offered him a drink. So I pressed him. "Go on!" I said. "Just the one, what harm can it do?" Just me and him. I'd see him home safe.

'Once he started you couldn't stop him, he was like a parched man in a desert. He had that bottle to his lips and he was drinking it like a baby. You should have heard him, all this stuff he was spouting about me and him. Like father and son, if you believed what he said. He said he was glad now that we'd taken a drink together to see how all the old misunderstandings could be washed away.

'He always was a stupid bugger. I never could stand the way she looked at him. When her eyes met his it was like there was no one else in the room. Neither of them heard a word I said. The number of times that happened when I was a child . . . I'd be telling her something and he'd walk in and she'd just forget what I was saying. I hated him. I used to see my old man, sometimes. Broken by it all he was, he never recovered.

'Poetic justice, don't you think? It was the drink that brought him over from Ireland and into our lives in the first place and it was the drink that got rid of him in the end.'

'Mabel said he never touched the stuff.'

'He did that night.'

'What did you do – force it down his throat?' My voice came out clearer this time, stronger.

'Give me some credit. I offered him a drink, you know, man to man, so we could discuss things. "Man to man", he couldn't resist that.'

'Had he seen you with Sylvia?'

'Come again?'

'Had he seen you with Sylvia?'

'Is that what you think this is all about, me and Sylvia? No. Ted had found out about the lorries and he wanted in. He wanted what he saw as his fair share. If I didn't pay up, he was threatening to tell Mabel. She'd have forgiven Ted for his attempted blackmail, but she'd never have forgiven me for taking a percentage off this multi-million-pound project which would never have got going without me in the first place. Mabel's straight as an arrow, as far as money is concerned. She'd have made the whole thing public. She'd have thought it was her duty.'

'What did you do to Ted?'

'No harm in telling you now, you won't be going anywhere. I let him carry on drinking until he'd passed out cold. Snoring away he was. A quick blow to the head and that was him.'

'You cold bastard.'

He inclined his head to one side as if I'd just paid him a compliment.

'And the other two young men who died?'

'They were getting greedy; I can't stand greed. Me and Micky had a cup of tea earlier that morning, I slipped two Rohypnol in his drink. Not enough to make someone completely incapable, just enough to cloud their judgement. Building sites are dangerous places, you need to have your wits about you, otherwise accidents happen. After that it was only a matter of time. Same thing went for Johnnie. I don't mind cutting people in, but I can't stand greed.'

'So what has Sylvia got to do with all that? I still don't understand.'

'Nothing. Nothing at all. Sylvia hasn't got anything to do with anything. Is that what Tilly told you? She's got you barking up the wrong tree.'

'And Charlie?'

'Charlie was different. I'm sorry about Charlie. He was a young man and he had a life ahead of him. But it's amazing. People you wouldn't expect to be on the take, turn out to be just as greedy as all the others.

'He wanted a house, he wanted a car. I'd already got him the flat for taking Sylvia off my hands. I told him, wait six months, see how you go. But armed with that photograph, he fancied he could put a bit of pressure on me. I went along with him, agreed with him, the way you do. Then, when he turned back to his fishing and there was no one about, it seemed like too good an opportunity to waste.'

'Charlie knew that Sylvia was carrying your baby?'

'He had a fair idea it wasn't his. You needn't look so shocked. We have our own way of doing things and it worked out fine until you came along. Charlie and Sylvia were due to get married. What did it matter if the baby were his or not? They say that the only person who can be certain about the father is the mother, and in Sylvia's case even she couldn't be sure.'

'Charlie wouldn't have married Sylvia if she hadn't been pregnant.'

'Oh? And who would he have married then? Little Miss Big-shot Film-maker? I wouldn't be so sure.'

'Charlie was only marrying Sylvia because she was pregnant and he thought it was his. That's what he said.' I could hear the desperation in my voice. I didn't want to believe this about Charlie, it couldn't be true.

'That's what he said, was it? Charlie would have made Sylvia a good husband and she'd have made him a good wife. She was quite happy to do as she was told. She knew that her mother and me had her best interests at heart. In a couple of years' time, they'd have had a few more kids and all this would have been history.'

I stared at him in disbelief. The pain in my head was throbbing behind my eyes like a great malignant toad.

'How could you do that? Sylvia was your daughter.'

'I didn't do anything Sylvia didn't want me to do.'

'And what about Maggie?'

'Maggie's gone through her change. She's not as keen as she used to be. She was the one who suggested Sylv. She knows what makes me happy.'

'You bastard.'

'Not at all. I've looked after that family. I love them.'

'And what about Mabel? Do you love Mabel?'

'Yes, Mabel. What a lot of lives you've touched in your short time here. Something you said to her about Ted started her thinking. She could always get the truth out of me, Mabel. And that was a shame for both of us. I watched a light die in her eyes and for just that one thing, I'll never forgive you.'

'How could you have done that? She was more than a mother to you, how could you have tried to kill her? You knew she had a bad heart, she kept the medicines within reach. I saw them.'

'Maybe she decided that she didn't want to reach them; maybe she decided she had nothing left to live for.'

'How is she?'

'She hasn't regained consciousness. They don't think she ever will.'

From down below I could hear a band playing; it sounded like fairground music, the hurdy-gurdy of a old-fashioned carousel – horses rising and falling as they spun round. Gay colours, painted piebald, flashing lights, the music seemed louder to my ears than the droning voice in my ear.

I was fading in and out of consciousness and I no longer wanted to fight the desire to slip away. So, when trying to describe what happened next I make an unreliable witness.

'Does it all seem worth the trouble, PJ?' I heard myself murmur.

'Funnily enough, it doesn't. Still, once you start something you've got to see it through, don't you? No going back.' He came and stood over me, silhouetted against the light like some monstrous monolith.

'Déjà vu? This is where you killed Ted, isn't it?' I said, trying to muster some spirit.

'I must be going. I wouldn't want the show to start without me, would I?' He squatted down and trickled some water into my parched mouth. I wanted nothing from him but my body took no notice. I gulped and spluttered, desperate for more of the delicious liquid which softened and eased my cracked lips and swollen tongue.

'Don't think I'm a cruel man.' That's what he said. That's what I think he said.

At this point it seemed to me the light was fading fast. The room had grown very, very dark. Surely that couldn't be right. It was the middle of the day. Weakened by hunger, and with traces of the drug still in my body, my vision was going. Or was I fainting? Tumbling headlong into pure oblivion.

The music had stopped. I ran my tongue over my lips and felt the deep fissures and tasted the blood on my tongue.

Outside, there was a loud crash and boom. The building reverberated with the shock. They haven't waited for him, was my thought. They have triggered the detonator. This is it. I am going to die.

PJ looked around him. He was scared.

I'm going to die and he is going to die with me. Even in this bleakest of bleak moments, I could take satisfaction from the knowledge that he was going with me. The rumbling continued, and still I felt nothing. I expected some awareness of death. Some sensation of collapsing from within, of being ripped, of being torn apart. Before death. Instead we stayed suspended within this huge column of deep sound.

On PJ's face was a look of frozen terror.

Then over and above the crashing booming sound came another noise. A whooshing, pattering . . . The sound of heavy rain.

And then Rob was there. In the room, not in my dreams – or was he? I called his name. He didn't answer. I shouted at him. Still he didn't hear me. If he had heard me, he would have come over to me.

'*Rob!*' I could scarcely hear my own voice. He looked at me, just flicked his eyes in my direction to make sure I was there, to make sure I was alive.

A flash of white light ripped the sky apart, illuminating the room. And immediately afterwards came another crashing boom. I could see the two men circle one another, Toro and Matador. PJ put his head down ready for the charge.

'The game's up,' Rob shouted above the noise of the thunder and the lightning and the pouring rain. When I heard him say that, I wanted to laugh. The line was straight from an old black and white 'B' movie. The hero says the line and then he and the gangster grapple and fight until one of them is dead.

PJ charged at Rob. I felt rather than saw their bodies collide and grip and tumble over and over. Rob was no match for PJ. The man was a colossus, a mountain, indestructible. He wrestled Rob to the ground and stood above him, panting. Then he turned and ran from the room. Rob struggled to his feet and raced after him.

I passed out.

They took me to Homerton Hospital.

I remember nothing of my rescue, nothing of the people who found me, strapped me into a stretcher and carried me down all those flights of stairs. I remember nothing of the dispersal of the gathered crowd. The instruments packed away. The street vendors clearing up and going home.

I didn't see the other ambulance parked at the foot of Angel Point, lifting someone up from the ground. Lifting him up from where he had landed, after soaring off the eleventh floor in the thunder and the pouring rain. Instead of soaring like a gull on a warm thermal, he fell like a dead weight, a broken television, an unwanted hi-fi, smashed to pieces in front of all those people, the communal intake of breath, time standing still on the wasteground below. The drop was vertiginous.

I remember nothing of them strapping his mangled limbs into a body bag and placing him on a trolley. Strapping him in for convenience, not protection. Someone who no longer needed the attention and care of the specialist services who had come to cart away his remains.

I didn't see the national news crews who had begun to turn up on the sniff of a good story. Anything meaty to get away from the bland stories of the summer season.

I saw none of this.

I awoke in a ward and the first thing I saw when I came to were the white bandages on my wrists. At the sight of these clean dressings I knew nothing more than that I was safe. I felt myself begin to drift back to sleep. Then I noticed the drip in my arm regulating the fluid supply to my badly dehydrated body.

A drip.

'Job,' I mumbled. No one heard me. 'Job!' I called out louder. Still there was no one there.

I tried to get out of bed. My legs were leaden. With difficulty I forced them to obey me. 'Job!' This time I shouted much louder. I swung my legs over the side of the bed.

At once three nurses swooped down on me.

'Where do you think you're going?'

'Get back into bed!'

'Lift her! One . . . two . . . three.'

To tell the truth, despite my great anxiety I was grateful to be carried back to bed. My legs felt as if they didn't belong to me and were unable to support my weight.

'Job!' I whispered.

'Is that his name? Go and tell him she's awake.'

I saw the woman's badge. Staff Nurse Jane Pitfield. I felt myself drifting back to sleep and concentrated hard on that badge; it was black plastic with white writing in capital letters.

'What day is it?' I asked her.

'Sunday,' she answered brightly, fluffing up my pillows. 'You've been asleep since they brought you in yesterday lunchtime. It's the effects of the drug you were given. Once it wears off you'll be fine.'

'What drug?'

'Rohypnol. Expect your memory to be a little out of synch. Things will come back to you in dribs and drabs. The police want to speak to you but Dr Chalcott has told them they must wait until at least tomorrow.'

Police . . . drug . . . I closed my eyes with the effort of trying to think about it all. And at once the image of two men fighting, silhouetted against a dark thundery sky flashed in front of my eyes. What had happened? How had I got here?

Rob?

I opened my eyes to ask the nurse to fill me in and saw Rob himself standing at the foot of my bed, grinning down at me. I didn't feel like grinning back.

'Job's alone in the flat,' I croaked. 'He's not well.'

'No, he's not. He's at the vet's.'

'Is he all right?' I tried to lift myself up, then collapsed with my head swimming against the crisp white pillow.

'Yes, he's fine. I went to see him this morning before I came here. In fact, he's looking quite frisky and wants to know when he's coming home.'

The relief was enormous. I felt my whole body ease and relax and almost managed a smile in Rob's direction. 'You're going to have to fill me in. How did Job get to the vet's?'

'I took him there.'

'How did you get into my flat?'

'You gave me a set of keys once, don't you remember?'

I did. It seemed such a long time ago.

Rob told me that Lexi Dee had contacted the Finest Cut when I didn't show. Rob was waiting for me in reception and overheard the phone call. He spoke to her.

'She said she was worried about you. You mentioned the fact that your boyfriend was dead. It came as news to me.'

I lowered my eyes to the regulation green coverlet on the bed. I couldn't look him in the face.

'I went to meet her and we looked at the photographs together. Lexi did a good job but still they looked like nothing special to me. Just pictures of PJ Pickford and some other men at Heaven's Gate with two trucks. I tried to call you. When I didn't get an answer on Friday or again on Saturday morning, I phoned the vet's. He told me you were at home with Job – which you obviously weren't. That's when I went round to the flat and let myself in.'

'How was Job?'

'Hungry, groggy but otherwise fine. For once I could even say he seemed pleased to see me.'

'Why did he need to go to the vet's?'

'I needed to concentrate all my energies on finding you. I phoned the police and gave them all the details but they didn't act as if the situation was urgent. So I went to PJ's home. His wife told me she'd seen you, but that PJ was missing. The only thing was to turn up at Heaven's Gate yesterday morning for the big Blowdown. When PJ didn't show, I wondered – I just wondered. Ted's body, Angel Point . . . it all had perfect symmetry. I broke through the barrier making sure I was seen by as many people as possible. I didn't want anybody to press any buttons by accident. The rest you know.'

I turned my head into the pillow to hide the onslaught of painful memories I knew Rob would see in my eyes.

Five dead men.

Ted O'Hagan.

Micky Holman.

John Martin.

Charlie Hammond.

And PJ.

Will you come into my parlour said the spider to the fly. I felt an overwhelming urge to cry.

Rob was stroking my cheek. Gently smoothing back my hair. Gentleness was more than I could bear.

'Take me home, Rob, please. I want to go home.'

Afterword

It is evening. September has begun and with it the slow descent into the twilight of the year. A hint of sharpness in the air foretells the bitter cold to come.

I am lying on the sofa in my living room with the windows to the garden wide open. Outside, the leaves are changing colour as the season turns. Beside me, in a tall slender glass, small roots form on my pelargonium.

Job is curled at my feet. Even in my sleep, my hand twists tight onto his collar. We are inseparable.

My ankle has healed, more or less, and Job is on the mend. We each draw comfort from the other. But I think that we carry other wounds which will take longer to go away.

Mabel pulled through. Perhaps some day I will go and see her. But not yet.

No, not yet.

Any second now I am expecting Rob. He comes round every day after work to make me something to eat. It is very kind of him. I know that.

The demolition has gone ahead, he tells me. Angel Point has gone. Albemarle Close no longer exists.

Lying here I feel a sudden wind spring up. Falling leaves gust and eddy, an unread newspaper at my side flaps, twirls, twists up into the air. Dust scatters, detritus from our fleeting lives. Grit stings my eyes, making them water.

A solitary tear slides down my cheek.

And I think of Charlie.